Queen

of the

Northern Mines

Kristi
To a fellow Civil
War buff

Richard H.
T. J. Meeker
Never Surrender!

Queen
of the
Northern Mines

~ A Novel of the Civil War in California ~

by

Richard Hurley and TJ Meekins

Bear River Books
Grass Valley, California

Bear River Books, 19221 Black Oak Lane, Grass Valley, CA 95949
http://www.bearriverbooks.com
© 2011 Bear River Books
All rights reserved. Published 2011.
Printed in the United States of America.

19 18 17 16 15 14 13 12 11   1 2 3 4 5

ISBN-13: 978-0-983-17980-1

Library of Congress Control Number: 2011906248

Front cover: *Portrait of Sophie Gray* by John Everett Millais, 1857,
courtesy of Peter Nahum at the Leicester Galleries.

Bear image in "Note on Names" from *15,000 Miles by Stage,*
by Carrie Adell Strahorn, re-printed by the University of Nebraska Press.
Artist: Charles M. Russell.

I do not know what we would do in this great national emergency were it not for the gold sent from California.

– *General Ulysses S. Grant*

In 1860, the ties that bound the Pacific to the Government at Washington were nowhere very strong.

– *Asbury Harpending, Confederate partisan in California*

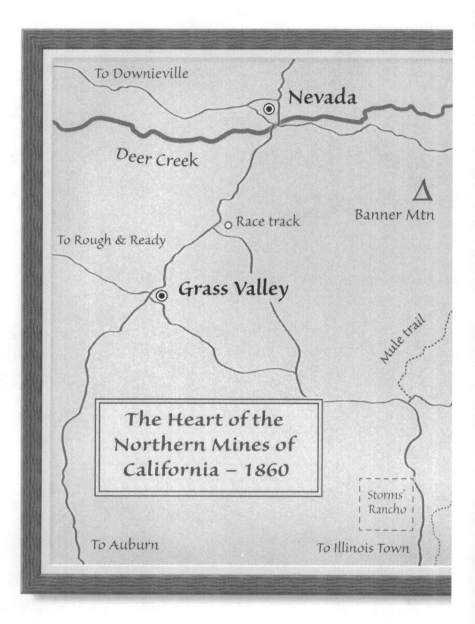

To Downieville

Nevada

Deer Creek

△
Banner Mtn

o Race track

To Rough & Ready

Grass Valley

Mule trail

The Heart of the
Northern Mines of
California – 1860

Storms'
Rancho

To Auburn

To Illinois Town

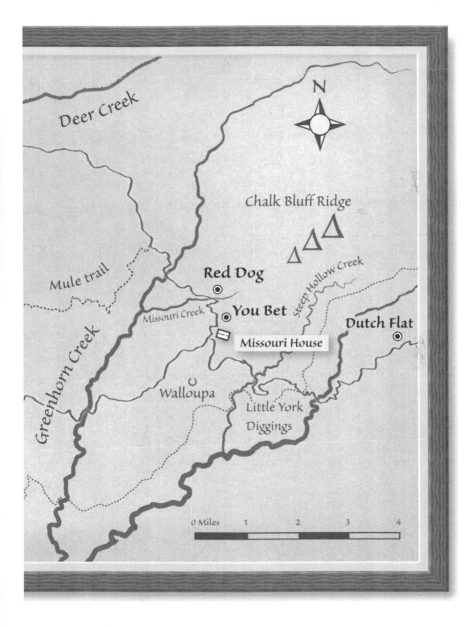

Acknowledgments

The authors would like to thank the following individuals for their help over the course of this project. Any errors remaining in the text are, of course, strictly chargeable to our own account.

19th-century weapons: Bob Butterfield, Charles Kritzon.

Cavalry consultant: 2nd California Cavalry Volunteers, Company F (Sacramento Rangers) – Rob Wangberg (aka Cpl. Thomas Whiting).

Chinese culture and language: Eileen Leung of the Sacramento Chinese Culture Foundation.

European languages: Christiane Bourgault, Bill O'Daly.

Horse transport: Grace Waldron.

Maidu culture and language: Farrell Cunningham.

Medical advice: Galen Martin, MD.

Red Dog/You Bet historical structures and roadways: David Comstock.

We also thank our kind readers, who reviewed these pages long before they were ready and offered many helpful suggestions: Karen Anderson, Patricia and Richard Calkins, Jeanie Harris, Steve Hurley, Charles Johnson, Warren Knox, Kitty Meekins, and Cheryl Rubin.

A Note on Names

In 1860, "Nevada" was the name of a bustling town on the western slope of the Sierra, hub of the astonishing mineral wonderland known as the Northern Mines of California.

The state we now call Nevada was known in those days as the Washoe Territory. When Washoe entered the Union in 1864, it lifted the name of the nearby California community and took it for its own – perhaps the most sweeping example of claim jumping the Gold Rush affords.

The characters in this story speak in the idiom of their time and are not clairvoyant. When they say "Nevada," or "Nevada City," they refer to the town in California, and when they say "Washoe," they mean the parched, sage-covered wasteland so many of them ran off to in search of the next great strike.

Chapter 1

Dutch Flat, California

November 1860

The stage reached the outskirts of the mining camp with the last light of day and rolled through a jumble of motley tents and tipsy shacks, all wreathed in the smoke of their evening fires. Through the window, Will Stafford saw a few substantial family homes appear, and a steepled church, tall and prim in white clapboard. Then the coach wheeled onto Main, where lanterns glowed and music poured from bustling saloons on both sides of the street. The driver reined up in front of the hotel, and the hostler dragged out a wooden step for the convenience of the passengers.

"This is Dutch Flat, folks," the grizzled driver announced, beating clouds of red dust from his sleeves, "though what's flat about it continues to puzzle the philosophic mind…"

"The beer," said the dispirited hostler.

"About half the billiard table," offered a lounger on the boardwalk steps.

"The wit of the locals, mostly," muttered the driver, opening the door of the coach. He helped an old missus and her Reverend husband descend, then stood back to let the able-bodied passengers tumble out.

Will Stafford smiled as he stepped down, glad to find enough level ground in Dutch Flat, California to stretch his back and rub his aching neck. He had just travelled five thousand stormy miles by sea and crossed Panama on a mule, but those hardships seemed tame compared with this day's battering in a crowded Sierra mud wagon.

But now the journey was over and its troubles already fading away. Soon he would be at his cousin Taylor's fireside, celebrating their new venture: *Burnham and Stafford, Attorneys-at-Law.* Will tested his legs and, finding sensation returning to his limbs, hobbled up the stairs to the express office to check his trunk and ask directions. Then he strode out into the crisp, pine-scented twilight.

A lantern shone over the porch of 12 School St., lighting up golden letters on the window that proclaimed the presence of *The Dutch Flat Enquirer.* Will bounded up the steps and rapped on the door.

"Help yourself!" came a voice from inside.

A wiry man in an ink-smeared apron stood by a printing press, rummaging through a tray of type. With a grunt of satisfaction, he snatched up a block and held it to the smoky oil lamp.

"Lincoln won," said the editor, without a glance at Will, "and I'd appreciate it if you'd spread the word, so folks will stop pestering me. If you want the details, you can read all about it in the *Election Special.*"

"I thank you for your news, sir," said Will, doffing his hat, "but I am looking for my cousin, Mr. Burnham. He wrote me that his office was at this address, but clearly there is some mistake."

The newsman lowered the type block.

"You want Taylor Burnham, the lawyer?"

"The same," said Will, smiling.

The editor pulled off his reading glasses and looked Will up and down. "And you would be...?"

"Will Stafford, late of Virginia, come to join his practice."

"My God!" The newsman hesitated. "Mr. Stafford, I'm sorry, there is no easy way to say this... Your cousin died weeks ago."

The strength fled from Will's limbs. He swayed, suddenly adrift in time and space.

"I sent a message to your family right away," continued the editor, "by the Pony Express. It must have just missed you. Taylor went off suddenly... a bilious fever..." The newsman saw the shock draining Will's face. "You're welcome to stay here, of course. You can have his room. We can clear off the bed directly."

"You are very kind, sir," said Will, replacing his hat with a shaky hand, "but this news comes hard… I must take time to consider."

∾

Will walked slowly back to the hotel in darkness, lost in memory. *Taylor and Will as playmates, full of devilry…sworn companions in life's adventure.* The margins of the present blurred and receded: he could see his Aunt Julia's grieving face, hear her voice say his name. *At least I won't have to break the news to her,* he thought wearily, as he trudged up the steps of the boardwalk and made his way through the crowd. He sidestepped a knot of men arguing politics and bumped into a boy with a scraggly goatee and shoulder-length blond hair, who was prancing around with a whiskey bottle in his hand.

"Beg pardon," murmured Will, his thoughts far, far away.

The youth cursed and spun around. "Watch out, top hat!" he snarled, eyeing Will's neat traveling suit with contempt. The boy tossed his hair and cocked his hand on his hip, inches from the Bowie knife in his belt. "We don't cotton to pretty boys around here," he sneered. "You'd better go home to Mama." The boy's companions sniggered.

The fog in Will's mind vanished and the present rushed back. His endless, brutal journey had been a fool's errand. Taylor was dead. And now, this noxious fool was capering between him and the drink he needed more than salvation. Will lifted his guard and stepped forward in a fighter's stance, his fists moving in slow, tight circles, like the tail of a cat about to spring.

"Go ahead," he said, "reach for the knife."

The blond kid eyed the height and broad shoulders of the man confronting him, the muscles standing out like ropes on the square jaw – and the boy's whiskey-fueled bravado began to evaporate. He felt the distance between his knife hilt and his fingers lengthen with each beat of his heart… pictured what might happen to his face before he could draw the blade… He glanced around until he caught the eye of Clay Cotton, his ally in many a moonlight holdup. Cotton nodded and began to edge around the crowd to slip in behind the dandy.

The kid drew a deep breath and relaxed. A leer spread across his lips.

"You didn't mind me, top hat! That's gonna cost you…"

"Probably not," said a gruff voice.

At the sound of well-oiled metal clicking into place, the kid turned and stared, cross-eyed, down the barrel of a heavy revolver at full cock.

"That's an expensive plate glass window behind you, sonny," said the grey-whiskered driver. "If I blow your brains out at this range, I'm gonna have to replace it."

"We're jist joshin' the greenhorn, mister..." the kid said, voice quavering. "Hell, cain't nobody take a joke around here?"

The stage driver flicked his gun sideways in dismissal, and the youths edged away, disappearing into a crowd of revelers setting out to cross the street. The driver slipped the six-shooter back inside his long linen duster.

"Mr. Bachelder, isn't it?" asked Will.

"Yup, though I prefer Henry."

"Henry, then..." said Will, "I believe I owe you a drink." He opened the hotel door and gestured the driver through.

"Nah," said Henry, "I'm sorry I butted in. I should've let you mash them sorry little dung beetles into paste. The town would've given you a medal..."

A whoop and a terrific crash drew their eyes to a boisterous crowd at the back of the room. They saw a miner leap down from a tabletop and another jump up to take his place. The new man tipped his head back and balanced a magnum of champagne on his forehead. Across the room, another contestant picked up a biscuit and let fly. The missile whistled past the bottle and exploded on the wall, to thunderous jeers and catcalls.

"Henry, I need a drink," declared Will, "or maybe lots of drinks...and some peace and quiet. Any suggestions?"

The driver cast a keen eye over the young man's face. "Dutch Flat not all you hoped for, eh?"

A pistol roared in the back of the room, followed by the sound of shattering glass and peals of laughter.

"I'm sure it's a wonderful town," said Will, "but my reason for coming here is dead."

"How far did you come to learn this?"

"From Virginia."

Henry whistled. "Well then, a drink's what's needful, and some proper vittles, too. I'm on my way to the Abbot House. You're welcome to join me.

Honest food, and Maggie won't put up with any hijinks from the clientele. Downright genteel, for a gold camp."

Will hesitated. He hadn't wanted company, but there was something reassuring about Henry Bachelder – and he really did owe the man a drink.

~

"The survival rate of passengers on our line," declaimed Henry, "is a source of pride and inspiration to the entire civilized world."

"Indeed," said Will, mopping up savory, red-eye gravy with a flaky biscuit.

"We may rough 'em up a bit," the driver conceded, with a wave of his steak-tipped fork. "A few broken arms 'n' legs here and there, but nothing serious. Not like some other stage lines I could name...but won't."

"Mighty Christian of you, Henry."

"Why, there's one line that kills 'em off quite lively on the Henness Pass, but our company's strict. We don't keep a driver that gets drunk and mashes up stagecoaches."

"Admirable," said Will, lifting his mug. "I honor anyone who carries passengers on roads like these and delivers them alive." Henry waved the compliment aside.

"It's not us teamsters that do the real work – no! It's the horses who deserve the credit, and no man who's ever held the ribbons will deny it. A good horse is the truest friend you'll ever have."

Will lifted an eyebrow, but didn't challenge the assertion.

"Old Joe was my nigh leader for the better part of five years," said Henry, "and there's not a road in these mountains we didn't travel together – smartest damn horse that ever pulled a stage. Sometimes I thought he'd turn around and speak to me. I'd say 'Gee-up, Joe. It shorely is dark tonight, and there's washouts on the road.' And he'd nod his head to say, 'Don't worry, Henry, I'll get you through all right.' Everybody loved that horse, and the kids all made a pet of him.

"Well, one night Old Joe and I were pulling along the Foresthill Divide, just a mile out of Yankee Jim's, and Mr. Walker pops out of the brush with his shotgun trained on me. All the drivers knew him – that is, we didn't know who he *was,* as he always wore a mask, but we called him 'Mr. Walker' 'cause he pulled his jobs on foot.

"'Throw down the box!' Walker shouts. 'Or I'll give you both barrels!'

"'Like Hell you will,' says I, and I touch Joe with the whip. Joe leans into his collar like a good 'un, and the team's gaining speed, when that black-hearted bandit draws down on Joe and kills him in the traces.

"So Joe goes down, and the stage tries to roll over the wheelers, and my leg's near broke from stompin' on the brake. Walker's climbing up and I can't see to shoot him, 'cause I'm bawlin' like a baby over Joe...

"Walker gets a hold of the treasure box and pulls it down, but as soon as he gets the feel of it, he knows it's empty. So he leaves it alongside the road and just vanishes into the brush. He's never stopped one of my coaches again. I believe he is ashamed."

Henry shook his head and wetted his whistle with a long draught of beer.

"Wells Fargo gave Old Joe a funeral, and a fancy one, like he was a duke or a lord. And they put up a marble gravestone with an epitaph: *Here lies Joe the Nigh Leader, lost his life in a hold-up, July 22, 1859.* You can see it along the road to Yankee Jim's, in a little stand of pines. Saddest day of my life since I came to California..."

"But you didn't lose heart," said Will, refilling Henry's mug. "You kept on driving."

"You bet. There's nothing beats the stages, by my lights. Couldn't picture myself doing anything else."

"Then you are a happy man, Henry. Myself, I wouldn't mind giving up the law. I'd like a clean start...maybe try my luck at mining. I've heard some fabulous tales about the Comstock silver veins."

"You and every other half-crazy prospector on the Pacific rim," snorted Henry, spearing a sweet potato with his Barlow knife and hoisting it to his plate. "I'm not saying you wouldn't strike it big," he added quickly, seeing the disappointment in Will's face. "You've got the right build for shoveling rocks. But there's surer and easier ways of making a living – and I suspect lawyering tops the list."

"I don't want to stay in Dutch Flat, though. Not after my cousin's death."

"Then try Auburn, Placerville, Nevada...they've all got rich gold fields. Mining's changing around here. Big companies are taking over, and they need armies of lawyers."

"Perhaps you're right, but I don't know one town from another. Except Auburn, that is, because you drove me through it. If you're heading back there, I'll give it a try."

Henry shook his tangled, shoulder-length mane.

"Nope… Can't take you to Auburn. I'm heading north tomorrow…leaving for the fair city of Nevada at first light."

"'Nevada?'"

"Yep. It's Spanish for snow-covered, which she will be soon enough. She's the county seat…calls herself the *Queen of the Northern Mines*. All the trappings of civilization, and then some."

"Well, then, Nevada it is!" said Will, with a weary smile. "The road there can't be any worse than the one we took today, can it?"

"I'd better turn in," said Henry, downing the last of his drink. "I need my beauty sleep…"

"That answer would be considered 'non-responsive' in court, Henry. If I were a judge, I'd toss you in jail."

Henry chuckled as they rose from the table.

"Well then, Your Honor, here's the whole truth, since you're so all-fired curious. Tomorrow we skip over to the Little York goldfields and take aboard a box packed with bullion – the surest bait there is for attracting road agents. There we'll be joined by my old friend Josh MacAdams, whose chief delight is sending stage robbers up the Golden Stairs. Then, for a little excitement, we'll cross Steep Hollow Canyon, where you'll learn what *steep* means in the Sierra Nevada. And if we miss a turn anywhere along the way, you'll find out why my coach is called *The Little York Flyer*."

Chapter 2

Steep Hollow Grade

November 1860

The midday sun filtered down through towering firs and madrones, mottling the empty wagon road and the tangled, brushy slope of Steep Hollow Canyon. A heavy-set man sat on a stump by the road cut, rocking backward as he tipped a whiskey jug to his lips. He took a long pull, then wiped his thick, black beard and moustache with the back of his hand and turned to his three companions.

"Now, listen up, ladies," said Big Jake in a lazy drawl, "'cuz what I'm about to say might save your sorry lives. And, what's more, it might save mine.

"There's two kinds of posses in this game. The first is Hell-bent on getting the bullion back and earning theirselves a big reward from the express company. *That's* the kind you want, 'cuz if things git awkward, you kin always jist drop your winnin's and vamoose…"

"We been through this, Jake," said Eldon Whitley, a tall, thin, pockmarked man with lank brown hair. He took the jug and wiped its mouth with his sleeve.

"The other kind," said Jake, ignoring the interruption, "is the posse you git if you kill the driver and messenger and shoot up the passengers. That's the posse you *don't* want, 'cuz they'll ride you down to the gates of Hell and riddle your sorry asses with lead."

Jake glowered at his companions. Eldon was busy with the jug, but the younger two appeared to be listening.

"Now, I've had both kinds after me," said Jake, "and I kin tell you which one I prefer. So if any of you ladies gits over-excited an' indulges in any *recreational* gunplay – then you better shoot me first, 'cuz I'll kill *you*, otherwise."

"Hell, they ain't gonna show fight," sneered the kid, who sported a rakish goatee and long yellow hair. The boy lounged against a giant boulder, carving off a chaw of tobacco. "Only a parson and his wife and a two-bit reporter are goin' on to Nevada. And them doddering ol' Yankees up on the driver's box wouldn't put the scare to a rabbit."

"Shut your damned flap, Turner," growled Jake, "and keep it shut till you know what you're talkin' about. Henry Bachelder's drivin' that stage. He may hail from Ohio, but he fought his way to Mexico City with General Scott while you was still suckin' tit-milk and shittin' yaller."

The tobacco tumbled from Turner's fingers as he pushed off the rock, his knife glinting in his hand.

"I'm tired of your mouthing, you mangy old…"

Before Turner could find his feet, Jake enormous hand clutched the boy's throat and slammed him against the rock.

"Easy, there, big brother," said the swarthy man at Jake's side. He was a close copy of Jake, right down to his red flannel shirt and blue denim pants – but on a smaller scale, younger, and clean shaven. "We're already short-handed for this job."

Turner's body was jerking. Jake eased his grip.

"I suppose you're right, brother Porter. Besides, this sorry son of a bitch ain't worth the bother."

Jake let the yellow-haired kid slide to the ground. The big outlaw drew a heavy gold watch from his denims.

"Well, well," he drawled, "this stage we're a-waitin' on is due at Missouri House at one o'clock, which means the ball's about to begin. *The Little York Flyer* is nothin' if not punctual, ladies, so you better tie on your bonnets an' git ready to dance."

Eldon reached into the satchel at his feet and pulled out four masks made from flour sacks. Turner rubbed his throat and eyed the crude masks with disdain.

"Be sure to give Goldilocks a hand, Eldon," Jake said. "We don't want them golden ringlets givin' us away."

Turner waved Eldon off with a sullen shake of his head.

"Listen, boy," said Jake quietly. "You think you're man enough to take a strongbox from Henry Bachelder? Well, this is your chance. Do you have the *sand?*"

Turner glared at Jake.

"I got as much sand as you."

"All right, then. You and Eldon burrow in by that madrone on the upside of the road. When the team comes along, you jump out and ask Mr. Bachelder to please throw down the box."

"I'll do that," said Turner sulkily.

"Eldon, show this greenhorn where to stand, so you don't have to shoot through him if things git rough. Porter and me, we'll be behind those rocks. We'll take the coach if they show fight."

Jake and Porter worked their way through the brush to a tall outcropping, where they could scan the steep grade that would slow the stage and take the wind out of the team.

"So," said Porter, "what do you think of handsome Bob Turner, the Terror of the Northern Mines?"

Jake snorted as he lit a cigar. "Likeliest man I ever seen for robbin' Sunday schools. Where'd you dig him up?"

"At Betty's, in Dutch Flat. He picked a fight with some greenhorn Yank, then laid him up alongside the head with a bar stool. So he's not completely useless."

"Got a mouth on him, though, don't he?" said Jake. "Talked hisself right into the place of honor on his very first holdup."

Porter laughed. "You played him pretty fine, Jake. I wouldn't want to be the one to stand up and ask Bachelder for his strongbox."

"Henry's hands will be full of reins. Everything depends on the new shotgun messenger, MacAdams. Know anything about him?"

"Jist that he rode for Wells Fargo in the Comstock, then showed up in Little York, packin' a sawed-off 10-gauge and a pair of…"

"*Hush up!*" hissed Jake.

Porter fell silent. They heard the sound of synchronized hoof beats in the distance. Jake dropped his cigar and ground it into the duff.

"Now we'll see what sort of stones our young cavalier has got," Jake said.

The brothers pulled on their masks and peered over the rock.

"Look at her," murmured Porter. "A fortune for each of us!"

The coach disappeared behind a stand of young pines for a moment – then reappeared, much closer. The brothers leaned forward against the rock and trained their shotguns on MacAdams, who was sitting on the driver's left, his short-barreled 10-gauge across his lap.

Turner leapt out from behind the madrone, two pistols raised.

"*HOLD!*" he cried, in a voice strained with fear.

Henry Bachelder cracked his whip behind the leader's ear. MacAdams swung the gun to his shoulder and fired. Turner spun around, one of his revolvers tumbling to the ground. Jake and Porter's shotguns roared from the hillside, and MacAdams flew through the air like a rag doll and disappeared over the edge of the coach. Henry lurched and clamped his elbow over the bright red stain on his side. The lead horses reared in their traces, eyes wild with fright.

Porter and Jake jumped out to rush the coach. There was a sharp crack and a burst of smoke and flame from the window. Porter staggered and hit the ground.

"*Jesus!*" cried Jake, dropping to his knees. Another pistol shot from the coach, and an angry ball tore the air over his head.

"Oh no…God. No!" Jake moaned. He rolled his brother over and pulled off Porter's mask. Porter's mouth hung open, eyes wide in astonishment. His body quivered, and a choking sound rose from deep in his throat. A dark blotch spread quickly across his chest.

"*Son of a bitch!*" Jake roared. He grabbed his shotgun and sprang to his feet, but the coach was already rolling away, the team gathering speed. Through the dust and smoke, he saw Turner writhing in the ditch, his mask torn away. And beyond stood Eldon Whitley, high on the road bank, deliberately emptying his six-shooter into the back of the fleeing stage.

≈

"Stay down!" Will yelled, as the bandit's revolver cracked and splinters whined through the air. Will cocked his Colt and leaned out the window. He saw the robber on the embankment, aiming directly for him. They fired at the same moment.

Smoke and flame, and a sound like an iron bar smashing through a chest of drawers.

Will concentrated with all his being on the tall, skinny man in his sights. Again the pistols went off together, and Will heard a high-pitched whine as a ball ricocheted off the luggage rack above his head.

The coach lurched and swung around a bend, and the bandit disappeared from view. Will gasped in a lung full of air…had no idea how long he had been holding his breath. The stage was still gaining speed, bumping and heaving up the twisting grade…but the wheels were skittering along the edge of the road cut, pushing sheets of small rocks over the rim of a hundred-foot drop.

"Henry!" Will yelled at the top of his lungs.

The coach lurched back into the worn ruts in the road, then bounced out again. The team was mad with fear. Henry's limp arm dangled over the edge of the driver's box.

Will grabbed the window frame and swung himself out of the coach. He stood on the window ledge, clutching the iron rail of the luggage rack above him. The careening stage was an arm's length from the rock face of the hillside. He swung his foot for the iron step below the driver's box and clung to the side of the coach like a spider. Then, with a yell, he heaved himself up and tumbled into the box.

He unwound the lines from Henry's hand and shoved the bleeding driver over to the messenger's seat. He frantically wove the lines through his own fingers. The coach was drifting steadily toward the drop-off.

Will shook the lines hard to let the horses know he was there, then reined in with all his might and crushed the brake pedal with his boot.

"Whoa! Gee-woah!"

The nigh leader pulled to the inside as he slowed. The coach swung violently, and Henry groaned. "There's a flat spot ahead…quarter mile," the driver gasped. "Let 'em stop there and blow."

"We'll get you down into the coach there," said Will.

"Nah…" said Henry, his head lolling with the pitching stage, "this is the best seat in the house…"

Chapter 3

The Shade of Mr. Meredith

November 1860

"Not before I kill you, poltroon!" cried d'Artagnan, thrusting an imaginary sword through Nutim. The Indian boy clutched his stomach and staggered backward, then fell to the parlor floor.

"Ha!" cried the young musketeer, brandishing her blade. "You will never insult my horse again!"

"How come I never get to be d'Artagnan?" said the corpse, lifting his head. "I'm tired of always losing."

"Because it takes the best acting to die!" said Ida. "C'mon, let's do it again! Only this time say, *'Morbleu!'* and twist your moustaches disdainfully..."

"*Nutim!*" cried Molly Hatfield from the porch. "Come here. I need your good eyes." The boy jumped up and raced for the front door, his tablecloth cape flapping. Ida followed close behind.

The three stood in silence, peering at the reddish-brown cloud rising over the pines and drawing rapidly nearer. "It's not smoke, mother...thick dust... moving fast," said the youngster, shading his eyes with his hand.

"That must be the stage," said Molly. "Either Henry's trying to kill his horses, or there's trouble. Nutim, fetch Mr. Johnson and Pedro, now!"

The boy sprinted the length of the porch and leapt down the steps. He stumbled as he hit the ground, but was up in a second and running to the stable, where the station's foreman and the cook's son were waiting with the replacement team.

Molly and Ida dashed for the office. Ida pulled a double-barreled 20-gauge from the gun cabinet and handed it to her mother. Molly checked the caps and issued instructions as she headed out the door.

"Load the spare shotgun first, Ida, and another revolver for Mr. Johnson. Pedro will help you when he gets here. Load every weapon that can kill a highwayman!"

~

Ida grabbed a Sharps rifle and a Colt revolver and staggered to the office window. She flung up the sash, knelt down, and ran out the massive barrel of the rifle. Pedro raised the window next to hers and rested the butt of a monstrous pepperbox pistol on the sill.

Ida's breath came quick and shallow. The Northern Mines were swarming with thieves and murderers, and stagecoaches were their favorite prey. She thought of Henry, high up on the driver's box, defenseless. *Henry…the closest thing in the world to a father to me.* Ida swung the front sight of the rifle into position. *Breathe deeply…squeeze the trigger at the end of the out-breath.*

"I can hear them," cried Pedro. The boy tightened his two-handed grip on the pistol.

Six wild-eyed, foam-lipped horses galloped around the bend, followed by a careening coach and a plume of boiling dust. As the team thundered in, Ida saw Mr. Johnson behind an oak, swinging his hat low across his knees to signal *no pursuit.*

A stranger in a spruce traveling suit reined in the team and looked down from the driver's box. Ida saw the man's fine clothes were torn and smeared with blood and dust.

"Where's Henry?" Molly cried.

"Mr. Bachelder's in the coach, ma'am. He's been wounded."

It seemed to Ida that everything happened at once: her mother pulling open the coach door, Mr. Johnson and the well-dressed stranger lifting Henry down, terrified passengers stumbling out. Pedro appeared, dragging an old door from the barn and helping the men load Henry onto it, while Esmeralda flew back to the house to get things ready for the wounded man.

Henry groaned as the pallet tipped on the way up the porch steps. Ida saw the big stranger easily lift the back end of the litter to keep it level.

"Into the first bedroom with him," said Molly, holding the front door open.

"Sorry, Molly," came a weak, rasping voice from the pallet. "I'll get blood everywhere…just get me…buckboard…haul me to Doc's…"

"You hush up this minute, Henry Bachelder. The sound of your jaw flapping has never helped intelligent people think."

Henry's feeble laugh turned into a full-throated moan as the stretcher grazed the door post. Ida saw his face blanch with pain. Molly wheeled and grasped her daughter's shoulders.

"You tend to the passengers, Ida. Feed 'em, water 'em, get 'em drunk – I don't care, so long as they don't get underfoot."

∾

Ida's charges were too few and too stunned to be any trouble. Just an old minister and his wife, and a reedy-looking man who claimed to be a writer for some paper back East. He was traveling up to the Northern Mines in search of "colorful life," and Ida reckoned he'd found it. She poured them coffee and ladled stew – and let her mind turn to the stranger who had brought in the stage.

She figured he was probably from Virginia. His voice had the same soft, fluid tones as Mr. Meredith, the handsome attorney who had gone off to the Washoe last year and got himself carved into little pieces in the Paiute war – leaving half the women in the county mourning. Like Meredith, the stranger had thick, wavy, brown hair that curled gently over his ears…arching brows, straight nose, neatly trimmed moustache… *But those eyes!* Ida stared dreamily through the passengers who were waving to get her attention. *Outside, they had glowed cornflower blue under long, dark lashes, then softened to a misty grey in the shadowy hall.* And he was older, too, like Mr. Meredith…at least 25…infinitely superior to the hapless boys who pestered her when she drove into town.

The passengers finished their lunch and retired to the parlor. Ida was stacking their dirty dishes when the bedroom door opened and the tall stranger stepped toward her.

"Allow me to present myself, Miss Hatfield. My name is William Stafford." He bowed, and Ida dipped her skirts in reply. "I'll be riding to Nevada, and

your mother has kindly offered me refreshment while a horse is saddled. She
referred me to your care."

Ida listened, enchanted by his slow, mellifluous speech. *Kine-ly?* Wherever had the *d* gone? And how did *care* become *kay-ah?*

"Oh…of course, sir. Won't you sit here?" She hefted the coffeepot. "I'll
heat this up," she said.

"Please don't go to any trouble. I must be on my way. Mr. Bachelder needs
help."

"How bad is he?" Ida asked, her eyes wide.

"He took some buckshot. It peeled the skin off his side…and likely broke
a couple of ribs. He is resting now, though. The laudanum has done its work."

Ida's stomach lurched. "Poor Henry! Any shot left in him?"

"We can't tell. I'm going for Doctor Hunt and then the Sheriff."

"You shouldn't go alone!"

"Don't fret, Miss Ida," Will said, suddenly smiling. "Your mother assures
me the horse knows the way."

Ida stared at him. *He's not afraid of the outlaws. He's as brave as Meredith… I hope he has better sense.*

Will read the concern in her deep blue eyes.

"I'll be all right," he said. "I want to do this for Mr. Bachelder. I owe him
a favor."

Ida piled his plate high with potatoes and smothered them in stew. She
slid the biscuits closer and scanned his place setting, looking for some way
of making herself useful.

"May I get you a glass of brandy?" she asked.

"That would be awfully kind," he said, buttering a biscuit with a hand that
was charmingly free of wedding bands.

Ida raced for the parlor, wrested the bottle from the startled reporter, and
sped back.

"Thank you, Ida," came Molly Hatfield's voice. Ida saw to her dismay that
her mother had materialized in the chair across from Stafford. "Will you
please go see how Pedro is doing? Mr. Stafford will be riding Incitatus to
Nevada, and the horse wants careful cinching."

Ida headed for the front door, seething. Pedro knew perfectly well – better than any of them! – how Incitatus enjoyed swelling himself up when you cinched his saddle. Her mother was clearing the field.

Not even out of mourning yet, Ida fumed. *Doesn't she realize she's **years** too old for a man like William Stafford?*

∽

"Ida's just fifteen, Mr. Stafford," said Molly Hatfield, as she poured him a generous glass of brandy, "and wild enough to frighten the paint off a Paiute war party."

"She was most kind and attentive to me, ma'am."

"I don't doubt it," said Molly, suppressing a smile. "I hope this incident hasn't thrown off your plans, Mr. Stafford."

"Not in the least, ma'am. My time is my own."

"You travel for pleasure?"

Will burst into laughter, and Molly, who knew more than most about the unspeakable agonies of stage travel, blushed.

"Not so far," he said, wiping his eyes. "But I continue to hope. Your Sierra trails are certainly picturesque, but in my country, we don't usually have to shoot our way into the stage stop."

Molly smiled. "You travel for business, then?"

"For lack of business, ma'am, if truth be told. I was an attorney back in Virginia. I came out West to join a cousin of mine in practice at Dutch Flat, but when I arrived at his doorstep, I learned a fever had carried him off. So I've decided to have a look at Nevada, then push on to the Washoe Territory and try my luck there. At mining, perhaps, or lawyering – if my hands prove too soft for honest work."

"Your cousin's death must have been a shock. Perhaps you should take some time deciding. Nevada's a wealthy town and the county seat – the perfect destination for a gentleman interested in mining law."

Lord! I sound like an advertisement from the Merchant's Association, she thought in chagrin, *...or like a lonely widow.* She hunted for a new subject.

"Is there any news of the election?" she asked.

"Why, yes, ma'am. Mr. Lincoln has won, as we all knew he must. Word reached Dutch Flat last night."

Molly frowned and bit her lip.

"I fear the news upsets you," said Will. "You are not an admirer of Mr. Lincoln?"

"I have nothing against the man, but his election worries me."

"Indeed, the secessionist fire-eaters have sworn to leave the Union if he takes office, though it is only South Carolina who appears ready to back her threats with action. I assure you, Mrs. Hatfield, there is little enthusiasm for secession in my country of Virginia."

"I am relieved to hear it. The news from back East has been alarming – talk of disunion…even war." Molly pushed away her empty coffee cup.

"Let us pray not," Will said. "We must place our hopes on cooler tempers and wiser heads…"

There was a somber pause, and then Will asked, "How do you all get along out here in California, with men from every state and territory?"

"Not as well as we could wish," said Molly, dryly. "It was just a year ago that Chief Justice Terry shot and killed Senator Broderick for opposing slavery in California. Since then the situation has grown steadily worse. The latest news is the legislature has voted to split off the southern counties and form a new slaveholding territory, with ex-Governor Latham to head it up. He wants to cut the State in two for his political ambitions."

"He isn't the first to use the crisis for his own advancement…"

Will fell silent as Pedro appeared at the dining room door.

"Incitatus is ready, *señora*. I put the large saddlebags on him, so the *señor* can carry some belongings. It will be too late to return tonight."

Will pushed back his chair. Molly rose with regret. She didn't want to part with William Stafford just yet – but Henry needed a doctor.

"Will you excuse me, ma'am?" Will said. "A change of clothes from my trunk, and I'll be on my way."

"By all means. Could you stop by my office before you leave, Mr. Stafford? I'd be obliged if you would take a note to town for me."

"Of course."

"And I hope you'll look over the Missouri House arsenal before you go, and take whatever weapons you need. Our road agents are enterprising – and given to revenge."

Chapter 4

Nutim's Story

November 1860

Molly sat in her rocking chair, pulling the tortoiseshell pins from her hair and brushing her heavy golden locks, banishing the tangles and cares of the day with soothing strokes. In the broad mirror above the washstand, she looked past her own reflection and saw Nutim's dark head poking in her bedroom door. She held out her arms, and he ran to her and climbed onto her lap. His eyes were very wide.

"Little Bit," she said, "I thought you were asleep hours ago." He shook his head, then buried his face in her shoulder and wrapped his arms around her neck.

"Don't be afraid, sugar, we're safe here," Molly said softly. "No one will hurt us."

The chair creaked under the boy's added weight. She rocked slowly and tried to banish the thought of the robbers who might be lurking nearby. She had been hearing stories of strange lights at the old Walloupa diggings. *Ghosts,* claimed the miners. *Outlaws,* more likely. Old Cerberus the watchdog had slept soundly through this afternoon's excitement. Maybe it was time to get another pup.

"Would you like a puppy dog of your own?" she said. Nutim sat up in her lap and smiled at her for an instant, then buried his head back in her neck. He mumbled something to the collar of her robe.

"Do you want me to tell the Nutim story?" she said. Nutim nodded his head. He hadn't asked for this story for some time. He'd been casting off his baby ways, no longer carrying his quilt around, or the toy horse that Zeke had carved for him. *Tonight he needs to be my baby again.*

She rocked him a few times, summoning the story from memory. She had made up the tale from guesswork, but the boy's reaction told her she'd come close to the truth.

"Little Nutim lived in the mountains with his mother and father, in a beautiful house made of cedar bark. In the daytime, he played in the forest among the big trees, and at night he slept under a blanket made of the softest rabbit fur.

"Early one morning soldiers came to the Indian camp. Nutim was asleep. His mother woke him. 'Hush, my son, and listen to me,' she whispered, 'the soldiers have come to take us away. We must run and hide.'

"Nutim and his mother ran into the forest, where she hid him under the low branches of a tree. 'Lie still, my Nutim,' she said, 'like a spotted fawn, and the soldiers will not see you. Do not move until I come back with grand-mother.'"

Molly could feel the tension in the child's arms around her neck. *What had he witnessed on that winter morning, five years ago?*

"Little Nutim lay in the forest all day. When darkness came, he went back to his house, but no one was there. He lay down under his rabbit fur blanket and tried to go to sleep. He was afraid, hungry and thirsty, and lonesome for his mother.

"He waited all the next day for someone to come for him, but no one came. At last, he decided to follow the trail of the soldiers and find his family.

"Nutim started walking on his little baby legs. The moon went down and the night grew dark, but Nutim was very brave. He found the white sand wagon road and followed it down Chalk Bluff Mountain. The North Wind blew down on Nutim from the snowdrifts on the ridge top. He shivered with cold, but he kept on walking.

"Early the next morning, when the sky was getting light, Molly came out with her milking pail on her arm. She pushed open the barn door and went inside. The barn was dark and warm, full of the smells of cows and hay. She lit the lantern that hung from the big hook by the milking stanchions. There was Dolly, the Jersey cow, lying asleep in her deep straw bedding, and curled up against her was a naked little child with long hair as dark as night.

"Molly picked up the tiny boy in her arms and carried him to the house. He put his arms around Molly's neck and held on to her like a cocklebur, all that whole day…"

Nutim was already asleep, his legs curled to fit between the arms of the chair. He was growing up so fast, losing the chipmunk expression he'd had when his adult teeth first came in. He was getting heavy, too. Soon she wouldn't be able to lift him like this. She laid him on the bed and smoothed the dark hair from his forehead. His skin was cool; she pulled the comforter over him.

He had been running a fever the morning she'd found him in the barn, and the next day his temperature had climbed frighteningly high. She had sat beside the delirious child night after night, sponging him with cold water, praying there would be no lasting damage. When the fever finally broke, weeks passed before his terror subsided and his skinny body began to fill out.

She had known all along she couldn't keep the child. On an early spring day, when he was strong again, she took the boy to Storms' Ranch to see the Indian Agent. Captain Storms was married to a daughter of Chief Wemah; he would know how to find the child's parents. Molly saw a haunted look come over Simmons Storms's face when he recognized the boy who was sitting on her lap. The agent's voice was flat and weary.

"This child is an orphan, Mrs. Hatfield. You will have no trouble getting his indenture papers made out to you. There is no one to object. Under the 1850 Indian Law, he will be bound to you until he is eighteen. You are required to treat him humanely and to answer for his behavior."

Molly flushed scarlet. "I did not purchase him, Captain Storms, and I do not intend to use him as a servant. The practice of kidnapping children is abhorrent to me. The boy must be returned to his family."

"That is praiseworthy in you, ma'am," the Agent said. "However, this boy's grandparents are also dead. There is no one here to look after him. His tribe has been removed to Nome Lackee Reserve, more than a hundred miles northwest."

Molly sat speechless. *Removed? The whole tribe gone?*

"Mrs. Hatfield, the Nevada Indians must be relocated away from the mining districts. Our good townsfolk will not tolerate their presence. At best, the Diggers are despised, at worst…well…you have seen the disgraceful conduct whiskey incites in both races. It is to everyone's benefit that they are segregated." Storms wiped his brow with his handkerchief. He was sweating, although the room was cold.

He stared out the window at the green meadow covered in spring clover, the bright stream winding through yellow willows. "Unfortunately, many of them refuse to work on the new land reserve. They straggle back here, a few more every week, even though there is no protection for them here…and no rations." He coughed. "At Nome Lackee, we can teach them to be useful and have a share in the future." Storms crumpled the handkerchief back into his pocket.

"Mrs. Hatfield, their primitive race must give way to a superior one. It is inevitable by the laws of history and nature. The poor Diggers must vanish so that civilization may appear. That you feel compassion for their deplorable condition does you credit, as does your rescue of this suffering child."

Storms pushed back his chair and stood up, signaling an end to the interview.

Molly rose to face him, the boy on her hip.

"Please understand, Captain Storms, that I am determined to make every effort to find this boy's relatives. Perhaps one of the new arrivals at your rancho will know who is searching for this child."

Storms shook his head in exasperation.

"No one is searching for that child, ma'am. But if you don't believe me, I can take you to Old Lucy. She gives the Indian children their adult names when they reach puberty. She knows everyone's family."

Storms guided Molly across the marshy meadow, to a bark house that stood on rising ground at the edge of a cedar grove. The conical, windowless structure was made of long slabs of cedar bark, propped up against each other and looking like the stump of an immense tree. Molly bunched her skirts and bent double to pass through the low entryway that sloped down to a single round room, dug halfway into the ground. The floor and walls were smooth, hard-packed clay, warmed and lighted by a crackling fire in a shallow pit in the center of the room. Storms motioned Molly to sit on a raised platform cushioned with boughs and spread with old canvas. An old woman and a half-grown girl with a scarred lip sat on the floor. A toddler with a distended belly tried to hide under the older girl's shawl.

Molly, nodding and smiling, presented her basket of cold chicken and bis-cuits, while Storms made introductions. Some Maidu words she recognized: *wólem kulem,* "white woman," that was herself; *kaletam bom ku,* "wagon road house," Missouri House.

"Do you know this boy?" Molly asked. She paused for Storms to translate. "Is anyone looking for him?"

Lucy held out her arms for the child, and he went to her willingly. The old lady had on a white woman's cast-off dress, washed so many times that its pattern was fading away. She wore a basketry cap over her silver hair, and vertical lines were tattooed on her chin. Her feet were bare and heavily cal-loused; her hands and fingers were knotted and broadened from work. Her eyes brightened and her wide face creased with a smile for the boy.

She pulled Nutim onto her lap and combed his hair with her fingers, whispering to him. She tickled his toes and sang in a low voice. Molly watched, relieved to hear the usually silent child laughing and speaking to the old woman. After a long time, Lucy stood him on his feet and gently guided him to Molly's knees.

"Tibim nuktim tébe..." the old woman began. Her voice was low and musi-cal, like water falling into a deep pool. *"...bomúmuknokas."*

Storms spoke over her in English.

"Such a little bit of a boy, I feel sorry for him."

"Unidi ókusàes..."

"Here we are hungry, and many of us are sick. There is no doctor at this place."

"Hubona ukoipada..."

"You go home and take good care of him. Bring him back to visit us."

"Betéimàakas hoiyam kodoidi."

"I will tell him the old stories, about the time before this world."

Lucy smiled and patted Nutim's head. She turned to Molly again, her black eyes searching Molly's green ones.

"Makitka?" she asked.

"Do you understand?"

∾

Nutim stirred in his sleep and turned over. Molly kissed his forehead and wondered how long she would be able to protect him. Five years had passed since that meeting with Storms. Now the news coming out of the Indian reservations was dreadful. Nome Lackee was shut down, and wars were raging. Starving Indians were taking livestock, and the militia were taking lives in exchange. She knew that Nutim brooded over these horrors. She dreaded that he would put himself in harm's way.

She lay down next to the sleeping boy, closed her eyes, and tried to compose her weary mind.

Almighty God, watch over my Nutim and protect him...and let his people... Let his people *what?* Blend in with the whites? Flee from them? Drive them away? What *could* God do to rescue His forgotten children?

Chapter 5

The Queen of the Northern Mines

November 1860

"A miner's kit in the old days consisted of a clasp knife and a bucket," said Mrs. Truscott, as she poured Will's coffee. "Or so Mr. Truscott used to say, rest his soul. He got here in '49, when Nevada was just a log store and gold sparkled up from the stream bed wherever you looked."

Will gulped down a savory mouthful of bacon and eggs and murmured an obliging, "Indeed, ma'am?"

"Oh, yes!" the landlady continued cheerfully. "The knife was for prying gold out of seams in the rock, and the bucket was for nuggets. Truscott camped down by Deer Creek with all the others, where the plaza is today.

"There was plenty more gold underground after the placer gold was taken. The town took off, growing right up the sides of the ravine and out over the surrounding hills. We're a commercial hub now, and lucky for you that we are! There wasn't much call for lawyers in the old days."

"No, ma'am?"

"Not a bit! If there was some judging to be done, the miners would get together over a keg of whiskey and drink their way to a verdict. Things are a lot more respectable now – we've got some first-rate law these days. But of course, you know that already…you've met Aidan Caldwell!"

"Yes, ma'am. I delivered a note to the Judge for Mrs. Hatfield, right after I spoke with the doctor and the sheriff."

"And got a job offer from Aidan on your first night in town! You've certainly landed on your feet, young man! More coffee, dear?"

~

The smell of fresh paint and newly sawn wood greeted Will as he ventured forth to celebrate the end of his journey. He strolled down streets that echoed with pounding hammers and the rumble of wagons laden with shingles, siding, and kegs of nails. Will saw several "Open for Business" signs hanging on the front doors of shops whose back doors had yet to be milled. Other establishments offered imposing, storey-and-a-half wood fronts to the street, but were only canvas tents in back. Along the main road that climbed out of the canyon toward Grass Valley, rows of dwellings perched on stilts, their front steps resting on the hillside, their backyards nothing but air. As he looked around, Will felt as if he had wandered onto a vast theater set being flung up for a play in progress, with swarms of stagehands and actors buzzing about and no director in sight.

"This isn't the first Nevada, nor will it be the last," opined Mr. Dickerson, the apothecary, in response to Will's remarks on the pace of construction. "Just about every building you see is a replacement for one that burned down in the last fire."

"How often do you all have fires in these parts?" asked Will, absentmindedly testing the bristles of a badger-hair shaving brush.

"How often do you want 'em?" scoffed the apothecary. "We burn through the place every three or four years."

Will raised a disbelieving eyebrow.

"It was worse in the early days," said Dickerson, with the complacency of an old-timer. "Nevada was mostly tents when I got here, packed full of candles and cross-eyed drunks. It didn't pay to sleep too soundly."

"Hard to burn up tents that are scattered around," said Will, setting the brush and a cake of soap on the counter.

"You'd be surprised, stranger. In '51, there was still tall timber around here, and we all strung up our canvas on lines stretched between the trees. As cool and shady in summertime as a picnic grove, but when some fool tipped over his lantern… Lord! How those big pines torched up – shooting flaming knots like skyrockets! They turned the whole sky into a ball of fire!"

Will stepped out onto the boardwalk and cast a newly appreciative eye over the treeless cityscape. Some merchants had evidently wearied of the constant rebuilding and were investing in more lasting structures – and larger ones, too. The National Exchange, a vast, three-storey "fireproof" hotel, anchored the foot of Broad Street, followed by a row of brick stores stepping up the hill toward the new brick firehouse, with its ornate, gingerbread bell tower. The proud thoroughfare also boasted fire hydrants, gas street lanterns, and newly laid wood planking over the roadway, to keep down summer dust and save humans and horses from sinking to their knees in winter mud.

Will walked up the north side of Broad Street, avoiding the crush of freight handlers and passengers around the stages drawn up in front of the National Hotel. Three long pack trains thundered past on their way to remote camps – perhaps two hundred mules in all and thirty swarthy, sombreroed drivers, all passionately cursing their long-eared charges in Spanish.

Near the corner of Pine, a middle-aged man was folding back the shutters from his storefront. With a strong New England twang, he invited Will to inspect his unrivaled stock of prospector's gear – all of the first quality, all a bargain. Was he right in guessing that the young visitor was bound for Virginia City, to seek his fortune in the Washoe mines?

"I am a newcomer, sir," said Will, "but I won't be heading on to the Comstock. I intend to stay here."

"Why, there's no mining to be done around here by a gentleman on his own," the startled shopkeeper told Will. "The claims are all taken up by companies with plenty of capital. The Washoe Territory is the only place where the spirit of the Argonaut lives on! Take it from me, young man, you should leave for Virginia City right away. The mountain passes will close soon – the snow won't hold off for long."

Will thanked the merchant for his advice and walked on. He was hailed by a grizzled lounger sitting in front of the café next door.

"Nevuh mind that Yankee, friend," said the man in a thick, Georgia drawl. "Count yoh'self lucky you nevuh caught gold fevuh. It gets in your blood, like swamp sickness, an' breaks out without waunuhn." He launched a jet of dark tobacco juice into the gutter. "Take a load off your feet, son, an' join me for a mug of coffee. It's hot, anyways."

Will thanked the man and settled himself on the rough wooden bench.

"Did you evuh hear of the prospector who died an' went to heaven?" the old timer asked.

Will regretted that he had not.

"Well…it seems when he arrived, he couldn't get in. The place was packed as tight as a sardine can.

"'*Full up?*' cries the prospector to Saint Pete. 'What do you mean?'

"'No room,' says Pete, turnin' to go, 'we're bustin' at the seams with prospectors.'

"'Wait a minute,' says the dead man, thinkin' fast, 'if I can make you more room, will you let me in?'

"'I suppose so…' says the Saint, kinda laffin' to hisself.

"So the prospector scribbles out a note and says, 'Here, give this to Old Soapy, or Two Fingers, or any of them that's playin' cards in there. It ought to do the trick.'

"Well suh, before long, all the prospectors in heaven are bangin' on the Pearly Gates, demandin' to be let out.

"'What's going on?' asks St. Peter.

"'*Let us out!*' they all cry. 'There's a big gold strike in Hell!' So Pete swings open the Gates, and the miners stampede out.

"'You can come in now,' he says to the prospector. 'There's plenty of room.'

"Well, before you know it, that same prospector is back and sets to hollerin' an' rattlin' those Pearly Gates.

"'What is it now?' asks Pete.

"'Let me out! I'm leavin' too!' says the prospector.

"'But why do you want to leave? You started that rumor about the gold strike in Hell in the first place!'

"'I know,' says the prospector, '*but there just might be something in it!*'"

~

By midmorning, Will had resigned himself to the fact that Nevada, *Queen of the Northern Mines,* was almost entirely male – with a dozen men for every woman. A tavern owner had evidently noticed this imbalance, too, and had hung an empty petticoat from his signboard to lure the lonely miners to his trade.

The men of Nevada hailed from every region of the globe. A French clerk at the haberdashery greeted him with a rousing *bonjour*. Passing the butcher's door, Will recognized the thick Liverpool English he had heard on shipboard. From the open-tent gambling halls of the Chinese quarter, he heard the singsong tones of Cantonese. In a downtown dry goods store, Will chanced upon a Maidu family bargaining with the moustachioed Italian owner, debating how to spend the gold they had panned out of a mountain stream. He was struck by the melodious flow of their language. It reminded him of the sound of his Latin teacher reading Ovid. *What a strange amalgam of races California is!*

After a superb lunch of grilled trout and Chablis at the National Hotel, Will left through the back exit and strolled down Spring Street. A crowd was gathering in front of one of the brothels, where two men circled each other, brandishing Bowie knives.

"Rose hates your sorry guts," sneered one.

"She puts up with you 'cause she'll get a whippin' if she don't," countered his opponent. Onlookers shouldered up, forming an arena, and egged the rivals on.

"Give it to 'im hot!" cried one. "Let some air out of 'im!" The combatants responded with a flurry of thrusts and slashes, though it seemed to Will that neither was wholly committed to dying for the lady's honor.

A voice of brass shattered the air. *"Get off my doorstep, you piss-ant sons of bitches!"* cried a blowzy, harried-looking woman, leveling a shotgun at the rivals. *"Clear off, or I'll shoot you in a way so's you'll never bother a female again!"*

The street cleared briskly as guilty and innocent alike remembered appointments elsewhere. *The Code of Honor in the mines,* Will mused as he joined the exodus, *may not be the formal, ritualized affair it is back in Virginia.* Every man he had seen so far carried some kind of weapon – and was evidently ready to use it without much preamble. He made a mental note to have his pistol looked to at the gunsmith's – and lay in some fresh powder.

Will wandered up and down the hilly streets, taking in the town's peculiar mix of crudeness and sophistication, its cheerful, unthinking embrace of the familiar and exotic. Crowded together downtown were churches, bars, bowling alleys, fortune-telling parlors, attorneys' offices, printers' shops, and a musical emporium that boasted an astonishing collection of sheet music. Jumbled in among the commercial establishments was an array of social clubs: a Masonic Lodge, an Odd Fellows Hall, and a "Hall of Comparative

Ovations." Gold lettering on the glass-windowed door proclaimed this last to be the home of *E Clampus Vitus,* whose motto, *"Credo Quia Absurdum,"* was proudly emblazoned below.

Will stood contemplating this message, wondering if his translation, "I believe because it is absurd," could possibly be right. The door opened and a representative of the lodge appeared, clad in a sober black coat and a red shirt. On his lapel he wore a star cut from a tin can lid. With a solemn glance toward heaven, the man raised both hands to his head, pressed his thumbs to the tips of his ears, and spread his fingers wide.

"Do you hear the *Braying of the Hewgag?*" he inquired of Will.

"I do not believe I do, sir," said Will.

"Aren't you the *Poor, Blind Candidate,* come to join the *Clampers?*" asked Tin Star, disconcerted.

Will replied that he was, to the best of his knowledge, neither poor, blind, nor a candidate, at which the lodge man disappeared back into the meeting hall, leaving Will to ponder the ways of the mysterious fraternity.

As the sun dipped, he strolled back to his boarding house, whistling cheerfully. For all its rough edges, Will found Nevada as exhilarating as champagne – a world of fresh beginnings and exciting possibilities. He was eager to discover if his landlady's supper would match the standard set by her excellent bacon and eggs that morning. Then he would sortie again in search of a companionable watering hole and a sampling of the town's after-hours amusements.

Chapter 6

Gone to Blaze's

November 1860

The saloon was full of a joyful hubbub that almost drowned out the exuberant piano in the corner. Will stepped up to the bar and lifted his voice to make himself heard by the giant who was wiping glasses on the other side.

"So I say to my new landlady, 'Could you direct me to a genteel saloon?' 'The What Cheer House,' she replies, 'is only two doors away.' So I step in there and ask the barkeep for a cocktail. 'This is a Temperance house, mister,' says he, 'may I set you up a sarsaparilla?' Well, that isn't what I have in mind, so I ask him if he can recommend an establishment where stronger beverages are served. 'Sir,' he says, 'if you want a drink, *you can go to Blaze's!*'"

Will launched his punch line into a lull in the tavern's usual din. Up and down the long, polished bar, the crowd *har-har-ed* their approval of the beloved local joke.

"Jim Blaze, at your service," said the grinning barkeep. He stuck out a fleshy hand and gave Will a bone-crushing shake. "What will you take, Mister?"

Before Will could reply, a florid-faced man next to him slapped a leather poke packed with gold dust on the bar.

"I'm standing this round, Blaze, in honor of this young wildcat!" He clapped a hand on Will's shoulder. "We read about him in the *Journal* this morning! Here we have the very man who brought the *Little York Flyer* in from Steep Hollow, with the reins in his teeth and both guns talking!"

"Well, now, it wasn't exactly that way..." Will started to protest, but he was drowned out by a barrage of questions from the patrons.

Jim Blaze poured shots of tanglefoot whiskey and sized up the latest arrival to his saloon. The young man was bright of eye, with a cheerful and unblemished countenance – no sign of brawling. The newcomer's hands looked soft and well kept. He wore no rings, nor did he sport the gaudy diamond shirt stud of a professional gambler. A strong frame filled out his handsomely tailored frock coat, and judging from the outline at his side, his personal armament was a .31-caliber Colt.

This gent's no professional gunman, Blaze reflected, *and he hasn't been in the mines for long. Too young for a banker...looks lively for a lawyer...but that's what he must be...*

A mud-spattered gold seeker holding aloft a canvas sack pushed through the swinging door of the saloon, followed by a pack of grinning loafers. The bartender turned toward the new excitement.

"Good evening to your honor," the grimy prospector began, settling the rucksack on the bar. "'Faith, here is such a thing as will astonish even a man so accustomed to marvels as yourself! And, if I may make so bold, I propose a swap – jar for jar – the contents of my sack for a *cruiskeen* of your honor's *pottheen!*"

Rubbing his hands with anticipation, Blaze loosened the knot at the mouth of the sack and lifted out a glass gallon jar packed with the rippling brown coils of a monstrous rattlesnake – who instantly lifted his tail and protested with loud, angry buzzing. Blaze banged the jar down and jumped back, while the patrons crushed in for a closer look.

Will Stafford heard a low-pitched voice at his side.

"You've already been introduced to our two-legged breed of rattlesnake, so that puny specimen must be a disappointment to you."

Will turned and shook the leather-tough hand offered by John Van Hagen, Sheriff of Nevada. The lawman's face was puffy with fatigue, and dark circles underscored his piercing blue eyes. He leaned his lanky frame against the bar and lifted a dusty boot to the rail.

"What news, Sheriff?' asked Will. "Is the stage driver patched up all right?"

"Doc Hunt dug three buckshot out of his ribs. Painful, but not too serious. Molly will get him back on his feet in no time."

"How about the Wells Fargo messenger?"

"Well, MacAdams got off one barrel, to his credit. But he was dead before he hit the ground."

The sheriff dug in his pocket for the price of a drink and looked up to catch the bartender's attention. Jim Blaze motioned Van Hagen to put his money away. The barkeep wiped the bar with a sopping rag, set up two fresh glasses, and poured the whiskey. The lawman took a deep drink and continued his tale.

"We followed the bandits down into Birdseye Canyon, steering by the trail of blood." He traced a simple map in the moisture left by the barman's rag. "They must have been trying to strike the old Emigrant Trail, but lost their bearings in the deep ravine. The geography there is well-nigh vertical, and the spiny live oak is thick as wool. Their tracks looped around until they were headed back to where they started." Van Hagen shook his head at the robbers' incompetence.

"The ground was rough and our horses were getting balky, so we dismounted and led them. In among some huge boulders, my mare had a conniption and broke loose. I was turned around, watching her disappear into the brush, when I saw the other boys grabbing for their guns. Right behind me, the biggest goddamn grizzly in creation reared up out of the rocks, blood dripping from his jaws!" The lawman paused for Blaze to refill his glass, then tossed off a gulp. "Be damned if my deputy didn't drop him with one shot – that man is stingy as Scrooge with his bullets!" Van Hagen grinned.

"We found the remains of Mr. Grizzly's last meal. There wasn't much you could recognize, except some long yellow hair. It must have been the kid who tried to halt the coach."

"My God! What an end!" Will blanched as he reached for his drink.

"Well, sir, you mustn't blame Mr. Grizzly for the youngster's demise. Nor the buckshot or the .31-caliber ball Doc Hunt fished from the body. It was a .36-caliber slug that ended the kid's career as a highwayman.

"Now, your Pocket Colt accounts for the .31-caliber bullet, and messenger MacAdams gets credit for the buckshot, but MacAdams never got a chance to draw his sidearm. Looks like the kid was hurt too bad to climb out of that canyon, so one of his own gang finished him off. They knew we would catch up to him. Now he'll tell no tales."

The sheriff shoved his empty glass to the back of the bar and watched in silence as Blaze filled it again. "One more drink," he said, lifting his glass to Will, "to knit the raveled sleeves of the last couple of days… Hell, the last couple of years." He took a fiery mouthful of whiskey. "There's more stage robbers infesting these hills than ticks on a stray dog – from lone despera-does to mounted gangs. They hit one express line after another, with every modus operandi under the sun. And now, this callous murder of MacAdams tops the list." The lawman shook his head. "I don't stand a Chinaman's chance of being re-elected, and I'm not sure I care. I'm tired of chasing vermin."

"This is wild country, Sheriff – lots of room for a road agent to hide in."

"Oh, they'll be caught, sooner or later," said Van Hagen. "Their trade rarely attracts a mastermind. But I don't mind telling you, Stafford, if an in-telligent and resourceful man like yourself were to set up in the stage robbing business, we'd be helpless."

The sheriff drained his glass and stepped back from the bar. He rested his hand on Will's shoulder. "William, a lot of folks around here are indebted to you for saving Henry Bachelder and that treasure box. If you decide to stick around, you'll find you already have some friends."

Chapter 7

Christmas on Piety Hill

December 1860

Judge Aidan Caldwell pulled off his gold pince-nez and held them up to the shaft of afternoon sunlight slipping through the curtains. He blew gently on the lenses, wiped them with his silk handkerchief, and wedged them back on. He lifted the top sheet from the deep pile of paper before him, scanned it, and let it fall with a grunt of disgust.

"'*How weary, stale, flat, and unprofitable...*'" he intoned in his resonant bass. "Shakespeare must have read law, Will. How else could he enumerate the horrors of its prose so precisely?"

Will smiled as he looked up from his seat in the alcove that served the office as a library. "Unprofitable, sir?"

"Unprofitable to the soul, I mean – corrosive to every moral and spiritual faculty that distinguishes man from the hyena. Take, as a peerless example, this deposition – a festering swamp of falsehood, a miasma of baseless allegations and innuendo, conjured up by Frank Dunn to conceal the guilt of a client who could teach Judas the finer points of treachery. By Gad, sir, if a single word of this document is true, I'll eat my hat!"

The Judge looked at the stovepipe hat that perched jauntily atop a marble bust of Cicero, as if sizing it up for consumption. His gaze drifted up to the clock above the great orator.

"Yes! It is just late enough to decently end the day's labors."

The Judge rose with a nimbleness surprising in a stout man in his 40's. "I'm done, Will…sated. I cannot absorb another word of mendacious twaddle.

I am granting myself a writ of *habeas potionem* – and I will serve it this minute on the barkeep at Blaze's. Care to join me?"

Will flipped the page of the tome before him. "In a moment, Judge. I believe I see light ahead in this winding discussion of drifting mineshafts."

"Suit yourself," said the Judge, scooping up hat, coat, and cane. "Just remember, my boy, that the Law is eternal. It will be there in the morning. Fine spirits, on the other hand, are by nature evanescent, and must be downed without delay when the opportunity arises."

The Judge paused on his way to the door. "You haven't forgotten Searls' dinner tonight, have you?"

"No, sir."

"Good! You'll like Niles. He looks too infernally young to have been here from the start – but he was. Trekked fifteen hundred miles in '49, battling deadly illness, the elements, and his fellow Argonauts every step of the way."

"I look forward to meeting him socially."

"The rest of the legal tribe will be there, and the wives, of course. And Mrs. Sargent – Aaron's out of town. And, oh…Molly Hatfield's coming, too, with Amanda and me. Her late husband, Zeke, was a good friend. We panned together on the Yuba in '50…" The Judge stopped and fingered the brim of his hat. "Shared the greatest adventure of our lives…"

"I've heard nothing but good of Mr. Hatfield," said Will gently. "And I am much indebted to Mrs. Hatfield for her kindness when I first arrived here. I am glad of the opportunity to thank her personally."

"Well, she's in mourning, of course. Not been around much… High time she got out and about." The Judge rapped his gold-headed cane smartly on the floor, causing it to bounce in the air, where he seized it and gave it a deft twirl.

"On second thought," he said, "I'm going to skip that drink at Blaze's. If Molly's coming, the house will be in an uproar: maids skirmishing with feather dusters and Amanda swooning over whether there is enough scent on the dressing table. I think I'll go home and add to the confusion."

"Of course, Judge. I'll close the office."

Will banked the fire in the wood stove and checked the gaslights. As he locked the door, his thoughts turned to Molly Hatfield. He had yet to meet another woman in California so richly endowed with wisdom and beauty. If this dinner marked her emergence from mourning, well…that added a new dimension to the evening's prospects. He ran his fingers over his bristling chin, wondering if his best coat was ready at the laundry. If he hurried, he might be able to pick it up and get to Rivaldo's Barber Shop before it closed.

$$\sim$$

The gently sloping roof of Searls' house stood out against the last light of day. Will passed a thick hedge of holly and turned in at the gate, only to stop and stare in surprise. Symmetrical tiers of tall windows looked back at him from a two-storey porch supported by smooth, slender columns. The spare elegance of the home was in the Federal style, so typical of plantation houses across the South. What Niles Searls, an Upstate New Yorker, was doing with such a dwelling, Will couldn't imagine – though he supposed he'd find out soon enough. Sectional differences were bound to be among the evening's topics, since word of South Carolina's official secession from the Union was expected any day now.

A maid showed him into the parlor, and Niles Searls stepped forward and stretched out his hand.

"Good to see you, Will. My wife's upstairs with the baby, so I am greeting the guests. You know Frank Dunn, of course, and this is Mrs. Dunn. Mary, allow me to present Mr. William Stafford, Aidan's rising disciple."

"Mr. Stafford," said Mary Dunn, with a graceful curtsey, "I am truly pleased to meet a gentleman from Virginia. Welcome to our little society."

Will bowed to the dark-haired beauty with the sweet South Carolina drawl. Mary's nose was a trifle short, her mouth small and dainty in its habitual mild pout. Her brown eyes were lustrous, quick, and very much inclined to take in what they wanted. Her husband Frank returned Will's bow, then immediately resumed his cross-examination of Searls, whom he suspected of heresy on a point of *usus fructus* in miners' water rights.

"My, but we do hear a lot of legal talk at these parties, don't we?" said Mary, smiling at Will. "Is this the first time you have visited here, Mr. Stafford? Let me show you a memento of the South."

She led him out of the parlor and down the wide, central hallway. She pulled up her shawl to cover her bare shoulders, and they stepped out onto a covered walkway that joined the mansion to a whitewashed cabin.

"Bless me!" said Will. "A dogtrot kitchen! I could imagine myself back in Virginia."

"This house is a refuge, is it not? Christmas always makes me homesick… makes the distance to Charleston seem to stretch out farther than the stars. We have wandered a long way from civilization, Mr. Stafford."

"Yes," said Will, "California is another world."

They looked out across Deer Creek Canyon to the winking lights of Nevada on the opposite rim. No trace of the original ancient forest remained to limit their view. All had been destroyed by fire or sacrificed to build the sprawling town and timber nearby mines. A sparse growth of new evergreens rose along the canyon wall, branches bowed beneath a mantle of new-fallen snow. Beyond, against the black sky, the raw scars of the diggings on the slopes of Sugar Loaf Hill were veiled with glistening white.

"All is calm, all is bright…" said Mary.

"Not much in the way of *heavenly peace,*" said Will, nodding his head in the direction of the stamp mills pounding away along Deer Creek.

Mary laughed. "That's the day and night music of the mines, Mr. Stafford. It's the sound of prosperity."

The door of the detached kitchen flew open, and a maid came out carrying a gleaming silver urn.

"I believe we may hope for fresh coffee!" said Will, offering his arm.

"Let us pursue it while it is hot," said Mary.

As they followed the maid into the parlor, Will felt Mary's grip on his arm tighten.

"Sakes alive!" she said. "If it isn't Molly Hatfield and the Caldwells! Good evening, Amanda, Judge. And you, too, Molly dear – I'm suprised to see you! I didn't think your year of mourning was quite over…"

"All my doing," said Judge Caldwell, before Molly could reply. "I insisted she come. I won't have friends spending Christmas time alone."

Amanda Caldwell took Molly's hand in both of hers. "We're so grateful she consented to join us."

"Yes, of course," said Mary. "And you do look enchanting this evening, Molly. I am so glad you didn't drape yourself in mourning jewelry. Your gold necklace looks quite charming on black, dear. Why, I'm told there are some men who find the combination quite alluring…"

Molly smiled the thinnest of smiles. "Where is Frank?" she said. "You haven't run off and left him at home, have you?"

"Not at all. He and Niles are in the library, playing lawyer. I stole Mr. Stafford while they weren't looking."

Will felt Mary's warm hands on his wrist and the pressure of her shoulder against his arm. The air seemed suddenly thick with the scent of competing perfumes.

"Forgive me, friends, for not greeting you," said Mrs. Searls, leaning out from a gallery above and speaking in a quiet voice. "I just got little Freddie to sleep."

The hostess floated down the staircase, filling it from rail to rail with her blue satin skirt. She stopped on the last stair and paused, casting a keen eye on Will.

"You must be the Mr. Stafford I have heard so much about," she said, holding out her hand to him. "Come, I need your opinion of a new champagne. Niles is considering investing in the vineyard." She swept off toward the refreshment table, and Will, feeling something like a human party favor, kept pace at her side.

"The Judge tells me you are a scholar," said Mrs. Searls, as she handed him a chilled glass.

"Reading and music are my chief amusements, ma'am – the balm of an indolent soul."

"It is not an indolent man who reads Homer in the original," said Mrs. Searls, running her eye over the fruit arrangement on the table. "Why look! A Grimes Golden!" She picked up the bright yellow apple. "This puts me in mind of a Greek myth I heard once…something about a contest…"

"*The Judgment of Paris*, ma'am. Strife threw a golden apple to the goddesses of Olympus, desiring it should be awarded to the fairest. Paris, a prince of Troy, was called upon to decide which of them deserved the prize."

"Yes, that's it! It ended rather badly, as I recall."

"Paris chose Aphrodite over Hera and Athena. The two disappointed goddesses rained down ten years of war on his city before razing it to the ground."

"Jealous females…" sighed Mrs. Searls. She turned and cast an appraising look at Mary Dunn across the room. "But Paris brought it on himself, did he not? He chose the vain goddess who delights in exercising her power over men, regardless of cost. I suspect a wiser man," she said, handing him the apple and smiling, "would choose a wiser goddess.

"Now," she said, taking his arm again. "Let me show you off to the rest of my guests."

Chapter 8

The Republic of the Pacific

December 1860

Afadter dessert, the ladies rose and fled the dining room under imminent threat of billowing cigar smoke and legal shoptalk. As the last hoop skirt swayed through the sliding doors to the parlor, the maid briskly cleared the table, leaving behind a tray of crystal glasses and four full decanters.

"So," said Judge Caldwell, unbuttoning a waistcoat that threatened to break free on its own, "what the devil *is* President Buchanan going to do? He's got almost three months left in office. The old ninny can't crouch under his desk much longer – not now that South Carolina is about to break away."

"I don't know, Judge," said Niles Searls. "Playing possum has always been Buchanan's strong suit. Remember, this is the gentleman who informs us that, while secession by any state is clearly illegal, the president has no right whatever to stop it. You could set the man's clothes on fire, and he would find you a dozen precedents for ignoring it entirely."

"Nonsense, Niles," said Frank Dunn, pouring himself a generous tumbler of whiskey. "Buchanan can't look the other way any longer. Forts Moultrie and Sumter command Charleston harbor, and they are still garrisoned by Federal troops. The Secessionists can't ignore them – not if they want anyone to take South Carolina's independence seriously. Mark my words, the Palmetto State militia will attack those forts if Buchanan doesn't hand them over."

"And Lincoln's Republicans will hang Buchanan from the nearest lamp-post if he does," said Searls, setting the humidor down in the middle of the table. "It almost makes you feel sorry for the old man."

"Has Lincoln weighed in on the crisis yet?" asked Dunn.

"The President-elect cannot make warlike noises without driving the Upper South out of the Union," said Will, "and he cannot make peaceful ones without setting the radical wing of his party howling for his blood. He has chosen silence, for the time being."

Judge Caldwell frowned and shook his head. "The fuse has been lit by those lunatics in South Carolina. Everyone can see the flame sizzling straight for the powder keg, but not a soul can think of a way to stop it."

"We could let the Deep South go," said Will. "Let them start their own country and good luck to them. Better a smaller, voluntary Union than a large one held together at gunpoint."

"I know some highly placed gentlemen," said Frank Dunn, "our governor among them, who would love to see the precedent of secession established. With the Eastern states split up, his notion of drawing off California and Oregon into a 'Republic of the Pacific' could become a reality."

"That might not be so bad," said Niles Searls, with an impish grin. "It would mean that all the wealth mined in California would stay right here. We'd be neck deep in gold dust in no time."

"No, sir, we would not," said the Judge. "The moment the United States Navy no longer protects us, we will find ourselves looking very uncomfortably at the British, Russian, and French fleets. And the Mexican government bears us no good will, either. It's damned awkward, I admit, for Northerners and Southerners to rub along together under the old flag, but the alternative is catastrophe – absolute catastrophe – in the form of endless war among ourselves and the Europeans for the wealth of North America."

A somber silence greeted this observation. Frank Dunn and Will Stafford knew their own home states of Kentucky and Virginia clung to the Union by the thinnest of threads. At any moment, their eastern brothers and cousins might find themselves marching to war against the Searls and Caldwell men of New York and Pennsylvania.

"The fate of the country balances on a bayonet point," said Niles Searls, "and there is nothing coming out of Washington now but bluster and ineptitude. Our best plan is to pray for a miracle."

~

Mary Dunn sat half-turned at the piano, quietly humming the melody of "I'll Twine 'Mid the Ringlets" while noiselessly working out a tenor harmony on the keys. In the half-hour since dinner, conversation among the women had descended inexorably to the accomplishments of their children – leaving Mary privately regretting the little prodigies hadn't been drowned at birth. She stifled a yawn as her hostess concluded a detailed history of her precocious five-year old's day.

Mrs. Searls beamed as she ladled mulled wine into crystal cups. "Where are your twins tonight, Amanda?" she asked, graciously yielding the floor to Mrs. Judge Caldwell.

"Kitty and Dora are out caroling with the church choir," said Amanda. "They have such a gift for harmony!"

"And your Ida is with them, isn't she?" Mrs. Searls asked Molly Hatfield, handing her a cup.

"Oh, yes," said Molly. "Ida loves to sing."

Amanda Caldwell leaned forward on the settee to bring herself in range of the petit fours. "It was so kind of dear Ida, " she gushed, "to volunteer to drive the Guild's Christmas baskets to the County Hospital this afternoon. Such a capable child! You must be very proud!"

Molly smiled weakly in acknowledgment. She knew her capable child would have happily delivered coal to the Prince of Darkness for a chance at the reins of the Caldwell's team and phaeton.

"Speaking of the hospital," said Ellen Sargent, in a quiet, even tone, "isn't it dreadful about Martha Clench?"

The room fell silent. Even Mary Dunn looked up from the piano. Ellen Sargent possessed a quiet gravity and a command of words that few ignored – especially the many who disagreed with her radical opinions on abolition and women's suffrage.

"Imagine poor Martha being widowed in her eighth month of confinement!" said Mrs. Searls, shaking her head in sympathy.

"You all know, of course," continued Ellen, "there is a guard by her door at the hospital, both day and night."

Molly Hatfield, who lived a day's ride from the Nevada gossip circuit, gave a cry of surprise.

"A *guard?* Whatever for?"

"Because she is deemed to be a hazard to herself and others," said Ellen, in an icy tone. "Martha has been *imprisoned* because she removed $700 from her husband's wall safe and handed it out to the families of the boys who died in his mine last summer. She then went to the office of the *Nevada Journal,* where she told the editor the children had been blown to atoms because Clench didn't want to pay a grown man's wages for dangerous work."

"We never saw anything of the kind in the *Journal!*" cried Amanda Caldwell.

"Of course not," snapped Ellen. "Clench threatened to horsewhip the editor if he spread the story – and then got Judge Thomas to declare Martha insane."

"He did that, even though Martha was with child at the time?" gasped Molly, appalled.

"Especially because she was with child at the time," said Ellen, her voice steely cold. "Clench's heart was failing – no surprise there! – and he wanted to tidy up his affairs before Lucifer called for his soul. He wrote a new will, leaving everything to a son by an earlier marriage and appointing him guardian of the unborn child. Now Old Clench is dead, and Young Clench is poised to seize the baby the moment it enters the world."

"This cannot be!" cried Molly. "Can't Niles do something?"

"He would contest the will *pro bono* – if there were any chance of success," said Mrs. Searls. "But he swears that, as the law stands, there is no basis for a challenge."

"It's *slavery,*" said Ellen Sargent, white with anger. "Dress it up with what terms you will, a woman's lot in California is no better than an African's in South Carolina."

Amanda Caldwell rattled her fan open and shut. Molly twisted her gold bracelets. Mrs. Searls busied herself with the punch bowl, pretending she hadn't heard the slight to Mary Dunn's home state. Mary smiled as she studied their discomfort.

"Well, bless mah soul!" she said at last, in an exaggerated, musical drawl. "Equality with the women of Califohniah! What joyful tidin's for our servants back home, I do declayah! Why, when I left, I don't remembah a single one of them wearin' such charmin' jewelry and satin as y'all. Their lot must have improved considerably!"

Ellen turned and faced Mary squarely.

"I had no intention, of course, of comparing our material lot with a slave's."

"Of course not, dahlin', because your husband is a fabulously wealthy man, who keeps you like a queen – even fundin' your splendid causes. Including, if I recall correctly, an impassioned crusade against the abuse of women by their cruel and spiteful husbands."

"I am fortunate in my marriage," said Ellen. "Martha Clench and thousands like her are not, due to wicked laws drawn up and enforced by men. As concerns the sanctity of her body and her maternal rights, she is no better off than a slave. Can you deny that?"

Mary surveyed Ellen with a mixture of pity and contempt.

"Of course I *do* feel for her. But challengin' her husband like that in the most public way... My, my!" Mary shook her head. "You realize, don't you, Mrs. Sargent, that the reason the Good Lord gave men those lovely, strong shoulders is because He felt sorry for the childish deficiency of their minds? Poor things, with their simple wants and needs. They are so easily managed by a woman of spirit! Though I will admit," she added after a moment's reflection, "that men can be disagreeable... I have to be quite severe at times with Frank."

"So," said Molly icily, "you are willing to be a slave to a man in the eyes of the law, so long as you can lead him around by the nose in private?"

"You state my position admirably, Mrs. Hatfield."

The ensuing silence was broken by the gentlemen's voices outside the door. They entered and found seats, the Judge next to Molly and Amanda. Will stood at the back of the room and watched the Caldwells talking softly with their friend, clearly solicitous for her in her first outing since her husband's death.

Mary Dunn turned to the keyboard and struck up "Joy to the World," singing the lead in her confident alto. The gentlemen joined in readily, and the ladies' voices followed as the old melody soothed their hearts. Amanda

Caldwell asked for "It Came Upon a Midnight Clear," and the party soldiered on through many verses until dry throats and forgotten lyrics caused the men to drop out, one by one. At the end, only Will Stafford's rich baritone supported the women's voices.

Mary Dunn, weary of sacred themes, searched through the rack of sheet music.

"Ah, here's 'Juanita,' that pretty Spanish song! Mr. Stafford, would you consent to join me in a duet?"

Mary played through the song, with its sudden pauses and melancholy mood. Will stood behind her, leaning over her shoulder and sight-reading the harmony.

> *Soft – o'er the fountain,*
> *Ling'ring falls the southern moon,*
> *Far – o'er the mountain,*
> *Breaks the day too soon!*

Molly watched Mary's beautiful hands moving over the keyboard, blue and white light flashing from the jewels that adorned them. They were extraordinarily gifted hands, and Molly was surprised and a bit ashamed of how badly she wanted to crush them under the keyboard cover.

Why? Why did she dislike Mary Dunn so?

Well, for one thing, Mary was a rich planter's daughter. Molly had known and detested a number of girls of that class during her school years at Madame LeFebvre's Female Academy. But that was ages ago, and she had long since stopped caring what slaveholders thought. So…if that wasn't the problem, what was? Why this sudden animus against a woman she barely knew?

Will Stafford, that's why!

She wanted to break those pretty, talented fingers because Mary had walked into the parlor with them draped all over Stafford's arm…and had flattered him throughout dinner…and – worst of all – was now singing romantic ballads with him.

Shame swept over Molly. It was eleven months since Zeke had died. She had let the Caldwells talk her into coming, but she had no business being out in society so soon – especially to moon over a handsome lawyer. She tried looking away but her curiosity betrayed her. She watched openly as Mary gazed up into Will's eyes as they sang, saw Mary nodding almost imperceptibly to cue him through the difficult timing.

> *Nita! Juanita!*
> *Ask thy soul if we should part!*
> *Nita! Juanita!*
> *Lean thou on my heart.*

Damnation! thought Molly, as the lovely Southern voices entwined. *I used to like that song.*

Chapter 9

Bomb Day

February 1861

T he sun was almost down and the air was crisp. Ida and Molly hurried down the path to the Caldwell's, where they were greeted at the front door by a breathless Dora.

"We'll be able to see everything from our own front porch!" said Dora, as she tugged them into the vestibule. "The Chinamen shoot a hundred bombs into the air, and when they explode, it rains down confetti and lucky rings that they scramble and fight for! They call it *Yee Yut Yee*, which means 'Bomb Day.' All the Chinamen from Marysville have come to Nevada City for a big parade tonight. It's been in the papers for a week! And they've brought their dragon – the only one in the whole United States – and he has a name. It's *Moo Lung!*" Dora opened the parlor door and stood aside to let her friends go in first. "*And* they've brought their idol, Bok Eye, who grants them wishes!"

Will Stafford rose swiftly to his feet as the women entered the room.

"Mr. Stafford," said Molly, "what a nice surprise!"

Ida seconded the sentiment with a joyful smile, her heart suddenly pounding like a six-stamp mill. But before she could maneuver herself closer to Will, Dora's twin sister Kitty came rushing in and grabbed her by the elbow. Together, the twins hauled Ida from the parlor and whisked her upstairs to their room.

"Take off your crinoline, Ida. I'll hang it up for you," said Kitty, as her own hoops cascaded to the floor. "We'll put them back on before we go down for supper."

Ida curled up in a wing-backed chair by the window overlooking the street. Kitty and Dora dove crosswise onto the bed, propped their chins on their hands, and waved their feet in the air.

"O-oh, isn't that William Stafford so *handsome!*" Kitty sighed. "Even more than Henry Meredith! And he's younger, too…only 28!"

"We saw him the first night he came to town, from that very window," said Dora breathlessly.

The bed frame creaked as Kitty bounced to her knees. "We tiptoed out to the head of the stairs," she said, "and heard him tell Clara he had a message for Judge Caldwell. Daddy took him into the study, and they were in there for an hour. When they left, we sneaked downstairs and peeked at the note!" Kitty's narrative broke down in a fit of giggles, so Dora bounced to her knees and took over.

"It was right there on Daddy's desk! It said, 'Dear Judge, This is the man you have been looking for. Hire him. Signed – Molly Hatfield.'"

Kitty let out a low whistle as she leered knowingly at Ida.

"I think your mama meant to say, 'This is the man *I've* been looking for!'"

The twins threw themselves into each other's arms in a pantomime of romance and dissolved into laughter. Ida turned her gaze out the window, tired of the gossipy twins. Judge Caldwell had been complaining for ages about his workload – everybody in town knew that. So why were Dora and Kitty carrying on so, simply because Ma had done something about it?

∾

The Caldwells' dining table offered spacious seating for ten, allowing the twins and their young guests to assemble at the foot, while the adults gathered around the jovial judge at the head of the table. It was a comfortable arrangement, allowing separate conversations for young and old. Comfortable, that is, for everyone but Ida, who developed a serious crick in her neck trying to peer around the loquacious Kitty for a better view of Will and Molly. The few glimpses Ida caught were deeply discouraging: Will Stafford smiling over his wineglass at Molly, Molly blushing like a schoolgirl under his gaze. Her honey-gold hair and ivory skin glowed in the shimmering lamp light, and her green eyes were bewitching.

By broad daylight, Ida thought with satisfaction, *my dear mother looks every one of the thirty years she admits to...and the thirty-one she really is!*

At the head of the table, Judge Caldwell rose to his feet and lifted his glass. "Here's to our bonny Mrs. Hatfield, to whom I owe the happy discovery of my new associate!" He beamed at Molly and at Will.

Ida gritted her teeth and mashed an innocent cake crumb with her fork. As soon as the ladies rose from the table, she slipped out the side door onto the veranda and slumped against a post. She hadn't managed to get in a single word with Will. *He doesn't even know I exist.*

She jumped as an eruption of fireworks shook the air. She clapped her hands over her ears as the opening salvo grew into a continuous roar that drove all thought from her mind. Then a thunder of deep-throated drums announced the start of the Chinese parade. Ida hurried around the corner of the house and joined Kitty and Dora as they rushed down the front walk.

Torches were lit along the street, and crowds of townspeople had gathered along both sides of the thoroughfare. A squad of men in black tunics and square red hats came marching down in front, carrying huge festoons of red, finger-sized firecrackers hung from the ends of tall poles. The clusters jerked and smoked and roared like gunfire. Next came two rows of men dangling glowing red silk lanterns, big as bushel baskets. Between the rows of lanterns, in the place of honor, tottered an ancient priest. The bent old man clutched a decorated box.

What's in there? Ida wondered. *Bones? A corked-up demon?*

A contingent of Chinese dignitaries, smiling, well-fed men, came next, resplendent in blue silk robes and shoes with white wooden soles.

"They must be from Marysville," said Dora. "I've never seen any of them around here, except for Ah Tie."

Ida recognized Ah Tie, who shipped the gold from his mine through the Missouri House express office. He was strolling along in the middle of the group, the tallest by far, and the only one in a business suit. A great shrine swayed past on the shoulders of two-dozen bearers in round, black-tasseled caps. Behind them came teams of scarlet-robed men, swinging huge incense burners on poles that poured out a curtain of thick smoke. Out of the smoke came a little man bearing a pumpkin-sized white ball on a scepter, with gold paper and glass jewels glued on.

"That's the Pearl of Wisdom," Dora shouted in Ida's ear.

Suddenly, a huge dragon's head lunged out of the smoke, snapping at the pearl and sending the little man reeling on his heels. The monster looked around in triumph as the crowd edged back. His head reared up, ten feet from the ground, red mouth open, swaying from side to side.

Ida was fascinated. She stepped out into the street in front of the dragon. Moo Lung dropped his massive head down and looked straight into Ida's face. He blinked his gigantic, painted eyes at her, puffed yellow smoke from his nostrils, and shook the jingling bells that hung from his horns. His jaws opened and closed, as if to speak. Then, distracted by the Pearl of Wisdom, he reared up and veered away, his long, silken body sliding through the smoke and snaking from one side of the street to the other, to a pulsing clamor of cymbals and drums.

Ida gave chase, skirting the edge of the crowd as she made her way through rolling clouds of incense and gunpowder smoke. Behind her, she heard Kitty and Dora calling, "Where are you going?" "Ida, come back!"

Let those ninnies wait! thought Ida, as she fell in behind the musicians.

The procession turned the corner at Pine and turned again to wind through the narrow lanes of China Hill, until it ended inside the high board fence of the temple courtyard. Ida found herself pressed into a line waiting to pay respects to Bok Eye, the visiting deity from Marysville, who protected the Chinese there from the river – *and granted their wishes!*

At the temple door, Ida offered the attendant a dime and received two red wax candles and twelve yellow sticks of incense. The little man pointed at her feet and to the doorsill, warning her in Cantonese to step high over the trick threshold that discouraged demons. She joined the crowd shuffling inside into a sandalwood-scented haze.

Bok Eye, God of the Northern River, sat serenely among his Immortal Companions in a gilded niche, considering the prayers being offered. His painted features had been freshly retouched with vermilion, and his long beard and moustaches were carefully combed. He smiled contentedly at a counter crowded with offerings: whole roasted piglets on platters, pyramids of golden fruit, vases of plum blossoms.

Ida watched carefully as the worshippers filed before the altar. When her turn came, she stepped up to the high table, lit her candles and joss sticks on one of the candles flickering there, and arranged them with other clusters in pewter basins filled with sand. Solemnly, she clapped her hands three times to get the attention of the god and bowed her head, as the other supplicants had done.

Excuse me, Mr. Bok Eye, if I don't know how to do this right...but here goes... I don't hold with forcing anybody to do anything...and I don't want to cheat anybody out of any happiness that belongs to them...I'm just asking for a fair chance for us to get acquainted, so he knows me for who I am...

Ida leapt as a tremendous explosion and a wailing of horns signaled the climax of the celebrations. Impatient worshippers nudged her along.

As she turned to leave, a young monk pulled her aside with a touch on her sleeve. He bowed and offered her a tall cup filled with slender bamboo sticks. She knelt at the end of a row of petitioners on a long kneeling bench padded in red velvet. Imitating the movements of the man beside her, Ida tipped the oracle sticks forward and gently shook them, rattling them in the cup until just one slid out and tumbled to the floor. She picked up the stick, and the monk took it from her and examined it. From a board hung with many sheaves of little colored paper fortunes, he selected a blue slip with Chinese characters printed in red ink. He bowed again, pressing the paper into Ida's hand.

"Please, mister, what does it say?" Ida inquired. The monk smiled and gestured toward the door, saying something she couldn't understand. Ida folded the fortune into her skirt pocket and let the crowd carry her out through the courtyard and into the maze of Chinatown.

Ida spotted a laundryman she knew as "Duck Egg." He was the pet of the Nevada schoolchildren, who delighted in alternately throwing snowballs at him and raiding his pockets for candy. He sat on a raised, narrow porch, bathed in yellow lantern light, a long-stemmed pipe clenched in his teeth. Duck Egg smiled and nodded as Ida approached. He took his pipe from his mouth.

"Hello, Missy, what I do for you today?"

"How d'ya do, Mr. Egg." Ida made a polite dip of her skirts. "Will you read this for me, please?" She held up the paper fortune.

Duck Egg looked surprised. He peered down at the paper and picked through the characters.

"*Pi – Ji – Tai – Lai*. Every China boy know, Missy. 'Out of misfortune come bliss.'" Duck Egg handed back the paper and returned his pipe to his mouth.

"Thanks, Mr. Egg," said Ida, and she started back up the street, brooding over his answer.

The remnant of the procession was mingling now with card players and revelers emerging from nearby saloons and Houses of Joy. Just ahead of her, Ah Tie in his business suit marched along, chatting and laughing with a jolly fat man in a blue silk robe and white-soled shoes.

Out of the back door of a gambling hall spilled a noisy gang of white miners, seriously "likkered up" and spoiling for a fight. Their tall, skinny ringleader, whose face was pitted with smallpox scars, pushed past Ida and swaggered up behind Ah Tie. He grabbed the back of Ah Tie's coat and twisted it into a handle.

"Why, here's a piss-ant yeller Chinaman dressed up like a white man. You wannee lookee like boss man? Well, first we're gonna get rid of that pigtail. C'mere, Treadwell, and hold him while I cut it off." Ida saw the man pull the Bowie knife from his belt.

Grabbing up her skirt, Ida took two quick steps and slammed the toe of her boot into the back of the drunken man's knee. His leg buckled. He twisted around and tumbled into her, and his knife went flying. They both sprawled in the dirt. Ida's hoop and petticoat flapped up around her waist, and the whiskey-soaked onlookers hooted with laughter. "Go to it, girl!" someone jeered. "Looks like Eldon's got a new sweetheart."

Ida's face scorched. She rolled over, got to her knees, and saw Ah Tie struggling in the midst of a gang of whites. Eldon grabbed her to give himself a boost up, forcing Ida back down. The drunks whistled and cheered some more. She grabbed Eldon's ankle and jerked his foot sideways, throwing him off balance and sending him flat on his back.

"Hooo-wee," taunted another wag, "look out now! She's gonna put her brand on you!"

Eldon scrambled to his feet, and Ida sprang up to face him, fire in her eyes.

"You cowardly varmint." She shook her fist in the ruffian's face.

Eldon stood mute, wall-eyed and sweating. He backed up, boiling with rage, but not quite drunk enough to insult a respectable white woman with a crowd looking on.

"You beady-eyed skunk!" Ida cried. "You oughta be stomped into a mud hole!" She delivered on her pronouncement, kicking the man hard in the shin with the pointed toe of her boot. He howled and snatched at her bonnet, but she was suddenly hoisted from her feet and dragged backward. Ida screamed and struggled, but her arms were pinned to her sides.

"Whoa, there," said Will Stafford, "can't you see he's licked?"

Will set Ida down, then stepped in front of her. His hand slipped into his coat and found the grip of his pistol. "Time to go home now," he said to Eldon.

Eldon sneered and spat in the dirt. He cast about for his knife and swore horribly as he realized that it had disappeared.

Across the street, a knot of angry Cantonese now surrounded Ah Tie. Two burly Celestials with bare, folded arms and impassive faces emerged from the crowd and stood on either side of Will. Eldon felt a cold shiver between his shoulder blades as he surveyed their black silk costumes. *Highbinders,* he thought, *sons of bitches who slit men's throats while they sleep.*

"C'mon, Eldon," the kid named Treadwell cajoled, "she's two-timin' you. Fergit her. There's lots likelier gals down at the Hog Farm!" The drunken gang swaggered off with a chorus of squeals and grunts, pulling Eldon with them.

Will led Ida a little way up Commercial Street, to where the back stairs of the New York Hotel ascended into darkness. They climbed to the first landing and sat down on a step, hidden from view. Ida's hands shook as she tried to wipe the grit out of her eyes with Will's handkerchief. He took it from her and gently dabbed at the dirt on her face.

"Why not pick on somebody your own size?" he grinned.

"He had it coming," Ida bristled. "He pulled a knife on Ah Tie!"

"I saw the whole thing, Miss Ida." Will put his arm around Ida and hugged her close to him. "You are a valiant young lady. Ah Tie owes you a vote of thanks."

Ida's heart was still pounding, but not with anger anymore. *'Out of misfortune comes bliss,'* sure enough!

She leaned her head against Will's shoulder, not daring to speak for fear of breaking the spell of the moment. She looked up at the cold sky of velvet black above them, with Jupiter blazing over the mountains. Will's arm was strong and warm around her.

Will felt her breath begin to slow and her shoulders relax.

"Time to get you back to your mother. She'll be worried."

"Aw, she'll keep."

"Just the same, I've had you to myself long enough. I'll be seeing you again soon – I'm invited to Missouri House for dinner next Sunday, so put on your fanciest rig for me!" Will gave Ida his hand down the stairs and his arm for the short walk to the Caldwell's.

Molly and the Judge were waiting on the veranda. They watched Ida hobble through the gate, clutching her ruined bonnet over a big rip in her muddy skirt. Molly flew down the walk and clasped her daughter in her arms.

"Ida, I was so worried! The twins said you disappeared into *Chinatown*. What were you thinking, taking off like that?" Molly smoothed Ida's hair and examined her face. "Are you all right?"

"It was nothing," said Will. "Our girl took a tumble is all. Those high sidewalks on Commercial Street can be a hazard in the dark."

"Thank God you found her!" Molly said.

I'm not sure it's old Jehovah who needs thanking, Ida mused as Molly led her indoors. She fingered the red-inked paper in her pocket and mouthed a silent thank-you to Bok Eye.

Chapter 10

Errands of Mercy

April 1861

Pedro led Molly's roan mare to the mounting block by the front gate, his face set in a look of strong disapproval. It was Molly's custom to use a man's work saddle when riding around her land, which meant that far too much of her sturdy bloomers showed during her mount. Seeing her sitting boldly astride the mare (like a *vaquero!*) was a sight that never failed to scandalize the boy. He kept his gaze fixedly on her face as he handed up the gun belt and pistol.

"The first three loads are ball, *señora*. The rest are shot."

This was the standard Missouri House issue: three rounds of heavy ball to discourage grizzlies, the next three cylinders packed with birdshot for rattlesnakes, who had the annoying habit of sunning themselves in the middle of riding trails this time of year.

"Thank you," said Molly. "I hope I won't be long. You and Mr. Johnson can meet the noon stage if I'm not back in time."

"*¡Mire, señora!*" said Pedro, nodding toward the road from You Bet.

A rider emerged from around the bend, his mount rocking in a steady lope. He wore a buckskin coat and denim pants, with a slouch hat pulled low over his eyes. He rode with the effortless grace of a man who had been on horseback since boyhood.

"Oh my God, it's Stafford," Molly murmured. It was one thing to dress as she pleased while working at home. It was another altogether to be caught by a gentleman while bestriding her horse, with her skirt wadded up and her bloomers showing shamelessly.

"Good morning, ma'am," said Will brightly as he reined in. He swept the hat from his head. "I trust I see you well!"

Molly felt her cheeks beginning to burn. *My face must look like a ripe cherry,* she thought, as she wrapped the gun belt around her waist. It had been Zeke's belt, and the heavy Colt hung lopsidedly off her right hip, completing the picture of Western barbarity to perfection.

"Good morning, sir," she said.

Will's blue eyes wandered over the details of her attire.

"I hope the road agents have not been misbehaving," he said, nodding at the pistol on her hip.

"No. I have to search through some rough country. My little Jersey heifer didn't come in last night. I need to find her and get her back to the barn before she drops her calf."

There, thought Molly, *now we can chat about the gory details of difficult calving. It's the only touch lacking.*

"I do hope she's all right," said Will. "As it happens, I, too, am on an errand of mercy. It seems to be the theme of this beautiful morning."

"You have a cow to rescue?"

"No, ma'am. I'm here to inspect a water ditch whose contents are being pilfered."

"You're going after young Clench?"

Will lifted his eyebrows in surprise. "The case is notorious, then?"

"That little skunk's been stealing Ah Tie's water, just like his father did before him. The whole diggings knows about it."

"Really? That should help with our case against him."

"Not necessarily. Clench has a right to some of that water. It will be hard to prove he's using more than his share – especially when the victim of the fraud is Chinese."

"Well," said Will, with a smile, "perhaps we can do something about that. I have convinced Ah Tie to enter into a consortium with a group of eminent white men. As it happens, it will be only the white men's names that appear in the case."

"I'll be damned!" Molly blurted, then blushed brighter still. *Now I'm cursing like a stevedore.*

"Instead of Ah Tie, Clench's attorney will find himself cross-examining Niles Searls and Aidan Caldwell," Will said. "Personally, I'd rather tackle a pair of rabid grizzlies. However, we must have ironclad proof. I must establish where and how the fraud is committed. I'm told the ditch is long and runs through rugged terrain."

"Ah Tie is a friend of Missouri House," said Molly. "I'd like to help. If you're willing to make a detour for my wandering heifer, I can lead you to your ditch – if you don't mind riding with an Amazon."

~

The warm spring sun had coaxed tender, emerald-green grass to ankle height and studded the meadow with blue and white flowers. The oaks were in first leaf and the redbud trees were bursting into fiery, brilliant bloom. Molly and Will rested on the soft earth while the Jersey heifer grazed contentedly nearby – unlike her rescuers, who were struggling with the provisions Will had thrown into his saddlebags that morning in Nevada.

"I will take my oath," said Will, staring balefully at the belt-tough jerky, "that this beast died years ago in the desert…of old age and abuse."

"I'm to blame," said Molly, flinging her hardtack to a blue jay, who eyed it doubtfully. "I have one of the best-stocked kitchens in the county. I could have packed us a feast in ten minutes."

They both drank thirstily from their canteens; the wretched jerky had been salted to preserve it for a distant posterity. Then they lay back on their elbows and watched a pair of hawks circling high over the meadow, calling back and forth with piercing cries.

"You deserve a better reward for your efforts," said Will. "I could never have spotted the tap in that ditch on my own. How did you know the pipe was buried there?"

"I know what's supposed to be green around here and what isn't. That pipe leaks. There were plants growing over it that had no business being where they were – unless they had extra water in summer. Old Clench must have put that pipe in years ago."

Will gazed at her profile as she watched the aerial courtship above. "You are a remarkable woman, Mrs. Hatfield," he said.

"I am what I have to be," she said. "California is a hard school."

"Aidan Caldwell tells me you are a native of Delaware. If you'll forgive my curiosity, how did you come to own an establishment called 'Missouri House'?"

"It's a long story," Molly said, wondering how many husbands to include in the tale.

"I'd like to hear it," he said.

"I grew up in Port Jervis, on the Delaware River. When my father retired from the sea, he bought a ship's chandler business and was very successful. He had two busy warehouses and enough money to send his daughters to the best schools. He wished to rise above his status as a merchant by marrying us into the old plantation families. The gentleman intended for me was older than my father…and had nothing at all to recommend him to a young and headstrong girl. I decided to elope with my childhood sweetheart, who was a master's mate on a trading vessel. We were married the night before his ship sailed for Kwangtung.

"We stopped for some time at the Pearl River trading forts…squalid, violent places. What I saw there opened my eyes to the suffering of the Chinese race. If I were a young man there, I would *swim* to California, if necessary.

"Returning from Hong Kong, there was fever aboard ship. My husband was one of the first to die and was buried at sea. The captain of the vessel saw no profit in carrying me further, so he put me ashore at Monterey.

"I had a little money and a chest of tea and porcelain. That kept me going until Ida was born. I loved Monterey – the coast was so wild and free! And I loved the Mexican people. They were generous to me…and the ladies were devoted to Ida.

"I married again – to Don Emilio Carrillo, a gentleman with grown sons. We lived a simple life on his rancho in the Salinas Valley.

"After the Bear Flag was raised, there was trouble between the *Anglos* and the *Californios*. My husband was ambushed and killed. His sons were drawn into the vendetta, and before long the Americans were hunting them down. The Carrillo family and the other rancheros weren't certain of my loyalty… and the Americans were suspicious of me, too.

"I believed it was dangerous to remain – so I made a desperate move. Esmeralda had been widowed, too, so we packed up her infant son Pedro and my Ida and quit Salinas, escorted by an American friend who had resigned his commission in the army. We rode to San Francisco just as the first rumors of gold were circulating. There were already ships stranded at the dock because their crews had deserted for the placers.

"We decided to pay a visit to Captain Sutter at Sacramento and hear the news first-hand. Sutter was famous for his flourishing orchards and vineyards, and I hoped to settle in some fertile valley nearby and resume ranching. Of course, the Gold Rush put an end to my fantasy.

"By the time we arrived, Sutter's Fort was chaos. Men were pouring in from everywhere, and there were camps all along the river. We were caught up in the excitement, like everyone else. We heard of *pound diggins* on the Yuba – claims so rich a man could take out a pound of gold in a day – and we decided to try our luck. We bought up what provisions we could find and set off for the mines. Esmeralda and I and the children were regarded as something of a wonder along the trail. We were treated with courtesy, but we had to guard our horses at night or they would have been stolen.

"As soon as we arrived at the diggings, my soldier friend struck it. Two feet down in red clay, he found a solid gold nugget something like a meteorite, all coated in iron oxide. It was judged to be worth more than $5,000. He departed for the States the next day…

"Esmeralda and I opened a restaurant. Our establishment was a canvas awning over a log bench, and our menu was pancakes and coffee. That's where I met Zeke Hatfield. We built Missouri House together. That was his dream, and he was happy as a king at You Bet."

Molly paused. "As to your original question…Zeke named the stage stop 'Missouri House' as a kind of joke between us, because, he said, marriage was a dangerous compromise.

"There were other reasons, too. Zeke grew up in Missouri, and he thought the name would be acceptable to Northerners and Southerners alike. He used to say that if the Union ever split apart, the rip would run through the heart of Missouri.

"My husband was shot over a disputed poker hand, Mr. Stafford, and the killer was never brought to justice. Some folks believe Zeke's murder was political, like poor Senator Broderick's, because they were both outspoken against secession." Molly paused in silent reflection.

"And now it's your turn to tell a story, Will Stafford," she said. "How did you decide on California?"

"I chose it for its distance, ma'am. It was as far away as I could get from my shame…

"I was in love with a distant cousin of mine, a charming young lady of many accomplishments. When my father passed away, and I came into my estate, I had the means and inclination to marry Charlotte. She had another suitor, however. I had been at school with him briefly, and I knew him for a good enough sort. We might have been friends, if she had not divided us. Instead, we became rivals.

"We met outside her door and had a drunken quarrel. I have no memory of what we said to each other, but we had gone too far…and were both too proud to back down. An *affaire d'honneur* was arranged – pistols at twenty paces – and I killed him. I meant to nick his arm, but he turned, and my bullet found his heart."

"And the lady?"

"Thriving. She now proudly bears the distinction of having a man die for her sake."

Molly heard the pain and anger in Will's voice – and shuddered. A swift change of subject was in order.

"How do you like our Northern Mines," she said, "and all their rough-hewn ways?"

Will smiled. "I could grow to like California very well. It has its cruelties and meanness, like any place. Yet it offers a fresh start to all newcomers. I have never before seen so many races and nationalities of men. It is obvious that many cordially dislike each other – most, I should say. But they are all here to be reborn. They have that in common, if nothing else, and the place fairly hums with the energy generated by so many dreams. Ida's birthright is a world as brave and new as Prospero's island. I wonder you didn't call her Miranda."

Molly laughed. "I considered it! But the name would have meant nothing to Ida's father, whose knowledge of books was limited to navigation. I doubt he ever read a word of Shakespeare."

"But Ida has," said Will, "and she has a wonderful memory for it. I over-heard her greeting the Caldwell twins with Banquo's words:

> *What are these,*
> *So wither'd and so wild in their attire,*
> *That look not like th'inhabitants o' th' earth..."*

Molly laughed. "Ida grew up reading Mr. Hatfield's library, and she has a real gift for recalling invective. She might have an acting career, if she could remember the rest of the play so well."

"I've heard that child stars are worshipped in the mines. Did you ever think of putting her on the stage?"

"No, I didn't. Perhaps I should have. Ida's friend, little Lotta Crabtree, was showered with gold dust when she danced for the miners, and there were times when the money would have been welcome. But these last years, there's been no need. Missouri House is very comfortable. We lack for nothing and want nothing more. At least, I don't. Ida is young – and has the restless feeling of the young. She probably sees the matter differently."

A cloud passed over the sun, and they felt the coolness of the waning day.

"We'd best be getting back," said Molly. "Will you join us tonight for sup-per? You'd be welcome to stay over, if you wish. There's not much of a moon tonight, and the road to Nevada is a long one."

"I could not presume on your hospitality – especially on such short notice..."

Molly shook her head. "I run a stage depot, Will. No notice is ever given, or asked, when I have guests. Besides, I want to make up for the lunch I failed to pack today. And hear your opinion of our piano. You play, don't you?"

Will's stomach growled. He abandoned all pretence of reluctance.

"I'd be honored. And I hope you'll allow me to sing for my supper, if it would give you and Ida pleasure."

Chapter 11

Chez la Modiste

May 1861

Ida shivered and swore under her breath as the buggy rattled across the slippery planks over Deer Creek and headed for Grass Valley. Today her extra petticoat and long cotton drawers weren't much use against the icy air settled in the ravine. *Women's clothes are obstacles to be overcome,* she railed to an indifferent universe, *while men's are designed for action and life!*

On the bright side, she had successfully shed the Caldwell twins and gotten off on her own – no small accomplishment with her mother in town. Molly saw highwaymen and ravishers behind every tree – she'd be horrified if she found out Ida was driving off alone. But this secret mission to Lavender LeJeune was worth any risk, for it was on Lavender's unrivaled skills as a seamstress that Ida staked her hopes of capturing the heart of Will Stafford. For this campaign, only the most devastating weapons of the female arsenal would suffice.

Lavender had arrived from New Orleans as companion to the stunningly beautiful Lola Montez, arguably the most notorious woman in the world. While on tour with her mistress, Lavender had created Lola's dazzling wardrobe: tarantella costumes with jeweled spiders that trembled on gossamer webs, deep-flounced Spanish skirts of black lace, even charming sailor-boy costumes for high-kicking reels and hornpipes. Now the fascinating Lola was gone, leaving Lavender behind to ply her needle for a clientele that ranged from the Honorable Mrs. Judge Caldwell of Nevada to the distinctly less honorable Madame Bonhore, proprietress of the U.S. Hotel, Grass Valley's premier bordello.

Lavender can make a silk purse out of a sow's ear, Ida assured herself as Daisy trotted on. *In two winks she can turn me into a Phantom of Delight, just like that gal in the poem.*

In her excitement, Ida had driven Daisy hard over the hill from Nevada, and the venerable mare stopped for a cool-down when they reached the spring-fed trough by the turnoff to the racetrack, the halfway mark of their trip. Ida could see the red earth oval of the track and the bright bunting fluttering on the grandstands, and hear the distant roar of the whiskey-soaked crowd as they cheered on their favorites.

A wagon lumbered into sight, coming up the road from Grass Valley. It was piled high with alfalfa, and as it rolled by, a pair of teenage boys hopped off. The youngsters didn't head straight for the races, but made a show of getting out their tobacco plugs and cutting off chaws. No one else was in sight, and Ida did not care for the boys' looks. She gathered up the reins and clucked to Daisy to back up, but the mare was not finished with her drink and ignored the command. Ida reached for the whip.

"Whoa, there, gal," cried the older-looking of the two boys. "Why be in such a hurry? That ol' hoss looks played out to me."

Ida said nothing. With a sinking heart, she recognized him as one of the louts who had been in the crowd that attacked Ah Tie after the Bomb Day parade. She could see in his eyes that the recognition was mutual.

"Say, I know you!" he said, suddenly smiling and casually strolling in Ida's direction. "You're the filly that tossed Eldon into the dirt when he tried to cut the pigtail off that Chinaman."

"The one you was laffin' about, Jim?" said his younger companion, making for the off-side of Ida's buggy.

"Yep. You should a seen 'em a-rollin' around on the ground together. Eldon was fit to be tied."

Ida cracked her whip over the mare's neck. Daisy lifted her head and backed the buggy away from the trough.

"Gee yup!" cried Ida.

Daisy pivoted, and the younger boy reached up for the bridle.

"I wouldn't touch that, if I were you," snapped Ida.

The boy grinned as he clutched at the leather strap. Daisy swung her head sideways and butted him in the chest. The boy staggered, lost his balance, and sprawled in the trough – soaking his middle and smacking his head on the wooden rim.

But the second boy was closing in. Ida drew back and cracked the whip in his face. He flung up his hands to protect his eyes, then jerked a knife from his belt.

Ida dropped the whip and thrust her hand into her coat. Out flashed Molly's little pepperbox pistol. The boy grabbed the dash rail and tried to spring on board the rolling buggy. Ida pushed the pistol against his boot and fired.

The boy screamed and dropped to the ground. Ida nearly tumbled overboard as Daisy bolted at the pistol shot. Ida crumpled herself down between the dashboard and the seat and held on for dear life, praying the boys wouldn't start shooting. Daisy was in full gallop now, and the buggy was pitching like a bucking mule.

No shots came. Ida hauled herself to her knees and managed to slow Daisy to a lope, then crawled back up into the seat.

I was lucky that time, she thought, with a shudder. *Those boys don't dare tell. They'd be lynched for trying to lay hands on me. But I can't tell on them, either, or Ma will never let me out of her sight.*

It took the whole mile to Hill's Flat for Daisy and Ida to work off their fright and simmer down. Ida corralled the pepperbox where it had fallen to the floorboards and slipped it back into her coat.

Ma might tan my hide for lifting the pistol and sneaking off, she thought, patting the weapon, *but at least she can't say I wasn't chaperoned.*

∽

By the time Daisy reached the outskirts of Grass Valley, she was ready for a rubdown and a nosebag of oats – and she knew where to get them. The mare broke unbidden into a stylish trot as she passed the U. S. Hotel on East Main, showing off for Madame Bonhore's "Soiled Doves," who were taking tea on the balcony. Rounding the turn onto the Auburn road, Daisy gathered speed as Ida sawed the reins in a futile bid for control. The mare whirled the little buggy into Woodworth's Livery and stopped at her usual stall. Soon

Daisy was unhitched and munching her oats, and Ida was stomping up Winchester Street, her boots slapping in the mud.

A hawthorne tree in bloom scented the air around the white picket gate, where a small, neatly painted sign announced the home and fitting rooms of *Mme LeJeune, Modiste.* Ida found the seamstress lounging on the porch, cocooned in a paisley shawl and smoking a thin cigar fitted into an ivory holder.

"Donne-moi un petit bec doux, chère," she cooed, as she raised her rouged brown cheek for Ida's kiss. *"Ça va bien?* Sit down, Ida, and unlace your *broguins."*

Lavender drew another puff and lazily blew a smoke ring. "How Madame Lola loved her cheroots!" she said wistfully. "We would go through boxes of them at our little *soirées...*"

"Don't mope, Lavender. The Countess will be back one of these days."

Shame on me for lying, thought Ida, surveying the melancholy seamstress, while privately wondering if she might work up the nerve to attempt one of her *cigarillos. It might calm me down.*

"...and magnums of champagne! Do you remember, when you lived in Grass Valley, how we drank toast after toast on Lola's birthday?"

"Like yesterday! I was only eight years old. I thought Ma would faint when I came home drunk. She wanted to strangle Lola!"

"Such good times we had!" said the créole woman, as she fished a small bottle from her bosom and took a grateful nip. "I love to lie here where I can see my Lolita's house...and think of those days gone by..." She let her head loll back against the rattan, tears glistening through her black lashes.

This won't do, thought Ida, watching her old friend's eyes becoming unfocused.

"Lavender," she pleaded, "please listen. You've got to help me. You're the only one I can turn to!"

Mme LeJeune roused herself in alarm, blinking. *"Bon Dieu, ma petite,* what can be the matter?"

"I need a dress to make me beautiful, *irresistible* – and pronto! There's no time to lose!"

Lavender breathed an inward sigh of relief. In her role as confidante to the female community, she had received more than one request for help from ladies with an unwelcome baby on the way. She straightened from her pillows and yawned demurely behind her hand.

"Ida, *chère,* you are beautiful as you stand. Youth is always beautiful, although the young don't know it."

"I mean *really* beautiful… *Please, Lavender!* I know you're busy, but I've got to have a ball gown that will turn heads. What's the sure-fire stuff? White samite? Silken fringes? I've got twenty dollars, all my own!"

Lavender smiled. "And where will you wear this head-turning gown, mam'selle? At the diggings?"

"Stop teasing me, Lavender. You know there's to be a grand ball and raffle to benefit the militia! Everybody's going!"

Lavender surveyed her young friend's eager face. What had brought on this sudden enthusiasm for the social whirl? Last year Ida had scoffed at party dresses. *Frilly dust mops,* she had called them.

"*Alors,* without a doubt we must make the effort *exceptionnel.* I will do my very best for you, *chère.* Come in the house now and let me measure you."

Inside, Lavender searched her shelves of fabric and lace. "*Voilà,*" she announced after some clattering of cupboards, "let us try this."

Ida stepped to the center of the studio, wondering how the tiny house could contain this grand room. Tall windows let in light from three directions. On the other wall stood a massive armoire, whose mirrored doors and sides could be opened to reflect every aspect of a woman's figure.

Lavender motioned Ida to stand before the mirrors.

"I have something saved for a special gown…although velvet is not suggested for the fashionable *demoiselles*…still…" Lavender draped a length of the soft fabric across Ida shoulders. "This palest blue, the color of the sky at early morning, when everything is quiet…see how it sings with the deeper blue of your eyes!"

The seamstress picked up the newest issue of *Madame Demorest's Mirror of Fashions* and opened it to a hand-colored plate of elegant evening dresses. She showed Ida a gown with a wide hoop skirt that was defiantly plain, without a single flounce or frill. The bodice of the dress was simple, too, cut very low and almost straight across, with small sleeves set just off the shoulders. "*Comme ça.* We will show off your tiny waist."

Ida noticed the lovely woman in the drawing was naked from her armpits up. A single wisp of transparent lace celebrated the line where the dress ended and the young lady began.

Now we're getting somewhere! Ida rejoiced inwardly.

She quickly undressed to her camisole, and Lavender measured her, jotting notes with a golden pencil attached to her chatelaine.

"I met the dancing-master from You Bet the other day," said Lavender, as the cloth tape encircled Ida's ribs. "Monsieur Doucet says you are his prize pupil – you and that young Joe Hardesty." Lavender waited for some reaction to her probe, but there was none. Clearly, poor Joe was yesterday's news.

The dressmaker reached up to unfasten the net holding Ida's long hair. "Heavy and thick, like your mother's," she said, running her fingers through Ida's dark auburn locks, lifting them and letting them fall in a fan across her shoulders. "You two are like the same drawing colored by different *artistes.*" Ida began to protest, but Lavender went on. "I saw *ta maman* yesterday. She, too, needs a new dress."

Lavender placed her hands on Ida's shoulders and turned her around to face the mirrors. *"Molly est très belle,* no?" said the seamstress. "So lovely… and *tout le monde* raves, night and day, over the hero, Monsieur Stafford, who has stolen the heart of every woman. How jealous they will be!"

Lavender fell silent, alarmed at the fiery blush that rose from Ida's neckline and set her cheeks ablaze. *Alors! So this is why our Joe is forgotten entirely!*

"Are you saying Mama and Will Stafford…?"

"Everyone says they make the perfect couple!"

Ida rounded on Lavender, glowering. "Horse apples! People love to make up stories."

The *modiste* hesitated, then shrugged. *"Tu as raison, ma petite,* perhaps it is only tattle."

But tattle from an excellent source, Lavender continued inwardly. Only yesterday the lonely Mme Hatfield had stayed for three cups of café au lait, pouring out her heart, confiding her dreams of a partner, friend, and protector – and praising William Stafford's qualifications for the job. According to Molly, the handsome lawyer was, in every way, what Mme Lola would have called "a likely man" – likely, that is, to end up in her bed. Lavender suppressed a heavy sigh. Clearly, silence was the only route in such a delicate affair. It certainly wasn't her business to shatter Ida's dreams – or Molly's, either.

"Come next week for a fitting, *chère*," she said, as she guided Ida's arm through her dress sleeve. "*Ta jolie robe* will be ready in time for the dance. You shall have the best patent hoop, a simple corset – no wires, the bosom and limbs must be free! Ruffled pantaloons…French heels, of course, to match…leave all to me…a capelet of lace…something for the hair…"

Ida fumbled at the hooks and eyes on her bodice.

Hellfire!

William Stafford my next stepfather?

Ridiculous!

Mama, Will, and me under one roof?

Over my dead body…

Chapter 12

The Grand Humbug

May 1861

Will relaxed into the plush wing chair, feeling as comfortable as could be expected with a flannel hood over his head. The heavy fabric made it hard to tell who was talking, but he suspected the voices belonged to Niles Searls and Aidan Caldwell.

"And now, William Stafford…"

"…for the ultimate question…"

"Do you believe in the Elevation of Man?"

Will hesitated, convinced he would regret any answer he gave.

"I consider myself a cautious optimist…"

"Yes or *no,* sir!"

Will sighed and took the plunge.

"Yes!"

Instantly, the chair shot upward, pitching Will into the air. Before his stomach caught up, he plummeted earthward, landing in a heap on the over-stuffed cushions. A crowd of unseen watchers laughed.

"Consider yourself elevated!"

"The Chairman of the Important Committee will now allow the Poor, Blind Candidate to see the Light!"

Will's hood disappeared, and he blinked as applause and catcalls erupted around the Clamper sanctum. Below a massive candelabrum of elk antlers ablaze at every point, Niles Searls sat on a giant wooden chair at least twice the height and size of a normal one, his feet dangling in the air.

"By the power invested in me as Ineffable Grand Humbug," Niles intoned, "I dub you Worshipful Knight of the Speedily Removed Garter and Member Perpetual of the Nevada Lodge of *E Clampus Vitus!*"

Cheers broke out, and red-shirted brethren crowded around Will to shake his hand.

"Congratulations," said Henry Bachelder, pinning a ragged tin star to Will's lapel and adjusting it with elaborate care. "We drank our way through a keg of spirits trying to think of an office for you, but grew confused and lost track. You'll have to settle for *Sovereign Grand Vizier of Virginia* – at least till we give it another shot."

"I believe it was *Grand Vizier of Sovereign Virginia*," said Judge Caldwell, clapping Will on the back, "but no matter. All Clamper offices are equally ignoble. We are all hierarchs here, a band of brothers, oath-bound to ignore each other's troubles unto death…"

"At which point," said Niles, "we send you off in style…and display a saintly commitment to the care of your widow and children."

"Especially your widow," added Jim Blaze. "But now, gents, I've got to get back to my establishment. Bring this greenhorn with you when you're ready, and I'll make sure you all leave on a shutter."

While the Clampers doffed their ceremonial garb and cleared away the ritual paraphernalia, Will looked around the "Hall of Comparative Ovations." A puffed blowfish glared back at him as it dangled from a beam, its spines pointing menacingly in all directions. Behind the fish, the silk-papered wall was decorated with fanned arrays of tomahawks and boomerangs, while on either side of the room, a gallery of cheerful, buxom women smiled benignly, apparently unconcerned at having mislaid most of their clothing. Adding to this glory were a dozen overstuffed chairs, a handsome billiard table, a piano, shelves of books, and a card table covered in green felt. It was, in Will's estimation, the perfect sanctuary for the male of the species, right down to the dust balls wandering freely across the floor.

"We're ready!" cried Henry. "C'mon," he said, handing Will his hat, "this is the good part. You're buying, of course, so drink hearty!"

～

The crowd was the usual mix at Blaze's saloon. The courthouse, just a block away, provided the lawyers and clerks, while Broad and Main Streets were represented by a throng of artisans and merchants, eager to invest the profits of the day in bottled refreshments and games of chance. A chorus of friendly shouts greeted the Clampers as they pushed through the swinging doors.

Will noticed Jonas Clench at a table near the door, pointedly ignoring their arrival. The mining heir had taken a thrashing in court over Ah Tie's water rights, and it was obvious the experience still rankled. Will saw Clench mutter a snide comment that was surely directed at himself, Searls, and Caldwell.

Will shrugged and turned to Blaze, who slid a foaming mug his way. Will lifted his drink to the monstrous pickled serpent staring down mournfully from its jar atop the back bar. *Between Clench and a rattlesnake,* Will reflected, *I'll take the rattlesnake any day.*

The door to the back room opened, and a Chinese man emerged, wearing a brimless cap, a ragged tunic, and the tough denim trousers and heavy boots of a miner.

"Judge Callwell?" the man asked.

The Judge, who was seated on the bar stool next to Will, lifted his eyes at the sound of his name.

"Yes?"

The Chinese miner looked cautiously around the bar at the sea of white faces, uncertain whether it was wise to proceed.

"Don't worry, my man. Come over here."

The man edged out around the bar, drawing a sheaf of papers from the waistband of his trousers.

"Your Honor, Ah Tie say come to you if trouble, and trouble come."

"I'm sorry to hear it," boomed the Judge, whose courtroom voice carried easily around the bar. "How can I help?"

"You look, please?"

The Judge took the papers, which were covered with formal handwriting, and scanned them swiftly, page by page.

"We have a deed, here, for some real property in the name of Mr. Keng Quee."

"I am Keng."

"I see. Well, I congratulate you, Keng. You appear to own three acres of stream frontage near You Bet, and the mineral and water rights thereon."

"Yes, my land."

"Unfortunately, you also appear to have a rather substantial debt...with a payment schedule specified. Would that be the problem? Have you not made these payments?"

Keng hung his head. "Sick...no pay."

"I'm sorry to hear it, Mr. Keng, because the terms of this note are rather harsh. Missing a payment makes the entire debt due and payable in ten days..."

"*Hai!*" Keng cried, pulling off his cap and wringing it in his hands.

Judge Caldwell shook his head. "If it was the May 10th payment you missed, I'm afraid you have until the end of business tomorrow to repay the entire loan, which is secured by your property."

Keng's face turned ashen. He stamped his feet. "My claim! It is...*every-thing!*"

Will took the documents and sifted through them. With sinking heart, he realized what the Judge said was true. Legally, Keng Quee had both legs in a bear trap.

"Perhaps you can sell the property right away," Will offered. "That way you can pay off the debt and still have money to start over. A paying claim should be worth quite a lot."

Keng shook his head violently. "Water go cross my claim – water Ah Tie need for *tong* cousin claim. If water not go, *tong* claim no damn good! I sell, Ah Tie *punish!*"

"Well, then," said Will, "why don't you sell your land to Ah Tie? I'm sure he would make a fair offer."

"Ah Tie go *Sanfow*...Marysville! Not come back. *Ai ya!* What I *do?*"

In his agitation, Keng cried out so the whole bar could hear. Will saw with dismay that Clench and his party had stopped talking and were listening avidly. Will signaled Keng to lower his voice, but the man evidently didn't understand the gesture.

"Ah Tie big boss!" he wailed. "I no sell!"

"Well now," said the Judge, "I don't know that you have much choice. If you don't pay off this Mr…" The Judge took the debt note back from Will. "… this Mr. Simmons by the end of business tomorrow, he will own your land, whether Ah Tie likes it or not."

Keng swayed dangerously, stumbled backward and slumped into an empty chair. Blaze poured a glass of water and pushed it across the bar.

"How much gold does your claim produce?" asked Will, handing Keng the glass.

"I work all day, catch twenty dollah. Sometime water freeze, sometime no water come, then no work." Keng hid his face in his hands.

Will did the math and whistled. "If you worked only half the year, Keng, you'd be taking out around $2500! Can you document this?"

Keng looked up, uncertainty supplanting the woe on his face. Will rephrased his question.

"*Proof.* Can you *show* how much gold you have found?"

Keng nodded.

"Ship gold Missouri House. Missus Hatfield say: 'Good clean-up, Keng, eh? Five hundred dollah again this month.'"

Will heard a chair scrape and glanced up. Jonas Clench had risen to his feet, a look of cruel expectancy lighting his face.

"We appear to have a business opportunity here," Clench remarked as he approached. "This Oriental gentleman appears to need cash in a hurry, and I could use another mine."

Will's heart sank. Clench had obviously heard the reference to Ah Tie and spotted the opportunity to injure his adversary.

"How much money does Keng need?" said Clench, barely suppressing the leer on his face.

"Eleven hundred dollars," Caldwell replied.

"Well, I see a satisfactory resolution at hand. Keng, what if I offer to buy your land at full market value? Then you can pay off your debt and have plenty of money left over. What do you say? I'll have the papers drawn up first thing."

Hope struggled with fear on Keng's face. He glanced back and forth nervously between Clench and Judge Caldwell.

"Wait a minute!" snapped Niles Searls. "How much do you intend to offer Mr. Keng, here, for his mine?"

"$2500," said Clench, eyeing Searls coolly. "The value of a year's production, by Mr. Stafford's estimate. More than fair, isn't it, Judge?"

Judge Caldwell's jaw worked. He looked like he was chewing glass.

"It's fair," he said grudgingly, "under the circumstances. One man working alone on a proven claim that size…could be plenty of gold still there."

Searls slammed his glass down on the bar. "Damn this!" he cried. "Judge, this vulture will cut off Ah Tie's water!"

The insult did not appear to offend Clench. On the contrary, his smile broadened. "Sorry you feel that way, Searls…"

"I'll buy the parcel myself," said Searls curtly. "Keng, don't sell to this man. He is a known enemy of Ah Tie. I will pay you $2600 for your property, in cash, as soon as the bank opens in the morning."

Clench shook his head. "That won't do. I have a particular interest in this property. I'll match your offer, plus the amount owed Simmons. That's $3700 altogether. What about it, Searls?" sneered Clench. "Are you prepared to pay eleven hundred dollars more to protect a Chinaman?"

Searls flushed, but remained silent.

"How about you, Judge?" Clench demanded. "Or you, Stafford?"

The Judge shook his head. All eyes turned to Will.

Rage boiled up inside him. He loathed Clench, loathed the bullying tone in his voice. For a moment, Will considered slapping the smug look off the man's face and sending his soul to Hell in the duel that must follow.

"Mr. Keng," said Will evenly, "I'll match that $3700 offer – and make sure Ah Tie gets his water."

Both Searls and Caldwell looked at him, aghast. They started to protest, but Will cut them off.

"Of course, I do not have that much in specie on this side of the continent, but that should not be a problem. Judge, would I be right in assuming your bank manager will accept a note from my bank in Virginia?"

The Judge hesitated. "I'm sorry, Will, but with the current political situation, I'm not sure he can do that."

Will stared at the Judge, hardly believing his ears. Aidan Caldwell was a senior director of the bank. The manager would surely cash any note the Judge asked him to.

"Out of the question, Will," Niles Searls added quickly. "The bank could not possibly take that risk."

Will flushed. Searls, too, was a director of the bank. *Were these two Yankees casting aspersions on a gold-backed note from Virginia?*

"I see," said Will coolly, turning away.

"Well, that's settled," said Clench brightly. "Keng, do you know where my office is on Pine Street?"

Keng nodded.

"Good, be there tomorrow at noon."

Keng bowed and hurried off with lowered head.

"And I'll expect you, too, Judge," continued Clench. "You'll want to make sure everything is on the up and up."

The Judge nodded grimly.

Will stared into his mug as Clench left. He did not want to see the smirk on the man's face – or meet Searls' or Caldwell's eyes, for that matter.

He had worked for Aidan Caldwell for six months and had known Searls for almost as long. He had counted them both friends…and yet, they had just *publicly* declined to cash his note at their bank.

Did they imagine that a Virginian bank would – under any circumstances whatsoever – decline to honor a note tendered by a Stafford? And even if the bank collapsed tomorrow – did they imagine that he would not make good the loss? Will was head of the Stafford clan since his father's death. Searls and Caldwell knew that. He could mortgage Greenbrier to cover the debt. There was no risk at all to their bank – *unless they considered him untrustworthy.*

His cheeks burned with humiliation and resentment at the gross personal insult. Perhaps such behavior was acceptable in the North, but for him, there could be no question of further friendship with men whose concept of honor was so debased.

Will looked up at the mirrored back bar and was distressed by the grim, unhappy face of the man looking back. He scowled as he lifted his mug to his lips.

"God help us! It looks like Virginia is voting to secede," said Searls.

Will almost choked on his beer. *There was a mocking tone in that voice!* He turned, pale with anger, only to see Caldwell and Searls smiling at him.

"Now, don't shoot…" cried Searls, raising his hands in feigned surrender.

"…and don't challenge us to a duel," said Caldwell.

Henry Bachelder's whiskered face appeared beside them. "And keep your voice down," Henry whispered, "or this time, you really will ruin the plan."

Will stared at the three of them as an inkling of the truth crept into his mind. "This…this was *arranged?*" he muttered.

No one answered, they just kept smiling at him.

"But Keng's deed…"

"Perfectly valid," said Niles.

"And his gold shipments…?"

"Molly will verify them under oath," said the Judge.

"And the debt to Simmons?" Will asked.

"Charley Simmons holds a note from Keng, all right," said Henry Bachelder, "just the same as the one the Judge holds from Charlie. The money's all scootin' sideways, you might say."

"I wrote both notes myself," said the Judge, "with an outstanding balance that happens, by uncanny coincidence, to equal the amount Ah Tie owes my office for services rendered – including your own excellent work, Will."

"So," said Will, with a hint of a smile appearing on his face, "you just got Jonas Clench to pay Ah Tie's legal fees…"

"To the penny," said the Judge, with visible satisfaction, "and an honorarium for Keng as well. Only fair, since it was his decision to sell his land and go back to China that sparked the idea – and his remarkable acting talent that carried it off."

"But what about Ah Tie's claim? What if Clench blocks his water?"

"Heavens," said Searls, turning to Caldwell, "that could be a problem… Did we make a mistake, there?"

"Perhaps," said the Judge, "though Ah Tie informs me his parcel has been mined to a fare-thee-well, and there's not a fleck of gold left on it."

"Nothing but lizards and poison oak," said Henry, grinning. "He'd probably give it to you, Will, if you ask politely…"

"What are you gents all huddled up about?" said Jim Blaze, working his way down the bar with a wet rag. "All this jawin' over here, and I can't hear a word of it."

"Nothing much, Jim," said Will, with a wry smile. "I'm just getting an eye-opening lesson in Yankee duplicity, that's all."

"Hell," said Blaze. "I could have saved you the trouble...could have told you flat out these three are snakes. What kind of organization do you think you joined, anyway?"

"There was nothing *serpentine* about this transaction," protested the Judge. "Indeed, I have rarely acted more honorably."

"That I can believe," muttered Blaze.

"As it happens," said Caldwell, with an air of wounded dignity, "I owe Ah Tie a considerable debt. I was prospecting on the Yuba some years ago, when a rock shifted, pinning me underwater. Ah Tie was good enough to roll the boulder off my leg, thereby saving my life. Since then, I have declined to charge him for legal services, while he is equally reluctant to let me work for free – Ah Tie being punctilious in his business obligations. So, in this most recent case, we compromised by letting Mr. Clench pay for his own chastisement in court. Seems to me, Blaze, that a more equitable solution can hardly be imagined."

Blaze rolled his eyes and ambled off toward a party of apprentices who had reached a belligerent stage in their evening's drinking. The Clampers watched the big barkeep hoist the chief miscreant by the back of his shirt and pants and sail him through the doors like a feed sack.

"Of course," said Searls, "you can cash your note at the bank anytime, Will. Funds are still transferring freely, but with this war in sight...well...if I were you, I'd turn every Virginian note I held into gold, right now."

Will's reviving spirits sank again at the mention of the nightmare unfolding back East – a continental-sized train wreck playing out over months, sending pieces of the shattered Union flying off with each new collision.

"Is there any news from the Old Dominion?" asked Judge Caldwell.

"Virginia goes to the polls in four days," said Will, "to vote on the Act of Secession. It is the last chance to pull back from the abyss, but every sign suggests the Act will pass." Will shook his head in disbelief. "For most of my life, secession was something old men grumbled about over brandy and cigars."

"What changed?" asked Searls.

Will shrugged. "Well, John Brown's raid didn't help. Virginians don't care for outsiders coming down to stir up insurrection. But the last straw was Lincoln's call for troops to put down what he terms a 'rebellion' in South Carolina. I confess I found it puzzling. For a man born in Kentucky, Mr. Lincoln shows an almost miraculous ignorance of the Southern mind. There was never the slightest chance of Virginia joining a campaign against a sister state."

"But couldn't she just remain neutral?" asked Niles Searls. "That is Kentucky's position."

"Perhaps. That would be the practical effect if the Act of Secession is voted down."

"A neutral Kentucky and Virginia…" Searls murmured. "It's hard to imagine how the Northern states could get at South Carolina, if that's how it plays out. General Scott would have to waft his army down the seaboard in hot air balloons…"

"The perfect way to wage war!" cried Henry, slapping the bar. "That's brilliant, Niles! The only thing that could possibly make me re-enlist!"

"Don't get your hopes up, Henry," said the Judge. "This notion of neutrality is humbug. If any responsible man is advocating it back East, it is only because he wishes to put off a decision by his state until the wind shifts in his favor."

"Yes," said Will grimly, "neutrality is a dismal option. Unfortunately, the alternatives…"

"…are *unthinkable*," said Niles.

"Amen!" said Henry.

"Well, now, gentlemen," said the Judge, "let us not forget the festive nature of the evening. Will, here, has been gathered into the fold of *illuminati*, and Jonas Clench has magnanimously atoned for abusing my friend, Ah Tie. *Ergo bibamus*, as my dear old nurse used to say."

"So did mine," muttered Henry, "but she never did tell me what it meant."

"'*Drink up!*'" said the Judge, lifting his glass and beaming at Henry. "She said, 'Drink up!' And I have honored her memory every day since!"

Chapter 13

The Union Ball

June 1861

Judge Aidan Caldwell escorted his wife, Amanda, and Molly Hatfield downtown to the Monumental Hotel, while Kitty, Dora, and Ida skipped before them, holding up their hoops and deftly vaulting over the gaps in the uneven boardwalk. Ida soared highest, buoyed by the fact that Molly hadn't gone to war over her new dress, but had – to Ida's amazement – complimented her on it instead. Molly had taken great care in arranging Ida's dark locks; she had even loaned her a favorite brooch – a cameo of the goddess Diana with the moon in her hair.

It was almost eight o'clock in the evening, and darkness was gathering as they entered the town plaza. The setting sun blazed momentarily off the hotel's plate glass windows as they climbed the wide front stairs. Then they were through the great double doors and into the lobby, where the air was thick with perfume and cigar smoke.

Judge Caldwell surrendered his charges to Clara, his maid, who was supervising the ladies' dressing room for the evening, then retreated to the male sanctuary of the bar, where he hung up his pistol and began hearing testimony on the quality of the aperitifs.

A quarter-hour of careful adjustment brought the women to fashion plate perfection. As Ida emerged from the dressing room, tow-headed Joe Hardesty raced to her side, openly devouring her with his blue eyes.

"I thought I'd grow old and grey waiting for you!" he said, as he seized her arm and steered her toward the refreshment tables. "Can you guess my news?

I'm enlisting!" he crowed, before Ida could reply. "We'll give those Rebels a whippin' and send 'em back to school to learn some manners!" He studied Ida's face. "You'll write to me, won't you, and tell me all the news from home? Promise you will? I won't mind so much being far away, if I know you are thinking of me."

"I thought you had to be eighteen to enlist!" Ida protested.

"Oh, nobody pays attention to that – what matters is I can handle a horse and rifle. I've got to act fast, Ida, or the fun will be over by the time I get there! It's a three-year hitch, but it won't take anyways near that long to settle the hash of those Secesh dogs!"

"Joe, why risk your life in somebody else's fight? What do we care about slavery? There are no slaves here."

"Why, my life wouldn't count for nothin' if I wasn't ready to put it on the line for the best government in the world! Besides, slavery is a blot on the honor of the United States. It's time it was removed, and it'll take Californians to do it!"

"Why on God's green earth would you court an early grave?" said Ida, glowering at Joe. "If you go, I'll write to you sure enough, and in every letter I'll make you miserable for leaving and remind you that it's your own fault you're gone."

Joe excitement faded. He looked surprised and hurt.

"I'm sorry, Joe," Ida said. "Don't you see, though? Everybody knows you've got grit. You don't need to prove anything."

"Shoot, Ida, the wide world is calling – and you want me to wither away in You Bet while life passes me by?"

                                   ~

Miss Liberty of 1861 and her Maids of Honor looked like lovely confections behind the huge, cut-glass bowls of iced punch. Soon they would reign in state over the Fourth of July festivities, but tonight the girls laughed and flirted as they served ginger ale and sweets to a throng of young men in black uniforms – the cavalrymen of the Nevada Rifles. Ida saw a tall, curly-headed youth in the crowd, and cried out in astonishment.

"Gareth Truesdale! I thought you were in Washoe!"

The young man pushed his way through the uniforms to greet her.

"You needn't look so alarmed, Ida. I'm not a ghost," said Gareth, flashing a handsome smile. "Does Dora know I'm here?"

"No, she'll be as surprised as I am!"

"Then I'll go spring myself on her and take advantage of her confusion," the young soldier said. "But first, surrender your dance card, so we can plan our maneuvers. Will you have me as a partner for 'The Lancers'?"

Gareth scrawled his name on Ida's program and held it out to her. Joe Hardesty intercepted it and scrutinized it with a scowl.

"What a wonderful night this will be for Dora!" Ida said, as Gareth strode off.

"It's a happy night for the whole Truesdale clan," said Joe. "The assay just came back on their new vein – $60 a ton! I'd say *happily ever after* was a sure bet for Gareth and Dora. As for you and me, Ida, we'll dance both Mazurkas." Joe scribbled in his JH twice and handed back her card. "Won't old Doucet swallow his monocle when he sees what we've got cooked up!"

At center stage, the orchestra was tuning up. Madame and Monsieur Doucet, instructors at the You Bet Dancing Academy, presided amid a sylvan glade of potted ferns and borrowed geraniums. Doucet held his violin to his ear and plucked the strings, while Madame pounded a single piano key at frequent intervals. Mademoiselle Doucet twisted the tuning pegs of her banjo and Sven Sorenson coaxed his double bass into tune. Supporting these familiar faces were the first-chair musicians of the Nevada Concert Band, testing reeds and noodling finger exercises.

Doucet called for silence, lifted his bow, and cued the cornet player. A fanfare stabbed the air, climaxing in elaborate flourishes, and Captain and Mrs. Harrington of the Nevada Rifles stepped proudly onto the dance floor, as the orchestra burst into "Yankee Doodle."

The Harringtons were followed closely – to Ida's astonishment – by her mother, on the arm of John Van Hagen. The sheriff looked particularly impressive in his black cavalry jacket with golden sergeant's stripes on his sleeve. Molly was dazzling in a gown of coral velvet and silver lace – *like the sunset sky with evening stars,* thought Ida.

The rest of the non-commissioned officers wheeled onto the floor with their ladies, whose immense hoop skirts were bright as butterflies, tiered with ruffles, and decorated with endless miles of ribbon. The community's civilian leaders followed, led by a beaming Judge Caldwell and a radiant Amanda. A stately procession of attorneys and bankers and their wives came next, of no interest to Ida – until she saw Will Stafford.

Will's hair was longer than when she had last seen him, and curled softly at the nape of his neck. He wore a swallow-tailed coat of black velvet over an ivory silk waistcoat that emphasized the slenderness of his hips. The petite brunette on his arm was strikingly good-looking in a fuschia silk gown, with a small constellation of diamonds glittering at her throat.

Who was that, now? Ida searched her memory. *Why, Mary Dunn, of course! Her husband must still be in the bar.*

Ida's heart flickered back and forth between jealousy – for Mary was indisputably lovely – and pity, since the whole town knew her brilliant husband was drowning himself in floods of old bourbon.

Ida fixed her eyes on Will until the tide of couples flowed around him and he was lost to view, just as Monsieur Doucet sang out, "Ladies and Gentlemen, the Virginia Reel!"

⁓

After the first set, the brightly lit and crowded ballroom felt hot and stuffy, and the revelers melted away to the cool veranda. John Van Hagen led Molly to the railing and stood close beside her.

"Molly Hatfield, I've never seen you look so fetching," said the sheriff, his eyes resting on the tiny golden horseshoe pinned to the center of her neckline. He looked up at the yellow roses in her hair. "I'm happy to see you're not still wearing widow's weeds."

"Zeke always said I looked dreadful in black," she said with a wry smile. "He didn't like it when I put on mourning for my father. He said the dead were selfish, and he hoped he would have better manners, if the occasion arose, and let me get on with living."

Van Hagen smiled. "Zeke always said that life was like beer...can't be tasted in a sip..."

The sheriff's voice dropped away. He had no wish to talk about Molly's late husband. He pulled in a deep breath to steady himself. He looked into her hazel eyes and took her hand. His heart was pounding so hard he wondered if she could hear it.

"Molly, when you think about marrying again, I hope you'll consider me."

"John! Is that a proposal?" Molly felt his strong fingers close over hers.

"It is, right enough. I'd be good to you, Molly, and I'd be a father to that youngster of yours – if the two of you will have me. We could travel…see the world! I've always wanted to see Paris. Will you go with me…as my wife?" His blue eyes held hers with a determined gaze. Molly gently drew back her hand.

"I'm honored, John…but…you take me completely by surprise! You must let me consider. I hadn't thought of marrying again." She turned her head, blushing at the lie, as Will Stafford stepped forward from the shadows.

"You'll excuse us, please, John," he said, holding his hand out to Molly. "I have come to claim my partner for the waltz."

Molly smiled her apology at Van Hagen as she swept through the door on Will's arm. There was nothing but bitter disappointment in the lawman's pale blue eyes as he returned her gaze.

The orchestra struck up a graceful waltz. Will circled Molly's waist with his right arm and covered her small, gloved hand gently with his own. She rested her left hand on his shoulder, and they swung into a series of swirling turns. *Musk rose and amber,* Will thought, as he breathed in the scent she always wore. *Passion and romance.*

She looked up into his eyes as they danced, her lips slightly parted, the pupils of her eyes so dilated that the green irises seemed entirely black. Will returned her gaze, hating the distance imposed by her crinoline. He wanted to waltz her out into the darkness, where he could crush her skirts and hold her body close to his.

They danced without words, lost in the music and each other, until the orchestra faded and Doucet dashed off into a soaring cadenza. Will leaned over and whispered close to her ear. "Please don't hurry away when the music is over tonight, Molly. I want to say good night to you."

$\sim$

The cornet split the air with a ringing fantasia, and the orchestra dashed off into a rousing Polka Mazurka. Joe Hardesty led Ida out onto the floor and whirled her away in large figure eights around the room: *step-close-HOP, step-close-LEAP* – flying into the air on every third beat.

Will Stafford watched the youngsters fly past, struck by Ida's effortless grace. Her shoulders and arms inscribed flowing lines, like Arabic verses written in air, and her dark blue eyes glowed with pleasure. Her swinging skirts played peek-a-boo with the tiers of white lace ruffles at her ankles, as her small feet tapped out the code of the dance. The couple alighted in front of the stage, where the dancing master was sure to see them. Joe dropped to one knee and Ida slowly circled him, the fingertips of their right hands touching, teasing, as if he were about to draw her down to him. Another seductive revolution, clockwise this time, and away they twirled down the hall once more. Ida smiled exultantly as she caught Will's eye.

Altogether lovely, thought Will, and not for the first time. *Ida is a new kind of creature, a western species, spontaneous and artless – with a soul born in freedom, pure as gold.*

The band leader's upraised bow signaled the end of the Mazurka, and Joe and Ida stopped deftly before the orchestra, frozen in a *tableau vivant.* Monsieur Doucet beamed with pleasure at his pupils' performance. Whisking violin and bow under his arm, he began clapping, inviting the applause of the other dancers.

～

Breathless, Ida rushed up to Will and playfully touched his lapel with the tip of her feathered fan.

"This is the Ladies' Choice," she proclaimed, "and you are mine!"

Will bowed obediently and offered his arm. Doucet struck three quick notes with his bow, and Mama Doucet soloed through the refrain on the piano as the gentlemen led out their partners for "The Jenny Lind Waltz."

"What a wonderful dancer you are, Miss Hatfield!" said Will as he spun her around. Ida flushed with delight.

"As are you, Mister Stafford! I pity the belles of Virginia, since we've stolen you away."

"The belles of Virginia fade away to nothing when compared to the young goddesses of California."

It's true, mused Will as they circled the floor. *I've barely thought of Charlotte Townsend since I arrived here, though I killed a man for her amusement.* He knew, even as bitter memories of the pointless duel flooded back, that neither Ida nor Molly would ever ask him to gamble his soul to feed their vanity. A rush of affection filled his heart.

"Miss Ida..." he began, but no words came. He pulled her a little closer to him, until he felt her arm relaxing on his shoulder, and then spun her into the dizzying finale.

Applause brought Will back to himself. The musicians were leaving the stage, and he and Ida were still circling in their own dance, looking in each other's eyes. As she glided off the floor on Will's arm, he spoke to her softly.

"Miss Ida, will you wait for me by the back door when the dancing is over, so I can say goodnight to you?"

Ida's head spun with joy. It was unbearably sweet to touch Will's arm, to feel him next to her as they strolled off the dance floor.

Chapter 14

For God and Country

June 1861

Dinner was served at midnight in the dining hall, where long, linen-draped tables blossomed with bowls of red roses and Union flags. Fleets of waiters crisscrossed the room, bearing savory supper dishes and pitchers of chilled cider. Joe, Ida, Dora and Gareth fell upon the feast, their small talk soon giving way to clattering cutlery and clinking glasses. At last, Ida laid down her fork, silently cursing the whalebone stays that forbade a second helping of strawberries and ice cream.

"Will the Rifles go back East?" she asked Gareth.

"No. The army will send the regulars back because they're trained and ready. Militia units like ours will do replacement duty in California. Some will be sent to Washoe to guard the Comstock bullion, but the Rifles will probably stay right here, to protect the big gold shipments from Allison Ranch – and from out by your place, Ida."

"Won't you be disappointed, staying in California?" Dora asked.

"Not if we have something to shoot at," said Joe, "Paiutes on the warpath, or highwaymen, or *secessionist traitors*." He lifted his knife and aimed at his water glass, as if it were a Rebel gunman. "If we have to content ourselves with keeping the Southern Chivalry in line, that's a real enough job. There are nests of sedition, even in the Northern Mines!"

"Exactly!" said Gareth. "We've got to keep an eye on Governor Downey – and Senator Gwin and his slave-holding cronies. The Southern faction may have run California since statehood, but their time is over!"

The young people's heads turned as Oliver Stidger, editor of the *North San Juan Hydraulic Press,* rapped with determination on the water glass atop the speaker's podium. The tide of conversation ebbed until the room was silent. Stidger gripped the lapels of his frock coat with both hands.

"Ladies and gentlemen," he began, in ringing tones, "it is my honor and privilege to speak with you on behalf of the sacred cause of National Union.

"'Now, that's all well and good, Oliver,' you may say, 'but what has the Union done for *us* lately, here on the far rim of the continent? Do we have mail service that we can rely on, yet? Or a telegraph line to the East? Has Congress made any effort at all to build the railroad we desperately need to bind us to the States?'"

The room erupted with cries of *"They're stone deaf back there!"* and *"They don't care if we float off into the Pacific!"*

"I agree, friends," said Stidger, cutting off the chorus of complaint. "Why, then, should we give two cents about the troubles of a distant and neglectful government – *when there is mining to be done?"*

General laughter broke the anger and tension that had been building in the room. Someone shouted out, *"Blamed if I know, Oliver! You tell us."*

Stidger drew himself to his full height and filled his lungs.

"I tell you, friends, that our National Union is no airy ideal, no quaint political theory. *No! It is the foundation on which our civilization rests!* Nor did we leave it behind when we crossed the icy mountains and perilous oceans to California! The Union is here as much as it in New York or Pennsylvania, or anywhere else Old Glory floats proudly in the breeze.

"We have travelled far from the scenes of our childhood, where we sat by the hearth and listened to white-bearded patriots tell of the terrible sacrifices that attended our country's birth. We all thrilled to those tales of ancient heroes who fought and died for Liberty and Union. It is now our sacred duty to preserve this government and bequeath it inviolate to our children, and our children's children..."

"That's tellin' 'em, pard!" came a booming voice from the back of the room. A growl of male approval shook the air.

"And now," said Stidger, his voice rising over the crowd, "our beloved country is threatened by conspiracy and rebellion! Will we, the citizens of

California, stand by and let our government, the Safeguard of our Liberty, be torn limb from limb?"

Cries of *"No!"* and *"Enough is enough!"* erupted around the room, as a pounding thunder of boot heels shook the floor. Stidger lifted his arms as if to embrace the crowd, which roared in response.

"Will we, the heirs of Freedom, dishonor the sacrifice our fathers made? Will we grovel before the repeated insults of the Slave Power...*and bend our knee to treason?"*

~

As Stidger stepped down to wild applause, Mary Dunn lifted her fan to her mouth and yawned.

"What joy!" she said. "I do believe Mr. Stidger has subsided at last. I declare, I will *never* forgive Frank for dragging me to this affair and then abandoning me to the horrors of patriotic oratory." She turned to Will, who was seated by her side. "What is the secret of your continuing calm and good humor, Mr. Stafford? Have your years in the courtroom inured you to mindless bombast?"

"I believe I feel it less keenly than most, ma'am..."

Molly Hatfield, who sat on the other side of Will, leaned forward and raked Mary with her eyes. "Did Mister Stidger's thoughts on the Union strike no chord at all in your heart?"

Mary pretended to untangle the tassel of her fan for a moment, then turned to Molly with a look in her eyes that made Will nearly drop his wine glass.

"I believe, Mrs. Hatfield," he interjected, "that Mr. Stidger forgets there are many here who hold their States in the same high esteem he reserves for the Union alone. As a Virginian, for instance, I am pleased to honor General Washington as the bringer of Liberty to both my countries. My loyalty and affection for my Commonwealth does not preclude a kind regard for the Union."

"But your Commonwealth has broken away from the Union," said Molly. "That would seem to me to force a..." She stopped, shaken by the look of pure misery on Will's face.

"Secession was a terrible mistake," he said somberly, "but my people have been buried in Virginia's soil for nine generations now, alongside our friends and neighbors. We are more of a tribe, ma'am, than a polity…"

"But of course, Mr. Stafford," cut in Mary, "you *do* acknowledge the right of Virginia to secede, do you not?

"Yes," said Will slowly, "…I do."

He rose to his feet before either woman could press him further.

"Ladies," he said, "I must beg your indulgence. I find I am in want of a smoke. Please forgive me."

He bowed to each in turn, and then made his way to the doors that opened onto the veranda.

~

Ida watched Will's exit with a pang in her heart. The night she had looked forward to for so long was now more than half over, and the precious minutes were fleeing. While a soldier with a sheaf of lottery tickets distracted Molly, Ida slipped from her chair. "Back in a minute," she explained to Joe, who was rising to follow her. "Save my place."

She scouted the covered porch for Will. Everywhere, dark clusters of men were deep in conversations punctuated by glowing cigars. She searched from group to group, wondering at the appalling, bloody-minded war talk she overheard. *They're all crazy – except Will,* she thought. *He won't get caught up in this lunatic war. He's a Californian now, and what's the difference to us if there's one government or two on the East Coast?*

She looked up, pleading, at the old moon stuck in the pine tops on Harmony Ridge. *Where is he?*

She felt a touch at her waist and whirled around, her breath frozen in her chest.

"Are you enjoying yourself, honey?" said Molly, smiling sweetly at her daughter. "I know I am. I wish this night would last forever."

After a moment of stunned silence, Ida let out her breath in a rush.

"I've been wishing that, too, Mama, 'cause I'm scared that nothing's going to be the same after tonight. Can you hear them, how excited they are about going to fight? If I was God, I'd get the biggest pail of cold water in Creation and slosh it over 'em, to snap them out of it."

"I wish He would."

"What docs Van Hagen say will happen? Did you ask him?"

"No," Molly laughed, "he was too busy asking me – to marry him!"

Ida's jaw dropped. "I had no idea!"

"Neither did I, until tonight. And what's more, he wants to take me to Paris for a honeymoon!"

Ida's heart jumped. If Molly accepted Van Hagen, there would be no question of rivalry over Will. "What did you say to him?" Her elation faded as she pictured the sheriff wrapping his arms around her mother. "You didn't say *yes,* did you?"

"Well, he's a fine figure of a man, and he doesn't chew tobacco..." Molly tried to keep a straight face as she watched Ida's look of growing horror. "No, honey," she relented, "I turned him down." Molly's teasing tone became rueful. "I don't think he'd fit in at Missouri House. He said he wanted to be a father to you – but what do you suppose he'd be to Nutim? Or Pedro?"

Mama's right, Ida thought. Van Hagen had led the bloody expedition to Pyramid Lake to punish the Indians for killing Henry Meredith. The sheriff thought the Maidu were treacherous, sneaking savages, and his opinion of Mexicans was only a notch higher. Missouri House's easy ways would end if John Van Hagen moved in.

"Let's go inside, honey," Molly said. "It's cold if you aren't dancing."

~

The evening's music ended and the orchestra rose to great applause. With a fluttering heart, Ida hurried to the back of the veranda. She perched on an iron bench where she could watch the door, interweaving breathless thoughts of Will with a passionate yearning to rub her aching feet.

A couple strolled out onto the veranda, arm in arm, black paper silhouettes against the hotel's blazing glass doors. They were only a few steps away when Ida recognized them as Will Stafford and her mother.

Dazed, Ida smoothed her skirt away to make room on the bench. "Here's a place for you, mother," she said faintly.

When Molly was settled in, Will stood before the two women and bowed.

"Mrs. Hatfield, Miss Hatfield, this surely has been a night to remember. I shall always recall it with the deepest pleasure. And I hope you all will think of me with kindness while I am away, for I leave this morning for Virginia."

"No!" cried Ida.

"You mustn't go!" Molly said, turning ashen.

"But I must," said Will, looking grave. "I have not seen my mother for some time, and these are trying days for her. All my arrangements are made. The express coach leaves at seven. Will you allow me to write to you from Greenbrier?"

"Of course," Molly stammered.

"Goodnight, then," said Will, holding them both in his gaze, pressing them into his memory. "God bless and keep you." He bowed again, turned, and stepped off quickly into the grey dawn.

Ida watched the tears trickle down her mother's face, while her own stomach clenched in cold panic. *He can't just disappear!* She reached for Molly's hand and held it as her own tears started to fall.

Chapter 15

Local News

March 1862

Cerberus, the aged watchdog of Missouri House, didn't have anything like a full set of teeth, much less multiple heads to put them in. He did, however, bark loudly enough for three ordinary dogs, and the morning air resounded with his challenge of Sam Gee. Esmeralda gave her bread dough a last punch, covered it with a damp cloth, and hurried to the back door of the kitchen.

"'Morning, Miss Esmela," Sam called as he hurried up the path, his hands steadying the pair of swinging baskets hanging from his yoke. The legs of his loose cotton trousers were wet and splashed with red mud, and his heavy boots were crusted with clay. "Best new garden today." Sam lowered his baskets onto the porch and proudly uncovered them.

"These are good-looking vegetables, Sam, but we paid Ah Tie for only one basket."

Sam shook his head emphatically. "Boss say, 'Missouri House, two basket.' Say, 'all best from garden.' You take, Miss Esmela, cook good food. Yes?" Sam unpacked his cargo into the tin tub on the porch: bunches of fresh green onions tied with string, bundles of tender snow peas, a stack of glossy cabbage heads.

"Wait, Sam, I have something for you."

Esmeralda dipped back into the kitchen and returned with a warm loaf wrapped in a dish towel. Sam inhaled the fragrance of the bread, eyes closed, before stowing his prize away. He bowed his thanks and trotted off toward town.

"*¡Señora!*" Esmeralda called through the open door. "*Ah Tie manda más verduras!*"

Molly emerged, her spectacles balanced on her nose, her fingertips stained with ink. Esmeralda grinned impishly at her.

"I think Ah Tie asks for your hand in marriage soon."

"He has a wife already," said Molly, surveying the brimming tub of produce, "and four daughters. I don't think he needs a foreign devil for a number-two bride. I'd say he was hoping to get some of your famous cooking – except that Ah Tie doesn't set foot in the dining room. It's all I can do to get him to come into the office while we weigh his gold." Molly slipped her glasses into her pocket and rubbed the small red marks on the bridge of her nose. "Maybe he's just impressed by common courtesy – Lord knows the Chinese see little enough of it."

"I still say he wants to marry you," said Esmeralda, as Molly followed her into the kitchen. "Wouldn't he be a better husband than Van Hagen?"

The lid bounced off the pot of boiling potatoes and water splashed onto the stove. "Mind your cooking!" Molly snapped, crossing the room and pushing through the swinging door to the dining room.

Esmeralda's smile faded as she pulled the bubbling pan back from the heat. Van Hagen was not a man to laugh about. He was *un hombre peligroso.* There had been such proud and fearless men in her family. Her father and uncles had been true *Californios:* men who did not take insults lightly, men who did not flinch at danger. They had killed their enemies without hesitation, without pity. And now they were all dead, killed by *los chingados yanquis.* Van Hagen would also find his death by violence. Shuddering, she quickly crossed herself. *It was unlucky to be the object of such a man's interest.*

She picked up her big knife and chopped through a solid cabbage head. She shredded the crisp, green-layered heart. *I don't need second sight to see why* la patrona *is so bad-humored these days,* she thought, rocking the wide blade back and forth along the milky edge of the cabbage. *Señora* Hatfield was clearly sick with love for Stafford, the handsome lawyer – preoccupied with him every day – and she was making a habit of her unhappiness. It was sad to watch the grim lines beginning to show at the corners of her beautiful mouth.

∽

"Ida, how do you spell *subterfuge*?" asked Nutim, looking up from his pencil drawing. The boy was seated at the dining room table and could reach his work easily. *Ten next birthday*, Ida thought. *Soon he'll be as tall as I am.*

"S-U-B-T-E-R-F-U-G-E," she replied, stealing a glance at Nutim's sketch on yellow paper. A dark-skinned maiden, arms stretched stiffly before her, resisted the advances of a bearded white man sporting a pistol and Bowie knife. From a rocky perch behind the unhappy pair, a black-haired lad aimed a feathered arrow at the unwanted suitor. Florid lettering curved over and under the scene: *The Return of the Waryer, or, Bear Hunter's Revenge!*

"Do you like it?" he asked. "This is the cover."

"It's dandy, Nutim. I love the tattoos on the maiden's chin."

"That was the hardest part," said Nutim gravely, "getting her face right. She has to look beautiful and angry, too."

"How is the story coming along?"

"I'm right at the part where she tells the bad white man to vamoose. Want to hear it?" He thumbed through the handful of old receipts he used for scratch paper, held one up, and declaimed in a stern voice:

> *"Skunk Cabbage Jack, you are thinking bad thoughts. Never, never, never will I be yours. There are fair maidens of your own kind. Go woo them and win them. If you can with those ugly wiskers. World Maker protects me. If you persue me, terrible bad luck will follow you."*

"I'm all suspenders! What happens next?"

"Oh, Bear Hunter shoots the nasty *wólem* full of arrows, and Red Clover Girl steals his horse. Trouble's all finished. They get married, eat acorn soup, have babies."

Just then, Molly's voice rang out from the kitchen. "Ida, Nutim, are your hands washed? If you're not at the table in two minutes, you can go without."

Nutim looked anxiously at Ida.

"Have you noticed," the boy said, his eyes wide, "that *Nikném* is very grouchy?"

"Why, yes, Mama has been a bit…"

"She said I wasn't to play war any more with Cerberus and my pup. She took away my rifle. It's just a toy, but she said war was wicked and I should be ashamed." Nutim looked troubled. "Do you remember the story of Bear Woman, the horrible sister of the old chief, who grew meaner and meaner until she turned into a *bear?*"

"You bet."

Nutim bent toward her and spoke in hushed tones. "Mother's fingernails are getting longer, and so is her hair!"

Ida considered for a moment, then put her hand on the boy's shoulder and whispered in his ear. "I've been noticing that, too. It might not take much more aggravation to turn her all the way into a *grizzly!*"

Nutim gaped at her in horror, then at the front and back of his hands. He leapt up from the table.

"Don't forget to use soap!" Ida called to the fleeing boy.

∾

Nutim's got a point, Ida admitted to herself as she sat down at the kitchen table. Ever since Will Stafford had left for Virginia, there had been something distinctly bear-like about Molly. *And I'm fretful, too, always worrying about Will. He could be killed in battle, and we wouldn't know about it for weeks! Or it could all be settled, and he could be on his way back to California tomorrow!* She liked to imagine him stepping down from the stage from Nevada, all smiles at having surprised her. How quickly she would run up and be folded into his arms!

Ida looked at the little blue man and woman in the scene on her dinner plate. They stood under an oak tree, looking across a lake to the spires of a beautiful city. *Will and Ida in Virginia, gazing off towards Richmond.* She wanted to meet Will's mother, his brother Tad, and all the colored servants. There was Lazarus, who was the same age as Will and had gone to war with him, and Aunt Dinah, who smoked a pipe. Will had described them all as family in his letters. But it was unsettling to think of them as the *property* of Will's family, as well. If she married Will, she would be a *slave mistress.*

What if the slaves secretly hated their generous master?

And what of Will's neighbors – the people they would dine with and go to church with – were they like John Van Hagen, who made no attempt to conceal his contempt for other races? Could she stifle her reactions for Will's sake? *What if the peaceful city of blue spires was about to be blown to smithereens over slavery?*

Esmeralda set a steaming bowl of mashed potatoes before her. Ida scooped up a mound and plopped it down on the spires of Richmond. Then she drowned the potatoes with gravy until there was no trace of the scene below. She had to get over her silly fears. Will would come back to California, and they would settle here, in the place they both loved, where war couldn't touch them. Molly was never short of admirers; she would find another husband, eminently suitable. Life would be perfect!

~

After dinner, Ida and Nutim cleared the dishes in record time – Nutim, so he could put the final, thrilling touches to the destruction of Skunk Cabbage Jack, Ida so she could finish her letter to Will in time for the stage to Nevada.

At Missouri House, March 12, 1862

Dear William,

Your letters came yesterday, three of them! We waited until we were all at supper so we could read them aloud.

We were so glad to hear that you and Tad have a snug cabin for the winter. How we laughed at your descriptions of the Great Snowball Fight – and your man Lazarus dancing the Buzzard Lope. Nutim didn't laugh, he said that Buzzard was a powerful spirit helper, so Lazarus must be an important person in the black tribe of Virginia!

All the mail here has been delayed and some of it completely lost because of a Great Flood. It rained <u>torrents</u> from the day after Christmas until New Year's Day, and it was so warm it melted all the snow pack off the mountains. All the streams and rivers flooded, and there were big mudslides. Marysville and Sacramento both ended up under water!

The Grass Valley quartz mines are <u>still</u> flooded, and the miners are out of work. They say it could be six months before the shafts can be pumped dry. Most all the bridges and roads in Nevada county washed away, except for Steep Hollow Crossing. So right now, there is no way to get to Nevada – except by passing our door! The stage stop is doing so well, Mama has promised us a trip to San Francisco next fall when the snow flies!

And she says I may have singing lessons, too. Dora and Kitty are taking lessons from Herr Kessel. Shall I tell? Dora said he heard you singing in the barroom in the National Exchange, and he thought that, if you had been sober, you would have been the best baritone in the Northern Mines! He wants to teach you for <u>free</u>, if you agree to sing Schubert for him! So you'd better get back here, right away, before he finds someone else.

I sort all the mail and pack it, now. I have learned to weigh gold, cleaning out the sand, etc., if necessary, for some persons think we are naïve and even add buckshot to their pokes! Of course I don't mean the big concerns like the Jehoshaphat or Ah Tie's diggings. Ah Tie's shipments are always exactly weighed and recorded. It is a shame I have to dump out his gold and check it, but that's my job. Then I seal the bags with red wax and write the weight on each bag. So far this year, I have weighed 4,472 ounces of nuggets and dust, which is quite high for this season!

Since there is so much water, the cementum mines are running at full tilt. Ah Tie's Lucky Stars Mine in Wilcox Canyon is turning into a heavy producer. He has 100 Chinese at work. Mama says she is afraid that they will be run off such a good location. John Van Hagen has the job of collecting the foreign miners' tax, so we see a lot of him these days. The Chinamen are afraid of him, and so are the Indians. Old Lucy hides in the chicken house when he comes by.

Lucy is a Digger Indian from Captain Storms's old ranch. She comes over to help us sometimes, so she can make a little money. I think she may be related to Nutim somehow. She is very old and doesn't speak much English, but she is very good with the poultry. The birds all come to her, and the banty hen tries to perch on her shoulder. Even

Mr. Buchanan the turkey minds Lucy, and she is not much taller than he is.

The old gal goes out with her digging stick every day and finds wild things to eat. Once I heard her singing while she was digging. Nutim said it was the worm-enticing song. She doesn't eat at the table with us, but fixes her own meals, because she doesn't like milk or butter. She likes her spot next to the cook stove in the kitchen, and she likes to feed the fire. She spends hours talking to Nutim and terrifies him with her stories about monsters and ghosts. Now he is afraid Mother is turning into a bear, because she's been so grumpy. He thinks in the springtime she will leave us entirely and go live in the woods!

I miss you, Will, and I hope you will be through with the Army <u>very soon</u> and come back to California. It is going to be a glorious summer. We can have picnics and go fishing up in the mountains.

I hope the stockings fit. I made them myself.

I must close now, because the stage is coming in. Please write soon.

Always your loving friend,

Ida Hatfield

Chapter 16

Yankees at the Gates!

June 1862

"I will not have those men in my house again," hissed Mary Dunn. She rapped her fan shut on her palm and flung it across the table – a hard sidearm throw that shattered the tumbler by Frank's hand. "They were coarse, underbred Yankees!"

Frank coolly reached for a wine glass and filled it with bourbon from a crystal decanter.

"Coarse...underbred...Yankees..." he said slowly, tasting each word in turn. "Sadly redundant, my dear. Not at all up to your usual standards of invective."

"Those grasping, boorish men..."

"Mr. Crocker and Mr. Hopkins," said Frank wearily.

"...those infernal *Yankees*..." she repeated, shuddering in disgust, "cannot form a simple sentence without the word *money* appearing at the beginning, middle, and end. And they're *Republicans*, Frank! Didn't you hear Crocker crowing about how he stole this state for Lincoln in '60?"

"It was no idle boast. And yes, I am aware of Mr. Crocker's politics. Perhaps a good deal more than you are."

"What do you mean by that?" said Mary, snatching up her wine glass. Frank eyed it warily, ready to duck.

"People can be Republican for a number of reasons..." he began.

"None that are honorable."

"...including a deep interest in 'developing internal markets.'"

"So I heard at endless length. I have never been so bored at a supper table…"

"And when they talk about *servicing* those markets, what they are actually referring to is Washington's plan for building a transcontinental railroad."

"And this matters to us because…?" Mary let the sarcastic question hang in the air.

"Well, my dear, it should be apparent – even to the feeblest understanding – that whoever builds the rail link between the Atlantic and the Pacific will be the richest man in North America…or one of the richest," he added, "since the project is beyond the resources of any one individual."

Mary glared at him, still livid with anger. Frank shrugged and went on.

"This evening wasn't about politics. It was about *commerce,* which is the Yankees' one true art form. I personally have no interest in Mr. Crocker's political affiliation. What matters is that there is a solidly Republican Congress back East that is about to make Crocker, Hopkins, and their friends the richest men since the Medici princes of Italy – and I am in an excellent position to join them."

"Of course you are." Mary's voice dripped with sarcasm. "Let me guess. They have offered to let you in on the 'ground floor' of their great venture – an opportunity granted only to their closest friends! And they assure you – in strictest confidence – that their influence in Washington guarantees success… My God, Frank, you are even simpler than I thought if you let this villainous passel of Northern swindlers…"

"*Enough!*" roared Frank, slamming the table with his fist and making the silverware jump. An ugly purple flush rose to his cheeks. "What do you know about any of this? By God, Mary, if I could bottle your ignorance and sell it to the Yanks, this war would be over in minutes."

"But *would you?* Would you sell my crippling stupidity to the Federals? Or would you slip a little of it into Jefferson Davis's whiskey, so you could go on plotting with your Yankee masters. Who cares if the South goes up in flames, so long as you can keep fantasizing about becoming someone important?"

Frank lunged to his feet, his thighs crashing into the table. He picked up his wine glass and flung it at Mary. She ducked, then stood up slowly – her face a mask of icy contempt. Frank pushed his chair aside. A moment later, the front door slammed.

So, Frank was off for another evening at Suzanne Bonhore's cat house...
and good riddance!

She did not know if Frank consoled himself with trollops at the U.S. Hotel, nor did she particularly care anymore. It was Frank's binge drinking and
his reckless gambling after every fight that terrified her. And now he was
preparing to hand over his fortune to a band of Yankee peddlers. Why, Huntington owned a *hardware store* in Sacramento, for Heaven's sake! How could
Frank debase himself with such associations? How could he grovel before
Yankee politicians who had sworn to destroy the South!

She stormed into the parlor, sat down heavily at her piano, and began
tapping out random bits of melodies as she struggled to order her thoughts.
A few notes coalesced into an odd, halting phrase, and she found her hands
drifting into the refrain of "Juanita," the song she had sung with Will Stafford
at the Searls' party in the last days of peace.

Stafford was displaying the courage and patriotism of a man of honor. He
was in uniform, risking his life for Virginia. Lord, how distinguished he must
look! Tall, broad-shouldered, with those beautiful grey eyes and that voice
like honey... For a delirious moment, she was tempted to write him, but
what could she say? *Come back and whisk me away from all this?* She laughed
aloud at the ridiculous idea. Such a one-sided declaration would gain her
nothing in the estimation of that vexingly complicated man. Stafford was
an enigma – every thought in his head seemed tangled, complex, absurdly
conditional. He was no vile Republican, but he was lukewarm or worse about
Secession, and hopelessly muddled on slavery. "We might do well to be shed
of our *peculiar institution,*" he had actually told her!

How could a sane man contemplate freeing millions of Negroes to wander over the South – with God knows what ideas of insurrection and revenge!
– while the Northern states close their borders and laugh at the ensuing may-
hem? What nonsense!

No, Will Stafford was a dreamer, hopelessly out of touch with reality.
Besides – Mary flushed scarlet as she thought this – *the damned fool prefers*
Molly Hatfield's threadbare charms to my own. She had guessed as much at
the Union Ball, and the fact that he was corresponding with that Yankee
mudsill confirmed it. Frank picked up tidbits from their letters second-hand
from Aidan Caldwell and hastened to pass them along. "Will Stafford sends

regards to all," Frank had chirped at breakfast that morning, "and dreams of Molly's Sunday dinners."

Mary slammed the dust cover down on the keyboard and swept the tall stack of sheet music to the floor. Tears welled in her eyes, and she sprang up before they could start falling. She would not give in to foolish vaporings. *Be damned to Will Stafford and be damned to Frank Dunn!* She was Mary Grahame, descended of a great laird of Scotland, and she would see them both in Hell before they would make her cry!

She rang for a servant and ordered her mare saddled immediately. There was still an hour of good light and plenty of ditches around Nevada to jump. She would ride until she was ready to drop, then treat herself to a steaming hot bath. And then, perhaps, to the summerhouse with *Madame Bovary* – a book she could easily lose herself in, despite its insipid heroine.

Madame Bovine! she thought savagely. *If the woman had possessed a thimbleful of spirit, she would have poisoned her pathetic husband out of hand!*

Chapter 17

The Hessian Girl

July 1862

Peter Kessel closed the picket gate of the Caldwell's fence, as he did every Friday after his lesson with Dora and Kitty, convinced that an hour's pay for an hour spent teaching the Caldwell twins was deeply unjust. The young ladies' incessant giggling and constant distractions called for his fee to be doubled at least, if not squared. *Caldwell triplets,* he thought with a shudder, *would call for cubing!* He also realized his reflections were pointless. He would not ask Judge Caldwell for a raise, and the twins would continue to take ruthless advantage of him, because they knew how much he enjoyed their company...how much he would have loved to have daughters of his own.

Kessel considered the happiness of the Caldwell household as he walked up Broad Street. Why did some marriages work so much better than others? The question intrigued him, even though he knew that, in his own case, it was entirely academic.

It was not that his qualifications for marriage were lacking. He was sober, considerate, and neat in his person (though not, perhaps, in his possessions, which tended to accumulate in deep drifts around him). The music store was successful, and between that and teaching, he earned enough to support a family in modest comfort. It was true that his appearance could only charitably be described as average – average in height and weight, in hair color (brown), eye color (also brown), and facial comeliness (good nose, weak chin). He might not be Adonis, but in many communities, he might have married long ago and been thought a reasonably good catch.

But in a frontier mining camp, a shy man with unrealistic expectations didn't stand a chance. Kessel was resigned, now, to the idea that no helpmeet was going to appear magically on the stage of his life. Such things happened in great operas – charmed works of the imagination – but not in the world of a middle-aged refugee on the American frontier.

He hiked up American Hill, restoring his spirits by whistling themes from Mozart's magnificent *Magic Flute.* Then, at the crest, he sang both parts alternately of the duet in which the absurd bird catcher meets his improbable bride. *Such enchanting music!* He imagined teaching Dora and Kitty to sing it with him, but then another possibility came to him – and instantly rang true.

Ida Hatfield as Papagena! The twins' friend was a more daring personality by far – someone who could step out onto a stage and take command of an audience. What a charming complement to the foolish bird catcher she would make!

But who for Papageno? Who could play the self-important, but oddly endearing bird man?

Why, Will Stafford, *natürlich!* The range was perfect for the Virginian's golden voice, and Stafford was generously blessed with the good humor necessary for the role. As for the chemistry between the two on stage, well... there was already a romantic undercurrent there, at least as far as the girl was concerned. He had noticed it whenever he had seen them together, though whether Stafford returned the girl's affection, Kessel could not tell. There were, after all, those rumors about Stafford and Molly Hatfield...

The beautiful widow, or her equally beautiful and attractive daughter? What a choice to have!

William Stafford is the luckiest man alive, he thought disconsolately. The man was gifted in so many ways that he could choose any woman he liked, even in a society where respectable females were rare as double rainbows. And yet, this same Stafford had flown off to risk his charmed life, fighting for the wrong side in the vicious war raging back East. Could there be any greater mystery than this?

The music teacher trekked on as the sky darkened, his mind teeming with thoughts on the peculiarities of America, on his friends, on music. And then the faint notes of a distant hurdy-gurdy drifted up the hill, and he stopped to listen, at once drawn and repelled by the primitive sound. He waited, longing for the music to stop and release him from its spell – but it did not. With a sigh, he turned and started back to town.

He descended Spring Street as evening fell, his way lit by glowing windows. The hurdy-gurdy's music welled around him, filling his imagination with scenes of peasant life in the old country. He pictured the curious instrument, about the size of a plump viola, with strings sounded by a hand-cranked wheel instead of a bow. It produced an amazing volume of sound, an eerie, hypnotic flow that filled the air around the tent at the corner of Pine Street, mingling there with the scuffling shoes and clashing tambourines of the "hurdy-gurdy girls."

The girls of the dancing troupe were from the Hessen states, judging by their accents. Most hurdy-gurdies were. Whole villages in that impoverished land were supported by money sent back by their young women as they performed throughout Europe, ostensibly to promote the sale of whiskbrooms manufactured at home. In America, however, this thin fiction had been dropped. There were no Hessian brooms being shipped halfway around the world to the gold camps of California. Out here, the girls danced only to promote themselves in the richest market in the world for their wares.

Kessel handed two bits to the seedy drunk propped up outside the tent and slipped under the flap into a solid wall of lamp smoke and whiskey fumes, overlaid by the reek of hard-working miners, many of whom bathed only when a misstep sent them into a stream or ditch. He had arrived during intermission, and the lamps in the back of the tent were turned up so the audience could stretch and exchange gibes and greetings.

Kessel eyed the left side of the tent. There was room for him there on the broad, thick plank spanning a row of nail kegs, just behind the hurdy-gurdy player's chair. This was his favorite spot, offering the best view of the beautiful *Mädchen* who danced at the end of the line. From here he could take in her long, flowing dark hair, her upturned nose, her lovely small breasts, and the pouting mouth that, when the reflectors on the oil lamps caught her face just right, raised a ghost from the sleeping depths of memory and summoned a world in which he no longer believed – the world of the poor but gifted music student, Peter Kessel, and the lovely Anneliese.

The hurdy-gurdy player emerged from the wings, his instrument tucked under his arm, his face ruddy from the refreshment he had taken backstage. He resumed his seat, rested the hurdy-gurdy on his lap, and brought it back into tune. Then the man who collected the entrance fees shuffled in and turned down the lamps. Chatter died away as the patrons drifted back to their seats.

Suddenly a tambourine shook wildly, and the men turned as one to the tattered, hanging carpet that served as an entrance wing. The musician cranked his hurdy-gurdy, and the drone strings filled the air with their wail. Then he began working the wedges on the melody strings, and a song in an ancient mode rose eerily over the tent. With a great shaking of tambourines, the girls launched themselves out onto the stage one by one, their spangled scarves, long hair, and flaring skirts flying around them. Each danced with abandon, halting only for a moment to cast a wild, seductive look at the miners and rap her tambourine with the heel of her hand. As the last girl stepped out onto the stage, Peter leaned forward, wide-eyed.

Lieber Gott, it could be her!

His heart pounded and his senses reeled, even as his reason cried out in protest. Anneliese would be in her thirties now! She would not move with the lithe grace of this young *Hessin,* who resembles her only when she twirls herself across the stage, eyes half closed, head tilted back…

For a fleeting moment, Kessel's heart stopped as he looked on the face of the young woman he had loved with all his soul. His thoughts flew back. Vienna…1848…the *Völkerfrühling* – the "springtime of the peoples," when the desperate underclasses of Europe had risen up and swept the cruel and arrogant *aristos* from power. Paris, Milan, Frankfurt, Berlin, Vienna – in city after city, princes had fallen or been brought to heel. The wretched serfs of Gallicia, enslaved as thoroughly as any black man in the New World, had been freed. The secret police, the soul-less censors, the spies – all had been exposed and driven off.

Young Peter Kessel had spent his last penny in a pawnshop, proudly buying an antique fowling piece. For he was a soldier – an officer! – of the Academic Legion that spearheaded the revolution in Vienna. And how Anneliese had admired him, with his absurd blunderbuss and his tricolor cockade that showed he was on the right side of history!

Then came the bitter divisions, the slow unraveling of the revolutionary alliance into bickering cliques, as the *aristos* watched and plotted. They had never lost control of the armies, and when dissension among the revolutionaries reached its peak, they struck, setting their hireling troops against a barely-armed populace. Vienna itself was besieged by Prince Windischgrätz, who shelled the city into a state of terror. The fighting was savage, the resistance heroic, but cobblestone barricades were no match for professional soldiers and artillery. One by one, the city's defenses were overwhelmed. Peter fought furiously, escaping death by inches, and Anneliese came again and again to the barricades, bringing food for the fighters and helping the wounded to shelter. On the last day of the siege, one of Windischgrätz's gunners lobbed a shell into a resisting suburb to "teach it manners" – and the blast cut Anneliese in two as she stepped out of her father's shop with a basket of bread...

Kessel emerged from his memories with a start. The dance was over and the girls were backstage, meeting their admirers and making plans for the rest of the evening. He rose and shuffled out of the tent with the crowd. He had plenty of money for a dancing girl, but the anger in his heart was too great. He needed to get out into the clean night air and look at the stars and the moon. That would clear his mind, and he would return to the piano in his showroom and the sonata he was working on, Beethoven's *Appassionata*. He needed to make dangerous music, music that knew and spoke the rage of a man at the barricade – but that insisted nonetheless there was beauty and love enough to make life worth living.

He walked swiftly along Pine Street, head bowed, playing the opening movement in his mind. He worked through the phrasing, tried to visualize the fingering. It was a consuming piece that he was just coming to grips with. It would be easy to lose himself in it till dawn.

Chapter 18

Ahearn's Tavern

May 1863

"Mordecai Atwater's the name, purveyor of fine millinery supplies and notions to discriminating merchants throughout the Central Valley. We're looking to expand sales up here in the foothills, now there's females enough to make the trip worthwhile."

"I saw you on the road from Marysville," said the other gentleman standing in the dust outside Woodworth's livery in Grass Valley. "I'm George Cartwright." Cartwright lifted his heavy carpetbag, which rattled and clanked. "Kitchen wares extraordinaire: apple peelers, cherry pitters, coffee grinders, and more. If it saves time in the kitchen, Cartwright Brothers stocks it!"

"Pleased to meet you!" said Atwater, wringing Cartwright's hand. "Do you know the lay of the land up here?"

"I'm afraid not. This is my first trip to the Northern Mines. See here, Atwater, what do you say we find a good watering hole and wash down the dust of the journey? We can compare notes on what we've heard about Grass Valley and Nevada."

"You bet!" said Atwater. "I saw a tavern just down the street. Want to give it a try?"

"I'm your man!"

The ride up from the Valley had indeed been long and dry, and the notion of downing a few tankards of cool ale lifted the salesmen's spirits. They strode off together to Ahearn's, which proved to be a more modest establishment than either had thought at first glance. A thick swarm of horseflies, drawn by the reek of human and equine urine, greeted them on the ramshackle porch and circled in the doorway as the salesmen passed into the dense cloud of whiskey fumes and cigar smoke inside.

"Dark as Hades," muttered the purveyor of fine millinery goods, as they settled at a table that still bore black grease marks from its early days as a cable spool.

"But cooler," noted the kitchenwares man.

As their eyes grew accustomed to the dark, they saw that the back wall of the pub had been carved out of the hillside and dressed with stone, which explained the remarkable coolness of the interior, as well as the tang of mold in the air and the abundant insect life that roamed the establishment.

"Good Lord," said Atwater, as he spotted a tight pattern of small holes blasted into the post behind his companion. Cartwright turned and stared at the splintered wood, which was exactly at head height as he sat.

"Buckshot?" he said faintly.

Atwater didn't answer. His gaze had strayed to the bar, where the dour, aquiline face of Jefferson Davis peered back at him from a framed engraving. Alarmed, Atwater surveyed the bar's patrons. They were a rough, bewhiskered crowd who favored Bowie knives the size of cavalry sabers and pistols by the brace.

"Perhaps we should take our trade to another establishment..." whispered Cartwright.

Before Atwater could reply, the bar boy stepped out of the shadows, wiping his fingers absentmindedly on the filthy rag that hung from his belt.

"What'll it be, gents?"

"I'll take the coolest ale you have," said Atwater, after a moment's thirsty reflection. Cartwright seconded the order with a nod, and the boy slouched away to the bar and disappeared through a timbered door frame into a storage room dug into the cool earth.

"Who's the gentleman next to Mr. Davis, I wonder?" Cartwright murmured.

Atwater looked again at the bar and saw another picture next to the Confederate President: a big, hand-tinted portrait of a handsome man with blond hair curling over his ears. His gilt plaster frame was wreathed in black crêpe.

"That's Albert Sydney Johnston," murmured Atwater, "the former commandant of the US Army on the Pacific Coast."

"That doesn't look like an army uniform."

"It isn't," said Atwater. "Leastways, not *our* army. Johnston rode out of California with a Secesh militia unit."

"To join the Rebels?"

"Yep. He made it all the way across the desert and through the Apaches to Texas. Came within a hair of destroying Grant's army last year at Shiloh. Johnston took a ball in the leg there…bled to death…"

Both men fell silent as the bar boy approached with their drinks. They paid and began to gulp down the ale with the idea of moving the party elsewhere as soon as possible.

Three young miners in tattered denim pants and red shirts swaggered through the swinging doors and elbowed their way to the bar, their eyes blazing with excitement. The tallest of the three shoved his ham-sized hand inside his shirt and lifted out a bulging poke.

"Twenty-six ounces *this week* from our coyote hole down on Wolf Creek, boys, as easy as kiss my ass! Let's have drinks all around! Who'll join me in three cheers for Jeff Davis and Bobby Lee?"

Rebel yells rent the air in the stampede to refill mugs and shot glasses at the bar.

The salesmen applied themselves to their ale with renewed determination. Glancing around as they drank, their hearts quailed as they saw twenty pairs of eyes glaring at them from bearded and moustached faces.

"Reckon you gents didn't hear me," said the young miner with the poke. "Ah said, Ah'm buyin', an' we're givin' President Davis three cheers."

"H-happy to…uh…share with you…the custom of the house…" stammered Atwater. Cartwright nodded. He appeared to have lost the power of speech.

"Why, that's right neighborly of ye," boomed Thomas Ahearn's thick brogue from behind the bar. "We thought for a moment ye might be a pair of soddin' Yanks from up Nevada way…"

Ahearn's comment was met by howls of merriment. Atwater's broad Boston accent was unmistakable, and the realization of this made the man tremble. He stood mute, trying to look as affable as a terrified man can.

"Someone git these two Southern patriots some whiskey," Jake Forrest bellowed. He and Eldon Whitley were seated at a table close by. Jake and Eldon rose and sauntered over to the salesmen.

Jake whipped out an immense Bowie knife and held it sideways. The grinning bar boy placed two glasses of whiskey on the broad blade. With both hands on the knife's handle, Jake held out the drinks to the salesmen. The men shrank back from the gleaming knife blade.

"Drink up, boys," said Eldon, in a low voice that carried around the hushed room. Everyone watched as the two strangers reached for the drinks, hands trembling. Eldon stepped behind them, his hand sliding toward the monstrous dragoon revolver in his belt.

The salesmen clutched the whiskey tumblers with both hands and raised them to their lips.

There was a flash of orange flame and a deafening explosion. Whiskey splashed over the strangers' faces as they dropped their tumblers and ran screaming for the door, struggling to be first out into the street. Peals of raucous laughter shook the room.

Jake pretended to fan away the cloud of gunsmoke that swirled around him. "I tol' you to be careful with that-there blunderbuss, Eldon Whitley! Now you gone an' frightened them two little piss-ants so bad they'll have to change their drawers."

"Sorry," said Eldon, to more hoots and laughs from the crowd. "Reckon I didn't know the blame thing was loaded. Anyways," he said, turning to Ahearn at the bar, "didn't somebody say *free whiskey?*"

A general cheer greeted this inquiry. Someone hoisted Atwater's abandoned sample case onto the bar and began to paw through the contents. While the delicate items of feminine apparel passed from hand to hand, inciting more antics and ribaldry, Jake and Eldon carried their glasses back to the corner and rejoined the jug-eared Irish miner who had been drinking with them before the entertainment started.

The miner sat with his chair tilted against the wall and his small feet cocked on the table. His high-heeled boots had metal toecaps and soles studded with brass hobnails. His blue denim pants stretched tightly over his brawny thighs. The sleeves were cut out of his collarless shirt, baring rock-hard biceps. His arms were tightly crossed, but he wiggled his boot toes with restless energy and darted his blue eyes around the room.

"Well, me lads," he said, "it was a grand awakening for those Yanks, so it was, or me name's not Fintan O'Conor." He retrieved his stein, raised it to Jake and Eldon, and drank. Then he wiped the foam from his moustache. "Shall I be telling you what happened this very day? How the light of wisdom dawned upon me?"

Jake leaned back in his chair and combed his fingers through his thick, black thatch of hair. The whiskey was softening his usually savage mood into something more playful, though just as dangerous. He sipped his drink, content to let the Irishman talk on.

"When I comes off me shift, the crew boss is waiting by the skiff before we goes up. 'Lookee, Fin,' says he, 'if ye're bringing out any *highgrade ore* tonight, stow it somewhere below, for ye'll be searched when ye get to the top. And, sure as I'm born, there were the owners, and other high and mighty bosses besides, all waiting in the changing rooms with Marshall Plummer and his wee snotty deputy. And didn't they make us strip mother-naked and spread our nether cheeks?" He jumped to his feet, scarlet with indignation.

"Have I not toiled seven years for them in the dark and cold? Did not Fergus and I drill and pack the black powder into the hanging face no Cornishman dared go near? I upon one knee, swinging the great hammer, and Fergus spinning the long drill, biting into the mother rock..." Fin pantomimed the motion. "Laying the fuses just so, never a cave in, never a man hurt..." Fin paused to cool his throat with a long draft of beer.

"Yeah, yeah," said Eldon, "you're the backbone of the world, you Irish."

Fin reached into his back pocket. Eldon's fingers darted toward the knife in his belt, then relaxed as Fin's hand emerged, brandishing a large, silver-plated serving spoon.

"What are you goin' to do with that, Fin, eat the bosses alive?" Jake grinned.

"I am going to get me fair share of the earth's riches," pronounced Fin. "Why, this is not some tawdry, run-of-the-mill spoon, boy-o."

"I guess not," said Eldon, "It says 'Holbrooke Hotel' on it."

"If ye know the secret, this spoon will work magic. Sure, ye've heard of the *amalgamated* spoon?"

Jake shook his head, "Cain't say as I have. Tell me about it."

Fin pulled his chair up to the table.

"Listen now, and I'll tell the secret of it. The first thing ye'll be needing is a jug of quicksilver, or mercury, as some say." He slid his beer mug to the center of the table to stand for the imaginary jug. "The true iron, or glass, or ironstone it must be to contain the slippery quicksilver – naught else.

"And next ye'll be wantin' a wee bit of crockery for wetting your magical spoon." He appropriated Jake's empty whiskey tumbler and set it next to the mug. Fin poured beer into the glass and dipped the big spoon in it.

"When your spoon's all *amalgamated* – all nicely coated with the shining quicksilver – why, then…" He held up the wet spoon for inspection, then gently stirred the bottom of the beer stein with it. "You dip it down into the sluice, just before the riffle bars, and spoon out the lovely gold. See, the mercury sticks to the spoon, and the gold sticks to the mercury. Ye'll be wiping it from the spoon with your fingers, for it clings tight!"

"Now, come Saturday next, when the highgrader's moon rises, there will be just enough light to see, but not be seen. Sure, this Saturday's the lucky day for the man bold enough to reach out and take his share of the earth's treasure."

Eldon took a measured sip of his whiskey, eyeing the spoon in Fin's hand.

"They shot two sluice robbers over at Sucker Flat last week," he said. "White men. And that Chinaman they caught at Timbuctoo Bend was near cut in two with buckshot. The night guards shoot first and ask questions later."

"Sure, they're paid to do their job," Fin agreed. "Still, no man can be in more than one place at a time. The wise night rover simply watches and waits his turn. For what would that wise man be preferring for his labors – an ounce of gold for a week's hard shoveling, or an ounce for twirling a spoon? I tell ye, there'll be no more toiling underground for the likes of Fin O'Conor.

"When next ye see me," he said, "'tis sporting the tallest silk hat in the Northern Mines I'll be, and upon me arm the fairest colleen in the county. And the world will stand back in amazement, sayin', *'There goes a lad whose fortune is made!'*"

Eldon smiled mechanically, but his eyes didn't move from the spoon lying in a puddle of golden beer.

Chapter 19

The Night Watch

May 1863

Wylie Yip moved the heavy iron pot to the edge of the ashes and banked the little cooking fire. "There," he said, "the rice is boiling. We have time for some practice before we eat. A Lion Dancer isn't made overnight!"

Jim Ling sat down and unlaced his boots. His shift was only half over and his feet were aching already from patrolling the mile-long tail sluice of the Lucky Stars Mine. He and Wylie had the best-paying jobs at the mine, and he liked working the night shift. Before long, summer would return and the days in Wilcox Canyon would become brutally hot. The evenings, however, were always cool and pleasant.

On nights like this one, when the water was turned out of the sluices for the cleanup, Jim liked to think of the heavy yellow gold piled deep against the riffle bars. At first light, the foreman and the day shift would come to extract the treasure. Until then, it was up to him and Wylie Yip to keep it safe.

"There will be a *bonanza* this time, when the sluice is cleaned out," Jim declared to his partner. "Ah Tie will give us extra pay!"

"You think too much about money," the older man admonished. "Come over here and try to pay attention to what I am teaching you." Wylie walked a little way from the campfire and stood on a flat stretch of gravel in the pale moonlight.

"Try the jump again, Jim," he said, as he handed his protégé a broomstick, "and this time pretend that you are holding the head of the Magnificent Lion."

Wylie adjusted his stance: feet planted wide apart, knees slightly bent, ready to receive the weight of his teammate. "Take a deep breath before you jump."

Jim grasped the broomstick in both hands like a trapeze bar and held it above his head. He faced away from his partner and leapt nimbly backwards, landing with bare toes on Wylie's muscular thighs and balancing there. While Wylie steadied him, Jim slowly rocked the broomstick from side to side in the air.

"That's good," said Wylie. "Slow movements with the lion's head are the most dramatic. Always take your time, stay with the drum. Now, step up to my shoulders. I will help you. One, two – good!" Jim tottered on his high perch, then recovered his balance with the help of Wylie's firm grip on his calves. He raised the broomstick to the starry sky, dipped it down, then raised it again.

"All right, step down, right foot first…now to the ground…well done!"

Jim tossed away the broomstick and turned a standing somersault to express his pleasure. He swung himself up onto the big sluice and walked on his hands along the wooden crossties.

"If I was young again," Wylie said, "I wouldn't waste my energy showing off for jackrabbits. This practice was easy, but it will be more difficult when you carry the Lion's Head in the New Year's parade. It is very heavy, and there are strings to work the eyes and jaws." Wylie peeked under the lid of the cooking pot. "Come down now, our rice is ready."

"I can't wait to be a Lion Dancer!" Jim spun effortlessly on one hand and vaulted down from the sluice. "We're going to be the ones everybody admires! 'Ooooh!' they'll say, 'look how fierce he is, the Red General, how he shakes his black beard. Aaaaah! Look how high he leaps for the lucky prize of delicious money!' Ha ha!" Jim's enthusiasm made Wylie laugh, too.

"And just think, cousin, when we are important Lion Dancers, why, when the New Year comes again, we may be leading the celebration in some great city like New York or Boston, all the way on the other side of the world from Kwangtung – as far away from home as we can possibly be!"

Jim tied up the laces of his boots and slipped into his jacket. The cool night wind had dried the sweat from his body and left him chilled.

"Do you ever get homesick?" Jim asked, poking sticks into the fire. The brightness of the little blaze made the darkness around them seem a denser, thicker black. "Do you ever wish you could go back to Kwangtung?"

Wylie's face grew somber. "When I am three years dead, then my bones will be dug up, and our Tong will ship them home to be buried with my ancestors. That is the way it should be. But until then, I have no reason to go back."

"But don't you have a mother or a sister at home who misses you?"

"No, there is no one in China who is lonesome for me." Wylie shook his head sadly. Then he grinned at Jim. "But in Marysville, there is a lovely young woman who prays for my return – so long as I bring my poke full of gold dust!" He laughed happily, stood, and walked away from the fire to relieve himself in the bushes.

Jim sat, savoring his tea. "Tell me, Wylie," he said, "does your lady in Marysville have a friend who is also pretty?" There was no reply. He heard heavy footsteps approaching.

He grabbed for his shotgun and jumped to his feet. He backed away from the fire and into the cover of the shadows. He stood still, peering at the trail where he heard the footsteps coming. Then he saw the glint of the knife swing into view and felt the heavy tug on his pigtail. He felt the sharp, deep slice of the blade under his ear and across his throat, and the stinging, brilliant pain. He was choking on his own hot blood…falling… *Goddess of Mercy, take pity on me…*

~

Jake Forrest and Eldon Whitley stared down at the body sprawled in the dirt. A vast, black stain spread out from the neck, barely visible in the moonlight.

"Who would have thought such a little monkey would have so much blood in him?" said Eldon. He crouched down and wiped his knife on the dead boy's pants. "Time to find out if that little Mick in Ahern's was spinning us a tale or not," he continued. "You got the kit?"

"Mercury, pots, spoon – yeah, I've got it all," said Jake. "I'm goin' to strike the dark lantern. We need to git to work."

"That dim-witted Mick," Eldon muttered, "spoutin' on about how sluice robbers has got to wait their chance... Hell, you don't have to dodge a guard if he's stone dead, and that's a *fact*."

"C'mon Eldon, the sooner we get started, the sooner we can head back to Grass Valley and buy ourselves each a bed full of the liveliest whores in California."

"That's so," said Eldon. "It is a mighty good thing to be rich. And if tonight's work pays off, why, I'll buy that dumb ass Fintan O'Conor a drink!"

Chapter 20

Tong Cousins

May 1863

Ah Tie was horrified by the blood that had run from the severed throat of the watchman. It soaked the dead boy's tunic and darkened the ground. Jim Ling lay twisted on the hard gravel, his head lolled back, his mouth open in silent accusation. Deerflies crawled over his corpse. Ten yards away in the manzanita, Wylie Yip's body lay face down. Near a circle of sooty rocks and a scattering of fire-blackened twigs, two bowls and two teacups showed where the guards had sat down to their last meal. Flies were lighting on the edges of the bowls. Ah Tie's face and hands felt clammy. These were his two best men.

Knowlton, the new sheriff, eyed the bodies with indifference.

"It's plain to see what happened here," Knowlton said. "While they were highgrading your sluice, they fought over the gold and killed each other. There's nothing for me to investigate. Too bad you can't get better help. You'd be smart to go back to China, where you belong."

"Their names were Jim Ling and Wylie Yip," Ah Tie said. "They were my *guards*. They did not carry knives."

Knowlton didn't reply. He mounted his horse and rode past Ah Tie, letting the toe of his boot in the stirrup brush the mine owner's sleeve. The deputy's horse, following close behind, forced Ah Tie to step off the road into the wet thistles and sticker grass.

Ah Tie stood helpless, his fury mounting. He pulled his handkerchief from his sleeve and twisted it, wishing it around Knowlton's neck. The men from the day shift, who had kept silent in the presence of the Sheriff, were now all talking at once in rapid Cantonese. They stood back from the corpses, careful not to touch the dead men, and glanced nervously at the walls of Wilcox Canyon, where the killers might still be lurking. One of the young men vomited into the bushes. Ah Tie waited for him to rejoin the group before he spoke.

"Evil deeds have been committed. We have been robbed, and our good friends are dead. The sheriff will not pursue the criminals. He says our countrymen have killed each other." The men gasped their disbelief.

"Listen to me," he said slowly, looking into the worried faces of his crewmen. "This could be the work of a dangerous gang. Be on your guard, night and day. If any of you wishes to leave, I will see that you are hired onto the crews that are grading the Henness Pass road. You can get top jobs there, with the experience you have gained here at the Lucky Stars."

The miners whispered among themselves. Ah Tie held tightly to the lapels of his suit jacket to keep his hands from trembling with anger. When all eyes turned toward him again, he continued.

"I shall find out who the murderers are, and I will see them punished. Until then, you must watch and listen carefully for any news about this crime. If you find out anything, come straight to me. Do you understand?"

Charlie the day foreman stepped forward. His wide face was ashen and his voice shook with emotion. "I will go after the killers now, while their tracks are fresh. My men will come with me. Give us the shotguns from the office." The day shift, rallying behind their brave leader, seconded him with angry shouts.

"I will kill them with my bare hands!"

"They shall die slowly!"

"We shall have their heads on pikes."

Ah Tie raised his hands for silence. "Calm yourselves, men. The murderers will pay for their crime. But we must discipline our emotions and use our wits.

"Now, I am raising the pay for guard duty, and I am hiring six more guards. Come see me at the office if you are interested in these jobs. Go finish drilling the new face for blasting. We will finish cleaning out the sluice after the midday meal. Charlie, you wait here. I need to speak with you."

When the men had gone, Ah Tie stood with Charlie, looking at Jim's body. Ah Tie kept his voice low.

"You are quite right in your wish to look immediately for clues. But this is best done by you and me alone, so the trail is not confused by too many footprints." He touched Charlie's sleeve. "We are old friends, you and I, and I can speak plainly." He looked earnestly at Charlie's face, which was swollen with anger, jaws clenched. "I do not doubt the courage or loyalty of any man here at the Lucky Stars. However, only our remaining six watchmen have been trained in the use of weapons. Am I right?" Charlie nodded assent, looking down at his feet.

"When amateurs go chasing after dangerous criminals, what is sure to happen?" Ah Tie continued. "And what will be the white citizenry's reaction when they catch sight of an armed company of Chinese vigilantes? More lives lost, arrests, fines, whippings! There is no need to risk added misfortune." Ah Tie paused, giving Charlie time to reflect on his words. "When the first shock of this awful thing passes, I am sure you will agree with me. Let us find out what we can now, and today I will send to my Tong cousins for help."

Ah Tie and Charlie looked closely around the bodies. Knowlton and his deputy had ridden their horses back and forth through the camp, churning up the ground. "Let us go a little farther down and look for tracks," Charlie suggested. "It's hopeless looking here."

They walked down beside the sluice, watching the ground.

"Here is our first clue," said Ah Tie, pointing to a spot where a leak in the sluice made muddy rivulets, "and the second is there."

Two perfect casts of huge booted feet, a long stride apart, were dug deep in the black slime. Ah Tie could even see the indentations of the hobnails on the toe and heel. There was another pair of marks, no more than dirty smears flattening patches of swampy grass. Ah Tie pointed at the smeared prints, then at the clearly marked ones.

"Two men came this way, they were in a hurry. This man wore slick-soled shoes, he will be difficult to track. But this one – such large boots! What cobbler could forget this client? And see here, two nails are missing on the right heel, just at the back. I will make a drawing." He took a notebook and pencil from his inside pocket and began to sketch. "Charlie, do you have a penknife? Will you measure this big print?"

Charlie cut a willow switch and squatted down to measure, notching the stick to record the width and length of the enormous boot.

"He is a burly man, this one, judging from his deep tracks," Ah Tie said. "The one with the slippery soles has smaller feet and longer legs."

Charlie caught a glint of metal in the grass. He stooped and picked up a bent serving spoon, the bowl crusted with dirt. It had a shell pattern on the handle and a fancy "TH" engraved in a cartouche.

"Look! This must be the spoon the robbers used to steal our gold. It still has traces of quicksilver on it!" Charlie sat back on his heels and looked up at Ah Tie. "Boss, every week my cousin Lee goes to the Traveler's Hotel in Grass Valley to pick up laundry. It is a brothel. I recognize this symbol."

~

When Ah Tie got back to the mine office, John Van Hagen was waiting in the deep shade of the porch. He moved back so Ah Tie could pass, then followed inside, ducking his head in the low doorway. Neither spoke as Ah Tie locked the door behind them, stepped around his counter, and opened his safe.

He laid two long buckskin pokes filled with fine gold, weighing three and a half pounds each, on the counter in front of Van Hagen, then opened the heavy ledger book and pointed to the place on the page where he wanted an official signature.

Van Hagen looked over the columns of careful accounting for the amount owed by the Lucky Stars Mine to Nevada County for the foreign miners tax: one ounce of gold each month for every Chinese employed in mining, for a total of $1,360. Taking the pen from its stand, he wrote, "rec'd by J. B. Van Hagen, Sunday, May 10, 1863." He collected the heavy bags and walked to the door, his spurs ringing on the plank floor.

"You won't see me next month," Van Hagen said as he exited. "The Nevada Rifles have been called up. The new sheriff will be here to collect. That's Knowlton, my deputy. You know him." The door banged behind him.

Yes, I am already acquainted with Sheriff Knowlton, thought Ah Tie. He stood silently by the window, watching Van Hagen ride off and feeling something like regret that he would no longer be dealing with the ex-lawman. Van Hagen possessed the virtue of uncompromising adherence to the law. This was deserving of respect. Sheriff Knowlton, however, seemed to think his badge made *him* the law. It would be folly to reason with such a man, or to complain of bad treatment. Trouble at the Lucky Stars would only increase if the malicious attention of Sheriff Knowlton focused on the Chinese of You Bet.

He rolled back the top of his desk and dipped his brush in the inkwell. *Two of your members are dead,* he informed the Sam Yup Company in Marysville. *As employer of the deceased men, I have made the funeral arrangements…*

Ah Tie rested his brush and pulled out his handkerchief to wipe his eyes. Jim Ling, especially, he had loved, and wished that he would someday have a son like him: a happy boy, handsome and strong, with a sweet nature that never bristled at the demands of custom and propriety. Jim would surely have been a successful, admirable man, had he grown up. But now he must bury Jim and Wylie, with music and offerings, in the Chinese Cemetery in Nevada, where their graves would be kept clean and their ghosts remembered at festivals.

The Company is assured that two corpse-handlers, a piper, and a priest will attend to the prescribed rites for your departed lodge brothers.

After three years, their bones would be exhumed and packed up for transport to China, carefully divested of any remnants of flesh by the corpse handlers, who used long sticks for the purpose. *Like monstrous chopsticks,* Ah Tie thought. He could never keep himself from making the unsavory comparison and was always sickened by this part of graveside ritual. *Ghosts are touchy,* he told himself. *It is good when such delicate rites are left to professionals.*

When he was finished, he pressed his square jade seal into the hot red wax on the letter cover. Ah Tie selected another piece of writing paper. This he addressed in English to the Chinese Asylum, Pine and Kearney Streets, San Francisco, and in characters: *Sze Yup Tong, Dai Fow.* Ah Tie faithfully paid his dues to the Tong, and the Brotherhood would punish without charge the white vermin who had murdered his men – though the gift he was enclosing would ease the journey of the individual sent to do the job.

Ah Tie put the letters in the mailbag and re-tied the drawstring. *White devils, you won't escape me!* He cinched the knot with an angry yank. "Ham gaa chaan," he snarled. *May their corpses be eaten by dogs.*

Ah Tie stood up, rubbing his weary back. He turned to face the shelf on the northwest office wall, where a figure of Kwan Ti, God of War and Business, presided over the transactions of the mine. Ah Tie lit four sticks of yellow incense and carefully placed them before the shrine.

O magnificent general, my ancestor, crown my efforts with success! Visit these evildoers with your wrath. Avenge my friends!

Chapter 21

Return to Nevada

June 1863

The sun was coming up as the buckboard splashed through the ford on Greenhorn Creek. The water was running milky white with sediments from the new hydraulic mines upstream in Birdseye Canyon. Ida and Mr. Johnson rode in silence on the lurching seat. Behind them, the eastern sky over the Chalk Bluffs shone the color of lemon pie, with white meringue clouds. Up where the light hit the tops of the trees, woodpeckers and blue jays were noisily trading the morning's gossip.

As the horses toiled up the steep eastern slope of Banner Mountain, Ida looked down to the white gravel tailings far below. She was exhilarated by the freshness of the morning and the possibilities of a day in town. First, she would collect Kitty and Dora and set sail for the downtown shops, with Goldfarb's Dry Goods the first port of call. There they would choose fabrics for Molly's summer dresses: a pale-flowered silk organza, perhaps, or a lavender-sprigged muslin, light as gossamer. Then it would be on to Kessel's music shop for Esmeralda's new guitar strings and an inspection of the latest sheet music. Kitty would coax the lonely old bachelor into an impromptu recital on his magnificent Chickering piano. Then out again, onto the busy boardwalk, past the enticing windows of Beitz's jewelry store, where Dora would feign indifference to the gleaming wedding bands that were her heart's desire.

They would, of course, pore over the playbills at the Monumental and the Nevada Theater to the last letter. Rumors had swirled for months of a return visit to California by the great Edwin Booth, who had risen to prominence in

San Francisco and then taken himself off to tour the great cities of the East. Ida couldn't bring herself to believe Edwin himself would come back, but she held out hope that Junius, or maybe the young John Wilkes, might make the trip. Shakespearean reviews – pastiches of favorite duels and love scenes from the plays – were immensely popular in the mines, and tickets to a good performance would sell out in hours. They would have to visit the theaters first – let the other delights of the day fall where they may.

∾

"Well," said Mr. Johnson, "I've got a busy day ahead, but you can reach me if you need to. I'll look in at the Empire Games of Chance from time to time…" Ida struggled to keep a straight face as the grizzled foreman cleared his throat. "To check for messages, that is…" he added lamely. "Gee up, there!"

Daisy and Incitatus lumbered out onto Broad Street, while Ida raced down the brick path and pounded up the porch steps of the Caldwell house.

"Oh, good mornin', Miss Hatfield," said Clara, the housemaid.

"Uh…hello, Clara. Are Dora and Kitty…"

"I'm sorry, Miss, but the whole family's away."

Ida's face fell so comically that Clara was moved to speech.

"Mister Judge is in court today, and Missus Judge has taken the young gals to the Ladies' Guild Picnic. They won't be home till supper time. Would you like to wait for them?"

"Well…" said Ida, a little puzzled by this invitation. Clara must know she had better things to do with her precious time in town than wait around for the twins.

"You're not the only visitor who has surprised me this mornin', Miss Ida. Perhaps you'd like to wait with the gentleman who arrived on the Overland."

Ida peered into Clara's ebony face, but the cagey woman gave nothing away. *A poker face that could win fortunes,* Ida thought enviously.

"I should like that," said Ida, keeping her own face as unreadable as possible. "Would you show me to him?"

Clara led the way through the house and onto the back porch. "He's out by the fountain, Miss," the maid said, gesturing down the grape arbor walkway.

"Thank you, Clara," Ida said, sweeping by in her most dignified imitation of a church matron.

Ida left the shade of the arbor and looked out toward the splashing water. Bright sunshine dazzled her eyes, and she did not recognize the figure standing farther off in the shadows. The man turned and stepped toward her. As he emerged into the light, Ida felt her whole body lift as if to leave the earth. Grabbing her skirts with both hands, she charged down the path.

"Will!" she cried. *What have they done to you?* she wanted to continue. Her eyes filled with tears.

Tall, powerful, handsome – that was how Will Stafford had appeared in her dreams these last two years. Vivid dreams, in which girlish fantasies had given way to adult desires, without shame.

But the man hobbling toward her was not that William, or anything like him. His cheeks were sunken and yellowed. He stooped and winced as his cane took the weight his leg could not bear.

Oh God, he's broken and old! she thought, then blushed furiously at her unkindness.

She looked into his eyes – those beautiful, blue-grey eyes – and a great dam of pity broke in her heart.

"Oh, Will," she whispered. He shifted his cane to take her hand and raised her fingertips to his lips. She said nothing, but drew his hand back to her and kissed it. Then she pressed it to her shoulder and laid her cheek against it.

They stood in silence, until a spasm in his leg made him stagger. He pulled his hand away and fumbled for his cane.

"Let's sit over here, in the shade," she said. "The damask roses are so lovely." She held his cane as he lowered himself onto the cushioned settee in the back of the bower.

"I'm not really a useless cripple, Ida. I just set out too soon. The trip from St. Louis set me back a ways." Beads of sweat had formed on his temples. He extracted a small flask from his coat pocket and took a pull.

"That's what they call a 'pocket pistol' in the Washoe," she said with a smile. She took the flask and sipped cautiously. The fiery brandy burned her tongue and made her eyes water.

"It's my portable medicine chest," said Will. "Perhaps too much so."

Ida put her hand on his and clasped it. They gazed in silence at the cascading roses and breathed in their sweet, heavy scent.

"I can't tell you how much I missed this place," Will said. "After I went East, Nevada seemed like an island of peace and sanity in a world gone mad."

"Nevada an island of peace and sanity?" she cried in mock disbelief. "The States must be in a bad way indeed!"

"You have no idea," he said, in a hard tone that shocked her. "They're drinking each other's blood back there."

"We don't get much first-hand news out here. Just letters from some local boys. But they're only on garrison duty."

"God grant they stay there."

Will reached for his flask again, then checked himself.

"I swear to you, Ida, I would crawl through Hell on my hands and knees to stoke the fire under the lunatics who started this war. Secession was a fool's errand from start to finish."

"How long have you been out of the army?" she said, turning to a more hopeful topic.

"I got my ticket out from a Yankee sniper at Fredericksburg, though my departure was delayed by a dose of camp fever."

"Oh, we heard about that fight. A tremendous Southern victory, wasn't it?"

Will laughed – a cold, heartless laugh Ida could never have imagined in him.

"You can call it a fight – and a victory, if you like – but you'd be wrong. It was an orgy of murder, brought on by the criminal insanity of the Federal commander. Burnside marched his men straight at us across an open plain. We were ranked three deep along a sunken road, with a thick stone wall for a parapet. The boys in back loaded their guns and passed 'em forward to those in front, who killed a Yankee with every shot. *Whap! Whap!* You could hear the Minié balls smackin' into them."

"God help us," Ida murmured, picturing torn and shattered bodies lying in heaps across a field.

"But the Yankees kept on comin'," said Will at last, "wave after wave – without the slightest chance of takin' us. Just marchin' forward to die. Our boys were black with powder and sweat, and worn to a frazzle from killin' and killin'. Finally we got mad and started yellin', 'Go back, you damned fools!' But the Yanks didn't listen."

Will brought out the flask again and drained it.

Ida sat appalled by the horrible images. "But it's over for you now, isn't it? They can't let you go back with your wound so bad. You mustn't!"

Will pressed his fingertips to his temples. "It *has* to end," he said, in a strangled voice of cold fury.

"Is there any chance of that?"

Will stared, unseeing, past the roses. "Lee's whipped the Army of the Potomac twice since Sharpsburg. He's on his way into Maryland and Pennsylvania right now. This may be the end. A few big Northern towns taken, the Federal army beaten again, and the whole bloody show will be over. I pray so, anyway."

"Leaving the country divided forever?"

"Yes. I can't see the South ever returning to the Union."

"But which way is your way, Will? Could you live in California if we stay in the Union?"

He turned to her, and she was shocked by the sheer misery in his face.

"On my eternal soul, Ida, I'd like nothing better."

"Then *do*, Will! Make *this* your home, and be damned to the Old Dominion! And damn Abe Lincoln, too, if that will make you feel better! Damn them all, North and South. You've *paid* your debt to the past. You can live as you choose. You're *free!*"

She searched his face for some clue to what he was feeling. He was being torn apart – by whom or what she could not tell. She only knew that her last words had been utterly wrong; if there was one thing on God's earth Will Stafford *wasn't*, it was *free*.

Chapter 22

White Sickness

June 1863

Missouri House was a tall, rangy structure that looked southwest over the toll road, protected from the ferocious summer sun by deep porches and a pair of majestic black oaks that were old when Columbus put to sea. The main house was surrounded by cedar-sided outbuildings of varying estate: from the noble, timber-framed barns and stables, through the honest bunkhouse and workmanlike blacksmith shop, to the score or so of humble coops and sheds.

The express office, the business hub of the establishment, was a comfortable room in the corner of the house and well lit by tall windows. Two desks faced each other in the center of the floor, the larger for Molly, the smaller for Ida. One wall was lined floor-to-ceiling with cubbyholes for letters and packages in transit. A black steel safe stood in the corner, draped with a colorful Mexican saddle blanket and topped with an Indian trade basket bright with shell beads and red woodpecker scalps. Across the room, the station's arsenal of shoulder arms and pistols was locked in a glass-fronted case. The walls were festooned with calendars, maps, and schedules, interspersed with a collection of watercolors in Molly's hand, depicting scenes from her wandering life: a wind-swept Delaware seacoast, a cypress-shaded plaza in Monterey, a Yankee clipper ship entering the Golden Gate.

This morning, the only sounds in the office came from the scratching of pens and the steady ticking of a Seth Thomas regulator clock. It was accounting day, and the women of Missouri House were trying to finish their sums before the noon stage rolled in. Molly's usually relentless pen faltered, however, as indignation boiled up inside her.

"I still say Amanda had no call to let him go. Will Stafford was in no condition to go anywhere but back to bed."

"He's a grown man, Mama. What were the Caldwells supposed to do, lock him up?"

"*I* would have," said Molly, ferociously blotting her page. "What's the point of having a judge in the family if you can't stop a lunatic from hurting himself?"

Ida's pen stopped, too, as her mind filled with visions of a court presided over by her imperious mother. Indoor tobacco chewers would surely suffer torments (the pillory the best they could hope for), while corset-makers would receive a stiffer penalty – slow strangulation by their own products. Will Stafford, criminally irresponsible for moving to an isolated cabin before recovering his health, might get off with six weeks, chained hand and foot to a sickbed and force-fed like a French goose.

Ida smiled and turned back to her petty cash receipts, but her thoughts soon drifted away. She was worried, too. The war had damaged Will; he had a haunted look and was hiding himself away in a lonesome cabin at Storms' Ranch east of Grass Valley – that openly Secessionist town. Did he think his Confederate service had offended his pro-Union friends in Nevada?

If that's what Will's thinking, he's a blockhead. Out here no one asks about your past in the States!

Ida's thoughts were interrupted by an exchange in Maidu outside her window, between a deep male voice and Nutim's, followed by the sound of bare feet across the porch and a light knock at the office door.

"Come in, Nutim," said Molly, without looking up.

The boy entered and stood beside Molly's desk, fidgeting silently until she lifted her head.

"Uncle Yoso's here with Yeponi Tom from Storms' Ranch," Nutim announced. "They say there was a strange wind from the south, and a great black hawk came. It tore apart the chicken house – killed all the hens and roosters. It swooped down on the ducklings, too, and carried them off!" Nutim glanced significantly at Ida, signaling there was more to the tale. *Shape-shifting spirits, most likely,* she thought.

"Uncle Yoso says the tribe will trade for as many birds as you can send," the boy continued. "They will be safe, now. The bad hawk is dead. Yoso shot him."

"Very well," Molly answered. "Tell Uncle Field Mouse and the *yeponi* we will be happy to help. Take them around to the kitchen and see they have something to eat. Then tell Esmeralda I want her."

Nutim dashed out the door, and Molly turned to Ida.

"My dear, you know the poultry as well as I do. Pick out the birds we can spare and get them into the wagon. Nutim and Pedro will help you."

An hour later, Nutim and Pedro were perched on the wagon seat, the bed piled high with slatted crates of gobbling, clucking, quacking, and crowing birds. A large hamper for Will, the result of Molly's conference with Esmeralda, was secured behind the driver's seat, wrapped in oilcloth and filled with cheese, smoked ham, pickles, preserves, a cold roast of venison, and an enormous cherry pie.

Damn the accounts, and damn the noon stage, thought Molly, as she and Ida watched the wagon disappear around the bend. *I should have gone myself.*

~

As the wagon neared the main house at Storms' Ranch, Nutim hopped off at the head of a winding lane and jogged down the narrow track, past open fields where the last wildflowers bloomed, and then through rows of pear trees, whose bright green leaves echoed the verdant grasses still growing in their shade. At last, he spotted the old settler's cabin where Stafford lived. A diminutive figure in a calico dress sat on the low front step.

"*He'he niki kulokbem,*" gasped Nutim, as he staggered to a stop, grinning, happy to see Lucy once more. "Hello, my little old woman." He bent forward, hands on his knees, to catch his breath. "Pedro and I have come with a giant basket of food...Pedro is bringing it in the wagon!"

Old Lucy looked up at him, and Nutim saw that her eyes were red and bleary. Her hand shook as she poked a dry mugwort twig into a smoky little fire built in the center of the pathway. Nutim recognized the pungent aroma of *munmunim,* the holy herb that subdued dangerous spirits. She rocked back and forth and began to sing softly.

"What's the matter, old woman?" he asked, sitting down at her side. "Are you sick?"

"The white man is dying," she sighed. "Evil has followed him from far away, hunting him. When he stopped at this cabin, it caught up with him." She snatched at the air with her hand, as if capturing an insect. She tilted her head back and looked to the zenith, pointing with one finger to the deep blue sky. "The *moloko* has come for him."

Nutim gazed upward. His sharp eyes made out the long black wings of the condor, very high up, circling the ranch. The *wólem's* end was surely near.

Lucy dropped another handful of twigs on the embers, making aromatic smoke swirl up. "All night I have sung and smoked tobacco to protect him," she said. "But I cannot keep awake much longer. When this fire goes out, the bad spirit will take him."

Nutim stepped into the cabin and saw Stafford stretched out on a pine bedstead. A heavy woolen blanket covered the big man to his chin. His face was pale, sunken, and covered with sweat. A sudden fear of white sickness raced through Nutim, nearly squeezing the breath from his lungs. He backed quickly out the door and moved downwind from Lucy's magic fire to let the sweet smoke purify and protect him.

"What should we do, old woman? Should we burn the cabin down?"

"The old-time people might have done it that way, child, but it would be bad manners, these days. Besides, you had better wait and see if I die, too, and then you can burn us both at once. I will crawl inside if I start to feel sick, so I will die in the cabin. There is a good stack of firewood out back. You should pile it against the wall with the window. Get a good blaze going, then throw some burning logs inside." She added more cedar twigs to her fire, and they flared up with an eager crackle.

"When the *wólem* first came to this country," she continued, "they brought deadly sickness. Whole villages died – even those who never saw the white ghost people! – for the poison spread from house to house. Many who survived the sickness died of grief afterwards. My children and grandchildren all died, except Clover." Lucy shook her head in resignation. "This could happen again."

Mama will grieve if Stafford dies, thought Nutim. *She cares very much for this white man. When his letters come, she looks young again.* Nutim fought to master his fear and steady his voice. "Old woman, I think we should not give up yet. I think we should take this *wólem* to my white mother. It would be wrong to burn him before she has a chance to doctor him. She has healing power, too. Maybe she can save him."

Old Lucy clasped Nutim's hand with her gnarled one. "I will ride along with you in the wagon. It is far to Missouri House, and I feel sad for this one. I will stay awake a little longer and sing for him until we get there."

Chapter 23

Molly's Healing Magic

July 1863

Two riders in blue uniform cantered up the toll road from Dutch Flat, red dust rising behind them. They swung around the tall Concord coach pulled up before Missouri House and tipped their kepis to Pedro and Mr. Johnson, who were unhitching the team that had just come in from Nevada. The cavalrymen dismounted and walked back to the stagecoach, spurs jingling, to where Henry Bachelder was rummaging through the boot for packages and mail for the express office.

"Why, it's Mr. Liberty of 1863!" said the blond trooper, grinning.

"Eh?" said Henry, straightening up, a mail sack in his arms. "Why, bless me! Joe Hardesty and Gareth Truesdale! Haven't seen you two in these parts for a while."

"Been guarding silver shipments in the Comstock," said Gareth. "We're on leave."

"Sure sorry we weren't back in time for the 4th of July parade," said Joe. "I hear the *E Clampus Vitus* lodge won the blue ribbon for the most artistic entry."

Henry Bachelder did not blush easily, but an unmistakable crimson glow suffused his bearded cheeks. "Don't know what you're talkin' about," he muttered. "Here, make yourself useful." Henry tossed Joe the heavy mail sack.

As they climbed the stairs, the men noticed Will Stafford in a rocking chair at the end of the porch, wrapped in a quilt.

"Hello, Mr. Stafford," said Joe and Gareth.

"'Afternoon, Will," said Henry. "How are you feeling?"

"On the mend," said Will, with a wan smile.

"Has Molly allowed you brandy and cigars yet?" Henry asked.

Will shook his head sadly.

"You poor devil!" said Henry, sympathetically. "I'd rather die – though I doubt I'd have the nerve, if Molly was aiming to cure me. Don't run off, now, Will. I'll come back and keep you company while Esmeralda feeds and waters the passengers."

Henry returned shortly from the crowded dining room with a heavily loaded plate and a tankard of beer. He sat down and offered Will the tankard.

"No thanks," said Will. "Say, what did young Hardesty mean by calling you 'Mr. Liberty'?"

Henry choked on a biscuit and coughed. "Well," he said, staring intently at his fried chicken, "there was a problem with the harness on Miss Liberty's carriage in the parade last Saturday. Her place was taken by a last-minute substitution...what we might call...an *alternative* Miss Liberty and her court."

Will arched his eyebrows.

"There's a rumor running round that Miss Liberty's beard looked a lot like mine," said Henry demurely. "Which shows how easily weak minds are deceived."

Will roared and tried to slap his knee, but got tangled in his quilt. He beamed at Henry Bachelder, whose regular visits to Missouri House were his lifeline to the outside world during his recovery.

"Any news from back East?" Will asked.

Henry's face grew somber.

"Yep. That fracas in Pennsylvania sounds pretty bad."

"We've heard about heavy fighting at some town called Gettysburg, near the Maryland border."

Henry nodded. "Looks like small detachments from Meade's and Lee's armies crossed paths on the first of July, and the fighting grew and grew as more units pitched in. Next day, the full armies pounded each other, with no advantage to either side. On the third, Lee sent Pickett, Pettigrew, and Trimble's divisions across a square mile of open space to try and break the Union center." Henry turned his plate for a fresh run at his mashed potatoes.

"And...?" prompted Will.

"Pickett's men were cut to pieces. It was the massacre at Fredericksburg all over again, played the other way around."

Will's stomach clenched. He closed his eyes and leaned back in his chair as Henry continued.

"Next day it rained, and both armies lay there, licking their wounds and growlin', mauled within an inch of their lives. Then Lee lit out for Virginia, and Meade went after him."

"Any word on casualties?" Will asked.

"Best guess is Lee lost a third of his army," Henry took a deep drink of beer.

"My God," said Will. "That's 25,000 men!"

"And Meade probably lost the same, since it was a draw till the last attack. Between 'em, 50,000 men gone…in three days."

Both men fell silent, imagining the horrors unfolding back East. There weren't enough doctors in Pennsylvania and Maryland to begin to help the wounded. Thousands would lie in the mud and rain till they died.

A stab of fear shot through Will. Tad was riding in Lee's cavalry under Jeb Stuart. What were his chances of surviving a slaughterhouse battle like this? Will shivered and wrapped the quilt tighter.

Henry pulled out his watch and grunted. "I better go collect my flock. Sorry for the news, Will," he said after a pause. "I know you've got kinfolk involved."

"Thanks, Henry. That's good of you."

Henry shrugged and set off for the kitchen to return his plate and tankard. Passengers began drifting out onto the porch. Will closed his eyes and pretended to be asleep. He must have actually dozed, because his next perception was of familiar voices nearby – the voices of Joe Hardesty and Gareth Truesdale taking leave of Molly and Ida.

"I'm off to see my folks, now," said Joe. "We've got a week's leave, and then we rejoin our unit in the Comstock. But we won't be there for long. Van Hagen says we've been ordered back to Nevada County."

"I'm glad to hear it," said Molly. "I know your folks will be relieved to see you boys back here, safe and sound."

Gareth Truesdale laughed with pleasure. "We'll be home by the end of October, Mrs. Hatfield! Look for us when the You Bet mines clean out their sluices. We're detailed to ride a big shipment down to Marysville in early November. After that, it's good times and parties, right through to Christmas…"

"And a wedding, too!" said Ida. Gareth smiled at her.

"My folks may have me underfoot the whole winter," said Joe. "There's talk of disbanding some units, now the war's turned around."

"Sounds like moonshine to me," said Ida. "Last month, everybody was jabbering about General Lee burning Philadelphia and Europe recognizing the Confederacy…"

"And the British fleet breaking up the blockade," said Joe. "I know, I know. But this is different, Ida. This is real! Lee has been *destroyed!* And General Grant has taken Vicksburg and bagged a whole Confederate army – *30,000 men!* Once Port Hudson falls, the Mississippi River will be clear of Rebels from Minnesota to New Orleans. It's the end, I tell you."

"Anything that ends this terrible war will be a blessing," said Molly. "I just want you boys to make it out safely."

"We'll be all right," said Gareth, as he swung himself into the saddle.

"You come to supper, Joe. You too, Gareth," said Molly, "just as soon as your folks let go of you."

"Yes, ma'am!" the young men answered.

Will kept his eyes closed as the hoof beats pounded away and the women retreated inside the house. He wanted to be alone with his dark thoughts.

So…had the South lost the war, after all?

The Northern press, politicians, and generals had all predicted General Lee's destruction before, and every time Lee had risen again. But what if this time was different? If a third of Lee's army was really gone, it could not be replaced. Virginia was already calling up children and old men.

And Vicksburg lost! Without Confederate batteries on the Mississippi, Yankee commanders could safely provision their armies by water. No Texas beef would cross the river to feed hungry Southern troops in the East. Union gunboats could fan out along the river's tributaries, seizing cotton and sending the precious bales up North.

Worst of all was the possibility that Meade would destroy Lee's army before it re-crossed the Potomac. If that happened, the war was over. The South would be a conquered province, prostrate before a Radical Republican government that had already declared the slaves in rebel states "forever free." Would Greenbrier be confiscated? The Yankees had already seized General Lee's beloved Arlington. And what about Robert Lee, himself? Would he end up dangling from the gallows?

But maybe the Yankees' terms won't be so savage, whispered another inner voice. *Maybe they'll just free the slaves and leave us be.* If the war ended now, thousands who were doomed to die would live instead. *And,* the voice went on, *Captain William Stafford would not have to feel guilty if he took no further part in the bloodletting.*

~

Nutim listened glumly to the stream of words, willing his bare feet not to swing and bang against the chair legs. Poetry evenings in the parlor were always a sore trial. It was not that he disliked long stories – there was a great one about Coyote that took four days to tell. But these *wólekim* tales – written in a dense, sacred language – simply bored and irritated him.

Tonight's yarn was a perfect example. It was the story of Hamlet, a chief's son who could not make up his mind about anything. The tale started off with a thrilling visit from the old chief's ghost, but plunged downhill after that. The hero wandered around, pretending to be crazy, while his wicked uncle prowled the lodge, stirring up evil at every turn.

Nutim sighed and stifled a yawn. Obviously, any warrior worth the name would have ripped out Uncle's entrails by this point and fed them to his dogs. But it was all talk, talk, talk in the tribe of the Danes. And all this from a storyteller named *Shakes Spear!*

Only Nutim's devotion to Molly Hatfield kept him upright in the uncomfortable chair. She had loved him and mothered him, and taught him to read and write. For this, he would walk through fire for her – or even pretend to be interested in a story about a foolish Prince.

But it was uphill work. The words began to flow together in a smooth, swift stream, and it became harder and harder to make sense of them. At last he gave up and turned his attention to the man reciting the wearisome verse.

Wilum looked better every day. His color was no longer so ghostly. Molly's healing magic had worked again.

Nutim liked having the man around. He was kindly and had applauded when Nutim put an arrow clean through a rabbit who had foolishly wandered out into the hay meadow. It had been a superb shot, from a distance worthy of a full-grown warrior, and Wilum had praised it. He had drilled Nutim as a soldier and shown him how to cut and thrust with an old cavalry saber that had belonged to Mr. Hatfield. Nutim enjoyed Wilum's stories of the fierce Rebels and thrilled to the tale of Bedford Forrest's single-handed saber fight with a Yankee brigade after Shiloh. He wished he were old enough to fight with the brave Confederates and take revenge on the blue soldiers.

Best of all was the effect of Wilum's presence on Molly. She sang more, scolded less, and seemed content. There was little chance of her turning into a bear if the big white man stayed around.

Wilum's voice meandered on, and Nutim heard it rasp with growing fatigue.

> *Thus doth conscience make cowards of us all;*
> *And thus the native hue of resolution*
> *Is sicklied o'er with the pale cast of thought…*

Will hesitated as the words began to swim on the page before him.

> *And enterprises of great pitch and moment…*

His heart raced, and he paused for breath until it calmed.

> *…turn awry…And lose the name of action…*

"Will, are you all right?" cried Ida.

"Would you like me to take over?" said Molly.

Will looked up. Both women were watching him with concern.

"Was I woolgathering?" he asked, forcing a smile to his lips. "I beg your pardon. I do feel a bit tired this evening."

He handed the book to Molly, settled back in his armchair, and shut his eyes.

Molly read beautifully – far better than he – and before long, her soft alto voice transported him from his tangled thoughts to the bedeviled Danish court – and to the quiet heroism of the prince who, in the end, did what he had to do.

∾

The moon had set. It was the darkest hour of the night. The stillness of Missouri House was torn by a man's voice, shrill with terror.

"Go back, you goddamn fools! Oh, Christ…GO BACK!"

Moments later, Molly Hatfield burst into the bedroom with a lamp.

Will was bolt upright in bed, eyes wide with horror. He raised a hand to shield his eyes from the light.

Molly set the lamp on the table and blew it out. She sat down on the edge of the bed.

"It must have been an awful dream," she said softly. She felt his cheek and neck with her hand. *Just a touch of fever tonight.* She ran her hand down over his nightshirt. It was soaked with sweat. She leaned over and gently kissed his cheek.

"It's okay now, Will, I'm here."

He locked his arms around her and hugged her close to him.

"Wait a minute, honey." She pushed away and stood up. She draped her robe across a chair. Then she turned the covers back, lay down beside him, and took him in her arms.

He lay there, motionless, clinging to her like a drowning man. Terrible images kept rising up and coming back to life. He was back behind the stone wall at Fredericksburg, staring down the slope as Northern troops advanced across the open field. A hail of rifle and cannon fire tore into them, smashing faces and ripping bodies apart, but the blue soldiers tramped on – some without arms, some without heads – until, at fifty paces, the writhing bundles of blood and bone broke into a trot, charging the wall with fixed bayonets, leers on their mangled faces. He remembered screaming in his dream. But he must have actually cried out, for here was Molly, warm and alive, holding him.

He could feel Molly stroking his hair, hear her murmured endearments. He shuddered and then began to breathe more freely. She had saved him again. The words of thanks that rose in his mind seemed too foolish and clumsy to speak aloud. He gently caressed her cheek. Then he bent his face to hers and kissed her. At the touch of her lips, he returned truly to this world, felt her soft body against his. He kissed her again, more firmly, and moved his hands over the soft curves of her neck and thigh. She returned the pressure of his lips and drew him to her. And, for the rest of the night, there was no war, no tormented country beyond the walls of the bedroom. There was nothing at all but Will and Molly, and the world they made for each other.

Chapter 24

The Highbinder

August 1863

Tired clumps of Tree of Heaven drooped over China Lane, shading the street and exuding their strong, musty fragrance in the hot air. The tin-roofed porch of the Asian Hotel cast a darker shadow from the blazing sun. It was almost noon, and the aroma of pork roasting with garlic wafted from the open front door.

A high board fence enclosed the hotel's back yard, and leafy tops of young plum trees rose above it, their clusters of ruby-red fruit bending the slender branches almost to breaking. On this private side, the hotel was all staircases and railed galleries, draped with climbing bean vines thick with scarlet blossoms. Close to the back door was a small swept-earth square, where ferny acacias spread a lacy canopy, inviting guests to linger and enjoy the garden. Ah Tie sat in the shade, watching a flock of tiny birds splashing in a shallow dish of water.

A short, bowlegged man stepped out of the office and stopped to watch the birds scatter at his approach. A wide-brimmed hat of plaited straw shadowed his face; a canvas duffel bag hung from his shoulder. His shirt sleeves and trousers were rolled up and ropy muscles stood out on his bare arms and calves. Spiraling blue scrollwork snaked down his biceps and looped around his forearm.

He is tattooed like a cannibal! thought Ah Tie. He had seen such incised tattoos before on seafaring men – it was South Sea Island work. The intricate indigo design almost concealed two horizontal black lines above the man's elbow. Ah Tie recognized those, too. They were Chinese prison brandings.

The stranger came closer, and Ah Tie saw the strong bones of his wide cheeks standing out in a hungry-looking face. A broad scar slanted down from the man's forehead to his earlobe and made one eyelid droop. Near his eye was another tattoo, a Chinese character that was the identifying mark of a prison.

The stranger crossed his arms and bowed to Ah Tie, showing three fingers extended on his left hand. Ah Tie gave the verbal countersign, "Three dots twenty-one." Ah Tie rose and led the man up an outside staircase to the Nevada office of the Lucky Stars Mining Company. Here the men sat down, and Ah Tie poured glasses of plum wine.

"I am Chung Ah Kit," said the stranger.

"Welcome to the Northern Mines," Ah Tie said. "Let us drink to our long-awaited meeting."

"I am glad to put San Francisco behind me," said Chung. "I was detained by a demon policeman who never sleeps. He kept me in his stinking jail and photographed me for his devil book. May he rot!"

Ah Tie frowned and shook his head. "I hear the war with the Hung Wo Tong goes badly – that informers are at work. Is that why you were arrested?"

"Yes. Some of our former friends in the Sze Yup have struck an alliance with the Hong Kong men, and there have been reprisals. Our loyal tong cousins think it is a good idea for me to stay away from First City until things settle down."

"Then I hope you will stay on as my guest, after our business is concluded. Your life will be secure in the tranquility of our mountain regions." Ah Tie smiled graciously.

Chung returned the smile, but faintly. This forced exile to a primitive mining district was not his idea of a vacation. He hated leaving First City and all the comforts of civilization: the Kwangchow Opera, elegant feminine companionship. And he hated snow.

Ah Tie got up and walked to his safe. He discreetly blocked the highbinder's view of the combination lock as he opened it. He came back with a heavy coin purse, a small notebook, a bent serving spoon, and a notched stick. Ah Tie arranged the items in a row on the table in front of Chung, who grinned.

"What's this?" said the highbinder. "A test? Am I supposed to choose one thing, like in the fairy tales? All right, then, I'll start by dumping the book. I'm a soldier, not a scholar – books are no use to me." He pushed the diary aside and picked up the spoon. "And I'm no chef, either." He swapped the spoon for the twig. He twirled it in his fingers, examining it. "This notched willow switch is more interesting – perhaps it is a secret sign – but I'm no spy master…so I'll choose the purse!"

Ah Tie laughed. "You shall have the purse, of course! And these other odd items, as well, for they will be useful to you. Let me explain their meaning. Each one is a clue to the identity of the *gwei lo* you are to kill." Ah Tie sat down and thumbed through the little notebook.

"Here are the notes and drawings I made on the morning my guards were killed." He fell silent and took small sips of wine until he could master his emotion. "We found the tracks of the *gwei lo* murderers in muddy places. On this page I have drawn the clearest prints." He handed the notebook to the highbinder.

"One man wore slick-soled boots. His tracks were smeared and useless… but the other outlaw's prints are quite remarkable. His toes and heels are studded with hobnails," Ah Tie pointed to the sketch with satisfaction, "and on the right heel there are two hobnails missing in a row, just at the back, there!"

"Very helpful," said Chung, "unless he bought new boots with the stolen gold."

"Old or new, his boots will give him away."

"How can that be?" asked Chung.

Ah Tie smiled and handed the willow switch to the highbinder.

"See, these two notches are the width and length of his tracks. Can you imagine his feet? What cobbler could forget this customer? He must be a giant!"

Chung measured the twig against his own foot. The *gwei lo's* boot was twice as long!

"What about this beat-up spoon?" he asked.

"The robbers used it to extract gold from the riffle bars of my sluice. My foreman recognized the symbol on its handle. That spoon came from the Traveler's Hotel in Grass Valley."

The old man is clever, Chung thought, *and his sorrow for his murdered guards is real. This is not such a bad job – I've slit throats for worse reasons. If the killers ever return to the Traveler's Hotel, I'll make certain they don't come out alive.*

"I have arranged a job for you at Woo's Pacific Laundry in Grass Valley," said Ah Tie, "because you must be able to account for yourself if the *gwei lo* police ask questions. Woo can get you inside the Traveler's Hotel – it is one of his accounts. Of course it will not do for you and I to be seen together until this business is safely concluded. Woo's deliverymen will carry our messages." Ah Tie studied Chung's weary face. "You will be very comfortable at our friend Woo's house – you will have a room all to yourself! But tonight you must sleep here. Have your meals sent up…and a hot bath…just ring the bell. I must go home to You Bet tonight. Tomorrow, Woo will come for you."

~

When Ah Tie left, the highbinder lay down on the bed in the corner. He was exhausted, but the room was too hot and stuffy for sleep. He staggered up and slumped into a bamboo chair on the veranda, where a slight breeze was rippling the blooming vines. There were bees humming around the scarlet flowers. He could hear someone sweeping the courtyard, and a man's voice singing an old song:

> *At the Lower Temple on Mount Lao*
> *The red camellias and white peonies*
> *Grow tall…*

He remembered his mother singing it to him, long ago: "The Scholar Cheng's Lament" for his lost bride, the white flower fairy, who was dug up and stolen away to a rich man's garden, where she withered and died. Chung's eyelids drooped, and his mother's face appeared to him, sad and worried, saying, "Our son has chosen to sip the wine of penalty over that of respect…"

Chung shook himself awake, sweating and trembling. What was causing these unhappy dreams? Were the familiar scents of this garden awakening memories of home?

He had left his childhood home in the Pearl River Delta long ago, but the old memories still haunted his nights. Fighting had raged through the port cities of his native Kwangtung province, as British importers, local smugglers, and the Emperor's police force fought a three-cornered war over the opium trade. When he was fourteen, British warships shelled his town, killing his father and grandparents. Shocked and grieving, he had shipped for the South Seas in the first berth he could find, aboard an old six-masted junk, bound for the Malay plantations.

Some years later, Chung was ashore in Hong Kong when news of the California gold strike reached China. He sailed the next day for *Gum San*, the Mountain of Gold. He got no farther than the First City. There the surging tide of Chinese immigrants needed lodging, interpreters, and jobs. Mutual aid societies, *tong-si*, were springing up to help them, and Chung had found work as a private policeman for the Sze Yup Tong, keeping order and protecting his countrymen along San Francisco's dangerous waterfront.

Soon the Sze Yups were busy with more than feeding and housing immigrants. There was serious money to be made in gambling, opium, and women. Chung's duties expanded to include collecting protection money and defending Sze Yup turf. For these more responsible assignments, he had been required to take the Highbinder's Oath, with two sword blades tickling his neck. It was a rough job, being a professional warrior for the tong: a highbinder was always on guard for his life.

It shouldn't take long to find this big-booted fool and slippery-soled devil and send them to gwei lo Hell. I'll get my business here done quickly and take some time to relax.

The highbinder untied his duffel bag and unrolled his all-black working clothes and his padded vest. The vest had a special pocket that held his steel lock picks, pins, and shims. He inspected his weapons. His flying claw, *fei jao*, was the size and shape of a hand with bent fingers. It had barbs on its iron palm and a long coil of supple rope attached to the wrist end. He could whirl it like a bull-roarer and throw it to entangle the limbs of an enemy, and it doubled as an excellent grappling hook. He checked its tackle and nestled it back into its pouch.

His single-edged *do,* or butterfly sword, had a wide, flat blade a little shorter than his forearm. Its heavy, hooked cross guard could catch and deflect an opponent's blade, and its finger guard could be used for punching, like brass knuckles. He drew it from its leather sheath and touched its shining tip. *This is the point of the present moment, where my complete attention must always be, if I wish to live to be an old man.* The *do* caught the sunlight and gleamed with dazzling brightness, as if delighted to be out of its scabbard.

Chapter 25

A Perfect, Gentle Knight

August 1863

I da lazily shooed an ant from *The Poems of Alfred Tennyson* – gently banishing the little marauder from the idyllic autumn landscape of the poem, where sturdy peasants scythed and barley fell in the fields around Shallot.

> *Willows whiten, aspens quiver,*
> *Little breezes dusk and shiver*
> *Thro' the wave that runs forever*
> *By the island in the river*
> *Flowing down to Camelot.*

In the prosaic world of You Bet, California, however, it was the middle of summer and hot enough to bake a lizard. Ida had fled Missouri House for her secret haunt by the creek, where the shade of an alder grove and the updraft in the canyon made it easier to breathe. There she could wear nothing but her old cotton dress with the sleeves cut off – and skinny out of that for a refreshing dip in the cold water.

> *A bow-shot from her bower-eaves,*
> *He rode between the barley sheaves,*
> *The sun came dazzling thro' the leaves,*
> *And flamed upon the brazen greaves*
> *Of bold Sir Lancelot.*

Ida lay sprawled across an old quilt spread over deep pine needles, her bottle of lemonade anchored in the stream to keep cool. She watched a water dipper bird in the shallows, encased in a silver bubble of air, hunting for food on the bottom of the stream. It moved as freely beneath the water as a song-bird in a tree. The little bird rose to the surface, chirping happily, and did a dipping, bobbing dance on a smooth rock.

> *From the bank and from the river*
> *He flashed into the crystal mirror,*
> *"Tirra lirra," by the river*
> *Sang Sir Lancelot.*

Am I dreaming or do I hear singing? Ida wondered. She looked up from her book and through the curtain of alder leaves. Will Stafford was riding upstream toward her in the shimmering canyon air, singing a slow and som-ber melody she had never heard before. He sat easily in the saddle, allowing his buckskin mare to pick her way along the edge of the stream. The horse splashed through the shallows, sending up diamond spray from her hooves.

Ida closed her book and watched Will dismount, a stone's throw down-stream from her hideout. He tied his mare in a shady willow clump and loos-ened the saddle girth. He unfastened his gun belt and hung it on a forked branch. Ida started to call his name, but her voice deserted her as Will began to unbutton his shirt. *This is my lucky day,* she decided, as Will doffed his clothes and walked slowly out into the rippling water.

Will leaned back against the current, arms outstretched, and stared up at the turquoise sky. A big orange dragonfly, curious, hovered and circled just over his head.

Ida allowed herself to breathe again. She hadn't seen Will for weeks – not since he'd been well enough to go back to his cabin at Storms' Ranch. She was surprised to see him here, so far from the beaten track. *No one comes here anymore but me.*

Will splashed water over a wave-smoothed boulder, cleaning it and cool-ing it off. Then he stretched himself face down on the warm granite and closed his eyes against the brilliant sun.

Ida saw him smiling and wondered what scene was playing in the theater behind his eyes. Her gaze traced the long, dark furrow left by the sniper's bullet from his knee to his hipbone. She watched his shoulders rise and fall lazily with his breath. One well-muscled arm curled beneath his head, the other fell to the water, fingers trailing in the stream. The sun had browned his body from the back of his neck to his heels. Glittering drops fell from the tendrils of his water-darkened hair and ran down between his shoulder blades, gathering in the hollow of his spine.

A perfect knight, thought Ida. Every part of him, body and mind, was in proportion. She watched the water droplets on his skin evaporate and saw the back of his neck begin to blush in the heat of the sun. He stood up and stretched, then plunged into the pool, swam two long strokes, and walked out on the dry sand, picking up his shirt.

Ida got up quietly and backtracked along the trail, careful to stay out of sight. She decided to count to a hundred by fives: "...sixty-five, seventy...Oh shoot! Ninety-a-hundred," then ran barefooted down the path and called his name.

"Will, is that you? Did I startle you?" she laughed, stopping beside him. "It's a good thing you're not a claim jumper, you know, 'cause this is *my* mining claim!"

Will stared in surprise.

"It is really mine," she chattered on. "Well, it belonged to my stepfather, but the placer gold was cleaned out long ago, so it's worthless, now, to anybody but me. C'mon," she said, pulling at his shirtsleeve. "Don't put your stockings on – I'll show you a secret! It's not far."

Will followed her upstream, burning his bare feet on the dry cobbles, then cooling them in the wavelets at the edge of the water. At the top of the swimming hole, Missouri Creek poured over a high ledge, roaring and foaming. Ida led him by the hand as they carefully skirted the upper rim of the pool. Then she waded straight into the edge of the splashing falls, drawing him after her.

There was just room for the two of them behind the waterfall, in a cavern overhung by a massive slab of speckled granite. A second monolith made a bench, cool and damp with mist. They sat in silver-blue light, Ida pressed close to Will.

"No one can see us behind the curtain of water," she said, "and no one can hear us above the music of the falls." She reached her arms around his neck and kissed his cheek.

"It's our own world in here," she whispered, her lips touching his earlobe.

He turned his head toward her, and she kissed him on the mouth, tasting his lips. He placed his hands on Ida's waist and gently moved her away.

"I wish that were true, my dear," he said. "More than you can imagine."

"It's our secret," she insisted, clinging to him and hoping for another kiss.

"A secret we could never keep from anyone." He smiled at her. "Your love-ly face, Ida, is an open book."

She blushed scarlet. "I'm so happy to see you well again…and…"

"Ida, please…" he said. His expression was deepening into sorrow.

I can't let him sink into unhappiness. I have to do something! Ida stood and dropped her hands to her hips, elbows turned out in an imitation of mascu-line swagger. She jutted her chin forward. "Will Stafford," she pronounced, staring him straight in the eye, "I *double-dog dare* you to follow me!"

She hurled herself headfirst through the sheet of water and into the still pool beyond. Will considered the churning white water under the falls, then dove in after her.

Ida stood up in thigh-deep water and looked around for Will. The only ripples on the pool were spreading out from her own body. *Oh my God, is he caught under the falls?* Then his hand grabbed her ankle, and she screamed at the unexpected clutch. He stood up, gasping with laughter, and caught a splash of water full in the face from Ida, who was scrambling toward the beach.

Ida found a perch on smooth, black bedrock, where she spread her skirt to dry. Will took off his shirt and wrung the water out.

"You wouldn't consider selling me your claim?" He grinned. "I believe it shows promise."

"Oh, no thank you, Mr. Stafford. I intend to hang on to it for awhile. It has begun to pay dividends."

Will laughed as he shook the water from his hair. "And what are your plans for investing your earnings?"

"Why, I intend to put them all into ice cream sodas and drink them," she declared, smiling sidelong at Will, who was spangled with shining water droplets. "Sometimes I like to imagine, when I duck behind the waterfall, that I find a glittering cavern of gold and an immense nugget, worth a prince's ransom, that makes me rich as Mrs. Croesus. Then I'd have the kind of money that means I can do whatever I please."

"And what would that be, Your Highness?"

"Why, I'd build a grand theater of my own design, and be an impresario... I'd book all the great actors and singers, and they'd come to Nevada to perform. I could watch a virtuoso every night! Sometimes I pretend this beach is my stage. I can see the audience crowding into the theater, excited, all talking at once..."

She got up and walked out onto the crescent of white sand at the edge of the pool.

"Then I step out into the lights and raise my white-gloved hands to hush the crowd, and every eye is on me as I graciously welcome them and cue the red velvet curtain, and as it goes up I say, 'In an exclusive Nevada engagement – all three Booth Brothers, reunited at last!'" Ida extended her arms as if to embrace the world and laughed aloud. "Franz Liszt would come all the way from Vienna to play my grand piano...and after five encores, accept a tribute of red roses from my hands." Ida sashayed her damp skirts and twirled around. "I would send champagne to their hotel rooms; they would embrace me and call me *dear Ida*." Ida stopped dancing and looked down at the gravel, blushing.

"I'm surprised you don't want to be the star of the show yourself," Will said. "You have the talent – and beauty, as well."

"As for that..." Ida paused to savor Will's compliment. "I suppose performing is always a thrill. It makes you feel so *alive!* But I'm no earth-shaking genius, and I'm happy not to have such an all-consuming gift. Sometimes I wonder if the stage isn't where an actor or actress feels most at home, because they don't really live anywhere. They're always traveling from one city to the next, never staying for long. I'm not like that."

She watched him brush the drying sand from his toes. Will began to hum, and Ida recognized the melody he had been singing on his ride up the canyon.

"That tune," she said, "what is it?"

"It's called 'The Wanderer,' by Franz Schubert."

"Schubert must have been feeling all-fired low when he wrote that."

Will considered as he pulled on his boots. "There's a power of melancholy in the music, I won't deny it. You'd never know it from the lyrics, though. Peter Kessel translated them for me. They're mostly about how happy the poet is. The song is about a fellow who's fixin' to wander, because the Moon has warned him that his life will be a dark one if he stays in his homeland."

"The moon? Truly? Won't you sing it for me? Wait, I'll introduce you!" She lifter her arms to the brushy canyon walls. *"Ladies and gentlemen,* the Missouri Canyon Theater proudly presents Herr Maestro Wilhelm Stafford..." Ida softly clapped her hands as she backed away from the center of the sandy stage.

Will climbed to his feet and made a formal bow. *"Der Wanderer,"* he announced to the waterfall. He took a slow, deep breath, and sang:

> *Wie deutlich des Mondes Licht*
> *Zu mir spricht,*
> *Mich beseelend zu der Reise;*
> *"Folge treu dem alten Gleise,*
> *Wähle keine Heimat nicht..."*

When Will finished the first stanza, he sat down next to Ida on the rock. The hot wind rustled the willows. "The second stanza," he said, after a long pause, "is about how happy he is that he's made up his mind to go, even if it means traveling alone."

"Happy!" Ida exclaimed. "If that's a German's notion of happy, what do they play at funerals?"

"Nothing."

"What?"

"There's never been a dirge that was finished. Every time a German composer starts in on one, he gets miserabler and miserabler until he flings himself off a bridge or drinks poison – Prussic acid being the general favorite."

Ida punched Will hard in the shoulder.

"You're just a liar, Will Stafford – a wicked abuser of your trusting friends."

Ida waited for a teasing response, but got none. She felt his mood sinking again – and guessed that "Wanderer" song cut too close to Will's heart. Times were dark in his homeland of Virginia.

They watched the cottonwood leaves down river turning silver-side up in the afternoon breeze. The sun was already dipping toward the canyon rim. "I'd better be headin' back," Will said, "or the moon will set 'fore I get to Storms' Ranch." He untied the mare and let her drink.

Ida watched him as he tightened the saddle girth. She considered trying to lift his spirits with another kiss. *You don't have to wander alone,* she ached to tell him. *I'll go with you, Hell or high water.* Instead, she held out her hand.

He raised it to his lips and kissed it tenderly. Then he swung into the saddle and rode out through the willow break, not looking back.

Chapter 26

A Visitor to the Mines

October 1863

The National Exchange Hotel of Nevada was a loose jumble of buildings, lassoed together with iron scrollwork and painted in a way to suggest a more intentional architecture than was really the case. The three-storey main structure towered over a full block of Broad Street and the plaza beyond. A wide, covered boardwalk ran the length of the hotel, allowing travelers to board the bustling stagecoaches in comfort. Its roof served as an elegant dining terrace, where the town's quality looked down with cocktails and sandwiches in hand on parades and celebrations, with only occasional bursts of gunfire from below to interrupt the flow of conversation.

A gleaming white flagstaff soared 135 feet into the air in front of the hotel. The pole was capped with a blazing gold eagle and flew the largest Stars and Stripes in the Northern Mines, testament to the hotel's unswerving devotion to the Union cause.

Will gazed up at the huge flag and regretted he could not share that devotion. He was, however, entirely at one with the hotel's passion for good food, and found it within the bounds of conscience to submerge his political opinions in superb white wine and the finest turtle soup this side of Charleston.

He ducked into the National's dark lobby, nodded at the barkeep, and climbed the stairs to the dining room.

"Willkommen, Wilhelm!" came a cheerful greeting from the center of the room, where a party of German shopkeepers crowded around a table covered with platters of broiled rabbit and tankards of beer.

"*Guten Tag, Peter.* Have the new *Lieder* come in yet?"

"Yes! I have so much new sheet music! You must learn *'Der Schiffer,'* 'The Boatman!'" Kessel lifted his mug and began to wave it in time.

Im Winde, im Sturme befahr ich den Fluß,
Die Kleider durchweichet der Regen im Guß…

"*Himmel,* Peter!" cried Aaron Goldfarb, eyeing Kessel's flying beer with alarm, "You should the storm and the soaking in the song leave." He edged his chair away and turned to Will.

"You are learning the Schubert *Lieder,* sir?" said Goldfarb. "Good! A new world will for you open, when you the words and music together understand… when you the *Lieder's* meaning…" Goldfarb cupped his hands together, miming the verb he was groping for. "…*grasp*…grasp *im Herzen*…in the heart!"

"Herr Stafford's musical understanding is admirable!" said Kessel warmly. "He will do justice to our dear Schubert!"

Will bowed, abashed by the praise, then took leave of the party and made his way out the doors to the terrace, where a man in a black coat sat alone, gazing out over the street.

"Dr. Forbes?" Will enquired.

The man with shoulder-length white hair turned his head, revealing a craggy, weather-bronzed face and glacier-blue eyes that peered over gold-rimmed spectacles.

"Mr. Stafford?"

The stranger rose to his feet. He was tall – fully the same height as Will – but his frame was spare. He extended a long, thin arm to shake Will's hand. There was surprising force in his grip.

"Forgive my lack of proper address, Captain," said Forbes in a low voice. "I did not wish to use your military title until I was sure whom I was addressin'. Pray, join me."

The man spoke with the accents of the deepest South – Alabama, most likely. Will pulled up a chair and took a seat by the railing.

"I trust your journey was not too arduous, Doctor."

"Not at all, sir. The packet from Stockton to Marysville made a record passage."

Albert, the National's waiter, appeared with a pitcher of ice water, a pair of crystal glasses, and menus.

"There's a barrel of fresh oysters just in from San Francisco, gentlemen," he proclaimed, with the pride of a man announcing the birth of an heir and namesake. "And the venison ragout is a masterpiece!"

Albert guided them artfully through the offerings of the day and retreated gracefully, having secured their consent to the feast he had planned for them all along. Forbes waited to speak until he was satisfied the waiter was well out of earshot.

"I have many things to discuss with you, Captain. One subject, however, demands priority above all others, and I fear it is a painful one."

Will closed his eyes. *Please, God,* he prayed, *let it be anything, anything at all, but what I dread.*

"I am truly sorry, sir – desolated – to inform you that your brother, Lieutenant Thaddeus Stafford, has died in captivity."

Will stared past Forbes at the plaza, which seemed suddenly unfamiliar, like the background of a nightmare. He closed his eyes and pressed his palms against them, but the darkness gave no comfort. His voice, when it came at last, sounded like a stranger's in his own ears.

"We knew Tad was badly wounded…left on the field at Gettysburg."

"It grieves me," said Forbes, "to be the bearer of such news. You have my deepest condolences. Please understand, sir, that the delay in telling you cannot be ascribed to our War Department. The Yankees have insisted on the most insulting terms for prisoner exchange – their *nigger* troops for our *white ones,* on an equal basis! They have all but ignored us since we declined their terms. Thousands of our brave men languish in foul prison camps, and we know almost nothing of their fate."

Will's mind was far away from Forbes, whose angry words buzzed in his ears like wasps at a windowpane. He thought instead of games he and Tad had played on the nursery floor with lead soldiers and cavalrymen. Although their lives had drifted apart, the outbreak of war had drawn them together again, riding with the 6th Virginia Cavalry to Fredericksburg and, in Tad's case, beyond – to the fatal field at Gettysburg…

"The rumors we hear of conditions in Yankee prisons are horrifying, sir," Forbes droned on. "Widespread negligence at best; at worst, a cruelty so base no Christian people would allow it! There will be a reckoning when this war is over, I promise you. The United States *will* pay for their crimes."

Will lifted his head wearily and looked at the doctor – and was shocked by the ferocity of the man's expression. Forbes's hard, blue eyes glittered; his face was rigid with hate.

The waiter appeared on the terrace, pushing a food cart topped with a gleaming silver ice bucket and soup tureen. Just behind came Mr. Lancaster, the hotel's owner. Will braced himself for Forbes's reaction to the town's most ardent Unionist.

"Good day to you, gentlemen," said Lancaster.

"And good day to you, sir," said Will. "Allow me to name Dr. Forbes, a visitor to this fair city."

Forbes rose and shook hands with the hotel owner.

"A truly remarkable establishment you have here," said the doctor warmly. "Elegant to the last degree!"

"Yes sir!" said Lancaster. "The bar and the piano in the lounge made the trip around the Horn from New York..."

Will listened to the men talk, unsettled by how swiftly Forbes set aside his rage. The man was evidently a gifted actor, ready to assume whatever pose the moment required. He watched Forbes dispatch Lancaster with a volley of compliments and then settle down to his lunch with gusto.

"Well," said the doctor, after a busy silence, "I must say, these Yankees do know their way around clam chowder. I find my spirits revivin'. In fact, I find myself able to undertake a much happier portion of my duty today."

Will glanced up from his chowder, mystified.

"It is my sincere pleasure, sir, to inform you that you have been named Major of Volunteers in the Army of Northern Virginia. Allow me to be the first to congratulate you!" Forbes raised his bubbling glass and drank to Will. "Very gratifying," he continued. "Your promotion will have a good effect on the men. It underscores the critical importance of your assignment."

"You do me too much honor, sir."

"I speak the simple truth, Major. Allow me to state my case, and then tell me if I am wrong. Our recent setbacks in Mississippi and Pennsylvania, though serious, have not undermined the military position of the Confederacy. Far from it! Even as we speak, General Bragg stands poised to destroy a Federal army that is cut off and starving in Chattanooga – a triumph that will fully undo the reverses of this summer.

"No, sir, the greatest danger to our cause is not military. It is *financial*. We have precious little gold, and our currency shrivels before our very eyes. The people call our notes *shinplasters,* and who can blame them, with salt selling for $60 a sack in Richmond? Our credit overseas is ruined; British and French arms dealers want nothing to do with our bonds. It is gold they desire, and a serious *guerrilla* here in the Sierra is our best chance of getting it."

Will agreed with the doctor's diagnosis. The grip of the Union naval blockade was slowly choking the Confederacy. Warehouses full of cotton lay rotting in seaports, denying the South its chief source of revenue.

"A healthy influx of California gold is the cure," the doctor continued. "As a physician, I have long recommended removing a substantial amount of it from Mr. Lincoln and administering it to Mr. Davis, thereby doubling the medicine's good effect. A campaign of lightning raids here, modeled on Mosby's work in Virginia, would deliver a staggering blow to the Northern war machine."

"So," said Will, "you've heard of Mosby?"

"Certainly! My friends in the War Office keep me posted on his progress." Forbes lifted his glass again. "Major John Singleton Mosby, the hero who is setting Northern Virginia on fire – and who captured a Yankee general sound asleep in bed."

"A brilliant officer!" said Will, draining his glass in reply.

"I understand," continued the doctor, "that Mosby, too, was a lawyer in Virginia. Your country seems to produce an exceptionally dangerous breed."

"Courtroom training hardens the heart," said Will, "which is useful in war. But I suspect Mosby owes his success more to the support of the local people. His men know the country intimately and can disappear without a trace when confronted by superior force."

"The same potential exists here!" said Forbes, with a feverish glow in his eyes. "True Southern men comprise an overwhelming majority in Fresno, Stockton, and Los Angeles, and more are spread throughout the state, ready to strike."

"How does recruitment go down in the Southern Mines?"

"We have over fifteen hundred men of substance who have taken the oath to defend the Confederacy, and many more have expressed their willingness to join once our standard is raised."

"And arms for your new recruits?"

"We have enough for all, mostly Mississippi rifles."

Will pondered the implications of this. Mississippi rifles were old Mexican War issue – .54 caliber muzzle-loaders that took a patched ball. Large numbers had come west with the emigrants, and it was these, presumably, that Forbes had bought up piecemeal. Quality weapons, originally, but out of date and sadly worn by now.

"Serviceable for infantry," said Will at last, "but not what I'd like for cavalry. Our force will have to be highly mobile, at least in the early stages of the campaign."

"You are surely right, sir. We are making every effort to acquire shotguns, carbines, and revolvers, but we are desperately short of funds. As you know, sir, Richmond has always seen this operation as self-supporting. There we must rely on you. An initial seizure of treasure would indeed do wonders for our efforts in California, Major." Forbes's slow and melodious voice took on a tone of impatience. "That is why we have all been waiting so anxiously for your return to health. When you were sent West on this mission, the target date for activity on this front was set for July."

Ah, here we come to the real reason for this visit, thought Will. *This is a reconnaissance to see if I have been malingering.*

"I have been ill, sir, but am now in health – and intend to strike soon at a good-sized gold shipment. We will carry the treasure as far as Marysville. Can you provide water transport from there for twenty men?"

"I give you my word, sir," said Forbes, brightening. "We have a highly competent agent in a shipping company there and the use of a private landing on the Feather River. We will take you south to Stockton on a fast steam packet. But you must approach discreetly – it would be madness for a large party of Southerners to be seen together in the immediate aftermath of the... action."

Will winced, sensing the word *robbery* that had nearly escaped the doctor's lips. Forbes watched him shrewdly and spoke to his discomfort.

"Once you have struck the first blow, Major, we can move openly. We will raise our standard proudly!"

"Proudly but briefly, Doctor. The point of this first action is to secure the means to wage war. We won't be able to take the field again until I've had time to train a substantial force in the Southern Mines."

"President Davis understands this completely. He expects no gold from your campaign until you have established yourself."

"Even with the gold in hand," said Will, "we will still need help from Richmond. A few light field pieces would be invaluable. More shoulder arms and ammunition…sea transport to take the gold back East…"

"Do not fear, Major! We have active plans afoot for naval reinforcement, ultimately including the fastest blockade-runner in the service – all yours, once we have begun our campaign in earnest. I have discussed this at length with the President's personal representative, who assures me that Mr. Davis takes the keenest interest in our project. 'There is,' he says, 'scarcely a more important…'"

Will lifted his eyes at the sound of approaching footsteps, and his face went white.

"Ida!" he cried, in a voice both higher and louder than his wont. He sprang to his feet.

"Good afternoon, Mr. Stafford! I saw you from across the street and thought I'd say hello. I hope I am not intruding…"

Forbes, too, rose swiftly to his feet.

"Miss Ida," said Will, in more measured tones, "allow me to name Doctor Ambrose Ransome Forbes, a visitor to our region. Dr. Forbes, this is Miss Ida Hatfield of Missouri House."

Dr. Forbes bowed.

"Mr. Stafford has boasted of this country's charms, Miss Hatfield, but I see even his eloquent words fall far short of the truth!"

Ida blushed and curtseyed. The florid compliment put her off balance; Will saved her with a swift invitation to join them. He drew up a chair for her.

"Well, just for a minute," she said, setting down her package. "Welcome to the Northern Mines, Dr. Forbes. Do you come to us from afar?"

"From Los Angeles. My associates and I have some funds at our disposal, and we are considering investing in gold mining companies. I am in Nevada to seek advice from my young friend, here."

"But Mr. Stafford has been away for a long while," Ida protested. "If it is mining news you want, you must talk with Judge Caldwell."

"I would not presume to trouble a stranger, Miss Hatfield."

"Not at all," said Ida, with a laugh. "The Judge was Mr. Stafford's employer before he went back East, and retains the highest regard for him. Any friend of his would be received in the Caldwell house like family."

"You are most obliging, but I hardly think…"

Ida interrupted the doctor's protests.

"What do you think, Will? Wouldn't the Judge be the first stop for an investor in mines?"

"Yes, he would," said Will, smiling at Ida's enthusiasm.

"Well, then, it's settled," said Ida. "Though you should know, Doctor, you may hear some harsh words about your friend, here. His Honor has been boiling with impatience, waiting for Mr. Stafford to return to his duties."

"Really?" said Forbes, with a searching look at Ida. "And do you think he is fit to resume his work?"

"Certainly," said Ida, with evident pride in her voice. "Why, sir, he was ninety-nine parts dead when he came back to us. Mr. Weaver had him measured for a hundred dollar casket…"

Ida stopped. There was something rather Old Testament about Dr. Forbes, for all his gracious manners, and she resolved not to adopt so familiar a tone again.

"I'm sorry to hear my young friend was in such danger," said Forbes. "As a medical man, I can only attribute his recovery to a most powerful agent – the beauty of the women of Nevada, perhaps."

"*Stuff!*" said Ida, dismissing her seconds-old vow of decorum. "It was Missouri House soup that pulled him through!"

Will laughed and raised his glass to Ida. "It was *Esmeralda's Miracle Broth* that raised this Lazarus from the grave!"

"Indeed?" said Forbes. "I admit I have not heard of the cure. Should I lay in a supply for my patients?"

"Esmeralda is our cook at Missouri House," said Ida, "a stage depot owned by my mother, out by You Bet, less than a day's ride away. You can sample our table when you come to inspect the diggings and judge for yourself. It's right on your way to the Comstock."

"A truly kind invitation, Miss Hatfield. I look forward to accepting your hospitality, if my journey takes me your way."

Ida started to say *of course you must come,* but held her tongue. It was altogether beyond her why anyone interested in mines would fail to visit You Bet and the Comstock, but Dr. Forbes was old enough to be her father and presumably knew his own business.

She sat in silence as the men discussed the dangers of mining the deep quartz veins around Grass Valley. It was silly of her, perhaps, but she couldn't help suspecting the discussion was for her benefit. Something, at any rate, made her ill at ease, and it was with a sense of relief she noticed the clock hand on the half-hour mark.

"Forgive me," she said rising, "but I promised to meet my mother at Dr. Chapman's. We have a female dentist here in Nevada, Doctor. Did you know that?"

Forbes rose, professing surprise at her news, pleasure at meeting her, gratitude for her kind offer of assistance in his business. Ida answered civilly and kept glancing at Will, wishing him to return her gaze. But their eyes met only briefly, as they shook hands.

As she passed through the lobby, she tried to reconstruct the conversation she had overheard as she had approached the table. She was almost sure Forbes had used the words *blockade runner, President,* and *Davis.* But what of it? Why wouldn't two Southern men discuss the fortunes of the Confederacy? But hadn't she also heard the words *our project?* True, the phrase might apply to Forbes's investment scheme. But if it did, what was it doing in a discussion so clearly centered on the war?

She tried to recapture exactly what she had heard, but details receded from her grasp. What did not fade was her sense that Will had not been himself. And his friend Forbes – if he *was* Will's friend – was a man who played his cards very close to his vest.

Chapter 27

A Letter Home

October 1863

Storms' Ranch near Grass Valley, California
October 3, 1863

Dearest Mother,

I don't know how to soften what I have to write. Forgive me the pain I bring, if this is the first you have heard of this news.

A gentleman in a position to know came today from Southern California and told me Tad has died of his wounds at Fort Delaware.

It breaks my heart to be so far from you at such a time. Embrace Kate and young Robert for me, and give them my love. Son, brother, husband, father – how many losses we four have suffered in this one loss! And ours is but a single entry in an endless book of sorrows. Poor, bleeding Virginia! What will be left at the end of our country's suffering?

Most in our family did not seek Secession. For my part, I was willing to cede almost every point to save the Union. If the Yankees wanted to throttle slavery in the territories, I was willing to look the other way. If they wanted to ignore the fugitive slave law in their own country, I accepted that as their right, just as it is a Virginian's right to own slaves in ours. What could not be admitted is that the Federal government is lord and master over all, with the right to force Virginia to join in the destruction of her sister Southern States who wished to leave the Union. That is where Tad and I drew the line in '61, and so long as I breathe, I will not dishonor the sacrifice he made, nor abandon the Cause for which he died.

This grieves me, Mother, because I feel strongly the lure of a new life out here, free from the conflicts that are tearing Virginia apart. I have friends in California as dear to me as the ones I left behind, and I find myself now in the position of betraying them in order not to betray Tad and all our kin who have sacrificed everything for Virginia. This is a heavy burden.

I am weary beyond words, and wish I could fling into the fiery pit the fools who so eagerly sought this conflagration. They were Judases...

The candle on the rough plank table guttered in the last quarter-inch of wick. Will set down his pen and rubbed his eyes.

He rose, taking care to place his weight on his good leg. A few steps took him across his new domain and into a small pantry, where a row of sagging shelves held all his dry goods and kitchen stores: a few cups and plates, some dried beans and flour in tins, salted bacon, wrapped and hung from the low rafters away from the rats. If Molly Hatfield were to visit him here, he thought, she would wonder at this austerity and probably laugh at the sight of his bachelor establishment...

After they had made love, came the immediate, unbidden thought.

He had never met a more desirable woman. Molly had the fierceness of spirit he needed in a lover, along with a body created by pagan gods to lie naked on an altar. He was surprised that she had desired him in the depths of his illness – and humbled that she still did, even after he had declared his intention of returning to this lonely cabin. Every gesture of her body, every look of her eyes told him so. They both understood this – were both versed in these matters in ways that dear, young Ida was not.

Ah, Ida! Will pictured her as he drew a new taper from the candle box. *There was a perfect beauty in the making, with a heart as fierce and free as her mother's.* He did not imagine love with her, the way he did so freely and often with Molly. Ida's innocence and grace touched him. He did not feel like a father to her, though – thank God. An impure older brother was more the mark, though he could feel the relationship changing as the girl grew into a woman.

And her feelings toward him? It was hard to say. When he first arrived in California, her childish infatuation with him was obvious, and it had taken great care on his part not to wound her feelings. Nor had there been any doubt about her revulsion at his appearance when he returned from the war. He did not blame her. It was not in the nature of a young girl to stay moonstruck over a man who looked like he had just been pulled from the grave. The incident at the falls had surprised him – shocked him, in truth. It was certainly flattering to be the subject of a girl's curiosity, but it would be foolish to make more of it than that.

He pried the candle stub out of the holder with his clasp knife, then twisted in the new taper and lit it. The little cabin had grown cool. He stirred the embers in the Franklin stove and laid on two hefty chunks of oak. The humble chore made him think of his mother, and how she would roll her eyes at this rough life without servants or comforts. She would never know how congenial her pampered son found it in his current humor.

He returned to the table and re-read his letter carefully, first with the eyes of a loving son, then with those of an outsider.

"I find myself now in the position of betraying them in order not to betray you and Tad... I will not dishonor the sacrifice he made, I will not abandon the Cause for which he died."

It wouldn't do. The letter had 3000 miles to travel by stage and train to Washington, where his Uncle Patterson would send it across the battle lines in the hands of a colored servant. It could be intercepted at any point along the way, compromising himself and his entire family.

This isn't a game, Will Stafford. Spies are hanged. And until you are back in uniform, you are a spy.

He lit a cigar on the candle, leaned back in his seat, and exhaled a long plume of smoke. Then he picked up his pen and wrote a new letter, filled with loving remembrances of his brother – who, for all the message revealed, might have died in a hunting accident.

Chapter 28

The Knights of the Golden Circle

October 1863

"Welcome back to Grass Valley, Dr. Forbes. I hope our arrangements are to your liking," said Madame Bonhore, proprietress of the U.S. Hotel. "Kahni, my houseboy, will bring your guests up as they arrive and make sure you are not disturbed."

Ambrose Forbes bowed deeply. "I am much obliged, ma'am."

"My associates and I are here to see to your every wish, Doctor. I hope you will join us tonight after your scientific meeting – you and your handsome friends." She smiled sweetly past Forbes at his two young companions, then left the room.

Forbes motioned Will Stafford and Asbury Harpending to make themselves comfortable. The upstairs room was hot from the fire crackling in the cast-iron parlor stove, giving off a sharp perfume of split cedar and fresh stove blacking. Harpending raised a window sash a few inches and stood breathing in the cool, rainy air.

"It has been a long time, Doctor," said Harpending, unfastening his fur-collared coat and doffing his tall silk hat. "I have missed California."

"Four years, if I am not mistaken," said Forbes. "Perhaps that does seem like a long time to a young man."

"Like back-to-back lifetimes," said Harpending, smiling. "I like to stay busy."

Will settled into the horsehair sofa and listened as Forbes and Harpending reminisced. Harpending looked like a freckle-faced child dressed up as a tycoon for a masquerade. It seemed incredible that the boy actually was a self-made millionaire several times over and – according to Forbes – the most dangerous conspirator on the Pacific Coast.

Crazy for adventure was how the doctor had described the youth. Before his sixteenth birthday, the boy had run off to join William Walker's bloody expedition to Nicaragua, intent on founding a slave state that could be annexed to the South. At seventeen, Harpending had been in California, striking it rich on a tributary of the Yuba River. Another golden bonanza had followed the next year in the Sierra Madre of Mexico. After Fort Sumter and Secession, the lad's Southern patriotism had burned white hot. By the time he was twenty-one, his astonishing successes and fierce commitment had brought him to the notice of the President.

Will knew a *letter of marque* in Jefferson Davis's own hand lay in Harpending's breast pocket, protecting him against charges of piracy. The boy was in California to purchase and outfit an armed privateer to prey upon the Pacific Mail Steamships that carried California's treasure shipments back East. Tens of millions of dollars in gold would pour into the coffers of the Confederacy if the daring scheme succeeded.

Harpending turned to Will and inclined his head. "The Doctor and I both have surprises for you tonight, Major. Let me tell mine now, since it is for your ears only.

"As you know, I have mining interests in Mexico. Through my agent in Mazatlán, I have been able to buy artillery and ammunition. The first consignment includes two twelve-pounder Napoleons for my personal project, and a pair of three-inch ordnance rifles for yours. Your guns, limbers, caissons, and the teams to pull them will be waiting for you in Stockton."

"This is a handsome gift, sir!" cried Will. "Those rifled guns are light and mobile – and dead accurate. I've seen a steady gunner knock the top out of a flour barrel with one at a half-mile."

"I am glad you approve, Major. I trust a ball from one will serve as an excellent calling card when you go visiting the Yankees!"

The clock struck nine. Kahni knocked softly on the door, then opened it to admit a silent crowd of men from the hall. Among the arrivals were many white heads and balding pates. Comfortable paunches were well represented, as were gold-headed walking sticks. Many coats displayed veterans' medals from the Mexican War. The men found themselves seats until all the chairs around the room were filled but one.

Another knock, and Kahni glided in again on slippered feet. He offered Forbes a small silver tray bearing a *carte de visite* with a photograph of a handsome youth with fair, flowing locks.

Harpending glanced over at the card and spoke to Will. "Major, this is the other half of your surprise. Lieutenant Clayton is an old friend of mine who may be of use to you."

A tall young man in a long-tailed riding coat strode into the room, and Forbes rose to greet him. "You are most welcome, sir. Now that our number is complete, we must proceed in the usual way." Forbes raised his voice so all could hear. *"The Seneschal shall secure the door."*

A burly man with a bulldog face took up his station outside in the hall, with his back to the room. Forbes closed the door and locked it. Then he strode somberly to a round table draped with red cloth and displaying a burning candle, a Bible, and a scroll tied with red ribbon. The gathering rose silently.

"Darcy Clayton, please step forward." Forbes handed him the Bible. "You have been deemed worthy to receive the solemn secrets of the Knights of the Golden Circle. Do you swear by Almighty God that whatsoever this night may be said or shown to you will be kept secret, never to be revealed to any living being?"

"I do swear."

Forbes took back the Bible and untied the scroll. "Then take this page and read the oath aloud."

Darcy unrolled the single page of closely-written script. The rest of the gathering placed their right hands over their hearts and recited in unison as Darcy read:

> *I do solemnly swear in the name of the Southern States, within whose limits I was born and reared, that I will never, by word, sign, or deed, hint at or divulge what I may hear tonight. Not to my dearest friend, not to the wife of my bosom, will I communicate the nature of the secret.*
>
> *By my honor as a Southern Gentleman, I swear that no consideration of property or friendship shall influence my secrecy. And may I*

meet, at the hands of those I betray, the vengeance due to a traitor, if I
fail in this solemn obligation. So help me God, as I prove true.

Forbes took the written oath from Clayton, opened the stove and dropped the oath inside. The paper burst into flames, casting a red glow over Forbes' face. He straightened and turned again to the young soldier.

"Lieutenant Clayton, you have proven yourself upon the field in Nicaragua and in the defense of your native land of South Carolina, at all times displaying the noblest attributes of our Southern Chivalry. Therefore, it is my honor to offer you a commission as First Lieutenant in the Army of Northern Virginia, with assignment to Major Stafford's command. Do you accept this duty? Will you second the Major in his upcoming campaign?"

"You may count me in to the limit!" said Darcy, with a broad smile.

Forbes motioned the young man to the empty chair next to his own, then turned again to the Knights.

"Tonight, gentlemen, we welcome a distinguished visitor who has made the journey from Richmond at the personal request of President Davis. This young man is a noble scion of the great Commonwealth of Kentucky. My esteemed fellow Knights, I give you...*Mr. Asbury Harpending.*"

Harpending took the floor. His voice was eager, his winsome face flushed with excitement as he addressed the crowd.

"Gentlemen, I am honored to be among you tonight. In this room we gather in the heart of the golden treasure laid down by Providence in trust for the Southern Cause. The Divine Hand that guides our destiny is pointing at this very room, singling out the Grass Valley Castle of the Knights of the Golden Circle for the honor of striking the Confederacy's first blow on the Pacific Coast!

"The Federal army in California is little more than a shadow. Only a handful of troops guard the arsenals where arms for fifty thousand are stored. We will overwhelm and seize every military installation between Washoe and San Francisco and stock them with Southern fighting men. Properly garrisoned, San Francisco's fortifications are impregnable. The Pacific Coast will be ours, and the outward flow of gold, on which the Yankees depend, will turn to Richmond instead."

Heads nodded in approval as murmurs rippled through the room.

"Thanks to your generosity, gentlemen, the means to launch this great enterprise are now assembled. We will soon step forth to enact such deeds of daring and heroism that the nations of the earth will vie to recognize the rightful claim of the Confederate States of America to a place among them!"

Harpending bowed and returned to his seat amid hearty applause.

Dr. Forbes rose, still clapping, and looked proudly around the room until the noise died away.

"I am sure," he intoned, "that I speak for all of us in thanking Mr. Harpending for his stirring words on the potential of our Cause in the West – a fitting prelude to the theme of our next speaker, Major William Stafford. This gallant officer will lay before you the principles of guerrilla warfare, as developed during the Revolution, and as currently practiced to such glorious effect by the Army of Northern Virginia in the Shenandoah Valley. Major Stafford cannot, of course, discuss details of possible operations in California, but his comments will leave you in no doubt of the golden prospects that await the bold practitioner of this unique form of warfare."

≈

"Well, Lieutenant Clayton," said Will, after Kahni set down a decanter of brandy and disappeared out the door. "I propose a toast to the Sierra Rangers and the beginning of our association."

They raised their glasses and clinked them together over the small, round table that had served as Forbes's altar to the Cause. The Bible, candle, and red drape were gone, as were the rest of the Knights, having departed for home or the pleasures of Madame Bonhore's casino and parlor house. Will offered Darcy a cigar, and they set about notching the ends and lighting up.

"So," said Will, "how do you come to wage war on the far side of the continent?"

Darcy leaned back in his chair and blew a perfect smoke ring.

"I was in the Sandwich Islands when the shooting started back home. I got back to South Carolina after all the promising regiments had been filled and sent to Virginia. So I spent a year with General States Rights Gist, roaming the blackwater swamps…"

"*States Rights!* Is that his real name?"

"On my sacred honor," said Darcy, laying his hand across his heart.

"Oh well…" said Will. "'What's in a name?'"

"Perhaps an excess of zeal, in this case," Darcy deadpanned. Will laughed.

"Forgive me, Lieutenant. You were about to describe your campaign…"

"We played hide-and-go-seek with the Yanks, who occupied the sea islands. Whenever they got bored with the sand fleas, they'd venture onto the mainland for a little excitement, and we'd chase them through the quicksand and palmetto stumps." Clayton dragged another chair into position and cocked his boots up on it.

"Then I heard that Asbury was visiting Richmond. We're old friends. When we were youngsters, we both tried to sneak off to join Walker's expedition down in Nicaragua. We were sent home to our folks, but they couldn't keep us pinned down for long. Asbury went gold mining, and I went with Walker's second campaign. So – when I learned Asbury was intending to raise Cain in California, I got him to use his influence with Mr. Davis to get me released from my regiment so I could tag along."

"I hope our little adventure doesn't prove a disappointment to you," Will said. "I fear Doctor Forbes may have overstated our prospects."

Darcy laughed and flicked his ash at the stove.

"*Overstated?* On the contrary, sir! I was deeply impressed by his restraint. It was mighty good of him not to boast of our plans to float the San Francisco mint out to sea and tow it around the Horn to Charleston."

"The good doctor's task this evening," said Will, "was to encourage the generosity of our local Knights. We were part of the show."

"I understand," said Darcy, nodding equitably. He arched an expressive brow and leaned toward Will. "Never fear you will alarm me with the true state of affairs. Remember, I thrive on desperate, ill-advised adventures."

"Then, sir, I believe we can satisfy your taste," said Will. "Here's the situation: we have currently fourteen men, mostly eager young 'uns, who know how to ride and shoot – though rarely at the same time and in the same direction. We will need another six men, at least, to tackle a fair-sized gold shipment. So your assistance in recruitment is essential.

"You will find most men in Grass Valley sympathetic to our Cause," Will continued, "while Nevada is largely Unionist. The quartz mining industry is depressed, so the prospect of a good wage has strong appeal. On top of their regular pay, we can offer a twenty-dollar bounty on enlistment, and I will see that our recruits receive more when our first action is successful."

Will swirled the liquor in his glass, choosing his next words.

"Please understand, sir, that I do not want this advertised as a campaign of plunder. A man who signs on just for the gold may be more dangerous to us than to the enemy."

Will drained his glass. Darcy leaned forward and refreshed it, and then topped off his own. "I imagine, Major, that raising a Confederate battle flag in the Northern Mines will create something of a stir."

"Like kicking over a red ants' nest," Will agreed. "The regulars are back East now, but the state is swarming with militia. They've had two years of training, and a lot of them have seen Indian fighting. They'll make us take to our heels after our first action. We'll head down to Southern California, where our friends are plentiful. With a brimming war chest, we can recruit and arm for a serious campaign in the Southern Mines."

"Currently, however," Darcy mused, "we enjoy the services of a major, a lieutenant, and fourteen privates. Too many Big Chiefs and not enough Indians, by my count."

"As things stand now," Will said with a wry smile, "the Sierra Rangers may be the most top-heavy military formation on the North American continent."

"I suppose we'll just have to postpone scooping up all those Federal arsenals until we have some more men," Darcy sighed. "Asbury *will* be disappointed."

"The odd thing is," Will said, "that this notion of a *guerrilla* isn't really a pipe dream. Mosby faces similar odds in Northern Virginia, and the Federals still haven't caught up with him, though they chase him night and day. He knows the terrain and strikes like lightning, then disappears in a puff of smoke. A genius blessed with luck."

"*Amen!*" said Darcy. "And speaking of luck, I believe I hear the call of an overburdened Faro table, begging to be relieved of its treasures. What do you say to joining forces in an assault on the coffers of the U.S. Hotel?"

Will shook his head. "Not tonight, my friend. I'll join you for breakfast."

When Darcy was gone, Will re-filled his glass. His thoughts were turning to Molly Hatfield, and he knew it would take a powerful dose of nepenthe to numb the pain in his heart.

What would Molly have made of the evening's program? What would she say of a roomful of Southern gentlemen – Will Stafford prominent among them – posing as Knights of the Round Table? He imagined her taking off her pince-nez and rubbing the bridge of her nose, heard the quiet skepticism in her voice: "So, Will, do you *really* consider the fight to preserve Negro property to be the moral equivalent of the Grail Quest?"

He missed her insistence on speaking the truth as she saw it – and her willingness to listen in turn. They had always spoken to each other as equals, never had to hide their thoughts from each other – until now.

He had seen the hurt in her eyes when he told her he was moving back to his cabin. But she had been too proud – and too much a true friend – to show resentment, and he was grateful for that. He ached to tell her how much he regretted leaving Missouri House, the place on earth where he felt most at home. But how could he reveal the reasons for his departure without making her a co-conspirator? It would be unforgivable to compromise her and her family just to ease the pain in his heart.

He could, of course, refuse the mission – betray the oath he had sworn to protect Virginia. But so many had already died for the Cause! How could he turn his back on them? His dreams were already haunted by visions of his mother and sister-in-law begging for mercy from a ruthless enemy. Desertion in such circumstances was unthinkable. The sacrifice of his personal happiness was nothing, compared to what others had offered up.

And who knows? Perhaps, if he went ahead and did his duty, a merciful fate might intervene, might show him some unimagined path to return to Missouri House.

If that happened, would Molly ever understand the choice I made? Would she ever forgive me?

Chapter 29

Frank's Bad Luck

October 1863

Madame Suzanne Bonhore descended the rose-carpeted staircase of her casino, resplendent in a golden silk-taffeta gown, her fiery mane of hennaed curls held high. Across her ample white bosom draped a heavy chain of twenty-dollar gold pieces, and diamonds sparkled from her earlobes and on her fingers that trailed along the polished balustrade.

The Professor looked up from his piano keys and saw her gold-fringed hemline sweeping along the landing. He left "Darlin' Nellie Grey" on an improvised bridge of two-handed chords and struck up "Oh! Susanna."

"How y'all doin', gents?" the madam inquired in a voice of brass. "Welcome to the U.S. Hotel."

She threaded her way through the crowded saloon, greeting new patrons, joking and flirting with the regulars, and checking to see that her Doves were busy dancing or complaining to their escorts of thirst. She paused at the passageway under the stairs so Kahni, her Hawaiian houseboy, could pull back the drapes and admit her to the card room, where gaslights flared on red-papered walls. Inside, the madam sat down in a high-backed cushioned chair beneath a gilt-framed painting of herself as Goya's *Naked Maja*. Men began crowding into the room, eager for a place at Madame's Faro table.

"You know the rules of the house, gentlemen, and if you don't, they are posted by the door. Hang up your hats. No swearing, no spitting. When I say the game is over, it's over. Anyone who breaks the rules will find himself on the street on a rainy night – when it's so much nicer inside." She smiled and winked at a dapper little man in an evening suit, who blushed to his ears.

"Now, gents, twenty dollars is the minimum. Just place your bets on one of the cards painted on the table. I'll deal two cards up. If your bet's on the first card, you lose. If your bet's on the second card, you win! What could be simpler?"

Players placed their markers on the painted game board. Madame Suzanne laughed or moaned at the play of each card, pretending to be happy when the gentlemen won or rueful when she raked in chips for the house.

"Lady Luck has been good to you today, Frank," she said to an elegantly dressed man in his early thirties, who slouched comfortably in his chair. His dark hair was long and wavy and fell over the sides of his pallid face from a center part. "My congratulations," she said, "on your big win in the court-room this morning."

"Thank you, my dear," Frank Dunn replied, "although luck had no part in it. The opposing argument…"

"And here's our charming Mr. Clayton," the madam interrupted, riffling the cards, "come to rob me of my heart and my fortune once more."

Madame Bonhore stopped shuffling and let her eyes wander over Darcy Clayton's athletic form as he relaxed into the chair and unfolded his long legs beneath the table. A paisley silk ascot wrapped his neck; his vest was care-lessly held together with one gold button. *A blond Adonis,* she mused, admiring his curly, tangled locks, soft golden moustache, and the strong line of his jaw. His mouth turned up in an easy grin, and his blue eyes were impertinent as he met her gaze.

"I'm just another moth drawn to your flame, Miss Suzanne. Do you pity us when we singe our wings?"

"There's nothing pitiful about you, Mr. Clayton," said the madam, placing the deck into the shoe. "You arouse different emotions." She smiled at Darcy while the gamblers placed their bets.

Frank Dunn looked curiously at his new neighbor at the table and then raised a questioning eyebrow at Suzanne.

"Frank," she purred, "let me introduce my guest, Mister Darcy Clayton. Darcy's just taken rooms with us."

Dunn sat up and made a polite inclination of his person. "I am pleased to make your acquaintance, sir. I am Francis J. Dunn, generally and justly held to be the most brilliant lawyer on the Pacific Slope." He paused and watched ruefully as Madame Bonhore raked away his chips. "Will you take a glass of Bourbon whiskey with me, Mister Clayton? *Corn* whiskey, sir, the nectar of Old Kentucky."

"With pleasure, sir," Darcy replied, keeping his eyes on Suzanne Bonhore's fingers as she whisked another card from the shoe. Frank Dunn lifted a dusty bottle and poured two brimming shots.

"The ace wins again." Suzanne winked as she matched Darcy's bet with a tall stack of twenty-dollar chips. Darcy took one from the top of his winnings and slid it across to her. She picked it up, tapped it twice on the table to signal her thanks, and tucked it into the lace between her breasts.

"Now there's a lucky chip, I do declare," said Darcy. Suzanne half-closed her heavy lashes and smiled. Her lips formed a little kiss.

For the next hour, Darcy mentally tallied the cards as they were dealt, deftly moving his bets around the Faro board. He won steadily, while Frank stubbornly staked the black queen, losing dismally. With a dark scowl, Frank shoved his remaining markers onto the board, covering the queen. He reached to refill his glass, and his unsteady hand knocked the bottle over. Darcy righted it with a lightning reflex, but not before a pool of liquor had darkened the green felt.

The madam spoke in a firm voice as she pushed Dunn's bet back to him.

"Frank, the time has come for you and that bottle of fine bourbon to return to your own cozy den, where you can enjoy it in peaceful surround-ings."

She turned to her Kanaka boy. "Kahni, *wiki-wiki*, Mr. Dunn's trap and Mr. Clayton's horse, side door."

She batted her long lashes at Darcy. "Darcy, darlin', please be an angel and see Mr. Dunn home." She tapped the neckline of her dress. "And when you come back, I'll see you have a chance to retrieve this lucky chip."

⁓

Darcy half carried Frank Dunn to the front door of his house on Nevada's Aristocracy Hill. Darcy knocked and waited, while the attorney addressed remarks to an invisible court.

"'The mining laws of California do not diverge. The end lines of each claim shall be parallel to each other...'"

The front door opened. Mary Dunn, in a scarlet satin dressing gown and slippers, held a silver hairbrush in one hand. Her long black hair tumbled over her shoulders in a luxuriant cloak. She looked at her husband's puffy, ashen face, then at Darcy's shining, cheerful one, and stepped back to admit them to the hall. Her nose wrinkled at the stale odor of bourbon and cigar smoke on the men's clothes.

"Please bring him this way," she said to Darcy, leading him to a front room and motioning to a red plush sofa. Darcy lowered Dunn to the couch and stooped to remove Frank's boots.

"'...unless such form is prevented...by adjoining rights or boundaries...'"

Darcy gently settled the lawyer back with an embroidered cushion under his head.

"Therefore, gentlemen of the jury, the end lines of a mining claim extend... *up* to Heaven and *down* to Hell!" Dunn triumphantly thumped his chest. "I rest my case," he sighed with satisfaction. He closed his bloodshot eyes and let his head sink into the cushion.

Mary Dunn surveyed the alcoholic tincture of husband now snoring on the settee. "Thank you, sir, for bringing Frank home," she said. Her mouth closed in a thin, straight line.

"Yes, ma'am," Darcy replied absently, feasting his eyes on her un-corseted form.

Mary smiled, blushing. "Since you are here, allow me to offer you some refreshment, Mister, um..." She was aware of the heat of his body as he moved close beside her.

"I'm Darcy Clayton, ma'am," he said. *And you could teach the torches to burn bright,* he added to himself, dazzled by the woman's sparkling black eyes and the dark curls flowing over her shoulders. Her soft drawl was thick as syrup.

He followed her down the hall. Entering a cool room in the darkness, Darcy was aware of the odor of books behind the jasmine sweetness of Mary's perfume. Both were dispelled after a few moments by the sulfur smell of a Lucifer match. Mary settled the shade back on the lamp.

"Please sit down," she invited, indicating a leather-upholstered armchair. "This is Frank's law library. There are several volumes here of particular interest. Let us begin with this one." From the nearest shelf she pulled out a massive volume titled in gold: *The Spirit of the Law*. She laid it down on the roll-top desk and opened the cover. Inside, instead of pages, nestled a square decanter.

"Frank keeps his best sippin' whiskey in here," she said, producing two glasses from a cubbyhole. She poured them nearly full and tested one. "Your voice reminds me of home, Mr. Clayton," she said softly, as she handed him a glass.

Darcy smiled. "My folks are from the Old Cheraw, Miz Dunn. Hagen's Prong. I often think of them."

"Hagen's Prong! Why, you must know the McRaes!"

"Very well, ma'am! The Colonel had an unmarried niece he thought would be perfect for me…"

"Not the dreadful Attelia!"

"That was the lady's name," said Darcy, with a twinkle in his eye. "But I decided to try and overthrow the government of Nicaragua instead. It seemed the safer choice."

"I am sure you are right. Have you heard any news of her cousins? The sandy-haired twins?"

"I liked them both, and the Colonel, too."

"And…"

"George died at Sharpsburg; Charlie at the siege of Jackson."

They both fell silent, sipping their drinks.

"I'm afraid the country I left doesn't exist any longer," said Mary at last. "Even so, I'd like to go back someday. I do get terribly homesick…and lonely." She closed her eyes and rubbed her temple with her fingertips. "You'd think my husband and I would have more in common, he being a Southerner, too. But Kentucky is not the Old South, Mr. Clayton. I sometimes think he is more Yankee at heart."

Darcy watched her, rapt, as she opened her eyes and swept back the hair from her brow.

"We've come a long way from home, haven't we?" Mary sighed. "But to what end? Perhaps we should never have left our country."

"I have traveled far, ma'am, and have come to believe that happiness depends on who you journey with, more than on where you end up."

"Yes, I can believe that," said Mary. "Perhaps it is not home I miss so much as the freedom of my youth." She stared into the amber fluid swirling gently in her glass. "Now I only search for ways to fill the empty days.

"Forgive me," she said, raising the glass to her lips. "I have no right to burden you with my unhappiness."

"Any man who was really worthy of you would move heaven and earth to make you happy."

She looked into his handsome, open face.

"Do you really think so?"

"Upon my soul, I do."

She ran her delicate fingers through her shining hair as she considered. Then she brushed back the luxuriant mane from her shoulders and looked around at the tall stacks of dark, leather-bound volumes.

"This is a gloomy room, isn't it? Would you like to see my summerhouse? It is just at the bottom of the garden. It is quite lovely there when the rain is falling…and my mandolin is there. I could play for you."

She led him through a garden swathed in low misting rain. The tiny summerhouse was dry and cozy. Mary put the lamp on the table and turned the flame down low. She took Darcy's hand and led him to the window seat, where she drew an instrument case from beneath the table and lifted out a gourd-shaped mandolin. She sat beside him and began to pluck the double strings with a long, flexible pick, raising a tremolo that ebbed and flowed beneath her warm alto voice. She sang softly, first in Italian, and then in English:

> *Donatemi una ciocca di capelli*
> *Che per memoria gli terrò sul core.*
> *Voltate verso me quegli occhi belli;*
> *Mi sentirete sospirar d'amore.*

Give me a lock of your hair
I will keep it over my heart.
Turn toward me those beautiful eyes;
You will hear me sighing with love.

She stopped playing and smiled at him. Darcy took the instrument from her and carefully laid it on the low table.

He leaned close and gently raised her chin with one finger, looking into her eyes as he brought his lips close to hers. He brushed her mouth softly with his.

Mary felt her heart begin a strong, steady rhythm. Her sudden longing for this man was almost the pain of a wound. She touched his lips with her fingertips; he took her hand and kissed the palm. Then he showed her where his lips had touched her hand.

"See? Tonight is marked here…on the line of your heart."

He slipped one arm behind her and the other under her knees and lifted her onto his lap. She wound her arms about his neck.

"Have you ever seen a day change so suddenly from dark to bright?" she whispered. "Like the sun coming out from behind a cloud."

Chapter 30

Attack of the Highbinder

October 1863

Chung Ah Kit stood hidden in the shadows of the livery yard, chafing his hands in the cold night air, invisible to the *gwei lo* passing by on their way to the Travelers' Hotel. The highbinder watched the window on the hotel's second floor, where his quarry wallowed in whiskey paid for by Ah Tie's stolen gold. He knew the outlaws' names now. *Big Boots* was Jake Forrest, *Slippery Soles* was Eldon Whitley – and they were ruthless and brutal men.

The highbinder waited as the quarter moon edged down toward the rooftop. The shadows of both men crossed the window shade – and then a woman's. Then, for a long time, there was nothing but the dim glow of a lamp. Finally, the light in Jake and Eldon's room went out.

Chung stretched and ran in place until his body felt warm and lithe. He needed to be at his best for the work ahead.

He slipped through the shadows to the oak tree by the hotel, drew out his flying claw and coil of rope, and lofted the claw over a long limb that reached out toward the corner of the building. He gave the rope a sharp tug and saw the black outline of the branch sway against the starry sky. The claw was firmly bedded.

Chung kicked off his shoes and stuffed them into his vest. Then he seized the grappling line and hauled himself up, hand over hand, until he reached the claw and freed it. He stood up on the swaying branch, arms stretched wide, bare feet splayed. He felt his way along with his toes, gradually shifting his weight to keep the slender limb from rocking. Then, balancing on his wrist-thin perch, he sprang into the air and onto the hotel's roof.

The highbinder landed noiselessly on the rough and splintery cedar shakes. He climbed to the ridge and crept along it until he reached the second chimney. He stood listening to the sounds inside the hotel. He could hear music and laughter from the casino downstairs, and loud snores from the room under his feet. He hooked his claw around the chimney and backed down the roof, slowly letting out his line. Balancing at the eave, he stepped off the edge and deftly found his footing against the outside wall, rapelling down until he hung outside the outlaws' window.

He tested the window sash; it was stuck shut. Chung drew his sword, slid the blade between sash and sill, and pressed down on the hilt.

With a sharp *crack,* the window popped up a quarter of an inch. Chung held his breath. All he heard were the hog-like snores of the *gwei lo* within. He gently lifted the sash, swung his feet through the open window, and slid in on his back.

The room was black, the air thick with stale liquor and sweat. Two iron-frame beds piled with bedclothes loomed in the darkness. The mound on the right was larger; from it came the louder snores. This must be the giant's, who should be attacked first. He glided forward, sword raised. He took hold of the blanket and whipped it back…

Wide-open eyes stared up at him as Chung slashed. Even as the hot blood spurted over his hands, he realized the body writhing on the bed belonged to a woman.

The blanket jerked from Chung's hand as Big Jake twisted away. His towering form rose on the far side of the bed.

"Wha's goin' on?" came Eldon's voice in the darkness. Chung heard the click of a gun being cocked.

He sprang to the window and dove out headfirst. The rope in his hand jerked and spun him around, cracking his head against the wall. Jake's huge, hairy arm reached out the window and Chung slashed at it. The highbinder loosened his grip on the line and shot toward the earth, tearing the skin from his palm. A deafening explosion shook the night sky as a pistol ball howled past his ear. He sprinted into the shadows and was gone.

Chapter 31

Cold Holler Farm

October 1863

Cold Holler Farm delivered everything its name promised by way of discomfort. The dark, brushy strip of land lay along the north side of a ridge, above a slough that filled the air with a dank chill. The muddy trail to the cabin wove through scraggly stands of second-growth pine, festooned with tendrils of poison oak that were shedding their last red leaves. Jake and Eldon ducked repeatedly as they rode through the tangle, swearing reflexively to pass the time.

"You sure there ain't no better way to this sorry hellhole?" drawled Jake. "Never heard of a farm with no wagon road."

"Well, I'm sorry the facilities don't meet with your approval," said Eldon, bending low under a berry vine. "Growin' up on the estate of your forbears must have made you uncommon particular…"

"You know where I growed up, Eldon. I know as much as a body ken about bein' pore. I jist cain't figure how ol' man Mays gets his crops to market, if this is how he sets about it…"

"He feeds hisself," said Eldon, "an' sometimes he feeds his boy. And if everything goes just so, why…then there might be an apple core or two left over for the hogs. The old man's main crop is hard cider, and when he gets done sampling it, there ain't much left to sell. Besides, old Mays ain't what you'd call overly social. It's okay with him if he don't waste a lot of time hobnobbing with the quality at the farmers' market."

A pair of hogs squealed nearby, a sign the men were nearing the cabin. Eldon dropped his voice. "Look here, Jake. Don't you go wavin' that iron claw around and spoutin' off about how we nearly got our throats opened by a highbinder. Old man Mays won't be too happy havin' us here if he knows there's a yellow devil on our trail. Just let him think the law's after us. That will strike him as a lark, and he won't bellyache if we lay up for a while."

As they rounded the last curve, a high, querulous voice sang out in a hill-country Arkansas twang, *"Who's tha-yatt?"*

"Howdy, old man," yelled Eldon. "No need to set the dogs on us. We're friends."

They turned the last corner and reined up. Before them stood a wiry old man on the porch of a rickety cabin. He wore a shapeless black hat riddled with holes and a scraggly grey beard. There was a rusty 10-gauge in his arms, pointing straight at them.

"Evenin' Merle," said Eldon. He slid off his horse and led her toward the house.

"Evenin' yerself," said the farmer. His suspicious expression did not change, but he lowered his gun.

"Is Young John around?"

"No, he ain't. He's off on a fool's errand, an' I never seen a boy better qualified for the job."

"How's that?" asked Jake, hitching his horse to the porch railing.

"Him and that Treadwell boy, they's taken up *soldierin'*." The old man didn't hide the contempt in his voice.

"*What?*" cried Jake. "They ain't gone and jined the militia!"

"Ain't they?" said old Mays bitterly. He launched a stream of dark tobacco juice over the porch rail.

"Cain't have," said Eldon. "Them boys hates Yankees – jes' as soon shoot one as look at 'im."

"That's why they joined the Secesh militia…the damned fools."

"*Secesh* militia?" said Jake. "Ain't no setch thing. Not in these parts."

"That's all y'all know," said the old man, with a contemptuous grunt.

Eldon shook his head. "Well, maybe there is. But why in Hell would those boys join it? I don't see them riskin' their hides for the glory of the South."

"They jined 'cause they're young and stupider than a bag of rocks, that's why," spat Mays, "leaving me all alone to break my back in my declining years, when a man's offspring should be his comfort and support."

If any back had been broken in Cold Holler, Eldon reflected, it must have happened while someone was lifting jugs by the still. The rest of the farm showed few signs of effort. The apple orchard had become a thicket, where pigs rooted for shriveled fruit that lay rotting on the ground. The garden gate swung crookedly on one hinge, protecting nothing but some spindly pole beans that were slimy from frost.

"Well, well," said Eldon, "Jim Treadwell and Young John, gone off a-soldierin' for the Confederacy. Where they off to, old man?"

"Nowheres," snorted Mays. "They got some hideout 'round here where they sneaks off to. Then they comes back, hungry as wolves, an' eats me out of house and home. This whole militia business is a story, I reckon, to cover up their worthless loafin'."

But it was not a story, as Eldon soon learned when the boys came riding in. They were both armed to the teeth, with new six-shooters and shotguns added to their pepperbox pistols and Bowie knives. And there was a new, war-like swagger to them when they swung off their mounts and climbed the porch, spurs jingling.

"Where's Pa?" asked John Mays, looking around.

"Down to the creek to check the trotline. He's invited us to supper," said Eldon.

"That's fine," said John, who was making quite a show of removing his new weapons and hanging them by the door.

"Say," said Eldon, "jes' between you an' me an' the gatepost… What's this 'Secesh militia' story you been spinnin' the old man? You boys ain't runnin' off a little free-lance bandit work on the sly, are you?"

"*Hell no!*" said Mays indignantly. "We're bona fide militia, commanded by a cavalry major from the Army of Northern Virginia – a real gent!"

"Well, your real gent seems to be a bit weak in geography," said Jake, as he drew out a plug of tobacco. "Last I heard, Virginia was a ways off to the east."

"Of course it is," said Treadwell. "That's jist where he got his commission. Our fightin's goin' to be right here in Nevada County."

"Pshaw!" spat Jake. "What fightin' would that be? You boys ain't stupid enough to pick a fight with Van Hagen, are you? He'd eat you for breakfast."

"We're not goin' to fight Van Hagen," said young Mays. "Leastways, not if we can help it…"

"Yeah," said Treadwell, "we're jist fixin' to take his gold – take it an' ske-daddle. The Major is planning to rob the big fall shipment from the mines…"

Mays and Treadwell looked at each other nervously, but with a touch of pride at their revelation of the bold scheme.

"Well, now," said Eldon, "I'm beginnin' to think a little better of your unexpected heroics, boys. How about you, Jake? You feel a sudden surge of Southern nationalism a-blazin' in your heart?"

"Nothin' sudden about it, Eldon," said Jake. The dark hair on his face rippled, suggesting a grin somewhere below. "I always thought it was a sorry spectacle, watchin' all them wagons packed with gold a-rumblin' down the hill to San Francisco to fill Abe Lincoln's pockets. Seems to me, a true patriot would want to put a stop to setch things."

"Amen!" said Eldon. He turned to Mays and Treadwell. "This fine officer of yours, would he be lookin' for new recruits? Jake and me, we're beginnin' to tire of our life of ease and plenty. We're on the lookout for something new…"

"And a change of scenery, too," added Jake. "I reckon you boys don't do your militia drill at the Plaza, do you?"

"I reckon not," scoffed Mays. "Major Stafford's got a cabin out by Storms's old place. We drill in a meadow out there…"

"*Stafford…?*" cried Jake, his usually dim eye suddenly ablaze. "William Stafford? A Virginian?"

"That's the man," said Mays proudly. "He went back East and rode with Jeb Stuart!"

"Well, well," said Jake slowly. "I'd shorely love to see combat with Major William Stafford."

"You know him?" asked Treadwell.

"Oh yes. Me and my brother Porter ran into him when he first arrived in these parts." Jake cut off a chaw with a deft flick of his Bowie knife. "I'd be right pleased to make Mr. Stafford's acquaintance again," he added softly.

Chapter 32

Mary's Flight

November 1863

Mary Dunn pulled back her shoulders, lifted her chin in imitation of Frank's cocky courtroom pose, and eyed her reflection with approval. *Clothes make the man, all right,* she mused. It was uncanny how much she looked like her husband, once she was dressed in his clothing.

She seemed taller in the suit – even commanding. The shoulder padding she had added and the long tail of the dark coat hid her female curves. Something was missing though…*a hat!* She tried on Frank's top hat. It settled over her ears absurdly and made her laugh. A soft brown felt with a wide brim was just right, when the band had been stuffed with tissue paper. With long hatpins, she secured it to her hair fore and aft, so that it could not blow off and reveal her secret.

It was odd to feel the weight of her clothing hanging from her shoulders rather than her hips. Freed of her suffocating corset and heavy skirts, she could bend and breathe with comfort. She could move in silence, quickly.

But there wasn't any hurry. District Court was in session, and Frank had several cases on the calendar. He would have his liquid lunch at the National Hotel with his cronies from lawyer's row, and he wouldn't be home until suppertime – if he came home at all.

Mary rummaged though Frank's chiffonier, selecting collars and shirts and carefully packing them in his big carpet valise, along with her own hairbrushes and nightgowns. Once she was safely out of the Northern Mines, she would resume her female identity. She would outfit herself *á la mode* as soon as she reached San Francisco.

She carried the bulging valise into Frank's study and set it down in the middle of the floor. Then she climbed the moveable library steps and began a systematic search of the bookshelves. On the top shelf, a new leather binding entitled *Origin of Specie* yielded a heavy sack of double eagles. On another shelf, between the covers of *God and Mammon,* she found a thick wad of banknotes and a soft doeskin money belt.

A square black bottle of brandy was her next prize, simply titled *Animae Sucus.* How would that translate? *Soul Juice?* She padded the bottle carefully and added it to the carpetbag. The spines of Frank's favorite volumes, *Tanglefoot Tales* and *The Spirit of the Law,* concealed his best bourbon. They were plainly marked with the patina of frequent handling. Those she left alone. Farther down the same shelf, she was surprised to find that *Extraordinary Legal Remedies* held a boxed set of derringers.

She tried putting these into her coat pockets, but they weighed down the jacket, stretching the fabric and revealing her figure. She put them in the carpetbag instead, between layers of clothing, each pistol wrapped in a thick worsted stocking. The small powder flask, lead bar, bullet mold, and tiny box of percussion caps she tied up in a handkerchief. *Better that Frank doesn't have any guns handy when he discovers his missing possessions – including me.* She imagined Frank and Darcy raising pistols, a voice counting, the two men firing…both falling…red roses of blood blooming on their white shirts…

She sank onto the desk chair, feeling faint and anxious. *I'm being silly, Frank knows nothing. There's no way he could know our plans. There'll be no confrontation, no scene… I'll write to him when we're safely away…*

She went to Frank's big roll-top desk and raised the lid. The cubbyholes and bins gave up nothing. In the back of the bottom right-hand drawer, she found a .31-caliber Colt with holster and belt. She spread a newspaper over the blotter on the desktop and loaded four chambers, leaving the hammer down on the empty one.

She walked back to her bedroom and stopped in front of the mirror to fasten the gun belt around her hips and tie the holster to her thigh. The .31 drew smoothly from the tooled leather. She pointed the barrel at her own reflection, trying to look threatening; her lower lip pouted, her brows knotted. "Now git, you varmint," she drawled, motioning with the gun barrel. She laughed and holstered the pistol. She felt light-headed. She was gambling everything; once she left this house there would be no going back. *Did Frank feel the same thrill at the Faro table? Was she as foolish as he was?*

She was suddenly swept by a wave of panic. What was she doing, dressed up in men's clothes, poised to run off with someone she barely knew? Was this simply insane?

She closed her eyes, and her father's thick Scots accent sounded in her memory. "Mind the words of the great Montrose, Mary!

> *He either fears his fate too much,*
> *Or his deserts are small,*
> *That puts it not unto the touch*
> *To win or lose it all."*

Was it really only four weeks ago that she and Darcy had seen each other for the first time? Her pulse beat strongly as she thought of him: golden, glowing, brimming with life. He made her feel like a child on Christmas morning.

Gathering up her luggage, she slipped out to the stable where the white mare was saddled and waiting. She tied her bundles behind Frank's saddle, mounted, and turned the sturdy mare down the trail behind Aristocracy Hill, to the upper ford on Deer Creek. She could cross there without being recognized and strike the road to You Bet near the Masonic cemetery. It was just eleven miles, an easy day's ride over the mountain, to Walloupa, where Darcy would meet her secretly.

Early tomorrow they would set off together – *our grand adventure.* In just a few days, they would be sailing out the Golden Gate, bound for Honolulu. She imagined them strolling together beneath waving palm trees, on a white sand beach, far away over the blue Pacific.

Chapter 33

The War Returns

November 1863

"That's the tree, Major Stafford. What do you think?" The big soldier pointed with his pipe at a towering yellow pine.

"Can you lay it straight across the road, Sikes?"

"That's how she wants to fall. We'll just give her a nudge."

"Carry on, then."

Sikes crouched at the base of the ponderosa. Gabriel Watkins, a small, wiry youth, put his palms against the tree and his boot into the stirrup Sikes made with his hands. Watkins hitched up the heavy coil of rope draped over his shoulder, then nodded to Sikes.

"One…two…*hup!*"

Sikes heaved his powerful frame upwards and launched Watkins into the lower branches of the pine. There was a frantic scrabbling of boots on bark as the youth hauled himself up, and then a shout of triumph.

"Looks as easy as a staircase from here, Major!"

"Secure your rope two-thirds of the way up, then drop the free end so we can send up another line. We need two stays to hold the tree till we want it to fall."

"Yes, sir!"

As Watkins spiraled up through the radiating branches, Sikes surveyed the lean of the tree. Then he drew a hatchet from his belt and notched the trunk at about waist height.

"Cutting marks, Major," he said, in response to Will's quizzical look. "If you undercut this tree just right, you won't hardly need stays. You could push the blame thing over with your hands at the first sight of a Yankee."

"Humor me, Sikes. I want stays. I'm naturally cautious."

Sikes chuckled as he slid the hatchet back into his belt.

"Hell, I don't blame you, Major. What would the Blue Bellies think of us if we set to whoopin' an' shootin' an' the tree don't fall?"

Drumming hoof beats approached; Darcy Clayton appeared atop a magnificent sorrel. He spotted Will and the sawyers among the trees, leapt his horse over the road ditch, and charged up the slope at them. Darcy touched the reins lightly, and the gelding drew up in a cloud of dust.

"Peculiar time to be layin' in firewood," he drawled, gazing down at Sikes, who was carefully dressing a long, two-handed saw.

"Just bein' polite," said Will. "I'm leavin' this tree as a consolation for the Yanks, in exchange for their gold. Did you get those men into the outlying positions?"

"Yes, sir. Two on the road to Nevada City, three on the road to Red Dog – about a quarter-mile away, with good lines of fire. They're just itchin' for the Yanks to come out and play."

"All right. Tether your horse with the others, Lieutenant. They're up the draw there. You'll see the tracks."

A cloud of disappointment passed over Darcy's face. He leaned forward in the saddle to protest, but Will's look made him think better of the idea. He whirled his horse around and set the sorrel flying with a touch of his spurs.

Another damned Ivanhoe who thinks it unmanly for an officer to fight on foot, Will thought, as he watched Darcy gallop off with the grace of a circus rider.

Will breathed in a waft of sweet pine sap. Sikes and Granger – an even bigger man, with a long, heavy beard that could comfortably nest swallows – were heaving the crosscut saw back and forth across the ponderosa, shooting out jets of sawdust with every stroke. Behind them, Watkins and another boy were hauling the free ends of the rope stays up the steep hillside, away from the road.

"Run those lines out with about thirty degrees of separation," Will called. The youths looked back at him blankly, clearly innocent of the faintest notion of geometry.

"Watkins, this-a-way." Will raised his left arm and pointed. "Jenkins, that-a-way," he said, raising his right. "Pull till the ropes are almost tight, then wrap 'em twice around a stout trunk and hold on."

Sikes and Granger sawed out a deep notch in the front of the tree and began a straight cut across the back, just a hand's breadth higher. As the saw approached the center of the trunk, Sikes cried, *"Easy, now!"* He and Granger changed to a slow, deliberate rhythm, pausing and looking up after every stroke.

"That's it!" Sikes roared. "Let out a foot of rope, slowly," he yelled to the boys.

Will detected no movement in the ponderosa, but when he looked at the stays, he noticed the slight curves in the rope had disappeared.

"Let out another foot of rope, slowly and together."

The boys obeyed, and this time Will detected a gentle rocking in the upper branches as the treetop shifted.

"There we are, Major," said Sikes. "When we release the stays, she'll drop square across the road."

∾

Will assembled his Sierra Rangers in line along the edge of the road. They numbered fourteen, not counting Darcy and the outliers. They were young and wiry, and their sun-faded clothes and worn boots bespoke hard outdoor living. Will suspected half of them had lied their way past his 18-year old age limit.

They stood proudly at something like attention as Will walked down the line. Apart from the shotguns he had provided, the men presented the most unlikely assortment of weapons imaginable: rusty pepperboxes, ancient flintlock pistols and muskets, knives of every size and description. He tried to gauge their frame of mind and saw fear and excitement in their flushed cheeks and bright eyes. Their fire would be wild, but in a brief, close action, they should give a good account of themselves.

Halfway down the line, he encountered two hard-bitten specimens who seemed a different breed altogether. Their clothing was certainly dirtier. But each carried a first-quality Bach shotgun, a broad, heavy Bowie knife, and a pair of huge dragoon revolvers in his belt. These weapons showed signs of considerable wear – and careful maintenance. The two men themselves showed no trace of nervousness, but rather gave off an impression of bored amusement. Both reeked of whiskey, especially the tall one with the pock-marked face and lank brown hair. Will looked carefully at the man – and recognition dawned. Slouching before him was the drunken lout who had insulted Ah Tie and knocked Ida to the ground during the Bomb Day parade some years ago. As Will stared, the lanky man smiled, revealing a row of crooked, tobacco-stained teeth.

"Eldon Whitley, sir. We've met before."

Will moved on to the black-haired giant standing next to Whitley. An impudent grin split the man's filthy beard.

"Jake Forrest," said the big man, who turned his back and launched a stream of tobacco juice at a stump.

Will looked at Forrest and Whitley in disgust, struggling with a powerful instinct to shoot them both on the spot. *An indulgence I can't afford,* he decided. The troop needed every man it could muster, and these varmints looked like they knew how to fight – especially from ambush.

Darcy stood tall at the end of the line in the full uniform of a South Carolina cavalry officer. His neatly tailored broadcloth jacket was trimmed with yellow piping and Austrian knots – elaborate, looping patterns of braid on his sleeves that proclaimed his rank. A golden sash and a leather sword belt wrapped his middle; a plumed slouch hat covered his flowing locks. Darcy raised his saber in salute, sunlight glinting off the polished blade.

We've been fighting a different war, thought Will, as he returned the salute. He looked shabby compared to Darcy. His grey coat was faded and his leather belt worn and cracked. His sword was in a trunk somewhere in his mother's attic. The only sign of his rank was some tattered braid on his sleeves and an outdated pair of yellow captain's stripes sewn to his collar. Will shrugged inwardly. Whatever its failings, his uniform was comfortable – and, at a deeply superstitious level, had kept him alive in some desperate situations.

He strode to the far side of the road and faced his troops.

"Gentlemen, there's a mountain of gold on the way. Our job is to take it and clear off before the Yanks know what hit 'em. There'll be an escort on horseback, most likely, and guards on the wagon. If we start trading lead, shoot the horsemen first, 'cause the wagon won't be goin' anywhere after that tree comes down.

"If we're lucky, we'll outnumber them, and I'll sing out and give 'em a chance to surrender. If they accept, well and good. If they don't – and I yell *fire* – pour it into them until I tell y'all to stop."

Will's voice trailed off as the meaning of *pour it into them* swept over him. He had never before planned an action against men he knew and liked. *What would it feel like to see Henry Bachelder with a shattered spine? Or Ida's young beau, Joe Hardesty, moaning on the ground with half his face blown off?*

The troops exchanged glances with one another in the silence. When Will spoke again, his face seemed set in stone.

"If the enemy resists, kill him. Aim for his belly. A ball over his head serves no purpose, while a miss the other way will bring down his horse.

"Now, if the Yanks surrender and I yell *cease fire,* then, by God, you'd better do it! We're here to win a war – not to collect scalps."

Will looked up and down the line of men. They were somber and attentive – a good jury. Will breathed deeply and relaxed for his summation.

"Now, listen, boys. Fightin' has a way of gettin' complicated, no matter how hard you try to keep it simple. All y'all have to do is obey orders – mine or Lieutenant Clayton's. And my first order is: *shoot any Yank who tries to get away on a horse, no matter what else is goin' on.* We're not going to get out of here if someone escapes and raises the countryside… Any questions?"

There was a pause, and then a gangly, straw-haired boy stepped forward with a passable imitation of military crispness.

"If we git the gold, Major, ken we spend the night at Madam Bonhore's 'fore we take off into the hills?"

An explosion of whoops and laughter greeted the question. Will waved the tumult down.

"We're not hidin' in any hills, boys – that's what the Yankees expect. We're fixin' to do the opposite. We're ridin' down to Marysville in the Valley and takin' a boat headed south – a good, long ways south – where more men and some prime field artillery are waiting for us…"

Will could see the men hadn't expected this. They looked puzzled, some looked concerned. Will pressed on without missing a beat.

"...*and*, from what I hear, Madame Bonhore's even prettier sister lives down that-a-way. So, if we do a good job with the gold, I reckon President Davis won't mind payin' for a spot of rest and recreation."

The men cheered. Will tore off his slouch hat and beat the air with it.

"Hush up, you damn fools!" he growled. "There won't *be* any gold if y'all scare off the wagon!"

The noise died away, with the few remaining jokers pummeled into silence by indignant friends.

"One more thing," Will continued. "If you get separated after the action, make your way to Flora's Faro Palace in Marysville. Someone will be on hand, lookin' out for you. Put on a mourning band 'fore you go in, and tell anyone who asks it's your Aunt Mary who has passed away. If he says he knew her well, that's your man. Y'all understand? *Aunt Mary* and *knew her well*."

The men murmured their affirmatives.

"All right then. Sikes, Jenkins, Watkins, Granger, McLaren, y'all come with me. The rest of you head off with Lieutenant Clayton. Quietly, now."

While Darcy concealed his men in the thick brush above the road, Will laid out the short arm of the L-shaped ambush, which would form along the roadblock. He placed McLaren and Granger, steady, full-grown men, behind thick cedars on the far side of the road, just in front of where the ponderosa would fall. From there, they could rake the whole Yankee column. He took his station in the corner of the L, behind the massive upended stump of an ancient oak, ready to move out along either arm of the ambush as needed.

There were a thousand ways for the plan to go wrong, and Will thought his way through most of them as anxious minutes dragged by. Was the drop-off on the far side of the road steep enough to tumble a horse and rider trying to escape that way? And what about those two men Darcy had signed up at the last minute? The skinny one was an ugly, drunken beast, and his beefy companion seemed cast in the same depressing mold. But that said nothing about their fighting ability. They were an asset at the moment, though they might prove awkward during the escape – especially if they were overly fond of gold.

The escape. That was the real problem. It was going to take time to secure prisoners, deal with the wounded, and load the gold onto pack mules. Could he slip away with his troops before word spread to nearby mining camps? If not…well, it was too late to worry about that. There was nothing for it now but to play out the hand as best he could.

He turned gratefully from problems of command and let his mind wander back to Missouri House – to passionate, gorgeous Molly and daring young Ida. Some said there was such a thing as having too much luck with the ladies, and he supposed that was true. *But if you have to have problems in life,* he reflected, extracting the flask from his coat, *that's the very one to have.*

The excellent brandy warmed his mouth with a sensual delight that was always keenest in the moments before battle. He took another swig and savored the beauty of the Northern California forest in fall: canyon maples turning gold, dogwoods bursting into red, dark green conifers glowing with overtones of blue. It was a perfect setting for an afternoon with Molly or Ida. But here he was, instead, back in the game of death.

He had expected, after so long away from action, that his heart would pound and his breath come short, but so far, neither had happened. His brother's death seemed to have detached him in some subtle way from life and was pulling him toward an alternate world of memory and spirit. He felt Tad's presence strongly in this dream-like return to war.

He became aware of a sound – a faint jingling in the distance. How long had it been there?

Another jingle. And another. The creak of an axle, growing closer.

Now his pulse began to pound in earnest. He scanned the road and the thick brush alongside it, vividly colored in both sun and shadow. A horse neighed in the distance. Will heard it as if its muzzle lay next to his ear.

The war was back.

Chapter 34

The Campaign Begins

November 1863

Will crouched behind the stump, watching the bend in the road. He heard hoof beats clearly now, along with the creak of harness leather and the shouts of men. Four blue troopers burst from the brush by the bend, riding two abreast. Will recognized Van Hagen in his sergeant's stripes in the second row. Behind the horsemen came a four-horse team pulling a "celerity wagon," a squat, canvas-roofed coach much favored in the mountains. Henry Bachelder sat high in the driver's box, crying out to encourage the team. A swarthy man in a buckskin jacket and broad-brimmed hat sat next to Henry, a double-barreled shotgun propped against his knees.

The canvas sides of the coach were rolled up. Two gun barrels were visible. *Probably two more guards on the other side.* Then the four mounted troopers of the rear-guard swung into view, riding two abreast.

Thirteen guns against us.

The blue troopers were carrying carbines – not the shotguns that were so deadly at close range. Van Hagen's militiamen would be well trained – no doubt of that – but the Rangers had the advantage of surprise, cover, and the greater accuracy of men firing from solid ground. *If I play my cards right, I can give Van Hagen a chance to surrender.*

The advance troopers rode on, oblivious to the Confederates hidden in the brush to their left. Will took off his hat and glanced at Sikes, who was poised to relay Will's signal. Sikes grinned and nodded. The man was clearly enjoying himself.

The Yankee horsemen were close now, no more than thirty yards away. Will realized, with a sinking heart, that the front trooper on the left was Joe Hardesty. Next to him rode Gareth Truesdale.

Just a few yards more…

Will swung his hat down sharply to signal Sikes. A sharp *crack* behind him was followed by a slow, rending sound. The tree began to lean – then jerked to a halt, its long branches swaying.

Only one rope had released!

The pine's trunk tore with reports as loud as pistol shots. Will watched in horror as the tree began to pivot away from the road and towards him and the men waiting in ambush.

The boy clutching the stuck rope pulled frantically, but the immense weight of the leaning tree locked the knot in place. Sikes charged up the slope, hatchet raised high over his head. For an instant, Will thought the sawyer was going to brain the hapless youth, but the hatchet crashed down on the knot instead. The rope end whipped through the air, and the ponderosa gave way with an almighty groan.

The huge tree was in free fall, heading straight for the Yankee riders. Will saw Joe Hardesty wrench his horse's reins and bury his spurs in the beast's flank. Too late. Horse and rider were smashed to the ground in an avalanche of pine boughs.

"VAN HAGEN!" Will roared, standing up to give the man a view of him. "You're surrounded! Give it up!"

"*Stafford?*" Van Hagen cried in disbelief, as he struggled to control his plunging mount.

The shotgun messenger on the driver's box swung his weapon to his shoulder. Will dove for the dirt as a barrel full of buckshot shattered the oak root next to his head.

Instantly, a volley from the hidden Confederates crashed out of the brush. Will scrambled to his feet.

A riderless horse galloping past the wagon, a blue trooper on the ground. Van Hagen coolly firing his revolver into the smoke erupting out of the brush, while Gareth Truesdale clutched the neck of his rearing, spinning horse.

Will lifted his pistol and aimed at Van Hagen, but as he squeezed the trigger, Gareth's frenzied horse came down and took the ball in the shoulder.

The terrified animal charged across the road and over the edge, its blue rider toppling backward out of the saddle.

Van Hagen spun his horse around and set his spurs to it, racing for shelter on the far side of the coach. Will got off a second shot, but missed as Van Hagen leapt from the saddle, his horse galloping off down the road.

The gunfire grew into a steady roar as the Yankees returned fire. Will strained to see what was happening, but the coach and hillside were wrapped in roiling clouds of gunsmoke.

"We've got to flank the wagon," he shouted to Sikes and the boys. "Follow me!" Will crouched low and sprinted across the road behind the fallen ponderosa. *A slapping sound and a grunt behind him.* No time to look back.

McLaren and Granger were crouched in the pine boughs, firing at the exposed Yankee flank. McLaren turned to speak, but his head jerked sideways and his jaw disappeared in a red spray. Will leapt over the writhing body and crouched next to Granger. Through the boughs, Will saw a huddled clump of men in blue. Most were firing at Darcy's men on the hillside. Two were turned and firing at his position. Will flinched as a ball shrieked by his ear.

"Spread out, boys, and find some cover. Kill the Blue Bellies who are shooting at us."

Will planted the butt of his Colt on the pine trunk, gripped it with both hands, and drew back the hammer. The Yankee in his sights fired at the same time, then jerked backward and tumbled to the ground. Three guns went off around Will, and the second Yankee spun around with a shriek. Van Hagen whirled and raised his pistol in Will's direction.

"Give it up, John!" Will shouted.

A shotgun blast from the hillside sent a body flying out of the coach and onto Van Hagen, knocking him sprawling in the dirt.

"CEASE FIRE!" Will yelled. *"Henry! Stop your men!* CEASE FIRE!"

Will's voice echoed through the smoke. Two more pistol shots rang out.

"PUT DOWN YOUR ARMS," Will roared, tearing his throat.

Slowly, one by one, the surviving Yankees laid their weapons on the ground.

"You in the coach there, come out with your hands up."

There was a moment of silence. Then Henry Bachelder sang out.

"Nobody left in the coach, Will."

"All right, then. *Everybody get your hands up…high!*"

Will scrambled over the fallen tree, his three remaining men following him. As they approached the wagon, pistols leveled, Van Hagen staggered to his feet, his face and shoulders spattered with blood.

"God damn you for a fool, Will Stafford," he snarled.

"Put the pistol down, John."

Van Hagen looked down, surprised to find his Colt Dragoon still clutched in his hand. He glared at Will as he laid the pistol on the ground.

"Jenkins," said Will, "collect their weapons and put them in the coach. Sikes, Granger, gather the prisoners. Sit them down in the road behind the wagon. Help them move their wounded."

As the prisoners moved off, Darcy Clayton appeared around the corner of the coach. His fine jacket was torn, and there was a gaping hole in the crown of his plumed hat.

"Darcy, what happened to the rear guard? I couldn't see."

"We dropped two of 'em," Darcy drawled. "The other two turned tail and took off. I heard fire from down the road aways."

"How many men did you lose?

"One dead, three badly wounded. Those boys in the coach showed fight, for sure."

"All right, Lieutenant. Have two of your men take Yankee horses and make for the outliers as fast as they can. But tell them to *walk* their mounts the last hundred yards, waving their hats, so they don't get shot by our own men. The outliers are to head for the telegraph lines, securing any travelers they meet along the road. They are not to hurt anyone – just leave 'em horseless and bootless and tied to a tree. And report right away when you know what happened to those two Yanks who skedaddled."

Chapter 35

After the Battle

November 1863

The roan lay sprawled in the road, its legs sticking out at odd angles, its head and neck crushed under a massive bough. Joe Hardesty sat leaning against the horse's haunch, his face ghostly white. Beads of sweat formed on his brow and upper lip.

"I hear you survived the battle," said Henry Bachelder.

"I guess I did," said the boy. "My dancing days may be over, though. My ankle smarts something awful when I try to wiggle my toes."

"Then don't wiggle 'em," said the driver, kneeling down and offering his canteen. The youth seized it and drank until water ran down his chin.

"Listen, Joe," said Henry, "I'm going to cut this boot off right now, before your leg swells." The driver opened his Barlow knife and slipped the blade into the boot top.

"Have you seen Gareth?" said Joe.

Henry didn't reply, but gripped the knee-high boot with his left hand and began to slice down through the leather. Joe's face contorted.

"I want you to do me a favor," said Henry.

"Sure," grunted the boy.

"I want you to listen to some free advice from a man old enough to be your pa."

Sweat trickled down Joe's face as he nodded.

"Broken bones take a long time to mend," said Henry. "There's no hurry to get back in the saddle, and the end of your hitch is coming up soon…"

Joe cried out as the boot came free. Henry kept talking as he gently lowered the foot. "When it does, you should accept the thanks of a grateful nation and fold that uniform away at the bottom of a deep cedar trunk…"

"Sound advice," said Will, who had silently approached the pair. His uniform was torn and dusty, and smeared with blood.

"*You…*" snarled Joe. "I should have known you'd betray your friends…just like you betrayed your country!"

Will pointed to the back of the wagon with his flask. "Henry," he said, "I've got to talk with you and John over yonder. You head on; I'll catch up." Will crouched down and offered Joe his flask. The boy turned his face away. Will shrugged and took a generous shot.

"Henry gave you some good advice…and I'll add a thought of my own. As soon as you can haul yourself up on your crutches, you should hobble down the aisle with that beautiful young Hatfield girl, before anyone else does. That's my advice." Will rose heavily to his feet. "And the next time you're at Missouri House," he added, "I'd be obliged if you'd remember me to Molly."

◇

The laudanum had done its work. The wounded men were silent – except for McClaren, whose jaw was so badly shattered it could not hold the alcoholic tincture. His moans were growing weaker, though, as he slipped off into shock. Will stopped to let two Yankee militiamen drag a body by. The dead boy's curly head lolled horribly, his neck clearly broken. It was Gareth Truesdale – Dora Caldwell's fiancé. Will watched the troopers add the boy to the row of corpses on the far side of the road, then walked on.

Henry Bachelder held his canteen high, tipping it so John Van Hagen could drink. The sergeant's arms were tied behind his back and lashed to the rear wheel of the wagon.

"Gentlemen," said Will. "I am conferring with you as the civil and military leaders of the opposition…"

Van Hagen spat out a jet of water that splashed over Will's boots.

"Go to Hell, Stafford."

"Speak your piece, Will," said Henry Bachelder.

"Henry, this is for you," said Will. He reached into his ammo pouch and extracted a sheaf of papers. Henry unfolded the top one and gaped.

"A receipt from the Confederate States of America, by God! A true-born lawyer to the very end!"

Will shrugged. "This war will be over someday, and when it is, the wreckage will be sifted by lawyers – packs an' packs of 'em. That piece of paper may save a mint of money for the folks who are shipping this gold, if it comes down to indemnities."

Henry shook his head in disbelief. "A man with a headpiece like yours, throwin' away a charmed life… It's a rare privilege to witness folly on such a majestic scale!"

Will smiled sardonically. "You seem to think I'm in charge of my life, Henry, but I'm not. There's a Yankee army burning and looting Virginia and slaughtering my kinfolk. That limits my options."

"That's what happens to traitors," snarled Van Hagen. The sergeant's pale eyes glowed with rage.

"John," said Will, "I'm leaving my wounded with you. I want your word they will be treated as prisoners of war."

"They're road agents, and they've killed men. You know the punishment for that."

"They're Confederate soldiers, sworn into service and commanded by an officer of the Army of Northern Virginia. If you hang them, then you are the murderer."

"What the Hell do I care what you call me?"

"Don't be a fool, John! If you hang my men, I'll have to retaliate. Is that the kind of war you want?"

"Will," said Henry quickly. "I'll do what I can to see your boys are treated as soldiers. But what happens to them isn't in John's hands or mine. That decision will come from a lot higher up."

"All right. Just make sure Sheriff Knowlton doesn't hang 'em in the meantime," said Will, "…for sport."

"This is nothing more than armed robbery and murder, Stafford," said Van Hagen. "And when you're marched to the scaffold, I'll be the one to pull the hood over your head."

"Your privilege, if you catch me," Will said coolly. "For my part, John, if you hang my men, I'll hunt you down and watch you die."

$\backsim$

On the other side of the coach, the last of three mules looked placidly down the road toward Red Dog, while young Jenkins caught the heavy doe-skin bags of gold Sikes tossed down from the wagon bed.

"You wouldn't believe how much these things weigh, Major," said the boy, as he lowered the bag into the mule's saddle pack. "These critters will sink to their hocks if we go over soft ground."

Darcy sauntered up next to Will and caught the next bag. He eyed it with undisguised avarice.

"A truly inspirin' sight, I do declare."

"What do you have to report?" said Will curtly.

Darcy motioned to the far side of the road and saved his answer until they were out of earshot.

"Those two Yankees in the rear guard – the ones that bolted – they never made it, Major. There's your good news."

"By God, Darcy, that's a relief! We'll get a good start now, before word gets out." Darcy's face remained grim. "But I suspect," said Will, "I'm not going to like the rest of the report."

"No, sir," said Darcy, shaking his head. "The Yanks were sprawled in the road, right where they fell. But our men didn't fare so well, either.

"We had Wallace and two boys posted as outliers on the road to Red Dog. When my man got there, Wallace was stone dead – a hole in his forehead and powder burns all over his face. The other two were nowhere to be seen."

"*Hellfire!*" growled Will. "What happened?"

"Well, Wallace was dragged into the brush and hidden. Looks like Mays and Treadwell killed him and ran off."

Will shook his head, appalled.

"That's not all, sir. Jake Forrest and Eldon Whitley are missing, too, and their horses are gone."

"*Christ…!* No time to track 'em down; we've got to get out of here. I'll send Sikes and Jenkins to Dutch Flat to clear the road and cut the telegraph line. That leaves you, me, and four men to protect the gold – six should be enough."

"I'm afraid you'll have to make that five"

"What do you mean?" Will growled.

Darcy took off his hat and fingered the brim.

"To be honest, sir, I'm in a spot of lady trouble… I promised to meet my friend down at the Walloupa diggins and get her out of the county. Turns out her husband's the vindictive sort. Should have shot the man while I had the chance, but it's too late now. Besides, the lady just wants to clear off and be done with him…"

"*Damn you, Darcy!* You can't just walk off. It's desertion!"

"Well, I suppose it is, in a technical sort of way. But I *have* just helped you seize a pile of Yankee gold, at considerable risk to myself and my wardrobe." Darcy poked his finger through the hole in his hat and stared at it mournfully. "I was hopin' you'd make allowances, a lady bein' involved, and all."

"We've just started a *war*. These hills will be swarmin' with men fixin' to kill us. You can't jeopardize the mission for a romantic adventure!"

Darcy looked at Will's face with maddening calmness – and smiled.

"Will Stafford, your campaign is off to a brilliant start. You've captured a fortune for Jeff Davis, and you've got four good men left to help you get away. A small party's better, anyhow – quicker, an' easier for y'all to hide. My lady and I will rejoin at Marysville, but I can't leave her wanderin' around, wonderin' if I'm dead."

Will opened his mouth to speak, but Darcy cut him off.

"I'm ridin' off now," he said. "You can shoot me if you feel duty-bound. But you strike me as a man who would scorn such an unnecessary gesture." Darcy replaced his hat atop his head and patted it into place. Then he turned and walked toward the tree where his sorrel was tethered.

Will felt a wild urge to chase the man down and beat him senseless, but Darcy was right. There just wasn't any point to the idea.

Chapter 36

A Fortune on the Loose

November 1863

Four outlaws sat by the edge of the trail, while their horses drank at a muddy pool nearby. The two ragged teenagers, Mays and Treadwell, exchanged skeptical looks as their older companions harangued them.

"There's jist a handful of Stafford's men left," growled Jake Forrest, glaring at the boys between swigs from his canteen. "Four or five at most to guard more gold than y'all ken begin to imagine. Ain't that so, Eldon?"

Eldon held the butt of his big revolver clamped between his knees and tapped a charge from his powder flask into each chamber.

"That's so, Jake," he said, not lifting his eyes from his work. "Them Yanks shot us to pieces 'fore they gave it up. That gold won't have nothin' but a scarecrow guard."

"We know jist where they're headed and ken lay for 'em," Jake continued. "It'll be a turkey shoot."

Treadwell, the older of the two boys, frowned as he sawed off a plug of tobacco with his knife.

"I dunno. It seems like pressin' our luck. The numbers is pretty even…"

"What did you ladies sign on for, if you weren't lookin' to make a fortune?" Jake dug into his pocket and hauled out his own tobacco, which was flocked with lint. "Did you really want to go ridin' around, gettin' shot at for the sacred cause of Southern nationhood?"

"Hell no, Jake. We want the gold as bad as you do," said Treadwell.

"Well, then?"

"Well…we figured we'd help ourselves to some of it along the trail. We didn't reckon on shooting it out with Major Stafford an' Lieutenant Clayton."

"Damn you, Treadwell!" Jake punctuated the oath with a jet of tobacco juice. "This is your last chance for the gold – you won't git another. Wallace took a bullet between the eyes and you're deserters. Do you really think Stafford's goin' to have you back? Think he's gonna say, 'Good work drillin' them Yanks, boys, so we'll jist let bygones be bygones about poor Wallace…?'"

"But we didn't shoot him!" Mays burst out.

Jake laughed. "Of course they're goin' to believe you, Mays! All you got to do is tell 'em you was a-standin' by when we did it, and all will be forgiven."

The youngsters shifted nervously.

"It's now or never, boys," drawled Eldon. "That gold is headin' for Southern California, quick as Stafford can carry it. So y'all either help us stop him now, or jes' go on back an' wait for Van Hagen to string you up for armed robbery and murder."

The two teenagers looked at each other, aghast. "What do you think?" murmured Mays.

Treadwell's knife slipped and nicked his thumb. He cursed and frowned. "I reckon…I'm in. How about you?"

Mays' pale, pimply face bobbed up and down. "Yeah, I guess."

"Where you fixin' to lay for 'em?" Treadwell asked, deepening his voice in an effort to sound tough and nonchalant.

"Well, now you're talkin'," said Jake, with a broad grin. "If Stafford figures to git to Marysville without ridin' through any towns, he'll have to follow the old Emigrant Trail. And to git there, he'll have to work his way south along the Greenhorn, on this-here mule trail we're a-settin' on. It gits steep and brushy about half a mile from here, jist across from the mouth of Missouri Canyon. I reckon that's our likeliest spot."

"You boys might want to give an eye to your canteens," said Eldon. "Once we get the gold, we'll be off in a hurry and won't be stoppin'. There's a flume jes' up the hill. Here, fill ours, too, while we re-load."

Jake and Eldon passed over their canteens. Mays and Treadwell skirted the muddy pool and began to climb toward the sound of trickling water.

"Scrawny little poults, the pair of 'em," Eldon snorted, as the youngsters passed out of earshot. "There's been a sad falling off in the quality of highway-men."

"They'll draw off some fire, leastways," said Jake, drawing two heavy pistols from his belt. "'Part from that, I don't see much use in 'em."

"It'd be a sorry waste of gold to cut them in," said Eldon, dropping his pistol barrel back into place and jamming in the wedge.

"I reckon you're right. They'd jist spend it all on whores an' stunt their growth." Jake opened his ammo pouch and laid it on the ground beside him. "Now, speakin' of divvyin' up the proceeds, we've got to figure out which of us gits to blow the brains out of that sorry son of a bitch, Stafford. I've got a brother six feet in the ground 'cuz of him, and I reckon that gives me rights."

Eldon frowned as he placed another ball in his six-shooter.

"So it does," he said, gripping the loading lever and driving the ball home. "But I got cause, too, Jake – *good* cause. Why don't we be fair and sportin' about the thing – and *both* shoot him?"

Chapter 37

A Change of Plans

November 1863

Darcy Clayton tugged his slouch hat low and kicked his long-legged hunter into a gallop. Horse and rider flew down the deeply rutted track to the old Walloupa diggings, dodging the tall rabbit brush that was swiftly reclaiming the road. Soon the abandoned camp came into view. Rusty barrel hoops, tin cans, and smashed crockery lay strewn about the site, presided over by a lonely log cabin with a collapsing roof. A snowy white mare browsed nearby, tethered to the post of what once had been a porch. Darcy dismounted and tied his gelding alongside.

"Darcy, is that you?" came Mary Dunn's voice, unusually soft and low.

Through the empty doorframe, he saw Mary seated in the gloom. Her hair was down, and she was running her fingers through stray wisps that had fallen across her eyes. A pistol and riding crop lay by her side.

Darcy crossed the floor, leaned over, and kissed her, his long, blond hair swinging down and mingling with her dark curls.

"Darcy, honey," she whispered. "Thank God you're here!"

He caressed her cheek.

"Nothing could have kept me away, love."

He took her hand and pressed it to his lips.

"I couldn't sleep last night," she said. "I must have dozed off after dawn."

She pushed the oilskin slicker off her legs and rose stiffly to her feet, yawning and stretching. "I do look forward to finding a better hotel in Marysville tonight, dear. This one has uncommonly bold rats."

"You'll have to go on without me, love," said Darcy. "I won't be far behind… It's just that I've been studyin' on Will's situation, and it isn't a healthy one. And I'm afraid it's my fault."

"What on God's green earth does Will Stafford's *situation* have to do with us?"

Darcy bit his lip – and unfastened his long cloak. Mary's eyes widened in disbelief as she took in his Confederate uniform.

"It just so happens," he said, "that Will and I started us a little war this morning. We borrowed the big fall gold shipment over by Greenhorn crossing for Jeff Davis, and we're fixin' to take it south. That's why I couldn't leave with you last night…"

Mary reeled as the implications of Darcy's pronouncement crashed over her.

"You damn fools!"

"I couldn't tell you, darlin'," Darcy pleaded, as the stunned expression on Mary's face gave way to outrage. "I was sworn to secrecy!"

Mary couldn't trust herself to speak. She snatched up the riding crop and began to rap it sharply against her palm.

"We captured a fortune in gold!" said Darcy brightly. "Enough to launch us a first-rate campaign! We can turn the Federals inside out once we get some more boys."

Mary's toes writhed in her boots.

"And just how, Darcy dear, did you and Will plan to get away with all that gold, with the whole countryside in arms against you?"

"Will's got a right smart plan figured out. He's just a natural in this *guerrilla* line!"

"I am relieved to hear it."

"We're off for Stockton, where *our* people live," said Darcy, oblivious to the sarcasm. "Will's taking the gold across the back of Banner Mountain right now, heading for the old Emigrant Trail. We've got a fast boat waiting below Marysville. There won't be any pursuit – leastways not for a while. *And you're comin' with us!*"

Mary bit her lip and drew in a deep, deep breath. It would do no good to explode now, she told herself. *There's no way to put the genie back in the bottle.*

She smiled – rather stiffly – and rapped the riding crop against her thigh so she wouldn't use it on Darcy.

"Well then," she said, "I suppose we should be on our way, once you have changed out of that conspicuous uniform."

Darcy's face fell like a little boy who'd just opened a brightly wrapped Christmas gift to find woolen socks and a Bible. He stared at Mary and slowly rubbed his chin, seeking inspiration in the stubble sprouting there.

"I'd love to, honey. But I've got to get back to Will. I may have kicked a hornet's nest his way, and there's no one left to help him…"

Mary's eyebrows shot up. Darcy blundered on.

"We had four men run off, and they killed one of our boys…"

"I see," said Mary coolly. "And you desert me in the middle of this wilderness because…?"

"Because they're all four working together, and Will doesn't know about it!"

"Darcy, dear, do try and talk sense."

Darcy flushed. "Well…I've been thinkin' on things as I rode over, and I reckon I may have made a mistake…may have signed up a gang of road agents." He turned away in embarrassment. "You wouldn't have anything to eat, would you?"

Mary pointed at the haversack hanging from a peg and watched as Darcy rummaged inside.

"So, what you're telling me," she said coolly, "is that Will Stafford is about to ride into an ambush."

"Like as not." Darcy looked wretched as he passed her a sandwich. "That's why I need for you to head on to Marysville, while I go back and warn him."

Mary nibbled thoughtfully at the bread in her hand. Then she sighed and gave Darcy a radiant smile.

"Of course you must go, my darlin'. Honor demands it."

Darcy beamed. He stooped and kissed her, then strode out the door. A moment later, she heard the big sorrel's hoof beats pounding up the road.

Mary flung aside her sandwich with an oath. It was maddening, just *maddening* to think of Darcy riding off to bail Will Stafford out of the God-awful mess he'd stirred up. But there was no point in trying to stop Darcy – not when a point of honor was at stake.

Here she was, *a day's ride from freedom,* and those blockheaded men were doing their level best to get themselves killed over a pile of gold that would never, ever see the inside of the Confederate treasury. She splintered the back of a broken chair with her riding crop – then began to pack.

Chapter 38

The Second Fight

November 1863

Darcy heard gunfire ahead and dug his spurs into his horse's flanks. The narrow, winding mule trail was thick with live oak and manzanita, and he bent low over the sorrel's neck to avoid being swept from the saddle. The firing slackened as he approached – no more than three or four men still in the fight, he guessed, all down to reloading their six-shooters.

He spotted the pack mules ahead and reined up hard. The beasts were standing by the side of the trail, looking around anxiously. Their heavy packs were intact, their lead rope snagged on a fallen limb. Next to them stood Will's buckskin mare, grazing calmly as revolvers cracked in the brush a hundred yards farther down the trail. Darcy swung down from his mount and drew his carbine from its scabbard.

He sprinted past the mules, crouching low as he struck up the trail. He could smell gunpowder now. He drew his six-shooter, ready to cut down the bushwhackers, but it was Will he saw first, partially hidden behind a stand of wild lilac. Will rose up, fired, and ducked down again. A shot from farther down the trail rang out, and Darcy heard the whine of a ricochet and saw a cloud of dust rise from the top of the big rock, where Will's head had been a half-second before. But Will was safely crouched down and hard at work reloading a second pistol. His motions were awkward, his left arm appeared all but useless.

"Will," Darcy called out. "It's me."

Will lifted his head, and the hard expression of his face transformed as Darcy sprinted forward, bent low.

"Good of you to drop by," said Will.

Darcy grabbed the pistol and powder flask from Will and set to work.

"Not at all," he said. "Just wanted to warn you that you might be ambushed by the scum that ran off after the fight."

"Thanks for the tip."

Another explosion from a heavy revolver, this time from above the trail. A shower of bark burst from the live oak trunk by Darcy's head.

"There's two of them left," said Will. "One above the trail, one below. They're working their way around to get a clean shot."

"What about our men?"

"All down."

Darcy drove home powder and ball into each cylinder and handed the revolver back to Will.

"How'd you ever reload with that wound?" he asked, nodding at the bright red stain on Will's coat.

"Slowly," said Will. "I'm right glad you showed up."

"You feel up to giving them a target?" Darcy picked up a stick, set his hat on top, and handed it to Will. Then he crept over to the side of the rock, his carbine at the ready. He nodded; Will lifted the hat into the air.

A pistol shot rang out, and hat and stick went flying. Darcy sprang up and fired into the thickest of the gun smoke. There was a piercing shriek and a loud oath. He dropped back down and whipped out a fresh cartridge from his ammo pouch.

"Nothing in the world more gratifying than the sound of vermin in pain," he muttered, dumping powder down the carbine's barrel. Will slumped down with his back against the rock. His face was deathly white.

"You're bleeding, Will."

"Just a ricochet."

"I'll take one more shot, then we'll fix you up..."

"Later."

"There won't be any *later* if you don't mind that wound."

"No time."

"Then get out of here! Your horse is down the trail aways, with the mules. If you head for Missouri House, Molly can hide you and stop up that hole in your chest."

"I'm not going without the gold," Will muttered.

"Suit yourself. I'll stay here and amuse our guests for as long as I can."

Will considered for a moment.

"I'll take the mules off the trail, straight down to the Greenhorn, and make for the Emigrant Trail and Marysville. Follow me when you shake off these bushwhackers."

"You won't make it by yourself, Will."

"Got to try. It's our only chance."

Darcy shrugged. "All right. Let's give 'em another dose. Think they'll fall for the hat again?"

"No. We'll use live bait. I'll take off for the mules on *three*." Will laid his pistols and ammo pouch on the ground.

"What are you doing?" asked Darcy.

"Thy need is greater than mine," said Will. He reached out his good hand, and Darcy shook it warmly.

Will sprang up and sprinted from tree to tree. Shots crashed out, and Darcy replied with a furious burst from his six-shooter. When the Colt was empty, Darcy crouched down and looked back along the trail.

Will was gone.

Chapter 39

Mary's Dilemma

November 1863

Mary reined up at the end of the road out of Walloupa. To turn south was to set off for Marysville and wait there for Darcy – a horrible prospect, offering nothing more than the assurance of a sleepless night. If, on the other hand, she turned north and followed Darcy, she would be riding into danger, but she could see for herself what was happening and apply her wits – which she trusted far more than his. The white mare fretted as her rider weighed the decision. Then Mary pointed the eager mare north, toward the Greenhorn crossing, and set her into a lope.

They passed You Bet without seeing a soul. Apart from the ravens and blue jays, who cried out at her approach, Mary heard no sound but the steady drumming of the mare's hooves – until a whip crack up ahead made her start. She set the mare at the bank of the road cut, soared over it, and clambered upslope to hide in a thick stand of manzanita.

Pounding hooves and the creak of springs. Another whip crack, loud as a pistol shot.

Through the leaves, she saw John Van Hagen, pitched forward in the driver's seat of a careening buggy. The soldier gripped the reins in one hand and a whip in the other, his face contorted as he flogged the galloping horse. Beside him sat Betsy Hardesty, clutching the dashboard, her face white with terror. The off-side wheel crashed into a root; Betsy screamed as she flew in the air. Van Hagen took no notice, but kept up his savage lashing as the buggy raced by in a roiling cloud of dust.

Van Hagen must have met Betsy on the road and commandeered her buggy. The ex-sheriff was minutes from Red Dog, where he could form a posse of miners in less time than it took to say, "Fabulous reward!"

Mary set the mare down the grade to Greenhorn crossing at a full gallop. The horse plunged down a long, sandy chute and splashed into the water, sending up jets of glistening spray. Then the world lurched and spun sideways, and Mary was choking and spluttering in the churning rapids.

She scrambled to her feet, clothes streaming, her boots slipping on moss-covered rocks as the mare rose beside her. She grabbed the horse's stirrup leather, and they staggered across the wide stream and onto the far bank. Mary gripped the saddle horn and started to haul herself up, but the mare shied away, stumbling badly.

Mary scrambled around the horse and ran her hands up and down the beast's right foreleg. The horse didn't flinch as Mary kneaded the bones around its fetlock – even allowed her to inspect hoof and shoe, which were intact. But the mare refused to put weight on the leg – a bruised foot, most likely, from a rock in the river.

Mary trudged up the steep road, leading the balky animal. The chill creek water in her clothes was soon replaced by streaming sweat. She heard a rumble of distant thunder and stopped to look at the sky. The cloud cover was high and light – no hint of a thunderhead. She stared upward, puzzled, until a staccato volley made her realize it was gunfire roiling the air. She feverishly cursed Will and Darcy.

What were they thinking of, starting a war in the Yankee-infested Northern Mines? *And how could I have been so completely simple as to not see through Darcy's behavior? Yes,* he wanted me to go away with him, but *no,* we couldn't ride off together. *Yes,* he would join me in the morning at Walloupa *– after* he had flung the match into the powder keg that will blow us both to Hell!

Panting with fury and exertion, Mary turned onto a narrow trail, following the freshly churned up tracks of many mules and horses. She stretched out her pace, making better time on the level path that wound around the mountain.

Another burst of gunfire echoed up and down the canyon, louder now. Through a gap in the brush, she saw movement far ahead. Someone was leaving the trail and plunging straight down the side of the canyon toward Green-horn Creek, with a pack train trailing behind. She could just make out a man in grey astride a buckskin horse. It was Will Stafford, riding alone down into the canyon with the gold – which meant the fire ahead came from Darcy.

How could Stafford be so craven as to run off when his friend was fight-ing for his life? *But no…that's nonsense. Will's nothing like a coward. There must be more going on than I realize…*

More pistol shots. She climbed into the saddle and viciously raked the mare's flanks with her spurs. The beast gamely attempted a jog, but soon fell back into a limping walk that no amount of abuse could shake her out of.

The road swung out along a spur on the mountain, and a break in the tree cover gave Mary a full view of the broad Greenhorn canyon. She saw Will and the mules on the far side now, winding their way toward the dark mouth of Missouri Canyon a half-mile downstream. Then she turned her gaze upstream – and cried out in horror. At the ford where she had fallen, a swarm of dark figures was charging through the water, sending up sheets of gleaming spray.

Trapped between a charging posse and a gunfight!

There wasn't a ghost of a chance of reaching Darcy before Van Hagen did. She sprang from the saddle and hauled the reluctant mare over the side of the road and down the treacherous slope, slipping and sliding toward the Greenhorn glinting far below.

Chapter 40

Return to Missouri Canyon

November 1863

If the buckskin mare had kept on walking, Will would have drifted away entirely. He had done so many times with the 6th Virginia, after days of chasing Yankee horsemen through the thick underbrush and swift-flowing fords of the river country, pressing onward by moonlight, with life or death hinging on who could stay in the saddle longest. The mortal fatigue was the same this time, but the burning ache in his shoulder added a new, nightmarish overtone.

The rocking stopped; Will opened his eyes. The horse was gathering herself to jump over a half-buried log, to get out of the stream and onto firmer footing. Will clutched at the saddle horn as she leapt, and searing pain tore through his chest. He gasped and swore as the mare steadied on higher ground.

A glance showed Will the mare had judged well: the stream was narrowing fast and filled with large rocks that could easily bruise her leg. The wide, flat gravel she had chosen was firm and unlikely to retain a track.

Will's mind, briefly roused by the pain, began to drift again as he crossed the hot gravel. He stared down at the broad, red stain on his coat and felt the sticky blood in his pant leg and boot. Darcy was right. There would be no Marysville escape for Will Stafford, no day and night in the saddle, dodging pursuit. He was exhausted. His only chance was to head up Missouri Canyon and try to reach Molly.

He let the mare choose her own path through the tumbled rocks that marked the mouth of the canyon. When she turned up Missouri Creek, Will set her in the water again and heard the mules splashing in after him. It was essential to leave no trail to Molly's door.

He clung to the saddle horn with his good hand, as the mare picked her way under the willows by the edge of the stream. The falls came into view at last, full and loud. Will stopped by the edge of the little pool where he had sung for Ida – how long ago? He lifted his canteen and poured water over his parched lips, remembering that dream-like day. It had been hot, and Ida had been cool and beautiful in the thin cotton dress that clung to her like a second skin. He hadn't taken the girl, who had as good as offered herself to him, but he had thoroughly enjoyed every stolen glance at her lovely body. He should have looked away, he supposed, but he was a gentleman, not a saint…

Will started to laugh, but stopped abruptly as an idea came to him. This pool was Ida's claim – had once overflowed with gold. *Why shouldn't it become rich again?* Yes! He would hide the gold behind the falls, where Ida had stolen her kiss! He would not show up on Molly's doorstep with a mule train full of Yankee gold.

Dismounting, he discovered, was a damned awkward thing when you can use only one hand and your chest is on fire. But it was child's play compared to untying the packs and fetching out the heavy sacks of gold, each of which had to be carried, one-armed, through the falls and stacked on the ledge inside. By the third bag, he was silently weeping from the pain in his shoulder, which was bleeding freely again. The job was beyond him.

Maybe caching the gold was crazy. Even if he hid it successfully, the infernal mules would follow him to Missouri House, for lack of anything better to do. If they didn't, they'd hang around the waterfall, braying out the location of the treasure. Will's thoughts collapsed into a jumble. He stood there, swaying in the water, defeated.

A voice came over the tumult of the falls, but he could not make out what it was saying. It was a high, male voice…solicitous…familiar…

"Wilum! Wilum!"

Will lifted his gaze to the top of the falls and saw Nutim. The boy was signaling by waving his bow back and forth. Will saw a look of alarm pass over his face, saw the youth scramble down the rocks and come splashing barefoot along the edge of the water. Then the lad was by his side, staring aghast at the curtain of red running down his uniform.

"You must come to the sand and sit down, Wilum. We must take off your coat and shirt so I can stop this blood."

Good idea, Will thought vaguely. It would be easier to think if he were sitting on the ground. He put his good arm over Nutim's shoulder and let the boy guide him to shore.

Chapter 41

Worries Enough

November 1863

Mary waited in the brush until she heard the posse gallop past her on the slope above. Then she scrambled out of her hiding place, dragging the mare by the reins. The canyon bottom was awash with tailings from hydraulic diggings upstream, and her smooth-soled riding boots skidded as she stumbled over the loose gravel. Then she was into the stream, where the current brought her down, battering her hands and knees. When she reached the far shore, she made for the cover of a willow break and paused, chest heaving, to take stock.

Van Hagen's rage had been palpable; she had never seen a man in such a murderous fury. If he caught up with her, he would drag her back to Nevada and hand her over to Frank – as publicly as possible. And there was a far more dangerous possibility: it would not take the ex-lawman long to trace her connection to Darcy.

Van Hagen won't see me as a runaway wife. He'll see me as a Rebel spy – a co-conspirator in a capital crime! My God, he'd love to be the one to tie my skirts together so they don't fly up when I drop from the gallows!

She had to get to Marysville, where she could escape in any direction by stage or riverboat. But to gain her freedom, she needed a fresh mount – and Missouri House was the only place she could hope to get one.

Her eyes narrowed as she imagined begging help from the Yankee mudsill who had beaten her in the contest for Will Stafford's affections. She writhed at the humiliation awaiting her. But between Van Hagen, Frank, and Molly Hatfield, the choice was simple enough...

An eruption of gunfire from the mountainside scattered Mary's thoughts: Van Hagen's posse slamming into whatever was left of the Confederate army in Northern California... *DARCY!...lost to me forever...*

Tears welled, and she bit her lip to keep them from falling. This was no time for mourning: a brutal hike to Missouri House lay before her and a posse of angry Yanks was close behind.

Once she was out of sight of Banner Mountain, she stopped to let the mare drink, and her own hunger and fatigue hit her with the force of a runaway stage. She led the balky animal up through a dense tangle of wild honeysuckle and madrone, until she found a hidden shelf on the side of the canyon. With the last of her strength, she lifted down the canvas bag of victuals and sank to the ground. She ate wolfishly, stuffing cheese and bread into her mouth until she almost choked.

She stretched out on the thick carpet of leaves and stared up through a maze of twisting branches at the sky, where the cloud cover was thinning and small patches of blue peeked out. Drowsiness overcame her; she was desperately tempted to drift off for a little nap – but it would not do. The sun was edging into the western half of the sky, and soon the Yankees would be swarming over these canyons, hunting for the gold. She slung the canvas sack onto the saddle horn, then leapt back as the outraged mare snapped at her hand. The horse's ears were laid back, her huge teeth bared.

"You devil," Mary hissed, raising her riding crop.

But the mare's interest in the dispute vanished. She swiveled her neck instead and lifted her quivering nostrils to the breeze. Mary caught a flash of movement in the distance – a figure on horseback, splashing down Missouri Creek, with a train of mules trailing behind. The rider was shirtless and nut brown, with long, black hair, and he was riding a buckskin horse. *Will's mare!* she thought, with a shudder, seeing an image of Will lying dead and scalped on the bank of the stream.

But this was no full-grown brave riding toward her, but a mere youngster. She recalled that Molly Hatfield had an Indian servant about that age – a boy with a curious name. Mary smiled wryly. *How perfectly like a Yankee to bemoan black slavery, then snap up an Indian orphan while they were so cheap on the market.*

She watched the youth slide from the saddle at the junction of the Green-horn and load the mules' packs with rocks. He remounted and led the animals out of the stream and onto a wet sand bar, leaving a spectacular set of prints heading south. Mary smiled. Unless she was badly mistaken, John Van Hagen and his posse had just been sent on a wild goose chase.

Mary and the white mare skittered down the steep slope to the trail by the creek, sending rocks clattering in their haste. Will Stafford must be just ahead, and Mary would not rest until she found him.

Chapter 42

Comrades in Arms

November 1863

Needle-edged oak leaves slashed Jake's face as he plunged through the brush. Rifles crackled on the slope above; lead hummed in the air around him.

He staggered into cover at the canyon bottom, gasping and swearing. The ball from Lieutenant Clayton's carbine had smashed a rib and torn through his arm, and the wound felt like a white-hot knife. His lips were split, two teeth were loose, and the rest of him felt like he'd been clubbed. He groaned as he sank back against a willow trunk. Dimly, he became aware that the gunfire had stopped.

Was Eldon shot dead...? Captured...? Or was he already swinging from a stout limb?

Jake's mouth was filled with the coppery taste of blood; his lips were parched and sticky. He groped for his canteen, but it was gone, torn away in his flight. Through a veil of willow leaves, he saw sunlight glinting on the river's surface, heard the rippling waves pouring over rocks. But thirty yards of open ground separated him from the cool drink he craved.

He cursed quietly, vehemently, as he weighed his terrible thirst against the prospect of a bullet in the back. Then he heard a crunch of gravel, and his hand flew to the revolver still miraculously wedged in his belt.

"Don't get trigger-happy, pard," came a low voice from the edge of the willow break.

"Eldon! Is that you?"

"'Course not. It's the Angel Gabriel, a-comin' for to carry you home.'"

"Jeezus! I thought they had you for shore."

"They wasn't interested in me. Nor you, neither, since they could have had you for the trouble of walkin' down the hill. No, Van Hagen's got his boys searchin' the road fer signs of the mules. I reckon he wants the gold a whole lot more than he wants a pair of bushwhackers."

"I don't blame him," muttered Jake. "I'm three-quarters dead already. Not much of a catch."

Eldon knelt down in front of his partner. Jake was a god-awful mess, with thick clots of blood drying in his beard and a fresh stream running down his side.

"How bad you hurt, Jake?"

The giant grunted.

"Clayton nicked me in the ribs, damn him… tore up my arm."

"Ball ain't inside, is it?"

"Hell, no. Like I said, he jist winged me."

"That's good."

Eldon offered his canteen and watched as his partner drank greedily.

"You can move, cain't you?"

"'Course I ken. Don't ask fool questions."

Eldon let out a grunt of relief. It was poor practice to leave badly wounded accomplices around – especially one whose testimony could hang a man a dozen times over. Dispatching Jake with a pistol shot would be risky, given their current neighbors, but going after him with a knife would be plain foolish, since the man was strong as a grizzly and twice as mean. Even shot to pieces, Jake Forrest would be a tough customer to finish off.

"Well," said Eldon, "best be gettin' on. These hills will be crawlin' with eager deputies, once word gets out there's a fortune on the loose."

Jake cursed as Eldon helped him to his feet. "Think our horses is still hitched back where we left 'em?" the giant croaked.

"We'll know soon enough," said Eldon. "If they are, we'd best head towards Nevada."

"*Nevada?* Did you get a ball through yore brains? What do we want to hole up in a Union town for?"

"'Cuz Van Hagen saw us when we took the gold. He knows who we are and where we're likely to run to. There's no headin' back to Grass Valley for us, an' you're too smashed up to hide out here. Nevada's close, an' no one will be lookin' for you under a pile of Yankees. You can hole up at Bob Hatcher's. He owns the Bed Rock Saloon."

"I know Hatcher. What are we runnin' to him for?"

"'Cuz he owes me money, and 'cuz he knows I'll cut his throat if he turns you in."

"Turns me in? What about you?"

"I'm goin' to track Stafford and the gold. He must have dropped off into Greenhorn Canyon." Eldon pulled a flask from his coat and offered it to Jake. "You wait outside Nevada till it's dark. Then slip into town and make for the back of the Bed Rock. Hatcher sleeps in a little room on the ground floor. Bob can hide you there till you're healed up."

Jake winced as he worked Eldon's whiskey gingerly around his bleeding mouth. He needed a real bed and soft vittles for a few days, and that was a fact. He'd barely be able to move tomorrow, once his body seized up from the beating he had taken plunging down the canyon wall.

"All right," Jake said, "but you come git me if you git so much as a whiff of that gold, you hear? That's more money than you and I seen in our whole lives, and I got a claim on it. And don't you worry about how I'm feelin' when you find it. I'll crawl out of my grave, if need be."

"All right then. You rest up. I'll do the scoutin'."

Jake snorted. "What kind of chance you think you got, if Van Hagen's got a whole army out lookin' for Stafford?"

"Not much. But I know one thing Van Hagen don't. Stafford's wounded. I could tell 'cuz of how long he took to reload. If the posse tears after him, thinking he's headed for Marysville, they might shoot right past him. And if Stafford does hole up in these parts, well, he's got a Yankee lady friend out at Missouri House who might figure in his plans. That's where I'll start lookin' if I lose his trail."

Chapter 43

A Big Time

November 1863

Nutim hung on to the saddle and let the buckskin mare carry him up the steep incline. He kept on singing the song he had made up to taunt Van Hagen and cloud the soldier's mind:

> *Us-hi-lo-ye, us-hi-lo-ye-no –*
> *Hi-tuk-tuk-no, tuk-no-yep!*

> *You've lost the scent again –*
> *Keep sniffing along like a dog!*

The three mules bounded up the hillside behind the mare, frisky without the weight of the stones in their packs. They were good, sure-footed mules, who had not slipped once since they left the river and ascended the secret trail that wound up the sheer canyon wall. Now at last they were out of the gorge and onto lush, sloping meadows where the surviving families of the local Maidu were camped. Chief Wemah had a new grandbaby, and the child had already survived sixteen days. Custom required a party – a *Big Time*.

As his saddle horse crested the ridge, Nutim saw the thin smoke of cooking fires rising against a sky clearing to pale blue. Clover and her playmates came running out to greet him. He coaxed his pack train into a trot to show off the fine animals.

Wokodot Tom, "captain" of the tribe that once lived along Wolf Creek, ambled up to greet him. Tom looked over the tall buckskin mare and patted her forequarters, visibly impressed.

"Sit down here with us, young man, and tell how you have come to visit in such a splendid manner." Tom waved him toward the men folk, who were gathered under a brush arbor. Wemah was there, his white hair cut short because so many of his relatives had died. Some of the men wore *wólekim* hats, the brims pulled low over their faces. A few of the younger men wore their hair gathered into woven string nets that would anchor their feather headbands and ornaments in the dancing later on.

They reclined on spread-out blankets, watching the women gamble. "When one side loses, they will serve us some food," Captain Tom explained. He offered Nutim his tobacco pouch and a charred wooden pipe. "My tobacco is strong, my young friend. Do you wish to smoke?"

Nutim felt pleased to be treated like a grown-up. He leaned back on his elbow and allowed Tom to light the pipe for him. The tobacco made him dizzy.

"I have come to ask my relative, the head man, Yeponi Wemah, for a favor," Nutim said, after what he hoped was a dignified pause. "I have brought him gifts." The men nodded their approval.

"You all know me. I was born near here, at *Sumú*, on Sugar Pine Mountain. When I was a little boy, the soldiers came. My mother hid me in the brush to save my life. My mother and father died on the long walk to Nome Lackee. I was left alone. The mountain spirits helped me and caused the good *wólem kulem* to find me. Now I stay with her, between the two streams, where the red newts come in springtime." The men grunted, *"Heu."* They all knew the place.

"Many gold-catching men are camped at that spot now," Wemah said. "It is not safe for you to live there."

"Yes, *yeponi*, it is dangerous, but my white mother has power over the palefaced men." The men hummed in assent. There were many interesting stories about this woman.

"Isn't she married to the *wólem* who lives in the cabin at Storms' Ranch?" asked Uncle Yoso.

"Yes, Stafford is the husband of the wagon road house."

"There are two white women there, at the place where the wagons stop. Are both of them his?" Captain Tom asked.

Nutim shrugged. "I think that may be so."

"But why would a man live so far from his wives?"

Nutim hadn't really considered the question before. "Maybe because the mother is grouchy and the daughter is headstrong."

"*The mother?*" cried Yoso. "You mean he has married that woman *and* her daughter?" Yoso tapped his forehead and looked wryly at Captain Tom. "No wonder he sleeps far away. These whites are very foolish."

"I have come to tell you about this man," Nutim said. "He is in trouble."

"*Hes weh!*" The old men snorted. "It's his own fault."

"It isn't woman troubles. He has been hurt." The men fell silent. Their eyes drifted back to the women's game.

"Tell us how this came to be," Wemah requested politely of Nutim.

Nutim counted silently to five, then began his story in the modest third person.

"Nutim went hunting in the canyon. He was following the tracks of *Kapa Kulem,* the Grizzly Bear Woman. By the creek he saw Water Dipper bird flying about and crying for help.

"'*Hesadom maka,* Water Dipper bird?' he asked. 'What's the matter?'

"'Someone has moved in under my waterfall! I cannot get to my nest!'

"'I will help you,' Nutim said, and he crept up to the waterfall to see who was frightening Water Dipper. There he saw a man carrying heavy bags. It was his *wólem* father, Stafford. The man was hurt. Blood dripped down, making his shirt red. The man staggered as he carried the bags into the water.

"Nutim stepped out from his hiding place. '*Hesadom bey?*' he asked Stafford. 'Whatever are you doing? Why are you putting those heavy bags in the cave behind the waterfall?'

"'I have made war on the blue soldiers and taken their gold,' Stafford said. 'My wound hurts me, and I cannot go farther. I must store this treasure and go to the wagon road house and hide there. The soldiers are angry, for I have killed many of them. They will hunt me and kill me.'

"'I know what to do.' Nutim said. 'I will play a trick on Van Hagen. I will make a false trail, and he will follow me far away from here. You have been kind to my aunties and uncles who live at Storms' Rancho. They will help you now by eating these delicious mules.'"

Wemah looked at Nutim sternly. "Are the soldiers following you?" he asked. "You know how gold makes the whites act crazy! Van Hagen must not come here looking for your *wólem* friend! Evil will befall us!"

"Nothing bad will happen, *yeponi*," Nutim assured him. "These mules had plenty of rocks in their saddlebags to make their tracks clear and deep. I rode down the river past our trail, then unloaded the mules and backtracked in the water. And I brushed out all the tracks where I turned up the mountain. Van Hagen will never find our secret trail, for it is hidden in the live oak thicket. He will ride all the way to Johnson's Rancho before he knows he has been tricked!"

The men laughed with pleasure at the joke played on Van Hagen. Wemah spoke a quiet word to the man seated next to him, who rose and walked off toward one of the cooking fires. Soon a group of old women and little children came and led away the mules and the saddle horse.

"You are a clever one, my young friend," said Wemah, "but take my advice. Don't tell anyone else this story, not even your white mother. Whoever knows about that gold is in great danger. Keep it a secret. Do you understand?"

The other men voiced their agreement. "Listen to the *yeponi*, youngster," Captain Tom said. "Gold is nothing but coyote piss, it means bad luck and sorrow for us."

Nutim was suddenly afraid for Ida and Molly. They would be questioned and watched by whoever was hunting for the stolen gold. He needed to get back to Missouri House right away.

Wemah looked into Nutim's troubled face and patted the boy's shoulder.

"Our *yomi* here is a singing shaman, a real old-time doctor. He never eats meat or salt, so spirits obey him. He will blow smoke and ashes toward the wagon road house to protect your friends."

Nutim cast a worried look toward the shaman, who sat apart from the others, stern and proud, wrapped in a bearskin. Shamans were known to be touchy. He had heard of one killing a boy who farted in his presence. There was more to being a *yomi* than just curing. Sometimes they were hired as avengers, to kill with secret poisons they shot into your body with their magical left hands. Once a shaman pursued you, you were doomed, unless he died first. There were stories of entire families wiped out because of duels between shamans.

Wemah studied Nutim's expression. "I will speak to the doctor myself," the old man said, "and pay his fee. You have done well, young man. Stay with us now, and eat. Then you may go back to your white family."

Nutim swelled with pride. He could see Clover beside one of the fires, helping to cook acorn soup, carefully stirring the hot rocks in the basket to keep the boiling mush from scorching. In only one or two more years, when the spring flowers bloomed, she would become a woman. There would be a Big Time, and after the dancing, he would come and make his bed beside her shelter. She would say, "Why are you sleeping out there? There is plenty of room inside."

He wanted to jump up and dance, sing and shout! Instead he forced himself to sit still and dignified.

"It is good, *yeponi*," he said, his face impassive. "I will eat with you. Then I will go help my friends."

Chapter 44

Dreams

November 1863

Mary found Will sitting with his back against a tree, a quarter-mile above the waterfall. His head lolled back, and his bloody, unbuttoned coat was draped over his shoulders. His shirt had been torn into strips and wrapped tightly around his chest and shoulder.

"Will…Will, honey…can you hear me?"

She uncorked her canteen and wetted the handkerchief she pulled from her coat.

"Here," she said, gently dabbing his face, "this will feel good."

He opened his eyes and looked at her.

"Mary…" he murmured, "…dreaming?"

"You're not dreaming, Will. It's me. These clothes are a disguise. I'm leaving Frank."

She could not tell if he followed her words.

"I'm heading for Missouri House," she said. "Is that where you're going?"

"Molly…" he murmured.

"Do you want me to tell Molly you're here?"

Will smiled. Then his eyelids drooped.

Mary gazed over his deathly pale face and blood-soaked uniform. It was stained all the way down to his boots. She put her hand on his good arm and gave it a gentle squeeze.

"Will, darlin', you hid that Yankee gold, didn't you?"

He moaned.

"Can you tell me where it is?"

No answer.

"Will, I know you're tired, but you've got to help me. Darcy needs to know where the gold is."

At the mention of Darcy's name, Will struggled to open his eyes.

"He's fine, Will, but he's tied up right now. You have to tell me where the gold is, so I can tell him."

Will mumbled something indistinct.

"What did you say?"

"Ida's claim..." he murmured, "...rich as Croesus..."

"Try and make sense, Will. You don't want the Yankees to find that gold, do you?"

She could see his lips move. She bent close and heard him whisper, "Ida... dividend." Then he drifted away.

∾

Mary struggled up the steep trail, gasping for breath and cursing the blisters on her feet. She had walked for what seemed an eternity today, and there was plenty of hard climbing ahead to get out of Missouri Canyon. Once she reached the ridge, though, she would haul herself up on the mare, and it would not be far to Missouri House. She needed to sort out her thinking before she got there.

Will had understood that she was talking about the gold – that much was clear. But she could make no sense of his reference to *Ida's claim*. He must have been in some private world, and from the look of him, he might not come back.

But Will wasn't the only one who knew where the gold was. Molly's Digger Indian servant knew about it, too. That much was obvious, since Will could not have unloaded the mules by himself. The boy had taken the pack train down Greenhorn Canyon, laying a false trail for the Yankees. He would return to Missouri House, and Mary resolved to be there waiting for him, ready to extract his secret before he could tell anyone else. But how? How could she get the boy to confide in her, and her alone?

What about an offer to buy him from Molly and set him free?

Yes, that sounded promising. She could offer the boy his freedom and a pile of gold on one hand, or a trip to jail as an accomplice to armed robbery and murder on the other. That would get his attention. If she played her cards right, she could probably get him to pack the gold out of Nevada County for her.

Her heart began to race with excitement. *Hundreds of pounds of Yankee gold for the taking!* She could set herself up like a queen in the Sandwich Islands. There was a colony of Americans on Oahu; life would prove mighty pleasant there for a woman possessed of a small fortune. She would play the part of a wealthy widow, and neither Frank's malice nor Abe Lincoln's could touch her in the sovereign Kingdom of Hawai'i.

Then the radiant vision faded. If Will Stafford succeeded in reaching Missouri House, he would see to it the treasure got to Marysville – where some other Confederate "patriot" would snap it up for himself!

Would Will get to Molly's on his own? He was hovering at the edge of eternity, but Death was capricious. If Molly learned where Will was, she might raise him from the dead once again.

Mary tugged on the mare's reins and quickened her pace. There was no telling how the hand would play out after she reached Missouri House. She would need all her luck – and then some – to win.

⌁

"Are you all right?" Ida's voice was edged with concern. She raced down the porch steps to the traveler, who was swaying atop a white mare.

"Mrs. Dunn?" cried Ida, astonished. Mary slid out of the saddle. Ida put her arm around Mary's waist and supported her up the stairs and across the porch. As the girl pushed open the front door, Mary grabbed her wrist.

"Who's here?" Mary gasped. "I mustn't be seen."

"No one – apart from the help."

"Good. I need to talk to your mother."

"She's not here. Come in, Mrs. Dunn. Let's get you off your feet."

Mary cried out through clenched teeth as she sagged onto the settee in the parlor. She leaned forward and reached for her boot.

"Let me do that," said Ida, kneeling down and cradling the boot in her arms. As she drew it off, she heard a low moan of sympathy from behind her.

Esmeralda was standing in the doorway, staring wide-eyed at Mary's bloody stocking, then at her masculine attire.

"I will bring warm water and towels, *señorita* Ida. And the medicine kit." Esmeralda spun around and disappeared.

Ida peeled off the stocking and let the foot down gently.

"Where's Molly?" Mary gasped.

Ida ignored the question. She frowned with concentration as she drew off the second boot and sock. Then she lifted her gaze and stared straight into Mary's eyes.

"You know, don't you?"

"Know what?"

"About the raid…the gunfight."

Mary hesitated, then said, "As it happens, I do."

Ida's eyes glazed with tears, but she kept them fixed on Mary. "We heard about it from a militiaman who tore through here on his way to Dutch Flat. He hollered out as he rode through…that…that Will Stafford…"

Ida's voice gave way. She knelt there, straight-backed, fighting the howl of misery rising inside her.

"Is that why Molly isn't here?" Mary asked. "She hasn't gone to look for him, has she? The hills will be swarming with trigger-happy deputies."

Ida shook her head. "She's gone to You Bet, trying to get a straight story out of someone. She doesn't believe that…" Ida's voice faltered.

"…that Will Stafford could be such an almighty fool," snapped Mary. "Well, he could. I have it on good authority."

"How do you know?"

"I was in the midst of running away with Mr. Clayton when he informed me that he and Will had a little business to tend to for Jefferson Davis."

Ida stared at her in amazement. Mary waited for some reaction from the girl – a sniff of Yankee piety – but it did not come. Instead, Ida reached for the brandy decanter on the end table and poured a stiff drink.

"Where's Mr. Clayton?" she asked, handing Mary the tumbler.

"Killed or captured."

"What about Will? Do you know *anything*?"

Mary stared at the lovely young face, contorted now with fear. Tears welled in the girl's eyes, but she returned Mary's gaze without flinching.

"You love him..." Mary murmured, before realizing she was voicing the thought aloud.

Ida said nothing, and Mary blushed. Her comment was impertinent; the girl was right to ignore it.

Mary clutched her drink, her heart and mind in disarray. The girl's obvious passion for Will Stafford moved her, despite herself. *Will might be a fool,* she thought, *but he's a well-bred Southern fool, who doesn't deserve to die in the dirt.*

Trying desperately not to think of the fortune she was throwing away, Mary took a scorching mouthful of brandy and braced herself for her descent into good works.

"Will's on the trail leading out of Missouri Canyon..."

Ida's eyes grew wide. The color drained from her face.

"...and he's been shot."

Ida sprang up and tore the medicine kit from Esmeralda's arms. A moment later, Mary heard the front door slam.

Chapter 45

The Wanderer

November 1863

W ill lay in the shadow land between waking and dreaming, just as he had during his long bouts of camp fever. This time, he had pictured himself talking to Mary Dunn, though why she had appeared in his dream dressed in Frank's clothes, he could not imagine. It did not matter, though. Hallucinations didn't have to make sense.

He lay on his side at the edge of the trail, his head resting on his good arm. He took a slow breath, not too deep. He didn't want to worsen the pain in his chest. The light from the bright sky hurt his eyes, and he closed them, grateful for the soothing darkness.

He had no idea how much time passed before he heard the music. The song might have been a dream, or everything in his life before might have been a dream – he could not tell. The baritone voice was magically pure – the most beautiful voice he had ever heard. A thrill of joy shot through him as he recognized *"Der Wanderer,"* the song Kessel had worked so hard to make him understand.

He had felt nothing but sorrow in the song when Kessel first played it for him. Later, after Peter had translated the lyrics, he had been surprised by the calm, confident words, so much at odds with the music. But now, the voice floating through the air brought out clearly the inner joy Peter had insisted was there.

The singer was closer now. Will heard the lyrics perfectly, the German transparent to him. *Wähle keine Heimat nicht,* urged the angelic voice. "Choose no homeland whatsoever."

But how could a Stafford do that? Did nine generations buried in Virginia's clay count for nothing?

The melody rose and fell, by turns confident, wistful, reassuring. Will had never heard such singing before, never imagined it possible.

> *Fort zu andern*
> *Sollst du wechseln, sollst du wandern,*
> *Leicht entfliehend jeder Klage.*
>
> *Away to the other,*
> *You should change, you should wander,*
> *Lightly fleeing every woe.*

No, the song was not mournful. It was tender and clear-eyed. The music and words were one, and the world they created was hopeful.

"*Und die Welt erscheint mir gut,*" continued the radiant voice. "And the world seems good to me..."

Yes, that was the meaning in the heart of the music – transcendence of a world filled with sorrow. He must tell Peter he understood now...

The voice strode confidently into the last line of the song, deep in the bass register, then soared and arched gently downward again as it faded away, leaving the last words dissolving like mist in the air:

> *Froh umgeben, doch alleine.*
> *Surrounded by joy, but alone.*

Will smiled as he imagined Ida and Molly's faces as he explained this to them. *They would be so pleased!*

But first he must rest.

It felt so very good to rest...

~

Ida saw Will lying by the side of the path and hurried forward, her breath coming in shallow sobs, her eyes fixed on the back of his coat and the brown curls tumbling over its collar.

She knelt down and saw that his eyes were closed, his face relaxed. She laid her hand on his cheek. It was warm, and for a second, she allowed herself to hope. She moved her fingertips down and gently pressed the side of his neck.

There was no pulse.

She screamed and grabbed Will, shaking him and calling his name. Then she wept, rocking him in her arms, until grief overpowered her and she sank to the ground beside him. She laid her head on his outstretched arm, and put her hand on his cheek.

"*I love you so much,*" she whispered. "*Please hear me, Will! I love you.*"

She closed her eyes and memories whirled in her head: Will bringing in the stage on the day they met…Will singing in her imaginary theater by the creek…their kiss by the waterfall…*the happiest moment of my life!*

She remembered their waltz at the Union Ball, Will's strong arms around her…and how they had kept circling as the orchestra fell silent.

Why didn't Will just hold me when the music stopped? I could have stayed in his arms forever…

She lay still for an uncertain time, until she became conscious of the hard clay beneath her hip. As she struggled to her feet, her skirt felt wet and heavy. Lying so close to Will had soaked her in blood.

She stared at his dark-stained uniform, realizing for the first time that it *was* a uniform. For a moment, it puzzled her. *Uniforms were supposed to be blue. What was Will doing in grey?* And then she remembered the war – the insane and pointless war that had reached across the continent and struck down the man she loved.

Anger exploded inside her – anger at Forbes, who, she now realized, had goaded Will to his death. Anger at Lincoln, whose mystical visions of Union had turned the country into a slaughterhouse. Anger at the slave-holding Secesh, who had torn the country apart.

And she ached with sorrow that Will had not loved her enough to turn his back on that mad dance of death.

She looked at Will's face, and her reproaches died within her, replaced by a hot rush of shame at her unkindness. Will had loved her – and her mother, too – with an open and generous heart. She knew that now, without jealousy. It was himself he hadn't loved enough. He had sacrificed his life for a cause that meant nothing at all to her.

A feeling of infinite weariness stole over her. Nothing mattered – not even this respite from unendurable pain…

Nepenthe - that's what Will would say it was – another one of those six-bit words he used to roll out, as if everyone had studied Greek at their mother's knee. Well, I know now – thanks to you, Will – that nepenthe is what those old pagans drank to forget their sorrows… Just as I know there isn't enough of it in the world to make me forget how much I love you.

She knelt again and gently kissed his forehead, then began the long walk back to Missouri House. Later, she had no recollection of the rest of that day – apart from the look on her mother's face, and the animal cry Molly made when she learned why her daughter's dress was soaked in blood.

Chapter 46

The Wólem Shaman

November 1863

The night had been clear and cool. All along Missouri House ridge, oaks spread their yellow leaves to the morning sun. A late bounty of acorns loosened and rattled down, to the delight of the flickers, who scooped them up and packed them into the bark of an old pine snag.

Nutim stopped to drink from the wooden pipe that fed clear spring water into the horse trough. He washed his hands and face and splashed cold water over his head. His legs ached and his stomach complained angrily that it was empty. He hoped Esmeralda had the pancake griddle hot.

Stafford might already be here, hidden somewhere. If not, he would take Molly to Missouri Canyon right away. If she asked questions, he would evade them. He would not speak of the waterfall or the mules, or of his visit to the tribe.

He hurried inside to find Molly. She wasn't in the office or the kitchen – just Esmeralda, busy at the stove. He ran back down the hall and noticed the parlor door ajar. The heavy curtains were drawn and a candle burned low, dripping wax on the marble tabletop. Molly was on the sofa, her face hidden in her arms. A pine coffin lay across three chairs in the middle of the room. He took a step closer and saw Wilum, his head resting on a satin pillow, face pale and eyes closed, as if asleep.

Nutim's heart began pounding wildly. He slipped silently outdoors and ran full-tilt until he flopped down in the dust by the steps to the tack room, where *Wépam,* his yellow hound dog, liked to sleep. He wanted to hold him and tell him about this awful thing that had happened.

Tears filled Nutim's eyes. He had never imagined that Wilum might die. He should have saved Wilum, somehow. What could he say to Molly and Ida? He sobbed aloud, tears streaming down his face.

"He was your friend, wasn't he?"

It was a female voice, close by, low and musical.

Nutim wiped his eyes with his fists. The face looking down at him was white and translucent, with the delicate features of a woman. The clothing, though, was that of a rich white man: a brown *wólekim* hat, a soft coat and silky tie. Pale yellow gloves disguised the hands, and ragged house slippers hid the feet. *Where could this creature have come from so suddenly? Is it shifting from a man's form to a woman's?*

The odd being sat down beside Nutim and put a gloved hand on his shoulder to prevent him from getting up. Nutim shrank from the touch. *Is it a white shaman?* He had never heard of such a thing before, but the *wólem* were full of unpleasant surprises.

"Don't be afraid. I am William's friend, too," the creature said sweetly. "He told me I could trust you. He wants you to help me carry out his last wish: that I take the gold to Jefferson Davis, to buy guns for the South." The lustrous brown eyes searched his face. "And you will come with me," it said softly. "I will take you away from here."

Nutim pushed his toes into the dirt, wishing roots would grow from them, so the shape-shifter couldn't tear him loose from the soil of Missouri House. His heart was racing again. *How did it find me? How does it talk to Wilum?*

The mysterious being spoke again in a soothing tone.

"That's what William wants. He wants you to help me, and he wants me to buy you from Molly Hatfield and set you *free!*"

The chill of fear knotted Nutim's stomach. *It is lying. Wilum knows how much I love Ida and Molly. This is a cunning shaman, hired to get the treasure back. Yeponi Wemah was right! The stolen gold is already making trouble!*

"Show me where the gold is," the *wólem* shaman said, "and you will never be a servant again!" The dark eyes flashed with eagerness.

Nutim shook his head, his voice paralyzed with fright. *What sort of sha-man is this? How does it kill?* He watched, transfixed with fear, as it ran its fingers over the heavy gold chain that hung from its vest pocket. *Watch that dangerous left hand! Don't let it shoot poison into you, like a Maidu* yomi *does.*

"You are in more danger than you realize," said the soft voice, taking on an edge of menace. "You helped Will Stafford hide that gold. In the eyes of the law, that makes you guilty, too." The magician paused to let this thought sink in, while it slowly peeled off its yellow gloves, revealing pale fingers and long white nails. It pointed at him.

"If Van Hagen finds you, he will force you to show him where the gold is hidden, and then he will *hang* you." The eyes flashed. "But you can trust me." The creature turned its body toward him, reaching out to pet his hair.

Nutim hit the dirt and rolled away. He scrambled under the corner of the tack room and scurried away on his elbows and knees. He scuffled out into daylight on the far side and sprinted into the woods. He looked back to see if the shaman was after him. He saw it hobbling back toward Missouri House.

Its feet must be changing. Now is my chance to get away!

He followed a deer trail through the woods to his secret lodge in Missouri Canyon, loping across the open hillside, rustling the dry, papery leaves of *töm bakum* and stirring up their musky odor. He would sleep in his bark house tonight. Perhaps a dream would come to help him.

Chapter 47

Repercussions

November 1863

Sgt. Van Hagen halted the mounted patrol in front of Missouri House with a wave of his gauntlet. The riders' horses were blown; foam dripped from their bridle bits.

Molly heard him barking orders as he dismounted. Two troopers rode toward the horse stalls, roiling up dust. Through the side window, she saw another pair circle toward the back of the house, trampling her chrysanthemum beds. Van Hagen tossed his horse's reins to a dusty soldier and dashed up the front steps.

Molly stood up from her desk, still holding her pen. She stepped into the hall as Van Hagen's tall frame darkened the doorway. He seized her by the shoulders and shook her.

"Tell me you didn't know about it, Molly. Swear to me you weren't in on it! By God, if I thought for one minute…"

Molly wrenched herself from his grip and backed up into the office. He followed her, his voice ringing through the house.

"They're saying Frank Dunn's wife was involved. She's here, isn't she? Frank's mare is in your stable. Don't lie to me, Molly. If I find out that you…" His expression changed from outrage to dismay. "My God, Molly, you, of all people…"

Her eyes stung with tears. How could she tell the truth? *I thought Will moved out because he didn't want me? I was so blinded by my own heartache, I couldn't see what he was up to?*

She wanted to feel insulted by Van Hagen's accusations, but all she felt was despair. Her fingers couldn't hold the pen. It clattered to the floor, spraying drops of ink across the carpet.

"I didn't know, John," she said bitterly. "I was blind – stupid and blind." She let herself down onto her chair. "And Mary Dunn's gone," she added in a hollow voice. "I have no idea where…"

Van Hagen paced back and forth, struggling against his fury.

"You could be arrested this minute, Molly! I could take all of you into custody right now as conspirators…"

His voice seemed to recede behind the thoughts swirling in Molly's brain. *Will must have known I'd be suspected! He shielded me by staying away, by not even saying goodbye. He kept me in the dark, just like when he left for Virginia… Damn him! He threw it all away!*

Van Hagen slapped his glove on the edge of the desk. "You're not listening to me! Seventy-five thousand dollars in gold is missing, and folks in *both* towns think you know where it is!"

"And what do you think, John?"

He leaned toward her, pressing his knuckles into her desk blotter.

"What I believe is beside the point. *Your life is in danger!* And if you think I'm here to protect you, think again! I'm taking my patrol back to Nevada tonight to try to keep the town from blowing up."

"What are you talking about?"

He straightened up, the muscles in his neck and jaw rigid.

"For God's sake, Molly, the situation's just shy of panic! The *Journal* is predicting more Rebel attacks, and the cellar of the courthouse is being provisioned for a siege. Gareth Truesdale's father is savage as a meat axe. He's ready to ride full chisel against Grass Valley and burn out the Secesh!" Van Hagen took his hat off and wiped his brow with his shirtsleeve. He sank into the empty chair at Ida's desk.

"Poor little Dora Caldwell is prostrated," he continued, "and her mother's draped the whole town in black. Amanda's collecting subscription money for a memorial service for 'Our Fallen Rifles.' We're going to bury six of our boys on the same day! I don't know if Sheriff Knowlton has a plan to keep the crowd under control, or if he strictly wants to. Nevada wants vengeance.

Clayton will hang for sure, right after the funeral." He rotated his hat, pinching the brim, sickened by the thought of the lynch mob in action.

"How was Mary Dunn involved?" Molly asked.

"We don't know yet. She's disappeared off the map. If you know where she is, Molly, you can pass along a word of advice: anybody who knows anything about that gold better *watch their back*.

"Jake Forrest and Eldon Whitley were part of Stafford's gang, and they're still at large. They're the slime that murdered that Wells Fargo messenger, MacAdams, on Steephollow Grade. They're the worst of the worst."

"My God, John! You don't believe Will threw in with those murderers, do you? How could he? He fought them off and saved Henry!"

"That was three years gone by, Molly. They all rode together this time, according to Clayton's story. Right after Stafford took the gold from us, Forrest and Whitley tried to take it from him – and gave him his death wound."

Molly felt dizzy; her stomach rose as she heard herself speaking to Will long ago. *'Our road agents are enterprising – and given to revenge.'*

"If those two haven't found the gold already," Van Hagen continued, "you can bet they'll be hunting for Mrs. Dunn. And they'll be watching you and Ida. If you don't lead them to the loot soon, they'll get impatient. So lock your doors and don't go out by yourself – not even to the outhouse! *Do you hear me?*"

Molly sank her head in her hands. Van Hagen got up and started pacing again.

"Look, Molly, I know you set store by Stafford. But I'll say it straight: he got what he asked for. Nobody around here wants the kind of bloodletting that's going on back East. If he needed to play Sir Lancelot, he should have stayed in Virginia. Out here, what he did is called armed robbery and murder, and we cure that kind of behavior with a rope!" He turned, and the fallen pen cracked under his heel.

"Oh…*Jesus Christ!*" Van Hagen kicked the pen aside and strode from the office. Through the open parlor door, he caught a glimpse of the coffin and the flicker of a candle. He heaved the front door open and stomped down the steps, his spurs ringing against the planks.

Molly watched him ride off at the head of the patrol, the last trooper in line leading Frank Dunn's white mare. She ran to the kitchen, where Esmeralda was scouring her frying pans.

"Where's Ida?" Molly asked.

"She left an hour ago for her waterfall, the place she calls her claim."

"And Nutim? Have you seen him?"

"No." Esmeralda shook her head. "I felt sure he would come back this morning for breakfast, but he didn't come."

"Where's Pedro?"

"Gone to Red Dog with Mr. Johnson."

"I'm going after Ida." Molly said. "You stay put. Close the office and lock up in front. Latch the side doors. Keep a gun handy and don't let any strangers in."

Molly pulled down the shotgun from the gun case in the office and checked the caps. Then she slipped across the road and plunged into the cover of the young fir trees behind the watering trough.

Chapter 48

The Return of the Waryer

November 1863

It was a hunting vision that came to Nutim in the night, after he cried himself to sleep over Wilum. The dream was always the same. It started with the sudden, tingling knowledge that something was watching him as he stood in the forest. Then faint sounds grew louder and louder: heavy footfalls drumming down the mountain toward him, the snorting, rattling breath of a giant beast and the whip crack sounds of thrashing, snapping brush. He could feel the heat of the huge body hurtling past him, unseen except for the violent perturbation of the forest. Then quiet…a cool wind…perfect calm.

Nutim awoke in amazement, drenched in sweat. Before now, he had always invited the hunting dream, but tonight it had come unbidden, like a command. He clutched at the *ohmeikum* hung around his neck in a doeskin bag and asked the spirit in the stone if today was the day.

~

He waited for Grizzly Bear Woman as she came down Missouri Canyon. He had been stalking her for almost a month, getting to know her. Lately, the big sow liked to leave her den on Chalk Bluff Mountain in the afternoon and forage her way down to Missouri Creek for a long drink of clear water. Yesterday, he had discovered a deer carcass she had stashed in a drift of fallen leaves near the waterfall. She was on her way to visit it again.

He crouched under a thick manzanita clump and peeked out at the huge bear as she ambled across open ground. In the slanting sunlight, her undercoat was bright orange-red, and her heavily muscled shoulders rippled under her hide. She lay down on her back in a little swale in the clearing, scratching her hump against the earth and waving her toes in the air. She looked silly, like a kitten playing, but Nutim knew it was only one of Grizzly Bear Woman's clever tricks, meant to lure a foolish deer into coming too close.

Old Lucy told stories of long-ago hunters who had killed a grizzly single-handed. And *Kapa Hembo,* Bear Killer, had done it, of course. He had driven three arrows into the bear's heart, standing so close to the beast that his forehead was ripped open by a swipe of its claws. The old man still carried the scars.

Only men of consequence, like Bear Killer, possessed a grizzly pelt nowadays. The skin conferred courage and strength to the owner. It could even enable a shaman to shift shape from man to bear and back again. The skin of this bear would be Nutim's wedding present to Clover, and they would sleep snug and warm on it when winter snows came down.

He had been preparing for this hunt for many seasons. His free time had been devoted to learning from Uncle Yoso, who had consented to teach him. Nutim had sacrificed his greatest pleasures: lazy summer afternoons at the swimming hole and reading adventure stories by the stack.

Instead, under Yoso's careful eye, he had chosen a yew sapling as big around as his two hands could circle and split out a wide, clear stave. This he shaped and shaved with an obsidian knife. He heated and bent the bow into a wide flat curve, and held it to dry between forked branches set firmly into the ground.

He had dried and pounded the long back and leg tendons of four buck deer, and separated the fibrous sinew into small bundles of fine threads. He had saturated them with warm glue made of boiled hide scrapings, and had laminated them onto the back and sides of the bow with a smoothing tool of bone. He staggered the courses, creating a thin, dense layer that grew in strength for weeks as it dried and seasoned, infusing the weapon with the spring of a leaping stag.

For his feathered arrow shafts, Nutim had chosen *soksokotu,* the spice bush whose scent he loved. It grew in shady streambeds and had a pithy stem, just right for hollowing out a socket to receive a hardwood fore-shaft tipped with *boso* – obsidian from the sacred West Mountain. He had trimmed hawk feathers and wrapped them to the shafts with the finest, thinnest sinew fibers. Then he had painted both parts of each arrow with his personal design of red and black bands.

Grizzly Bear Woman was close now, just out of sight on the other side of the thicket. He could smell her scent, sweet like the *chitukam* grass when it starts to dry in autumn, along with a sinister whiff of something decayed she had been rolling in. He could hear her ripping apart a rotten stump to look for insects. Discarded chunks of punky wood rolled down the slope and vanished off the edge. Nutim tested the direction of the breeze to be sure she could not catch his scent. He stood motionless, listening to the bear snuffling as she ate.

Across the canyon, he saw a figure in skirts moving through the brush. Molly Hatfield, shotgun under her arm, was striding down the path to the waterfall. The grizzly snorted at her approach and took off uphill, galloping up the steep slope with uncanny ease and vanishing in the dark timber near the ridge.

He saw the hem of Molly's skirt rip on a bramble vine, saw her boot toe catch on a rock, watched her stumble and fall to one knee, then rise up, moving even faster – fear and urgency in every movement. He started running along the hillside, keeping Molly in sight on the opposite side of the creek. Where the trail began its final zigzag down to the streambed, she abandoned the track and ran straight down the steep incline, digging her boot heels into the ground with every step, plowing furrows in the earth.

Breathless, Nutim reached the jumble of boulders at the head of the falls. He crawled between two of them to get a look at the swimming hole below. On the little beach at the end of the pool, he saw Ida struggling with a tall white man. The *wóle* was leaning on Ida, pinning her hard against a rock outcrop and holding her wrists to keep her from clawing his face. Heart pounding, Nutim drew an arrow from his quiver.

Molly skidded down to the beach and staggered when her boots hit the deep, dry sand.

"Damn you, I'll blow your brains out," she cried, raising the shotgun and charging toward the struggling figures.

The *wóle* looked around at Molly in surprise. Ida broke free from his grip and flattened herself on the ground, but before Molly could get off a shot, the *wóle* threw himself down on top of Ida and drew his pistol. Molly hit the dirt. Ida rolled from under the man as he fired, spoiling his aim, and the bullet whined off the face of the falls, just under Nutim's hiding place. Quick as a snake, the *wóle* grabbed Ida and stood up, dragging her to her feet in front of him.

Molly raised up on her elbows, her gun pointed at the man's pock-marked face – but Ida's neck was caught under the man's arm in a stranglehold. Ida's horror-struck eyes were fixed on the wide black bore of Molly's scattergun.

"Let her go, you son of a bitch," Molly yelled.

The outlaw took slow aim at Molly with his revolver.

"Say your prayers, whore," he snarled. "I'm gonna do you a favor. You won't have to watch what happens to your little gal."

"Be good to me, Luck-Giver," Nutim whispered, as he pulled the bowstring back to his shoulder and let fly. The arrow hissed through the air.

The white man stared in astonishment at the feathered stump sticking out of his belly. Then he squinted in Nutim's direction, bewildered, seeing nothing. The pistol dropped from his hand and he grabbed the arrow butt, gasping.

Ida tore her head from under the man's arm and dived for the pistol. She swooped it up and ran to her mother. Molly seized Ida's outstretched hand and they scrambled for shelter behind the rocks. The outlaw sank down to the sand, scuffling his feet in agony.

Nutim scrambled down from the falls and sprinted along the beach, waving his bow and calling to Molly.

"Mother, it is I, *Nutim!"* He ran to her, tears streaming down his face.

Molly wrapped one arm around the boy and crushed Ida to her with the other. She held them both, and they huddled together behind the rock. They could hear the outlaw moaning and the gravel crunching beneath his boots as he struggled with death. Ida tried to tear away. "Let me go, Mama, I'll shoot him and it will be over."

"No!" said Molly, recoiling at the thought of Ida killing the man. "Stay where you are."

All three were crying. Molly found a handkerchief in her pocket. She wiped Nutim's face and kissed his eyes and forehead. She cradled Ida's head against her shoulder and smoothed her daughter's dark curls.

The terrible noises finally stopped. Nutim slipped from Molly's embrace and cautiously returned to the beach. The *wóle* was dead, sprawled on his back, mouth open, vacant eyes staring at the sky. Nutim put his foot on the man's belly and grabbed the arrow butt with both hands. He jerked the feathered half of the shaft out of the wound, leaving the fore-shaft and arrowhead still embedded. He looked up to see Ida and Molly peering around the rocks.

"Help me roll him over!" he called.

Nutim tugged at the dead man's arm. Ida pulled and Molly shoved until the body flopped over. The obsidian point stuck out the back of the blood-sodden shirt.

Nutim wrapped Molly's cotton handkerchief around the sharp arrowhead and grasped the point just under its flanges. He yanked the rest of the arrow from the flesh and waded into the stream to wash the blood away.

Molly pointed her shotgun at the dead man, the barrel almost touching the dark wound. "Stand back, Ida," she ordered.

Ida gasped and clutched at her mother's arm. "There's no need, Mama. He's dead!"

"Yes there is!" Molly jerked free of Ida's grip. "What do you think will happen if a white man is found dead of an arrow wound?" Molly's arms trembled with the weight of the gun. "There'll be Hell to pay!"

"Wait, Mother. I know what to do," said Nutim. "There will be no trouble when I am done. You and Ida go back to Missouri House now."

"What are you going to do with him?" Molly asked. "Boil him for glue?"

Nutim pointed to the huge bear tracks in the wet sand by the water's edge.

"I will ask Grizzly Bear Woman to help us."

~

The cached deer carcass was still hidden where Nutim had seen it the night before. It was easy to drag it downhill to the swimming hole, leaving a powerful scent trail. He draped the half-eaten carcass across the dead outlaw. Nutim stood up and faced the mountaintop where he had last seen the bear.

"Here is a meal for you, Grizzly Bear Woman. Come and eat! This *wóle* was evil, but his flesh will make good food. You will grow fat and sleepy, and your cubs will be born in the winter den. Do this for me, Bear Mother, and I will hunt you no more. We will be friends."

Nutim broke off a manzanita branch for a broom and carefully brushed out all the tracks, except the bear's and the man's.

Chapter 49

Nothing New at All

November 1863

Pedro smoothed his slicked-down hair, ran his thumbs under the edge of his finest red sash, and adjusted the revolver and Bowie knife tucked inside. "Have you loaded your *pistolas, pequeño?*" he asked Nutim. "*Bueno,* give them to me, and I will show you how to wear them."

Pedro tested the feel of the heavy derringers in his hands. They were handsome weapons, excellently crafted.

"*¡Qué guapo estás!*" said Pedro, wedging the pistols into Nutim's black silk cummerbund. "Now, when *los pinches yanquis* come to arrest us, we can fight back and prove that we are the true *Californios!*"

Nutim's voice cracked with anxiety. "Why should they arrest us?"

"Because they are beasts. They think we have hidden the gold in the coffin of *el señor Estaffor,* and they will spoil the funeral and dishonor the corpse. And when they do not find the treasure, they will take us to jail and beat us until we tell where it is hidden. Those *yanqui* devils want that gold back more than they want to go to Heaven!"

"It is true the *yanqui wólem* are crazy for the gold," Nutim said. "They hired a shaman to help them find it."

"*Un brujo?* A *witch?*" gasped Pedro, crossing himself. "How do you know this?"

"I talked to it here – on this spot! It appeared out of nowhere, the day after Wilum was shot, and it wanted to know about the gold."

Pedro frowned and fished a bottle from a hiding place under the tack room steps. He uncorked it and took a hearty slug of wine.

"Are you sure it was a witch?"

"Well, it was changing from a man to woman. And it claimed it could talk to Wilum, even though he was dead…but I think it was lying about that."

The boys fell silent. Nutim sat with his head hung down, his whole body filled with dread. It was only a matter of time until the *wólem* shaman carried out its threats. *It will betray me to Van Hagen, and he will hang me…or sell me as a slave!*

"*¡Sé valiente!*" said Pedro, shaking Nutim's shoulder. "Where is my brave friend of yesterday who killed the black-hearted desperado? Maybe this witch isn't very clever…maybe it has sent the *yanquis* off to chase the wild goose. Then, while Van Hagen is looking in the wrong place, we will look in the right one!"

Nutim scowled at Pedro. "Didn't you hear your mother tell us to stay home?"

"I heard her say we should stick together. That is very good advice, and we will follow it. Together, we will find the treasure. Think of it, *pequeño!* Five thousand dollars reward! We will be rich as princes, and buy our mothers jewels and furs. They will be proud to have such sharp-witted sons!"

~

In front of Missouri House, Daisy and Incitatus, washed and brushed to perfection, stood proudly in their traces. Mr. Johnson sat tall and straight at the lines, his rifle in its scabbard, hanging from the dash. The homemade coffin on the buckboard was wreathed in evergreen boughs and the last brave blooms from Molly's yellow rosebush.

Two black geldings with matching white stockings were hitched to the rockaway coach, whose wheels were painted black for the occasion. Molly slipped the office shotgun into the scabbard mount and handed Ida her little Manton pistol. "Put this in your pocket, dear," Molly said, and they climbed aboard.

"*Ándale,*" said Pedro, and the team set off, following Will's casket on the buckboard north, up the long, winding road to the cemetery hill – a funeral procession of two lonesome vehicles and six mourners, armed to the teeth.

Cemetery Lane circled high up on a narrow track to the burying ground at the top. Nutim jumped out in front of the wrought iron archway, opened the gate, and held it wide while the horses pulled through.

He lingered, gazing at the panorama that opened from the hilltop. To the northeast, he saw the sun lighting up the distant Chalks Bluffs. To the west, he saw the steep side of Banner Mountain rising, clad in golden leaves, and glimpsed the red clay bed of the Nevada road winding along the slope. He spotted a mountain stage rolling down to Greenhorn crossing, filled with black-coated, black-hatted men and bristling with guns. Behind him, he heard Mr. Johnson say in a grim voice, "Looks like we've got company, Mrs. Hatfield."

Nutim's heart sank.

These must be the yanqui wólem, *come to arrest me. But what if Molly doesn't give me up? What if there is a gun battle?*

His pulse began to race. The day of reckoning he had secretly longed for was at hand. Today he would take revenge on the *wólem* for their brutality to his people, for the murder of his mother and father. With Zeke's derringers, he could kill two *yanquis* and take their weapons...then kill some more...

But what if someone gets shot because of me! He suddenly pictured Van Hagen's six-gun roaring and Molly crumpling to the ground. A wave of blind panic swept over him.

I must run away! But if I run to Wemah's camp, Van Hagen will follow me, and more of my people will die!

He grasped his lucky stone in its pouch, begging for a sign. He heard Wind Man singing in the huge pines that towered over the graveyard. "Ooooh," Wind Man moaned, "oooooh, oooooh." Nutim felt a chill run down the back of his neck.

Wilum's ghost might be nearby, blowing about and crying! Ghosts were extremely dangerous – even those of loved ones. *If Wilum's spirit speaks to me, I will die.*

He gritted his teeth, forcing himself to think calmly.

There is nothing to fear. Wilum's ghost has already gone on. He would not hang back, hesitating to make the journey to Epinim Koyo. *He is already walking through fields of flowers, on his way to the Valley Above.*

Down in the canyon, the stage was splashing across the ford.

*It will be here soon, but I will not run! I will be strong-hearted – like Wilum!
– and face this danger!*

He ran to the buckboard and took his place beside Molly, who stood in
front of the coffin with a shotgun cradled in her arms. Behind her, Mr. Johnson and Pedro trained their guns on Cemetery Lane.

Nutim listened to the harness bells jingling as the stage crested the rise.
He saw Molly stiffen her grip on the gun. "Damn them," she murmured,
"won't they let us bury him in peace?"

Nutim drew the derringers from his waistband as armed men poured
out of the coach and massed silently in the road. A grey-bearded man strode
through the group.

"Oh my God!" Molly cried. "It's *Henry!*"

Henry Bachelder uncovered his silvering locks as he approached, and
almost as one, the armed men behind him swept off their hats.

"Missus Hatfield," said Henry, "the Nevada Chapter of *E Clampus Vitus*
would like to offer our services as pallbearers on this sad occasion."

Molly wiped away her tears, unable to speak. Behind Henry, a young
priest stood smoothing his white surplice and straightening his purple bene-
diction stole. He cleared his throat and spoke in a clear tenor.

"My name is Dunbar Chapin, ma'am," he said. "I'm the new curate at Emmanuel Episcopal in Grass Valley." The priest held up his *Book of Common
Prayer* by way of proof.

"Yes, I've heard of you," Molly said.

"I've come on my own initiative, ma'am, to say the words over the departed,
if you will allow me… He attended my church…" Chapin looked gravely at
Molly's shotgun and said nothing more.

"I'd be grateful, Father." She motioned the way to the mound of freshly
dug earth. Father Chapin led the way with his open book, while six Clampers
followed with Will's coffin on their shoulders.

"'I am the resurrection and the life…'"

The Missouri House delegation stood beside the grave. Molly reached for
Ida's hand and held it. Ida could feel the pulse of her mother's heart.

"'Thou knowest, Lord, the secrets of our hearts…' said Father Chapin.
"'Suffer us not, at our last hour…to fall from Thee…'"

When the priest closed his book and the coffin was gently lowered, Henry Bachelder stepped forward. He gripped his old bowler hat in his hands and began to speak.

"The passage of a man's life is a mysterious thing…where we come from…where we go. So far, there's been a wealth of speculation on the subject, but few first-hand reports sent back from the other side."

Henry cleared his throat and continued in a stronger voice.

"When a young man first climbs up on the box and takes the ribbons in his hands, he thinks he's the king of the road. But pretty soon he learns that the road holds a different view of the matter. It's got countless twists and turns waiting for him…and washouts and storms…and nights so black that all you have to steer by is the sound of your own wheels on the track.

"Now, I've traveled a few rough stretches in my time, but I've never seen a road as cruel as the one Will Stafford faced when the war came. Some may disagree with the route he took, but there's no one can say he didn't choose his path by the best of his lights…which is all a mortal can do.

"Will was a brave and kind-hearted man, and I'm proud to have known him."

Henry stooped and picked up a handful of earth. "Goodbye, my friend," he murmured, as the dirt slipped through his fingers and rattled on the coffin lid. When he spoke again, his voice was raspy and ready to break.

"*Padre*…ladies…as the departed was a soldier, we should give him a soldier's send-off." He turned to Molly. "Will you join in the salute? We'll fire at my signal."

Henry swung his sawed-off shotgun to his shoulder and took aim at a cloud. All the Clampers stepped forward and followed suit. Ida, Nutim, and Pedro drew their pistols, and Mr. Johnson and Molly raised their shotguns. Esmeralda covered her ears, while the priest bravely resisted the urge to do the same.

"Ready…*fire*."

The earsplitting salvo rang off Banner Mountain and echoed out over the diggings. A pungent cloud of gun smoke swirled over Will's grave, then lifted lazily and wafted toward the blue mountains in the north.

∾

Ida left the crowd at the graveside and walked slowly to the wagon. She wrapped her arms around Daisy's warm neck and buried her sobs in the old horse's mane.

"Ida, *chère*, don't cry so," said Lavender LeJeune. She dabbed at Ida's wet face with a lace handkerchief. "I regret I did not come sooner, but I have so much work...so much to do, sewing clothes for all the viewings and the funerals. I have been stitching black dresses all night by lamplight..."

"Don't apologize, Lavender," said Ida, taking her old friend's arm in hers. They set off together down the path that wound through the graveyard. "I'm awfully glad you came. There aren't a lot of folks who made the effort. You'd think we had whooping cough, the way they're staying away."

"Not all your friends forsake you. Dora Caldwell sends you this note." The seamstress drew a sealed letter from her reticule and handed it to Ida, who pocketed it without comment. She had already received one letter from Dora – a stream of bitter reproach – and was in no mood for another.

"How are the Caldwells?" Ida asked in a flat voice.

Lavender sighed.

"*Désolés*. The poor Judge steals off to the garden to weep for Monsieur Stafford..."

"That's hokum!" Ida snapped. "He didn't even come to Will's funeral..."

"Ida, do not be so hasty to condemn. Can't you see? Madame would not let him come here on the day before Gareth Truesdale is buried. She is near collapse!"

Ida said nothing, but Lavender saw the skepticism in her expression.

"The Judge's grief is real, *ma chère*. Mr. William was the son he never had." The seamstress stopped and gently turned Ida so they stood face to face. "Mr. William was a good man, a true friend to you and your *maman*, and to the Judge."

An awful ache welled up inside Ida. She turned away to hide her face.

"*Oui, chère*," said Lavender, "when you have lived as long as I, you will know how rare such a man is. So sad, so sad. Bad enough to lose a dear friend from sickness or accident, but to see him throw his life away... *Mon Dieu, quelle folie!*"

"Will hated the war, Lavender, but he felt he had to fight. He was defending his people and his homeland of Virginia."

The seamstress searched Ida's face.

"And tell me, child, what he was defending Virginia from?"

"Why, from the Northerners, of course."

"*Bien sûr*. But those Northerners, why did they want to attack Virginia?"

"To take away her rights."

"Ah, I see. And what rights would those be?"

"Well…," said Ida. She could tell where the conversation was going, and in loyalty to Will, tried to head it off. "…the rights her sovereignty entitles her to."

"Like, perhaps, the right of rich white folks to own slaves? That does seem to be the right the Secesh worry about most."

"And what of it?" said Ida. "That's not a crime…"

"Oh, yes it is! Not in the eyes of white folks, perhaps, but in the eyes of God, it's the worst crime there is."

Ida stopped and stared at the seamstress.

"How can you say that, Lavender? There's lots of things worse than…"

"No, Ida, there's *no* crime worse than slavery – 'cause all the other crimes are wrapped up inside, like leaves in a cabbage. Kidnap, rape, torture, murder…they're all in there, hot from the fires of Hell!"

Ida dropped the seamstress's arm.

"Shame on you, Lavender! You know Will would never condone any of those things, not ever, not for *anybody*, black or white!"

"Of course not. Mr. William was a kind man. I don't doubt the colored servants in his family were well treated."

"Then how can you say such things?"

"'Cause you don't have to be a good man like Mr. William to own slaves. All you have to be is white. And if you are, no one will say *boo* if you buy a slave girl and rape her every night of the week. You could be poxed up one side and down the other…"

"*I don't believe that any man…*"

"Doesn't matter what you believe, *chère*, because you know nothing about it. Have you ever even *seen* a slave?"

"I've seen colored folk who might have been slaves…"

"Well, I've seen slaves, child. Lots and lots of them – like my own *grand-mère,* who was fifteen when her massah gave her a baby. And believe me, she didn't ask for it!"

Ida shrank back from Lavender, who seemed to have grown taller in her anger.

"I'm sorry, Lavender. I don't hold with slavery – it's wicked. I just don't think that's why Will fought."

"That's not why he *thought* he fought, but his fighting makes it possible for slavery to go on and on. *Écoute-moi, chérie:* I don't give a bent needle for Virginia's rights – just as she cares not a straw for mine."

The two women stared at each other. Ida's eyes welled with tears, and her lips began to quiver. Lavender pulled her close.

"I don't mean to talk against Mr. William. He was a dear, kind man. He just happened to die for a bad cause. There is nothing new in that. Nothing new at all."

Chapter 50

Ah Tie's Story

November 1863

Big golden leaves came twirling down from the canyon maples and spread a glowing carpet across the white clay roadbed, as Ah Tie strolled down the Chalk Bluff Road toward Missouri House. A cool breeze rippled through the gold and silver willows along the drainage cuts. Across the diggings, he could see the stand of tall oaks around Missouri House turning orange and red, and the bright yellow Tree of Heaven grove surrounding Sam Gee's house.

The golden trees made Ah Tie think of his first autumn in the mines. That year the changing leaves had brought him a lucky turn of fortune. On the "played-out" placer claim he had purchased with the last of his savings, he unearthed a rich pocket of coarse gold, a hatful of smooth, glossy nuggets the size and shape of pumpkin seeds. After that, each time the leaves turned to gold, his riches had increased – until this fall. Today the golden leaves mocked him: where was his stolen gold?

This robbery had struck him with astonishment. That Will Stafford had appropriated the Lucky Stars' gold in an audacious raid in the name of the Confederate States of America might have been amusing, had the losses not been so staggering and the death toll so pitiful. There were many sorrowing mothers and fathers among the white families in Nevada and Grass Valley. The outrage in both towns was terrible. He had warned his miners and Sam Gee's gardeners to stay home and keep to themselves – the fury of the whites might be taken out on the Chinese, even though they were the victims, not the perpetrators, of the misfortune.

He was sorry for the death of Stafford. He had admired the man for his fairness and cleverness, and was grateful for his advocacy against Jonas Clench. Ah Tie had to smile: it was oddly satisfying that Clench's Jehoshaphat mine had lost even more gold in the robbery than the Lucky Stars.

Often, when Stafford came to You Bet to consult on legal affairs, he would stay to drink tea. Then they would laugh and talk about home and family, or sit in silence listening to the steady beat of the Lucky Stars' stamp mills – like an army of dragons roaring in the hills, shaking the earth. He would miss Stafford's easy companionship, his humorous observations on human nature.

Ah Tie had enjoyed translating poems for him – Stafford had especially liked the ancient patriotic verses by Lu Yu. "For My Son" was his favorite:

> *When dead and gone one finally knows the vanity of all things,*
> *But I still regret that I won't see the realm reunited.*
> *When our armies recover the Central Plain to the North,*
> *In the family devotions, don't forget to let your father know.*

Ah Tie pitied the Missouri House ladies. They would be grieving over the loss of their friend. Maybe one of them had a deeper sadness. Had Stafford been the lover of either woman? Everyone had expected him to marry the mother – she was rich and beautiful. Perhaps the man had preferred the daughter. The young lady had admirable qualities. He had been touched by her friendship when she came to his defense at the Bomb Day parade. She certainly had courage and a fierce love of justice. What a pity these auspicious traits had not been invested in a son!

He wondered if Stafford's death might have converted the Hatfield women into revolutionaries. It was just such bitter feeling that had caused the rebellion of his ancestors. His was the eighth generation to swear revenge for those who had died at the hands of the evil Manchu usurpers. Did he hope to see his sons take the same vow?

No, he hoped his children would prosper here. He had already written his wishes and instructions. He would be buried on this very mountain, with his feet toward the Steep Hollow water. He did not want his bones dug up and sent back to Kwangtung. His family's bones would rest here also. Here their leaves would fall and enrich the ground for their children's children.

~

The door to Missouri House stood open, propped with a crock full of rust-red chrysanthemums. He could hear someone playing the piano. Mrs. Hatfield came to the door, and Ah Tie swept off his hat.

"I am come to pay respect. I, also, am grieved by this death. Please accept this gift. In China it is custom to bring sweetness to banish sorrow."

"How kind of you," Molly said, as she accepted the hexagonal paper box of candy. "Please step inside, my friend, and join us." She took his hat and showed him to a chair by the parlor window, next to the table where her red geraniums bloomed in the afternoon sunshine.

Henry Bachelder was playing host with a dish towel tied around his middle for an apron. He handed Ah Tie a tumbler with two fingers of brandy and offered a tray of cigars. Ah Tie took a polite sip of the brandy and set it aside. He accepted a cigar, trimmed the end with a tiny penknife attached to his watch chain, and held it to his lips for Henry to light. Ah Tie sat dignified and erect on the edge of the chair, one plump hand resting on his knee.

Ida Hatfield came out of the kitchen with a teapot on a tray. She caught sight of Ah Tie and her expression changed from wistfulness to alarm. She stopped stock-still and stared.

"Yes, Miss Ida," he said. "No pigtail! I have cut my hair as the *Californians* do." He ruffled his bristly scalp and laughed. "I do not wish to return to China. My home is here, in You Bet." Ah Tie motioned to the chair beside his. "Will you sit down with me?"

Ida slid her tea tray onto the buffet table and took the chair next to Ah Tie.

"The music is beautiful," Ah Tie said, nodding toward the piano. "This man is an artist." Peter Kessel was playing "The Battle Cry of Freedom" in a slow tempo that made it seem almost a hymn.

"Yes, and he is a very good teacher," Ida said. "I hope to take lessons with him someday."

"That is a good wish." Ah Tie said. "We Chinese say music is like the wind, when it blows over the water and dissolves the waves into foam and mist. It softens the anger and pain in our hearts." He noticed the tears forming in Ida's dark blue eyes.

"I have a small gift for you, a distraction," he said swiftly. "It is a Chinese custom. Will you allow me?" He drew a narrow box from the inside breast pocket of his coat and presented it to Ida with both hands.

The box was thin, patterned cardboard. Inside was a smooth wooden case, and inside the case, a fan. Its sticks were carved from scented sandalwood, its red silk was gilded along the edge. Ida opened it gently. The artist had painted a branch hung with golden persimmons, arching over a tiny landscape of green mountains, with a foaming white waterfall pouring into a blue lake. In the still water of the foreground, two lovers drifted in a tiny boat. The lady held a parasol over her shoulder. The man played an instrument like a long-necked banjo.

"It is so lovely, Ah Tie! Does it tell a story?" Ida asked.

"Well, it is a painting of a real place, near where I was born. It is called the Yellow Fruit Tree Waterfall, and there are legends about it, of course. Many people come to see it, for it is the largest waterfall in all China! There are beautiful gardens there, and one path leads behind the falls, through a grotto filled with blue light. The water nymphs are said to live there and hold revels on summer nights."

Ida gazed at the fan, her mind far away. It was summer, and she was looking out through the waterfall in Missouri Canyon. Will's hands were on her waist, and he was smiling at her. Then a shadow crossed his face, and she wanted desperately to cheer him up…

She blinked her eyes and stared at Ah Tie. The fan trembled in her hand. She leaned close to him and spoke in a whisper.

"I think I know where your gold is!"

Chapter 51

A Token of Madame's Esteem

November 1863

Jed Woodson hated jail duty, with its endless, wearing routine and depressing company – drunks and lunatics, for the most part – two-legged skunks that made a man want a bath and change of clothes after being in the same room with them. But with his sciatica, there was nothing else for Jed in the law enforcement line – or any other, for that matter. Besides, the job gave him a steady living, which was more than mining ever had, and even had a few good points. In summer, the sheriff's cool, dark brick office offered shelter from the scorching heat. In winter, a pot-bellied stove kept the front room cozy, so the only time he shivered was when he went back to check the prisoners, which wasn't often. Packed with pillows from the cots in the cells, the sheriff's swivel chair was almost comfortable, and there was always a yellow-covered novel or two in the desk drawer, along with a pack of cards for solitaire.

Unfortunately, the deuce of hearts had been missing from this deck for a week now. If the damn card didn't show up soon, he'd to have to head down to the Empire Games of Chance for a new deck. *Christ, they might even charge me for it!* That's how low his status in the sheriff's office had fallen these days…

A knock on the door roused Jed from these unhappy thoughts. He slipped his revolver into his belt and rose gingerly to his feet, wincing at the wicked twinge in his hip. He shuffled across the room, peered through the peephole, and threw back the bolt.

There was no doubt about the profession of the young woman standing in the doorway. The blazing rouge on her cheeks and her startlingly low-cut neckline both proclaimed her a "daughter of joy," as the French miners put it. What amazed Jed, however – what struck him dumb – was the prettiness of the face beneath the paint and powder. Whores he had known by the score, both in his professional capacity as a lawman and in his private recreations as a citizen, but he had never yet met one with truly beautiful features.

"Aren't you going to ask a lady in?" asked the visitor in a coquettish drawl, batting her eyelashes at him.

"Uh...sure...come on in, miss."

Woodson goggled at the whore's swaying hips as she swept past him in a cloud of perfume.

"I'm Jenny Mae," said the vision, offering him her hand. She pinioned the deputy with a glowing smile. "Madame Bonhore sent me to see the poor prisoner who is bound for the gallows."

"Only prisoner I have..." Woodson mumbled, "...is that Rebel...Clayton..."

"Why, that's the man!" cried Jenny. She reached into her shoulder bag and drew out an elegant silver flask. "Madame B would like to see he gets this comfort for his final hours."

"I'm sorry, miss," Woodson murmured, "but it's against..."

"Of course, Madame wouldn't *think* of giving a prisoner such a gift without paying tribute to the brave gentleman guarding him." Jenny fetched out another flask, identical to the first. "Do take it, sir," she whispered confidentially. "It would be a shame to waste fine brandy."

Woodson hesitated, then reached for the shiny flask. "Well, I don't see what harm it could do," he mumbled.

"And there's another gift from Madame for the prisoner, which I have to give him myself. It is of a most private nature."

Jenny's soft, silvery laugh rippled through the dingy jail as she drew a wooden token from her cleavage and held it just above the exposed mounds of her flesh. Woodson leaned forward and saw the outline of a shapely woman, quite naked, carved on the chip and colored in with meticulous attention to detail.

Woodson's mouth went dry.

"Of course," Jenny said, "what's good for the prisoner is good for the keep-er." She pressed the token into Woodson's palm, which had extended almost involuntarily to receive it. She ran her fingertips up the inside of his wrist and caressed the soft skin there. "When you come to redeem it, honey, be sure to ask for Jenny," she breathed.

Woodson opened his mouth, but finding nothing at all coming out, closed it. He cleared his throat and tried again.

"I'm sorry, miss. But I don't think I can..."

"Of course you can, darlin'. All I'm asking for is a few little minutes alone with the prisoner to...relay Madame Bonhore's best wishes. Surely he is allowed visitors."

"Yes, miss, but...the door between the office and the cells has to stay open, and visitors ain't allowed in the cells themselves."

"Well, now," said Jenny Mae with a knowing wink, "that does limit the con-solation I can offer Mr. Clayton. But I expect we can get along well enough. And then – if you like – I could give you a chance to redeem that lucky chip, right here and now."

She stepped close and looked up into his eyes. Her sweet perfume swirled around him.

The deputy lurched to the desk and snatched up the key ring from the top drawer. With trembling hands, he unlocked the door to the cell corridor and turned to usher Jenny in.

"Don't make a sound," said Jenny Mae, cocking two heavy-caliber der-ringers.

The jailer turned white and began to back up.

"That's it. Now hand that key ring to Mr. Clayton and sit down on the floor – with your hands above your head."

Woodson dropped to the floor. Darcy grabbed the keys and began trying them in the door of his cell.

"By God!" said Darcy, as the lock turned on his cell door. "You do look fetching in that rig, my dear."

"Why, thank you, Mr. Clayton. Another compliment like that and I shall have to award you a token, too."

"Darlin', may I ask for enough of your petticoat to bind our deputy, here?"

"I will not harm a thread of this lovely outfit," she replied loftily. "But perhaps these will do just as well." She hoisted a pair of manacles from the peg by the door. Darcy tore off Woodson's shirtsleeve and gagged him. Then he swung the deputy's hands through the cell bars and snapped on the cuffs. Mary retreated to the office, where she shimmied out of her extra skirt and petticoat and unpinned a deep hem stuffed with garments.

"Thank Heaven," she said. "I could hardly move. Darcy dear, I'm afraid you cannot wear that uniform. The town is swarming with militia. Here is everything you need to transform yourself into an ungainly lady of the evening."

Darcy laughed. "Won't they stare just as much at the tallest whore in North America?"

"Not if you slouch properly. I have a buggy waiting down Coyote Street. We can hide most of you under the lap rug."

Mary inspected the fully transformed Darcy by the light of the grimy, barred window. The wide flare of crinoline beneath his dress gave him ample room to bend his knees. On the other hand, the blond stubble sprouting on his chin was a dead giveaway.

"Forgive me, Darcy, for this horrible sunbonnet," said Mary, reaching up on tiptoe to position the head covering bedecked with frills and silk flowers. "Hopelessly *outré*, but the more shadow we cast on your face, the better. And here is a veil. Bend down and I'll arrange it."

"Where do y'all park your weapons in this rig?" asked Darcy, searching in vain for a place to hide the deputy's .44-caliber six-shooter in the folds of his feminine apparel.

"A derringer fits nicely in a jacket pocket," Mary said, handing him one of hers, "and usually suffices, if you shoot straight. If you wish to bring that cannon along, we'll have to tie it under your petticoat."

~

There wasn't a soul on Court Street to wonder at Darcy's bent-kneed duckwalk as they made their way along the creaking boardwalk. They turned down Coyote Street – and almost collided with a wild-looking man in a seedy black coat, with black britches and boots. Darcy edged back and lowered his head to hide his face, while Mary and the man in black eyed each other warily.

"You are *Jezebel!*" the man cried, drawing a worn Bible from his coat, a mad gleam in his eyes. "The woman of sin! Cast off your wicked ways, I say! Repent...*or perish!*"

Mary's hand clenched instinctively around the handle of an imaginary riding crop.

"Cease that detestable prating, sir, and step aside," she hissed.

The man appeared to swell beneath his ill-fitting clothes, and a look of malignant triumph lit his sallow face. He crossed his arms and spread his feet, blocking the narrow boardwalk.

"YOU CANNOT HIDE FROM THE LORD ON JUDGMENT DAY," he declaimed in a roar to make sinners tremble. "NOR CAN YOU HIDE FROM HIS SERVANTS HERE ON EARTH!"

Mary shot a glance behind to check her line of retreat – and saw two boys poking their heads out of the dry goods store, eyes wide.

"Look'ee here, Pa!" sang out one of them. "Hellfire Bob's gone and found himself some more ladies!"

Mary slipped her hand into her jacket and drew out her derringer. Shielding it from the view of the children, she turned swiftly back to Black Coat.

"I advise you to stand clear this instant," she said coolly. "I have no notion of being persecuted by a lunatic."

The man's eyes opened wide as he stared at the gun pointed at his belly. Then he flung both hands in the air and lifted his gaze to heaven.

"THE LORD SCOURGETH EVERY SON WHOM HE RECEIVETH!" The man looked down at Mary, a glint of mad satisfaction in his eye. "Go ahead, vixen...shoot! I have no fear of suffering!"

Mary stared at him in disbelief for a moment. Then, with a shrug, she drew back the hammer. Black Coat lifted his eyes to heaven once more.

"Repent for your soul's sake, woman," he intoned. "REFUSE NOT HIM THAT SPEAKETH..."

Footsteps creaked on the boardwalk behind her. Ahead, store doors jingled as clerks and customers poured out to watch the fun. Mary uncocked the derringer and slipped it back into her pocket.

"Last time Bob went after a troupe of sportin' gals," came a reedy voice behind her, "they'd just bought a new pair of fire tongs. Doc Hunt used a whole spool of thread sewing him up!"

Darcy had been poised to spring on the man if Mary's derringer did not make him back off. But now, with a crowd gathering, he could only look to his defenses. Could the veil possibly disguise him at this range? He seized Mary's waist and drew her to him, burying his face in her shoulder and letting out a high, theatrical moan that made her cringe.

"Look!" cried a grizzled teamster, who had drawn up his wagon to enjoy the proceedings. "He's got one of 'em crying already!"

A sympathetic murmur rose from the crowd, which included a pair of prostitutes. *"For shame!"* cried one. *"Brute!"* cried the other. Darcy howled in acknowledgment of their support.

"Sophie, dear," said Mary through gritted teeth, "there's *no need to carry on so..."*

But Darcy, encouraged by the response from the working girls, loosed a volley of sobs and moans that rose steadily in pitch and volume.

It was badly done. Darcy's attempts at female impersonation were contemptible, even by the abject standards of a gold camp. Mary patted Darcy's broad, muscular shoulders and scanned the crowd, braced to meet suspicion, disbelief – even outrage. To her amazement, she saw nothing but concern, shot through with anger at her tormentor, who was still holding forth with eyes uplifted and arms outstretched.

"Hark ye, sinners...*I SHAKE NOT THE EARTH ONLY, BUT ALSO HEAVEN...*"

"Shove off, Bob," cried a lanky miner, shaking his fist. "Them girls has got as good a right to the street as you."

"*...FOR OUR GOD IS A CONSUMING FIRE...*"

"Better stow it, Hellfire," shouted an amused militiaman, leaning on his rifle. "Give it up before the ladies get mad."

"There, there," crooned Mary to Darcy, as she desperately surveyed the scene. There *had* to be an opening – some way to extricate themselves...

An enormous man wearing a buckskin jacket and the blue denim pants of a miner stood behind Hellfire Bob. The giant's hairy face had not known a razor for years, but the eyes above the tangled beard were kind – and fixed on Darcy with rapt attention.

"Poor Sophie has such delicate nerves," said Mary, gently rocking Darcy from side to side. She lifted her face to the colossal miner's and wiped away a tear. "Such an angel…not an unkind bone in her body."

There was a rustle in the miner's beard. His mouth turning down? And surely that was a frown of concern on his brow. Mary gazed soulfully into the giant's eyes as she improvised.

"But Madame caught her last night not charging one of the customers and beat her horribly… Her poor face…"

At this, Darcy started in again with his wretched noises. Mary slid her hand up under the veil, located his windpipe, and squeezed.

"*Hush, now,*" she said, lifting her voice over Darcy's choked coughing. "Dear Sophie! She just can't stand to see a miner go without, simply because he's down on his luck."

A murmur of deep, masculine approval rippled through the crowd. The boardwalk groaned as the huge miner stepped forward and pushed Hellfire aside.

"I'd be honored to escort you ladies back to your diggins," said the man, sweeping the cap from his head. The small portion of his face that was visible was blushing crimson.

"You are awfully kind, sir," said Mary. "If you will only be so good…as to see that we leave here unmolested…"

Mary stepped forward slowly, guiding Darcy as he walked backwards with his knees bent and his head on her shoulder. Hellfire Bob scowled and moved to block her, but was suddenly jerked sideways and slammed into the brick wall of the jailhouse. Mary heard the breath fly from his lungs.

"Thank you, my friend," she murmured to the miner, whose ham-sized fist pinned Hellfire to the wall. "You are a *gentleman.*"

She smiled up into the rough, hairy face – and was surprised to see tears welling in the miner's eye. "Thank you, ma'am," he replied thickly. "And you are surely a *lady.*"

As they reached the vacant lot, Mary heard a shattering crash and a loud splash. She spun around and saw, through a gap in the crowd, the splintered wreck of a hitching rail and a pair of black boots thrashing in the air over a horse trough.

"Come along, Sophie, dear," she said, clambering onto the buggy. "It's time we were on our way."

~

As they rolled by the Baptist Church, the voice of the congregation rose up to heaven in the triumphant refrain of "The Battle Hymn of the Republic":

> *Glory, glory Hallelujah!*
> *Glory, glory Hallelujah!*
> *Glory, glory Hallelujah!*
> *His Truth goes marching on!*

Darcy's usually cheerful face darkened into a scowl beneath his veil. Mary put her hand on his knee.

"Don't fret, my love. A just God will never favor a people with such appalling taste in music."

She coaxed the horse into a trot and whistled up a soft but spirited rendition of "Dixie," tapping out time with her boots on the footboard as the buggy rattled down the wooden planking on Main Street.

They crossed over the Deer Creek Bridge and turned south to Gold Flat and the swift saddle horses waiting there. As the buggy bounced and swayed, Darcy regaled Mary with tales of the life that awaited them over the Pacific.

"It was Captain Cook who brought the pineapple to Hawai'i," he said, hoisting his veil and firing up a cigar. "The natives clubbed him to death for his trouble – poor thanks, since the fruit grows better there than anywhere else in the world. The Kanakas scoop out the centers of perfect ripe pineapples, dice the sweet fruit, pour it back inside, and cover it with rum. I used to sit on the beach at sunset…"

Darcy reached over and gently brushed back a wisp of Mary's hair that had fallen over her eyes. "Forgive me, dear," he said. "I am remiss. I have not thanked you for saving my life."

"Nonsense. I never believed any of those rumors about lynching. The Yankees would have been very unpleasant, but even they wouldn't murder a captured officer."

Darcy shook his head. "Didn't you wonder why I was guarded by just one man – and a half-witted one at that? Knowlton wanted to make it easy for the mob to do what they liked with me. And so they would have, if Jennie Mae hadn't come calling."

"So, we are even," said Mary, "life for life – for Jennie Mae's wasn't worth living until she met you."

She lifted her head and began to sing:

> O Jenny's a' weet, poor body,
> Jenny's seldom dry:
> She draigl't a' her petticoatie,
> Comin thro' the rye!

She sang Burns's poem in a full-voiced, trilling Scots, without a trace of a drawl – feeling keenly the living presence of her father. He, too, had left all behind and set sail for a distant shore. He would have huffed and puffed about her abandoning her marriage, but she knew beyond a doubt that he would have secretly delighted in Jennie Mae. She was, after all, a lass after his own heart.

Chapter 52

The Beast at Bay

November 1863

Woo the laundryman swung his flat iron smoothly, and sweet, soap-scented steam sizzled from the damp cloth. The hot, humid air in the whitewashed basement room was suffocating. He thumped his iron down on a trivet and mopped his brow with his sleeve.

Ai ya! My nerves are so raw!

He inspected the dainty muslin nightgown on the padded board, trying to clear his mind and focus on his work. The Grass Valley madams were the Pacific Laundry's best customers. Scorches or stains on a bordello's finery meant insults and withheld payments.

He wiped the iron on the salt bag to clean it, then polished it on a soft rag before touching it to the garment again. Now the iron was too cold and crumpled the delicate fabric. He placed it back on the the big, wood-burning stove and stirred the steaming copper kettle full of blue starch that was just coming to a boil. He held his breath against the lye fumes as he lifted the lids on the wash boilers and skimmed the dead bedbugs from the surface.

He heard the clopping of many hooves and *gwei lo* voices shouting orders in the street. Through the louvered windows that opened at sidewalk level, he saw Sheriff Knowlton's mounted posse riding by again, six abreast, filling the Auburn Road from side to side. They had been patrolling since first light. As they left, he heard bells tolling from the *gwei lo* temples on the hillside, an ominous sound.

That morning, as soon as his early delivery boys had returned, Woo had sent everyone home from the laundry and instructed them to stay together and out of sight. He had locked the front door and pulled the curtain across its glass pane. He would look after the shop by himself at such a dangerous time.

So many days of bad news!

It had started when his deliverymen had come back, frightened and upset, to report a big robbery at You Bet and twenty *gwei lo* dead in a shoot-out! The next day, all of Grass Valley had been searched – even the homes of the dead rebels' grieving parents! The town was in an uproar. Today for sure the loyalist Americans of Nevada and the Secessionist rebels of Grass Valley would go to war.

All over town were posters with descriptions of the *gwei lo* that Chung Ah Kit was hunting. But the highbinder had disappeared before all this trouble started. Was he mixed up in it? Or was he dead?

Woo wiped the sweat from his face, then took the cover off the water bucket and drank a cool dipper full. *The best cure for shaky nerves is work!*

He filled his brass sprinkling can and blew a fine spray onto the white shirt on the top of the stack. He dampened a half-dozen more and rolled them up. Some laundrymen spat water from their mouths – an uncouth practice. To be a great laundryman was to be a man of refinement, of discernment as fine as the fabrics he handles. *A great laundryman is an artist!* Woo frilled a dainty lace collar with a hot fluting iron and dabbed it gently with a sponge.

A sudden tapping from the panel behind the soaking tubs made Woo jump. He rushed to open the hidden door, and Chung Ah Kit popped out of the tunnel that linked the basement to the heart of Grass Valley's Chinatown. The highbinder was grimy, rank, and unshaven. He'd lost weight and his eyes were red-rimmed. His saggy black clothes looked rusty with red dirt, and his boots were caked with mud.

Woo was horrified. He had to get the filthy man away from his clean laundry!

"Come to the back room, *túng báan*," said Woo, "you look like you could use a cup of tea."

The tiny back room felt chilly after the sweltering heat of the laundry. Woo opened his lunch hamper and offered the contents to Chung: rice balls with salted plums inside and cold pork buns. The highbinder stuffed them into his mouth and washed them down with scalding tea.

"Where have you been all this time? I was worried!" said Woo.

"Waiting in the cold and damp, watching that miserable cabin for Ah Tie's two *gwei lo*. They never came back. Do you have anything else to eat?"

"Ah Tie wants to see you right away at the Asian Hotel," Woo said, as he handed over the buns he had been saving for himself. "He has sent for you every day since you left here."

"Why?" The highbinder shoved another bun into his mouth.

"Don't you know? Those same murderers robbed the Lucky Stars again!" Woo saw chagrin and anger contort the highbinder's expression.

"*Bai lo!*" Chung cursed. He jumped to his feet, clenching his fists. "Tell me what happened!"

"Sit down, and I will tell you." Woo, alarmed at the violence of Chung's reaction, assumed a soothing tone. "Three days ago, Southern rebels took the fall gold shipment from the You Bet diggings. They ambushed the wagon and killed the escort. No Chinese were hurt, but many *gwei lo* are dead. The soldiers and the sheriff's men are searching everywhere for the rebels and the gold. They were here yesterday."

"Are you saying the *gwei lo* army is looking for Big Boots and Slippery Soles?"

"Yes, there are notices everywhere: they are wanted, dead or alive. There are checkpoints on all the roads, and soldiers are questioning everyone. You will have to account for yourself when you go to Nevada. I will give you a bill to take to Ah Tie for payment. That will suffice."

≈

The gwei lo *robbers have had days to run,* thought Chung Ah Kit. *They'll be far away by now! Besides, if the sheriff and the militia can't find them, my chances are next to nothing!*

The turnpike to Nevada was crowded, and everyone seemed to be in a hurry. No one noticed the highbinder dragging his heels along in the dust.

Chung dreaded the interview that was coming. *What can I say to Ah Tie? He's lost another fortune! How can I save face?*

He had stood in the bandits' room as they slept, his blade ready to taste their blood – and had let them escape! Retreat wasn't always dishonorable – but it was last on the list of the *36 Stratagems*.

Should I have stood my ground and fought? He might have taken both outlaws with an instant, determined attack...or not. *Ai ya! It is foolish and weak to keep second-guessing!*

The highbinder's way to Nevada lay over the bridge on Pine Street that hung from steel cables, a miracle of invention that had stood for an entire year now without collapsing. At the bridge, a pair of soldiers leaned against the railing.

"Halt!" cried one, snatching up his musket. "State your business."

"Boss send me Asian Hotel," Chung explained, showing them the invoice for Ah Tie. The soldier barely glanced at it.

"Who's your boss?"

"Woo...Pacific Laundry."

The young soldier waved Chung on. His companion on watch, who was holding a newspaper, thumped the page and whistled.

"Hey, Ted, did you read about the dead Secesh they found?"

"How could I?" snapped Ted. "You've been hogging the paper since we first came on duty."

Chung stood close by the soldiers, listening, while he waited for a jogging mule train to clatter down Pine Street and cross the span.

"Knowlton's posse found a body up on Missouri Creek, out there by You Bet. They think it's that Eldon Whitley that's on all the posters. Varmints got to him pretty bad, though. Not much left to identify."

"Any word on the gold?"

"'Course not! There'd be four-inch headlines if they'd found that! But listen to this, there's a reward – $5,000 for the recovery of the shipment!"

"*Damnation!* Sure wish I was out there! This sentry duty is cow flop. Seventy-five thousand in gold and a gang of crazy Rebs on the loose, and we're stuck here asking a half-wit coolie if he's come to burn down the town! What a damn-fool waste of time!"

The last mule trotted by and Chung walked on, stunned by the unexpected news. *Slippery Soles dead?* So, maybe the other killer, Big Jake, was still around! *Maybe the gold is still within reach…and I can recover it!* Chung's step grew lighter as he crossed the bridge.

He turned onto Spring St. and looked up in surprise at a huge canvas tent that had risen on a vacant lot. *A hundred men could fit inside,* he thought, gazing at the rippling structure.

A cluster of *gwei lo* women sat by the front flap on a bench in the sun. They were drinking coffee and brushing their hair, still wrapped shamelessly in their dressing gowns. *These must be the hurdy-gurdy girls, the dancing prostitutes!*

He listened to the women's barbarous speech as he approached – a dreary gurgle, punctuated by raspy sounds, as if they were clearing their throats. They were large women, with big noses and pale skin – in every way inferior to Chinese prostitutes. But the sing-song girls of Nevada had all been struck down by disease, and replacements from Marysville had not yet arrived. Perhaps he would overlook the white women's ugliness and take in a performance of the hurdy-gurdies.

He glanced at the door of the tent for a "No Chinese" sign – the first words he had learned in the curious *gwei lo* script. Sure enough, there it was, crudely painted on the flap itself. *These arrogant whites have an exaggerated view of their women's attractions,* he thought bitterly.

As he turned away, his gaze swept along the muddy ground by a horse trough. He was not conscious, at first, of what had caught his attention – just of a sudden jolt of excitement, a sense that something wonderful had happened. He looked again at the ground…and saw the enormous, hob-nailed boot print of Jake Forrest!

Heart pounding, Chung walked over to the trough. There were three prints clearly belonging to the giant.

Why was Big Jake here, in the town of his enemies?

To deceive his pursuers, of course! It was clever of the bandit to hide where they least expected to find him.

The prints led straight to a wooden shed built onto the back of the Bed Rock Saloon, where crates of empty bottles stood piled by the door. Chung walked over swiftly and tried the latch. *Unlocked!*

He stepped inside, into a narrow hallway lit by a greasy window. The place reeked of cats and turpentine, and was crowded with mops, brooms, and paint cans. *What luck!* he thought. *A bucket big enough to carry the giant's head…and rags to wrap it in!* He would earn a bonus from Ah Tie for bringing in such a splendid trophy!

There was a rough plank wall on his right, with a door at the far end. Chung found a knothole and peered through: a quilt…the legs of a bed…a pair of colossal boots…

Yes! There was Big Jake, propped up in bed against a pile of cushions. His left arm and massive torso were swathed in bandages. His head lolled on the pillows and his eyelids were closed. *How badly was he hurt?*

The highbinder took his time studying the little room. A spirit stove with a small flame dancing under a coffeepot stood on a shelf next to Jake. Next to the pot lay a huge knife and a pistol. Chung could see no hiding place for the loot, except under the bed.

A simple hook latched the door from the inside. Chung selected a slender steel pick from his kit, slipped it into the gap, and lifted the hook. Then he drew his sword and silently swung the door open.

He sprang forward, jerked the giant's head back by the hair, and swung the sword around to cut his throat. Jake's enormous hand struck Chung's wrist, gripping it and locking it. Chung braced himself against the bed frame and heaved with all his strength.

The razor-sharp blade quivered in mid-air. With his free hand, Jake groped for the weapons on the shelf. His wounded arm swept across it, knocking the pot sideways and soaking his bandages with boiling coffee. He roared with pain, and his grip faltered. The highbinder thrust down, slicing the sword into flesh, rocking the blade…*deeper, to make sure*… Jake's agonized shriek died away in a bubbling gurgle, and he slumped.

Chung stood up, arms shaking.

An acrid stench stung his nose – *burning wool?* He turned and saw smoke rising from the crack between bed and wall. The spirit stove had fallen into the bedding!

Chung dropped to one knee and checked under the cot. No gold. A flame shot up, and then another one, higher. The air was filling with thick black smoke.

He raced from the room, gasping and coughing, and slammed the door behind him. He seized a rag in the hallway, wiped his sword clean, and slid the blade back in its scabbard. Then he snatched up a mop and bucket and stepped out into the street.

Two soldiers walked straight at him, only a few steps away. Chung grinned foolishly at them, shouldered the mop like a rifle, and saluted them with the bucket still in his hand.

The militiamen laughed and returned the salute. Chung waited for them to pass, then set off down Spring Street at a deliberate pace. If he could just make it around the corner, all would be well. In a moment, the soldiers would have a lot more to think about than a simple-minded cleaning man. That wooden shed would burn like a torch. With any luck, the giant's body would roast to a cinder in its own fat.

Still, he thought, swinging the big bucket as he turned the corner onto Bridge Street, *it was a shame about that head*. It would have been a great comfort to Ah Tie to gaze into the sightless eyes of the barbarian who had killed his men.

Chapter 53

How Lovely to Meet You

November 1863

T he urgent, high-pitched clanging went unnoticed amid the tolling bells calling Nevada to Sunday worship. When the church bells fell silent, the clanging persisted, and men jumped to their feet and strode swiftly down the aisles. Then a second high-pitched bell joined in. The whispering in the pews became a general roar, and entire congregations rose, clutching their children as they headed for the doors.

Peter Kessel recognized the fire bell at the first stroke. He thundered down the stairs of his loft and sprinted up Commercial Street to Pine to look around. *Nothing amiss at the Court House.*

Turning his gaze south toward Broad Street, he gaped in horror at the thick, black plume of oily smoke boiling up over the rooftops. A crowd was gathering at the corner of Broad and Pine, and he raced to join them.

"It's bad," said Amos Beitz.

Kessel glanced at the little jeweler, who had witnessed every fire in town since the inferno of '51. What he saw in the man's ashen face made his heart sink.

"Don't worry," roared Jim Blaze, who stopped to clap Beitz on the shoulder. "We've got a new pumper and plenty of water – a whole reservoir's worth." The big bartender released Beitz and lumbered uphill to join the men swinging open the double doors of the fire station.

"I pray God it all works," murmured Beitz.

"Mein Gott!" gasped Kessel. "Can the firemen not stop this?"

Beitz shrugged. "I'm off to put every jewel and every fleck of gold I own into a carpetbag. I advise you to do the same, Peter."

Kessel's stomach, which had knotted tight, seemed to fall through space. There was no way to put a grand piano into a carpetbag – or guitars, drums, the tuba... Sheet music, perhaps...a flute...the tintype portrait of his parents... Y*es, that's what I'll save!* ...the cash box...his favorite fiddle...

He heard a burst of loud crackling and was shocked to see a sheet of orange flame leaping up, hurling embers and a blazing scrap of fabric that consumed itself as it twisted into the air.

Distant screams. A handful of figures dashing around the corner of Spring Street onto South Pine. People fleeing for their lives – and he would soon be one of them!

A young woman came round the corner, her hair down, her nightgown unbelted. He recognized her at once, watched as she dragged a small trunk, straining with all her might. Then the uneven boardwalk caught her foot, and she staggered and fell.

Kessel rocked backward and forward, hesitating, then hurled himself down Pine toward the fire, ducking and dodging through the terrified mob streaming the other way.

The woman was on her knees when he reached her. Her gown was torn and there was blood on her hand. He pulled her to her feet and started to help her away.

"*Mein Reisekoffer!*" she cried.

She pointed at the trunk. He pushed it off the boardwalk and jumped after it.

"*Komm, um Gottes willen!*" he yelled, holding out his hand.

She jumped down beside him. A terrific blast rent the air and hurled them both to the ground. Peter shielded her with his body as boards and shingles rained down around them.

"*Den Reisekoffer...bitte!*" she pleaded.

The trunk was heavy, and for a second, he considered leaving it. But the girl was half out of her mind and might refuse to go on without it.

The roar and crackle of the fire, which had been stunned by the blast, now rose up redoubled. Orange flames danced behind shattered windows in the store to his left. Smoke filled his nose and made his eyes sting as he gripped the trunk and dragged it, bumping and scraping, through smoldering wreckage.

Christ! he thought, *Zeno's gun shop is nearby. God knows how much powder he has in there!*

Broad Street was total pandemonium. Frenzied store owners heaved merchandise onto wagons as horses stamped and neighed. Horsemen galloped by, missing people by inches. A buggy swerved to avoid an overturned handcart and plowed into the lead horse of the team pulling the fire pumper. The beast went down, screaming.

To his store. He had to get to his store!

Desperately dodging traffic, he dragged the trunk across the wooden planking of Broad Street. *How long would it take for the street to catch fire?*

The wind shifted as they struggled along North Pine, choking them both with thick smoke. The woman was weeping disconsolately now, catching her breath in loud gasps that became increasingly violent. He had to distract her...ask her something – if only her name!

"*Wie heißen Sie?*" he shouted.

"*Ich heiße...Grete, mein Herr,*" she sobbed.

"*Angenehm, Grete. Ich bin Peter.*"

A big man bolted out of a doorway and crashed into Greta. Peter threw out an arm to keep her from sprawling. The trunk lurched in a deep pothole, wrenching his wrist.

"*Wie schön, Sie zu treffen!*" he yelled, shoving her back on her feet. "*How lovely to meet you!*" he added, in a singsong voice.

She stared at him blankly as they flattened themselves against the railing of the boardwalk. A runaway mare galloped by – lips foaming, eyes bulging.

"Just a bit farther," he said in English. The language was evidently difficult for her. Struggling with it seemed to distract her from the bedlam surrounding them.

"Welcome to my home!" he said, with a swift bow. "We will now fill our arms and run for our lives."

As he leaned past her to open the door, she took his arm and squeezed it. Startled, he turned to her, and the kiss she had aimed at his cheek landed awkwardly on his lips.

≈

Wisps of smoke rose from the pine planks overlaying Broad Street, as embers from the blaze gained a foothold in the gaps between the boards. The firemen ran off lengths of canvas hose from the cart, while the youngest of their number, a gangly youth, ran from hot spot to hot spot with a bucket, dousing the flames where they threatened to scorch the hose.

The crew assembled the hose with lightning speed while Jim Blaze twisted the nozzle cap off the hydrant. Then he grabbed a stout wrench from the hanger on the hose cart and gripped the operating nut atop the hydrant.

"You boys ready for some water?"

A chorus of shouts answered him. Teller, a big man from the livery stable, gripped the brass nozzle under his arm, like a wrestler clamping a powerful opponent in a headlock. Blaze swung the wrench and the valve opened. Instantly, the hose began to writhe like a giant snake. They heard the rushing, tumbling air and water shooting along – and a violent gurgling at the end of the nozzle. A jet of water shot out, arcing thirty feet through the air, and the firemen cheered. Then the surge subsided, the arc of water shortening, shortening, until it was barely ten feet long.

Blaze's stomach lurched. *It can't be! This is a brand new water system!* He must have not opened the valve all the way.

He closed the valve and muttered a prayer under his breath. Then he swung the wrench until he felt it come to a full stop, the valve in the wide-open position. He stared at the nozzle.

Still just a ten-foot throw! They might as well piss on the flames!

"This hydrant must be busted!" he roared. "We've got to try another."

"The next one is on the corner of Broad and Commercial," Teller shouted. The fire was horribly loud now: knots exploding in beams, glass shattering, and the all-pervading roar of flames sucking oxygen out of the air – a self-generating hurricane.

"We've got to coil the hose, boys," Blaze bellowed. "We can't drag it that far. It would be torn to shreds."

Instantly, the crew set to undoing the couplings, dragging hose lengths back to the cart, and swiftly coiling them onto the big spool. Blaze grabbed the bit of the terrified mare and pulled her toward the next hydrant.

A stupefying blast – *a thunderclap inside his skull* – and the ground heaved. The mare twisted in her traces and tried to rear. Blaze clung to the bit with both hands.

Zeno's gun shop, by God!

A rattling noise like heavy hail surrounded him. He felt a sharp blow on his back. He had to get the mare moving, this instant, before she lost her mind entirely!

He saw Teller grab the mare's bit on the far side. Together, they dragged her by main strength.

The mare lurched forward, and Blaze sprang aside to avoid her massive hooves. They dragged the animal into a jog, while the rest of the firemen trotted behind.

At the second hydrant, Blaze twisted off the nozzle cap and roared for the men to stand clear. Then he thrust the big wrench onto the nut and swung it with all his might. A jet of white water shot out of the hydrant – a level blast from one side of the street to the other. His heart leapt.

This one works!

Then cold horror gripped him as he saw the jet sag. He let the water flow until the pressure stabilized. Maybe fifteen feet of throw. They couldn't deliver a drop of water to the tinder-dry, wood shingle roofs two storeys above.

He wrenched the valve shut and looked at his companions, who stood in a half-circle around him.

"It's firebreaks, boys. We'll make a line by knocking down a row of buildings. Then we can wet the rubble with the water we've got."

～

Peter and Greta sat side by side, looking down on the remains of Nevada from atop Sugar Loaf Hill. The Chinese quarter and the business district were gone – just a few blackened brick shells stood forlornly at the base of Broad Street. Peter tried to spot the ruins of his store, but there was nothing but charred beams and smoldering rubble. Columns of thick grey smoke rose from the ruins, gathering into a blanket that hovered over the town.

Scores of other refugees sat with them in the clearing, consoling each other in quiet tones. Greta spoke, in a Hessian peasant dialect that Peter's Viennese ear could barely untangle.

"I'm sorry I made you drag that trunk. We should have thrown out my nonsense and packed it with instruments from your store. They were much more valuable." She wrapped a scarf around the handle of the enameled pot on the little spirit stove and poured tea into a pair of porcelain cups that had crossed the ocean with her.

"It is not possible," said Peter, "to make tea in a musical instrument – except perhaps the horns – and there would be little comfort in sleeping under a trumpet. I am heartily glad we saved your trunk."

Greta looked at him, sensing the effort it cost him to keep the unconvincing smile on his lips. This morning he had been as rich as a nobleman, with a grand piano to play anytime he wished.

"I recognized you right away," she said, "from the hurdy-gurdy tent. You watched me there…" She handed him a cup and saucer, "but never asked to meet me."

A blush rose up Peter's neck until his cheeks glowed.

"The girls liked you very much," Greta continued, taking no notice of his embarrassment. "They called you *der Musiker*… You were the subject of many secret passions," she added with a smile.

"*Me?*" cried Peter. He looked at her sharply. *Was she making fun of him?*

Greta laughed. "A German-speaking gentleman on the far side of the world, wealthy as a prince, and able to charm a girl's heart with music…? Why, there wasn't a dancer in the troupe who wouldn't have married you in a minute!"

"The life of a hurdy-gurdy girl must be dreary indeed to make me seem a catch."

The smile on Greta's face faded.

"It is a life that has many…disappointments, but it could be worse. Klaus, our manager, is drunk all the time, but he doesn't beat us, and he doesn't make us go with men we find horrible or frightening. Of course, with so many patrons milling around the tent, it makes no difference to Klaus if we are choosy."

"How long have you been with the troupe?"

"My parents died three years ago of typhoid fever. I was the eldest child, so it fell to me to earn a living."

The plunk of a banjo string distracted them, and they looked around. A black man sat on a stump across the clearing, tuning up, while his companions fetched out their instruments. A young boy held his hands to his mouth, and the twang of a Jew's harp cut through the air. These musicians were well known in town, staples of the parades and endless civic functions that Americans were so fond of.

The leader stood up, tapped his foot, and the banjo burst into the opening notes of "Kingdom Coming," a wild song of jubilee. Salton, the town's cabinet-maker, pulled his young wife to her feet. They clasped each other, leaned to one side, and flung themselves off in a wild *gallop* – their flying boots beating up clouds of dust as they whirled in time to the music. There were whoops and loud applause, and another couple followed. Soon the hilltop was alive with dancers and hand-clapping, foot-stomping spectators.

Peter drew his fiddle from its battered case and Greta pulled her tambourine from her trunk. They made their way to the little cluster of musicians, Peter tuning as he walked. Aaron, the band leader, waved for them to join in, and Peter launched into a soaring harmony that made the guitarist and the banjo player grin. Soon the musicians were passing improvisations back and forth, while the Jew's harp twanged and the spoons and tambourine anchored the beat.

They played on as the sun sank low. The air became cool and crisp; a campfire was built in the center of the clearing. Those who had food passed out victuals for all. At last, little groups began to drift away from the fire and lie down for the night.

Greta lit a candle, took Peter's hand, and led him to a small opening in a stand of manzanita. He saw that she had gathered armloads of bracken and spread them over the thick carpet of leaves. Her blanket was spread out on the ferns, her quilt on top, with pillows lying side by side.

"Home, sweet home," she said slowly in English, frowning as she formed the unfamiliar *w* with her lips.

"Very good, Greta!" he replied, also in English. "Can you also make the *th* sound?"

"I *think*...with some...*thought*..."

"*Wundervoll!*" cried Kessel. "Soon you will be American!"

Greta sat down on the bed and began drawing the hairpins that had survived the adventures of the day.

"I should…to myself…*the* hair…brush…"

"No," he said, kneeling beside her. He gently swept away a stray wisp from her forehead. "It is lovely, just as it is." His fingertips traced the soft, warm curve of her cheek until he touched her chin. He lifted her face to his and kissed her gently on the lips.

"This," he said, forming the English sounds with care, "is a lucky day."

"*This*," she mimicked, "is lucky…*yes*…"

Chapter 54

Ida Rewarded

December 1863

The red dun filly was pitching a fit right down the middle of the You Bet road, crow-hopping and kicking like a mule. Ida could see the saddle hanging upside down and the stirrups flopping and dragging in the mud. Ida ran down the front steps, just as Nutim's yellow hound came baying around the corner of the tack room. The frantic horse shied away and stepped on the trailing reins, nearly falling as the bridle bit yanked her mouth.

Ida collared the hound and marched him into the feed room. She snatched up a grain bucket, slipped out, and latched the dog inside. She strolled casually to the middle of the road, swinging her bucket, pretending not to notice the horse dancing toward her. The filly slowed down and sniffed the air hopefully. Ida spoke in a gentle voice, taking care not to look directly into the animal's large, frightened eyes.

"I see you're in a state of confusion, Miss Red, but I'll sort you out."

The filly's ears tipped forward. She stretched her long neck toward the bucket, and Ida took a firm grip on the bridle.

"Where did you come from?" she murmured, while the horse investigated the oats. "I've never seen you before. I'll bet your mother is Donovan's red dun mare. You've got all the markings."

The filly searched the bottom of the bucket for crumbs, then lifted her head to sample Ida's bonnet.

"Mind your manners," Ida snapped. "Were you born in a barn?" She freed the cinch and let the saddle drop. "This is a fancy rig, gal. Were you goin' to a party?"

Ida slung the muddy saddle over a rail by the spring-fed trough, while the red dun touched her nose to the water and drank. Ida stroked the horse's neck, feeling the fit, supple muscles.

"You're somebody's pet, all right. C'mon, let's go find your rider."

She soon spotted Sam Gee coming down the road from You Bet, limping and muttering, a saddle blanket under his arm. When he saw Ida, he sat down by the roadside and waited.

"Is this your horse, Sam?" Ida asked. "She sure is a beauty."

Sam threw down the blanket. "She not mine!" he said indignantly, pulling a crumpled letter from his pocket. "Ah Tie say, take *sweet gentle* pony to Ida Hatfield. Give her horse. Give her letter." Sam thrust the letter into Ida's hand. "*Ai ya!* I go home. Sam never ride pony again. Trust own two feet." Sam waved away an imaginary cloud of troubles circling his head and started trudging back toward town.

Ida was stunned. "Wait, Sam," she called. "I don't understand."

"You read letter." Sam looked sullen.

"Sam, did you saddle this horse yourself?" Ida asked gently.

"Young fellows at stable fix saddle for Sam."

"They sure did. Look at the big stickers in this blanket."

Sam grimaced, anger etched in every line of his face.

"I don't like those mean boys," Ida said. She felt sorry for Sam Gee. Any snot-nosed white kid in the mood for mischief could play a cruel joke on a Chinaman, and nobody would turn a hair.

"You are good girl, Miss Ida," said Sam.

Ida watched him go. There was something sad about Sam. *All the China-men must be lonesome,* she thought – except Ah Tie, who was so rich and powerful he could smuggle in a wife from Kwangtung. There were no Chinese families in the mines except his. The rest of Ah Tie's men kept bachelor quarters, a half-dozen or so bunking together. Still, they did better than most white men at keeping themselves washed and mended, and they were good cooks, too.

There was something heavy in the letter Sam had handed her. She pinched the paper and felt the outline of a key. She turned the letter over to see her name written, not in Ah Tie's careful hand, but in Aidan Caldwell's bold flourish.

The impatient filly nudged Ida in the back.

"You can't read," Ida said. "What are you so excited about?"

$\sim$

"Molly, my dear, don't look so serious, I have nothing but good news for you," said Aidan Caldwell, reaching his hand across his desk. "Ida, may I have the key?"

Ida shook the little brass key from the letter and laid it on the Judge's palm. He fitted it to a black metal box, extracted a sheaf of folded documents, and arranged them on the green blotter.

"This is all so mysterious, Aidan," Molly said, "what do you mean by telling us to 'come alone, while Amanda is at church'?"

"My client has instructed me to confer with just you three," the Judge said, "and, as my law office is a currently a pile of charred rubble, I thought it might be more convenient to meet here. This is a delicate matter, Molly, involving events you have no knowledge of. It is only because the situation has been altered…through the death of a mutual friend…that Ah Tie wishes to speak now."

The Judge paused to clean his pince-nez with his handkerchief, surreptitiously wiping away a tear as he did so. "Ah Tie insists that everything we discuss remain strictly confidential. Do you all agree to this?"

"Of course we agree, Aidan," Molly said, "but I don't see what Ah Tie…"

"Patience, Molly," said the Judge, "I'll explain as we go along." He unfolded a bundle of pages and smoothed out the creases.

"In February of 1861, my client, Mr. Yee Lo Dye, also known as Ah Tie, attended a Chinese festival in Nevada City. At the event, he was assaulted by ruffians and threatened with bodily harm. Miss Hatfield came to my client's aid and helped repel the assailants."

Ida could feel her mother's eyes boring into her. She looked straight ahead at the Judge and kept her expression blank.

"My client owes Miss Hatfield an immense debt," Caldwell continued, "and now wishes to show his gratitude with something more substantial than vegetables."

"So that's why..." Molly stammered. The mystified tone in her voice took on a sharp edge. "What happened that's worth bushels and bushels of vegetables...*and a horse?*"

Judge Caldwell did not seem to hear Molly. He continued to summarize the document.

"For saving the honor of his ancient surname, Ah Tie has endowed two Trusts, of which I am Trustee. One is for Ida, the other for Nutim. There are specific instructions as to how these Trusts are to be used. If you decline the terms, the funds revert to a charity...yes, here it is...the 'Dipsomania Relief Commission.'"

"*Rubbish, Aidan!*" cried Molly. "This sounds like the Grand Humbug at work!"

"I assure you," said Caldwell with dignity, "the Grand Humbug is entirely silent in this matter. I speak now in my character as an officer of the court, and I speak in earnest."

The Judge held up another document from his desk blotter.

"Ida, Ah Tie stipulates that a portion of your Trust be used to open a theater, in the location of your choice. I have in front of me the conveyance of a suitable Nevada property that can be yours for a song, if you'll permit me a little joke." Caldwell chuckled happily as he handed a deed to Ida.

Ida was speechless. *How could Ah Tie have learned about my theater?* She scanned the deed for the address of the lot: 101 Main Street. *That used to be the Monumental Hotel!*

"There's a substantial building fund as well," the Judge continued, "enough for all the velvet curtains and crystal chandeliers your heart could desire."

Molly scowled and rose from her chair. "Aidan, if this is a joke, it's in poor taste. I think it's time we..."

"*Peace, Molly!*" Caldwell looked sternly over his pince-nez. "If you don't believe me, perhaps Mr. Conroy's signature on these bearer bonds will convince you." He pushed the bank notes toward Molly, who stared at the amounts and at the bank president's signature. She sat back down, looking dazed.

Caldwell turned and smiled at Nutim. "There is something here for you, too, young man. Most of your money will be invested so you will have a regular allowance. The remainder, if you wish, may be used to purchase Sugar Pine Mountain. I have a Bill of Sale here, ready to be signed if you approve. You must understand, of course, that it is the Trust that will actually own the land. You will not be able to sell it or give it away…"

Nutim frowned and shook his head.

"Is there a problem, son?" the Judge asked.

"No one can own a mountain," Nutim said gravely. "The world does not belong to men, to buy and sell for money."

"Ah," said the Judge, eyeing the boy's glum expression. "Of course, in a larger sense, you are right," he said gently. "The earth does outlast us all. However, for present purposes, this deed is quite useful. It allows you – or rather me, in your name – to tell other people to go away and leave you in peace…"

"Aidan, what's going on here?' exclaimed Molly. "These are enormous sums that Ah Tie is settling on Ida and Nutim! How can he afford it after losing his fall gold shipment?"

Again, Caldwell's hearing appeared to fail. He extracted a page from the bundle on his desk and handed it to Nutim. "Here's your copy of the map of the property. See?" He pointed to a green line. "Here is a right-of-way from the main road that crosses through Ah Tie's holdings…"

"Ah Tie has recovered his gold, hasn't he?" said Molly, eyeing Caldwell's face. "And maybe more – maybe he found something belonging to that dirty dog, Jonas…"

"*Quieta non movere!*" barked the Judge, making Molly jump. He eyed her sternly. "That's Latin for 'don't rock the boat, Molly!' I assure you it would be entirely fruitless to speculate on facts beyond our ken…fruitless and *unwise.*"

Molly stared into the Judge's poker face. *He's not going to tell me a damned thing!*

"As soon as these papers are signed," said Caldwell briskly, sweeping up a selection of documents, "we'll take these youngsters for an ice cream soda to celebrate their good fortune. We'll treat ourselves, too, for we have our own cause for rejoicing! Our good friend Lucas Donovan of Little York has bought the Jehoshaphat Mine – lock, stock and barrel – from young Clench, who is off to the Dakota Territory to recoup his fortunes."

∽

Nutim leaned back in the armchair, waiting for the others to finish signing the documents. He held the map Judge Caldwell had given him and stared at the rectangle outlined in red ink. A black triangle marked the mountain peak, a little tadpole with a wiggling tail meant water, and a dotted line traced the Indian trail winding up behind Chalk Bluff. There, where the dots ended, once stood the village called *Sumú,* where he had been born.

He closed his eyes and pictured it, as he had done every day since he lost his mother and father. He could see the tall sugar pines behind the camp, their long branches drooping and swaying with the weight of huge seed cones. A spring trickled down through the meadow. He had lain on soft green mosses and watched the Water-strider Women crisscrossing its crystal pools. He recalled the feel of the black mud squishing up between his toes as he waded into a bog of blue camas flowers.

The smooth mound of the dance house had stood on rising ground; white-blossomed tobacco had grown on its earth-covered roof. Everyone bedded down inside on cold winter nights and listened by flickering firelight to storytellers conjuring up the old tales. There were scary stories, like the Hungry Head that rolled around looking for someone to eat, and funny ones, like when Coyote disguised himself and his penis as an old woman and her ugly baby. The storytellers were all gone now, and the dance house was in ruins. His early life at *Sumú* seemed a distant dream made of bird song and morning dew, and the sweet smoke of cedar-twig cooking fires. And sometimes, in that dream, he felt himself warm and happy beneath a rabbit fur blanket, listening to his mother singing at her tasks.

Sugar Pine Mountain was still home to many creatures. Near the top was a tiny snowmelt lake, where yellow water lilies floated. A powerful spirit lived there; no village child could play in its waters. Important persons came to the lake to burn herbs and make medicine.

Once, by the water's edge at dusk, he had seen a small hairy man no taller than himself kneel and drink. Grandmother said he had seen a *pitch head:* one of the little people who moved around at night. They were much stronger and sturdier than the Maidu – more like stumps or rocks, she said. Had they survived the coming of the *wólem*, high up on Sugar Pine Mountain? If so, maybe he could, too.

Chapter 55

Epilogue: Lupines

April 1864

Ida leaned forward and replaced the wilted bouquet with a fresh bunch of purple-blue wildflowers.

"I brought you lupines, Will," she said, smoothing her skirt. She was seated cross-legged on a saddle blanket laid out on the soft spring grass. "Looks like Ma brought the same. They're the prettiest things blooming now."

A butterfly landed on the flowers – an Echo Blue. It raised and lowered its wings, savoring the sweet scent, then flew away.

"We're ready to put the roof on the theater. We'll open this summer – only a year after I told you about my dream…"

Her voice faltered as she recalled their hours by the stream. But then a smile stole across her face.

"I saw you swimming there," she said softly, *"without a stitch on!"*

She blushed.

"Oh, Will, I will never forgive you for not compromising my virtue that day. There's such a thing as being too much of a gentleman…" She spoke the words lightly, trying to paper over the searing wound in her heart. Her voice dropped to a whisper. "You're the only man I ever loved, Will…the only one I wanted to give myself to. I can't bear the thought of holding someone else."

She reflected in silence. Then she shook her head, reached into her skirt pocket, and drew out a crumpled sheet of paper.

"I got a letter from Peter Kessel. He was awfully kind to me when he came to play at your send-off…told me that he had lost someone very close to him when he was my age…

"He's playing piano at a place called the Emporium, in San Francisco. It's a fancy gambling hall that's a whole block long and grand as an archduke's palace! He says the tips he brings in will get him started on a new store on Market Street. Imagine! And he married that Greta gal he met during the fire – says he's happier now than he has been in years…"

She unslung her canteen for a drink. The action brought Will's flask to mind – and how he had always offered it to her naturally, without comment. He had never once failed to treat her as an equal.

"There's romance in the air up here in You Bet, too," she said, wiping away the tear that had escaped and run down her cheek. "Do you remember Lucas Donovan, who owns those mines in Little York? Well, he's been dropping by Missouri House every chance he gets. I think he's smitten with dear old Ma…"

Ida shook her head.

"Not that she's even thinking of courting yet. Something broke in her when you died, Will…maybe her faith in the future… But it's good to know there's somebody waiting, if she perks up. And Mr. Donovan *is* waiting. He's not rushing her. He's just as kind and patient as…well…as you were, when you met her after Zeke died.

"I think her spirits will pick up. 'Life's for the living,' Zeke used to say. You would have liked him, Will."

Ida's voice trailed away. Was it kind to speak of Molly's love for another man? She shrugged. Will's heart was big enough to cope.

She rose and shook off the saddle blanket.

"I'd better be on my way. I've got to be back at Missouri House in time for the stage from Dutch Flat. Ma really needs my help."

Ida picked up Molly's faded bouquet and ran her fingers over the flowers.

"There's times I think Ma would like to climb onto the next stage and ride till she's somewhere new, where there's nothing to remind her of…*anything*. And mostly, I think that would be a good thing for her – though I can't bring myself to tell her so. I could stay and run Missouri House until she came back… I wish I could do that for her."

Ida leaned over the bouquet of fresh lupines and blew Will a kiss, then turned and walked down the path to the rusty iron gate. She stroked the neck of the red dun filly, then swung herself up into the saddle, eager to begin the long, flying gallop that would dry her tears before she reached Missouri House.

Afterword

Historical Sources

The following is a list of the real people and places whose extraordinary qualities earned them a place in our story.

AH TIE – Argonaut, *tong* boss, and philanthropist, Yee Ah Tye is an important figure in the history of the Chinese in California. In our novel, "Ah Tie" is a composite of Yee Ah Tye and his son, Sam Ah Tye, who also mined at You Bet. For their true story, see: *Bury My Bones in America, the Saga of a Gold Rush Family,* by Lani Ah Tye Farkas, 1998. Also, *You Bet Gold Fever: A True Documentation,* by Jerry Brady, 1983.

AHEARN'S SALOON – Ahearn's saloon was near Allison Ranch, south of Grass Valley. It was a well-known Secessionist hangout. At least one murder was committed there in the early days.

ALLISON RANCH MINE – John and William Daniel uncovered this gold-bearing ledge in 1853. "South of Grass Valley, on Wolf creek, is the village of Allison Ranch, noted the world over for having one of the richest quartz mines yet discovered. The gross yield of Allison Ranch for the three years ending December 30, 1865, was $1,000,000." – Edwin F. Bean's *History & Directory of Nevada County, 1867.*

THE BED ROCK SALOON – The city of Nevada "...suffered a total destruction of its business houses and public buildings on Sunday, November 8, 1863. About noon on that dreadful day the alarm of fire was sounded and flames were seen issuing from the rear of the Bed Rock Saloon, on the south side of Broad Street... The fire companies responded with alacrity, but for some unknown reason there was but little pressure of water and the hose threw a feeble and almost useless stream." – *History of Nevada County, 1880,* by Thompson & West.

JIM BLAZE – Barkeeper John Bazley was fondly known in Nevada as "Blaze." He liked to swap drinks for curiosities and wrote his own advertising copy, including the memorable: *"One hundred thousand square drinkers wanted at Blaze's, corner of Pine and Commercial. No Drunkards tolerated on the place."* – Thompson & West.

EDWIN THOMAS BOOTH – Actor Edwin Booth's experiences in the Northern Mines were attended with hardship and sorrow. He was snowbound and hungry in Grass Valley in 1855, when he heard the news of his father's death. He walked two days and a night to Marysville on snow-covered roads, rejoining his brother Junius in San Francisco "in a forlorn condition." In 1856, Edwin had to run from angry townsfolk in Downieville, who believed that he brought bad luck, or perhaps an arsonist, with him. On tour with "...a strolling manager named Moulton, who had organized a dramatic company... Booth travelled on horseback, halting now and then to act, and so making the mountain circuit. The expedition met with intermittent public favour, but it was uniformly attended by one startling incident: each town took fire as soon as Moulton's cavalcade had left it, and so regularly did this lurid phenomenon recur that at last it became the theme of general remark, and Booth was known and designated as The Fiery Star." – *Life and Art of Edwin Booth,* William Winter, 1893.

MADAME BONHORE – In 1855, a fire broke out on lower Main Street in Grass Valley, originating "...in the United States Hotel, kept by Madame Bonhore, and owned by Oakly and Hall, the latter now being Police Judge of Sacramento." – Bean's *History*.

BOURBON LODGE – This historic home, one of the oldest in Nevada City, still stands on Aristocracy Hill. According to Bean's History, the remarkable library at Bourbon Lodge, "every volume having a cork," actually belonged to a convivial soul named James Fitz-James. We moved Frank Dunn and his fictional wife, Mary Graham, into the venerable mansion.

THE BRODERICK-TERRY DUEL – "Perhaps, up to this time, no event ever filled Nevada with such gloom as the reported death of Broderick, Senator of the United States, who died on the 16th of September [1859], from wounds received in a duel with David S. Terry, on the 13th. Broderick had many friends among nearly all professions of political faith in Nevada, and large numbers of houses were draped in mourning and closed." – "Sketch of Nevada City and Township" by Edwin F. Bean, in Bean's *History*.

Speaking in 1936 before a meeting of the California Historical Society, San Francisco Judge Charles R. Boden said, "The duel was fought, and Broderick mortally wounded. On his death bed, he said: 'They killed me because I was opposed to the extension of slavery and the corruption of justice.'"

CHUNG AH KIT – Chung Ah Kit appears on an illustrated page of lurid vignettes including "The Chinese Highbinders in San Francisco," "A Haunt of the Highbinders in Chinatown," and "The Highbinder's Favorite Weapons," in *Harper's Weekly*, Vol XXX, No. 1521, February 1886, available at the Online Archive of California: http://www.oac.cdlib.org/.

JUDGE AIDAN CALDWELL – Our Judge Caldwell is a composite of several pioneer judges of Nevada. "From the earliest settlement of Nevada county its bar contained men of learning and ability. Rich mines hereabouts...were fertile in causes of litigation, giving abundant and profitable employment to the legal profession." – "Sketch of the Nevada County Bar," By Hon. A. A. Sargent, in *Thompson & West*.

REV. D. D. CHAPIN – Reverend Chapin's name is recorded by Thompson & West as an early Rector of the Parish at both Emmanuel Episcopal Church of Grass Valley and Trinity Episcopal of Nevada.

NELLIE CHAPMAN – The first woman dentist in the old West, Mrs. Chapman practiced in Nevada City. "Her patients made themselves comfortable in a grand red velvet chair, fitted with a porcelain bowl on a stand, an aspirator, and a holder for a crystal water glass. The drills she used...were powered by a treadle, which worked like a flywheel as it was pumped." – *The Doctor Wore Petticoats: Women Physicians of the Old West*, by Chris Enss, 2006.

CHARLES CROCKER AND MARK HOPKINS – In the summer of 1861, the Big Four (Charles Crocker, Mark Hopkins, Collis Huntington, and Leland Stanford) began wooing investors to their newly incorporated Central Pacific Railroad Company. Among the first to be courted were D. W. Strong of Dutch Flat and Charles Marsh of Nevada City, California. The Big Four backed the Railroad with their personal fortunes. "Among their Friends and acquaintances this was regarded as an act of insanity, that if they proceeded, it would result in their dropping all they had in the cañons of the Sierras." – "The Story of the Central Pacific. The

Rise of The Big Four: Huntington, Stanford, Crocker and Hopkins" by William F. Bailey, in *The Pacific Monthly,* January and February, 1908.

Lotta Mignon Crabtree – Lotta came to Grass Valley in the summer of 1853, where her mother opened a boarding house on Mill Street, very near the house occupied by Lola Montez. "Her [Lola's] house became a veritable salon, thronged with singing, laughing people. She… began a rather picturesque custom of playing with children, among whom was Lotta Crabtree… Soon Lola began teaching her to dance… to sing ballads and ride horseback. They went about the countryside together, Lotta on a pony, Lola on a horse. At Rough and Ready Camp, Lola once stood the diminutive child on a blacksmith's anvil and bade her dance before a group of miners, declaring she should go to Paris… Above all Lotta liked minstrel acts in which she could romp, dance and sing with hoydenish delight. Her songs or ballads came to life because she was adept at mimicry. Likewise she made an act of picking up her rewards at the end of a performance. Then she became a child, taking off her shoe and naively filling it with dollars, gold slugs, nuggets." – "Lotta Crabtree, Musette of the Gold Coast," Monograph XV from Theatre Research W.P.A. Proiect 8586, O.P. 465-05-5-286, Lawrence Estavan, Editor. San Francisco, October 1958.

Lotta retired from the stage at age 44, full of wealth and honors.

Zeno Philosopher Davis – Davis was a noted pioneer gunsmith. His shop fronted on Broad Street, and his family's living quarters were in back, off Spring Street, next to the National Hotel in Nevada City. Davis rode with the Nevada Rifles. He grew deaf in old age, reportedly the result of firing the cannon for Nevada City's 4th of July celebrations.

Duck Egg – Longtime resident of Nevada City, his sobriquet comes from his laconic defense against a charge of stealing chicken eggs. "Duck Egg" opened a laundry at the foot of Prospect Hill in 1858 that he operated for many years. See *Desert Magazine,* October 1965.

Frank Dunn – "Francis J. Dunn was…pleasant and accommodating when sober, and opinionated and surly when in his cups… Many anecdotes were current in the olden time concerning the convivial habits of the limbs of the law… A party of men going along the Downieville road came across a well-dressed man lying by the side of the road. They roused him and inquired, 'Who are you?' 'I am Francis J. Dunn; considered, and justly considered, the best lawyer in the State of California,' said the disturbed one, struggling to a perpendicular." – from Aaron

Augustus Sargent's "Sketch of the Nevada County Bar," in *Thompson & West.*

E CLAMPUS VITUS – (Also *E Clampsus Vitus* in California) "ECV was popular because it afforded the young men at the mines with a perfect excuse for horseplay. Furthermore…it ridiculed the stuffy secret fraternal, benevolent, and political societies…so important in the Gold Rush days. Not only were there chapters in such well-known towns as Yreka, Nevada City, Auburn…but in mining camps, some long gone. In San Francisco, it was here as early as 1852. In 1858, a meeting was called in Honolulu, and Clampers were active in Carson City and Virginia City, Nevada, during the Comstock Lode years. However, when the last century came to an end, gold mining and the Gold Rush towns faded. *E Clampus Vitus* also waned… Most likely World War I was a factor… By the end of the 1920's, the order was just a memory." In the 1930's, ECV was revived by Carl Irving Wheat. "After that…Poor Blind Candidates were supposed to have an interest in California history, and by 1936, the Clampers could boast of many of the era's most respected historians, bibliographers, historical society presidents, journal editors, printers, and collectors from throughout California." – Dr. Albert Shumate, a Humbug of Sublime, Noble, and Grand proportions, to the San Francisco Corral of Westerners, June 25, 1991. http://www.yerbabuena1.com/history.html.

THE EMPIRE GAMES OF CHANCE – "In 1851 Nevada had two of these (gambling saloons) establishments, of special magnificence and prominence. They were the Empire, on Main street, on the site of the Union Hotel, and Barker's Exchange, opposite the Empire, with entrances on both Main and Broad streets…These places had each its band of music, and from twelve to fifteen tables where games of chance were played." – *Thompson & West.*

JAMES GRAHAM, 5TH EARL AND 1ST MARQUESS OF MONTROSE – Skilled with sword and pen, Montrose raised the Highland Clans for Charles I in the Civil Wars and became Lord Lieutenant of Scotland in 1645. He was captured and executed by the Scots as a traitor in 1650. His monument in Edinburgh reads:

> "Scotland's glory, Britain's pride,
> As brave a subject as ere for monarch dy'd
> Kingdoms in Ruins often lye
> But great Montrose's Acts will never dye."

ASBURY HARPENDING – In early 1863, Captain E. W. Travers USN "discovered a plot to outfit and arm the schooner *J. M. Chapman*, which was to be used in the service of the rebellion to cruise on the high seas and commit hostilities upon the citizens, property and vessels of the United States… Several months previous, Asbury Harpending, the chief instigator, had gone to Richmond, Virginia, where he received from Jefferson Davis a letter of marque… The plans of the pirates were ambitious and extensive." – Aurora Hunt, *The Army of the Pacific; Its Operations in California, Texas, Arizona, New Mexico, Utah, Nevada, Oregon, Washington, Plains Region, Mexico, etc. 1860-1866,* 1951.

Harpending, a larger-than life adventurer, tells his own story in *The Great Diamond Hoax and Other Stirring Episodes in the Life of Asbury Harpending – an Epic of Early California,* edited by James H. Wilkins, 1913.

For another view of the *Chapman* conspiracy, see *The Dark and Tangled Threads of Crime,* by William Secrest, 2004.

CAPTAIN W. P. HARRINGTON – Until Harrington's election to command in 1861, the leadership of the Nevada Rifles was largely in the hands of Secessionists. Harrington, a staunch Unionist, was also Foreman of Eureka Hose Co. #2, founded in 1860, and a Town Trustee of Nevada in 1857. For a history of the Nevada Rifles, visit The California State Military Museum online at: http://www.militarymuseum.org/NevadaRifles.html.

DR. R. M. HUNT – Hunt, a pioneer physician, was administrator of the Nevada County Hospital from its completion in 1860. His son also practiced medicine in Nevada City. A photo of Dr. Hunt's mansion on Aristocracy Hill in Nevada City may be seen online, courtesy the Bancroft Library of California: http://sunsite.berkeley.edu/FindingAids/dynaweb/calher/goldrush/figures/I0041295A.jpg.

HURDY GURDY GIRLS – "In 1862 the already notorious Bed Rock Saloon on Broad Street, Nevada City, introduced a corps of Hurdy Gurdies, German dance-for-hire girls. The saloon immediately attracted a large and enthusiastic clientele, which to the horror of some townspeople included young men from the business and professional class." – *After the Gold Rush, Society in Grass Valley and Nevada City, California, 1849-1870,* by Ralph Mann, 1982.

OLD JOE – Marker #809, placed by the Native Sons of the Golden West, bears this inscription: "On the day of July 3, 1901 a stagecoach, driven by Henry Crockett, was on its way to the town of Foresthill when a hooded man appeared with a shotgun and ordered Crockett to stop, to which he replied, 'You are only foolin.' At that the robber shot and killed the wheel horse known as 'Old Joe.' He then robbed the stage and its passengers." The robber was never captured.

GENERAL ALBERT SIDNEY JOHNSTON – "The exemption of the Pacific coast from the calamities of civil war, and, in great measure, subsequently, from the bitterness engendered elsewhere thereby, was due to General Johnston, perhaps, more than to any other man, by reason of his firm and unshaken attitude as a commander until relieved, and afterwards by his counsels as a private citizen." *The Life of General Albert Sidney Johnston,* by his son, William Preston Johnston, 1878.

For another appraisal of Johnston's importance to the fate of California, see: *The Contest for California in 1861: How Colonel E. D. Baker Saved the Pacific,* by Elijah Robinson Kennedy, 1911.

KAPA HEMBO – Bear Slayer, the famous Nisenan hunter, lived near Coloma. His story comes from *Deeper than Gold: Indian Life in the Sierra Foothills,* by Brian Bibby and Dugan Aguilar, 2005.

THE KNIGHTS OF THE GOLDEN CIRCLE – A semi-secret military Secessionist society active in antebellum and wartime California (and elsewhere), dedicated to the overthrow of the US Government. Major-General Edward V. Sumner, who relieved Albert Sidney Johnston of command of the Department of the Pacific in 1861, believed the Knights of the Golden Circle in California numbered at least 16,000.

JAMES KNOWLTON – Knowlton was John Van Hagen's deputy, then succeeded him as Sheriff of Nevada, 1861-63. He was also Captain of the Nevada City Light Guard, organized April 1863 from the Nevada Rifles.

MAIDU – These indigenous people of California lived in an area roughly bounded by Mt. Lassen and Honey Lake in the north, the crest of the Sierra Nevada in the east, the Consumnes River to the south, and the Sacramento River on the west. They spoke related languages: Nisenan in the southern region, Konkow in the west, and Mountain Maidu in the northeast. The vocabulary in this book is mostly Mountain Maidu. Names of local plants, animals, and places are in Nisenan when possible. The word "maidu" can be translated into English as "person."

HENRY MEREDITH – Meredith was young, handsome, a promising attorney, and the flower of Nevada City Chivalry. He was one of the first to fall in Ormsby's ill-fated action against Paiute warriors at Pyramid Lake in 1860. John Van Hagen brought home his body. Meredith was laid to rest in the Pioneer Cemetery in Nevada City, the townsfolk all turning out to do him honor.

LOLA MONTEZ – This fiery-tempered, glamorous, and notorious danseuse was also a passionate revolutionary. Ludwig I of Bavaria created her "Countess of Landsfeldt" before their stormy affair toppled his government. Forced to leave Europe, Lola toured the United States, including northern California. She was enchanted by the Sierras and made her home on Mill Street, Grass Valley, from 1853 to 1855. She arrived with 50 trunks of finery. Lola kept a menagerie that included a bear cub. She is said to have employed a Kanaka manservant and a maid called Periwinkle, who had come with her from New Orleans. There are many biographies, including Bruce Seymour's *Lola Montez, a Life*, 1996.

MOO LUNG – The first Chinese parade dragon in the US, the original Moo Lung was more than 150 feet long. The dragon traveled all over the United States to appear in Chinese celebrations. The head of Moo Lung is displayed at the Bok Kai Temple in Marysville during their annual Bomb Day celebrations, where a successor Golden Dragon, Gum Lung, dances. For old photos of Moo Lung, visit the Bok Kai Festival website at: http://www.bokkaifestival.com/. Moo Lung's history is also documented at http://www.bokkaitemple.org/.

COLONEL JOHN SINGLETON MOSBY – "His great work was his distinctive warfare near Washington against the troops guarding the Potomac. Behind the Northern forces aiming at Richmond, for two years of almost incredible activity…he maintained his warfare, neutralizing at times some fifty thousand troops by compelling them to guard the rear of the enemy and his capital. The four counties of Virginia nearest Washington became known as 'Mosby's Confederacy.' Here his blows were almost incessant, followed always by the dispersing of his band or bands among the farmhouses of the sympathetic inhabitants… Usually from thirty to sixty (of Mosby's rangers) would be collected at a rendezvous…and after discharging, as it were, a lightning flash, be swallowed up in impenetrable darkness, leaving behind only a threat of some future raid… The execution of this bold plan was…long successful; its damage to the enemy enormous, and it exhibited a military genius of the highest order… Mosby is clearly entitled to occupy a preëminence among the partisan leaders of history." – *The Memoirs of John S. Mosby*, edited by Charles Wells Russell, 1917.

NATIONAL EXCHANGE HOTEL – This landmark is one of the oldest hotels west of the Rockies, in continuous operation since 1856, even though its elegantly furnished accomodations were damaged in the fire of November 1863. It was a stagecoach, mail, express and telegraph center in mining days. Mark Twain signed the register twice in the 1860's. Young Herbert Hoover boarded at the National in the 1890's. – see *The Way it Was: Looking Back at Nevada County*, by Robert M. Wyckoff, 2007.

NOME LACKEE INDIAN RESERVATION – In 1851, Wemah and other Maidu headmen signed a treaty with US Commissioners that awarded them twelve square miles of land in western Nevada County. Washington rejected the treaty in secret session and sealed the decision until 1907. The Maidu were removed to Nome Lackee Reservation in Tehama County during the years preceding the Civil War, where they were held in virtual slavery by corrupt Indian Agents and marked for extermination.

An eyewitness to the arrival of a band of Maidu at Nome Lackee made this report to a San Francisco newspaper: "The poor Indians began to show…regret in leaving the place of their birth. The women in the wagons set up that peculiar plaintive cry used by them at their funerals, while the men walked behind the wagons in mournful silence." – *San Francisco Evening Bulletin*, September 22, 1857.

ELLEN CLARK SARGENT – "Ellen Clark Sargent (1826-1911) moved to Nevada City, California from Massachusetts as a new bride in 1852, when Aaron Sargent owned and edited the local newspaper… In 1869 she founded the local suffrage association. During the twelve years she lived in Washington while her husband sat in the House and Senate, she was the most conspicuous suffragist among congressional wives. Susan B. Anthony often stayed with the family; and Ellen Sargent was for many years Treasurer of the National Women's Suffrage Association." – *The Selected Papers of Elizabeth Cady Stanton and Susan B. Anthony*, edited by Ann Dexter Gordon, 2003.

NILES SEARLS – Searls was a distinguished jurist and District Judge of Nevada 1855-61. He rode with the Nevada Rifles. During 1863 he was editor of the *Nevada Democrat*. A founding freemason, tradition names him also a prominent member of *E Clampus Vitus* in Nevada City. The story of Searls' family is told in David Comstock's trilogy, *The Nevada County Chronicles*.

WILLIAM MORRIS STEWART MANSION – The Nevada County Historical Marker reads: "Built 1855-56. Exact replica of wife's Ante-Bellum Colonial birthplace. Only edifice of this type in California. Stewart, an early Nevada County District Attorney, joined 1859

Comstock silver rush. Led battle for statehood and became Nevada's first U.S. Senator, served 29 years; known as the Silver Senator and Father of American Mining Law, authored 15th Constitutional Amendment."

Niles and Mary Searls lived in this house on Gethsemane Street in Nevada City in 1861. Author Ruth Herman lived there in the 1970's and wrote about the house and the Stewart family in her biography of Stewart: *Gold and Silver Colossus: William Morris Stewart and his Southern Bride.*

OLIVER P. STIDGER – A civic-minded and high-principled man, Stidger came to California in 1849. He published the *Marysville Herald* 1856-63, and the *North San Juan Press*, (formerly the *Hydraulic Press*) 1863-64. He did most of the writing for the *Nevada Daily Gazette*, beginning in the spring of 1864. Also a Judge and Justice of the Peace, he was an outspoken enemy of secession and narrowly escaped assassination for his views.

SIMMONS P. STORMS – Captain Simmons Peña Storms established an early trading post on the Yuba River near what is now called Jones Bar and learned the language of the Indians. He was appointed Indian Agent for the area in 1851. At the time Storms was put in charge of removing the Maidu to Nome Lackee Reservation, he lived at his Rancho at Chicago Park called The Hermitage. There he had an arena where races, bull and bear fights, and other amusements were held and both whites and Indians attended. – For more, see *When the Great Spirit Died: the Destruction of the California Indians, 1850-1860,* by William B. Secrest, 2003.

JOHN B. VAN HAGEN – John Bence Van Hagen was a career lawman and soldier. He was Captain of the Nevada Rifles in 1860, and Sheriff of Nevada, 1859-61.

WILLIAM WALKER – The "Grey-Eyed Man of Destiny" was born in Kentucky in 1824. Between 1853 and 1860, Walker led a series of military expeditions into Mexico and Central America. Although the US did not officially sanction his enterprise, popular opinion was overwhelmingly in favor of his plan, called "filibustering" or "freebooting." Walker's private armies of adventurers attempted to colonize the lands they conquered and establish an English-speaking, slave-holding empire. Walker's portrait and other images of his life are online at the Tennessee State Library and Archives, http://www.tn.gov/tsla/exhibits/walker/index.html.

WALLOUPA – Walloupa, or Guadelupe, for whom the mining town near You Bet was named, was a Nisenan Maidu *yeponi* (head man) who resisted the encroachments of white settlers. "I have not sketched the local excitement from…the capture of Wemah and his beautiful boy, 'Lulu,' to hold as hostages…nor of the inglorious defeat of another posse in the same campaign, by Walloupa and his naked, breech-clout warriors…" – "Sketch of Rough and Ready Township," by E. W. Roberts, in Bean's *History*.

WEMAH – (also spelled Weima in the old accounts) Wemah was another *yeponi* of the Nisenan Maidu at the time of the gold discovery. He led his people through the holocaust that followed. The present-day town of Weimar in Placer County is named for him. "The name of this well-known Indian was Guierlermus, and was given him at one of the old Missions, and had been corrupted by American pronunciation to Wemah." – *Thompson & West*.

We acknowledge the living descendants of Wemah, Walloupa, and Kapa Hembo.

PRINCE ALFRED ZU WINDISCHGRÄTZ – "Uprisings, revolution and civil war broke out in 1848 leading to the virtual collapse of the (Habsburg) monarchy. The revolutions…affected virtually every major European state… Popular uprisings in Prague, Vienna, Budapest, Venice and Milan sought an end to absolute monarchical rule…military high command slowly but systematically suppressed the revolts… Foremost among these generals was Alfred zu Windischgrätz, 'the Sword of the Monarchy,' who crushed rebels in Prague, Vienna and Budapest to restore the Habsburg dynasty." – The Official Website of Chip Wegar, author of *An American in Vienna,* http://anamericaninvienna.com/the-habsburgs/.

Made in the USA
Charleston, SC
04 June 2011